THE WRECKER'S GIRL

S. K. Tremayne is a bestselling novelist and award-winning travel writer, and a regular contributor to newspapers and magazines around the world. The author's first novel, *The Ice Twins*, was picked for the Richard and Judy Book Club and was a *Sunday Times* No.1 bestseller. Born in Devon, S. K. Tremayne now lives in London and has two daughters.

The Wrecker's Girl

S. K. Tremayne

Hemlock Press
An imprint of HarperCollins*Publishers* Ltd
1 London Bridge Street,
London SE1 9GF

www.harpercollins.co.uk

HarperCollins*Publishers*
Macken House, 39/40 Mayor Street Upper
Dublin 1, D01 C9W8, Ireland

First published by HarperCollins*Publishers* Ltd 2026

1

Copyright © S. K. Tremayne 2026

S. K. Tremayne asserts the moral right to
be identified as the author of this work.

A catalogue record for this book is available from the British Library.

PB ISBN: 978-0-00-858164-0
TPB ISBN: 978-0-00-858165-7

This novel is entirely a work of fiction. The names,
characters and incidents portrayed in it are the work
of the author's imagination. Any resemblance to actual persons,
living or dead, events or localities is entirely coincidental.

Set in Sabon LT Std by HarperCollins*Publishers* India

Printed and bound in the UK using 100% Renewable
Electricity at CPI Group (UK) Ltd

All rights reserved. No part of this publication may be
reproduced, stored in a retrieval system, or transmitted,
in any form or by any means, electronic, mechanical,
photocopying, recording or otherwise, without the prior
written permission of the publishers.

Without limiting the author's and publisher's exclusive rights,
any unauthorised use of this publication to train generative
artificial intelligence (AI) technologies is expressly prohibited.
HarperCollins also exercise their rights under Article 4(3) of the
Digital Single Market Directive 2019/790 and expressly reserve this
publication from the text and data mining exception.

Author's Note

My thanks to Dr Richard Taylor, psychiatrist and writer, for his invaluable insights into the worlds of forensic psychiatry and psychology.

Then

The rain, always the rain.

Emma stared through the open door and gazed up at the spiteful morning sky. Yes. Still raining.

Her sigh was heavy and heartfelt. She desperately needed a walk. The rooms were either too hot, or too small, or too cold; the conversation with her in-laws was so stifling, her husband Andrew kept disappearing, leaving her stranded in their small talk; the long-awaited break in far West Cornwall was anything but the relaxation he'd promised, back in London.

It will be romantic, darling. We'll go for walks along the cliffs together.

It was not romantic. She woke up every dawn under surly grey clouds, and the clouds always looked so relentlessly determined, as if they had a job to do. A job which they absolutely did, and then Andrew disappeared as if he couldn't stand to be in the same house as his own family, his own mother and father?

Rain.

Stalled at the door, Emma wondered, again, where Andrew had got to. Nipping down to the tiny village, again? Drinking in the Saracen, again? Whatever the case, she was alone, and as of this moment there was no one looking for her, no one pressing her with questions – scrutinizing her, assessing her, boring her – and she was standing at the door that led to the path that led to the beauty; it was one of the few precious chances she'd had, in this trip to Cornwall, to do her own exploring. And these moments were always the best.

For a second she wondered if she should tell someone, leave a note, call, but then Emma decided: no. She wanted a proper sense of escape, again; to be alone and herself, and gloriously unbothered.

And even as she watched, the rain seemed to be abating. The muted shush of the distant sea was now the only noise. And maybe a voice behind her, from deeper in the house, someone seeking her out?

No, that must not happen. She could not face another game of cards or another cup of tea, or another round of meandering chat, not when all that was *out there*. How could people live like this, so often indoors, yet surrounded by such magnificent wildness?

Enough.

Urgent and determined, Emma slipped on her coat, laced up her boots, and stepped outside: quietly closing the door behind her.

Turning left, past the stables, the glossy horses, Emma took the one available path down to the ocean. She already knew the route well. In between chilly monsoons, Emma had, this week, come to love this sweet, sad, beautiful place, with its tiny coves and bays: Penberth, Le Scathe, Porthguarnon, Zawn Dorlam. Where the wild moors descended to wildish woods which tottered down to perilous cliffs, and wastes of ocean, and wheeling seabirds, patrolling their private granite stacks.

After half an hour, Emma came to the expected crossway of the paths. She knew at once which way to go.

Her favourite.

Zawn Dorlam. The Cove of the Waterfall! Everyone kept telling her it was dangerous, slippery, notorious; a lovely place but with menacing, broken cliffs, the enclosing, decomposing woods, and the rotting old rock walls. She did not care. Because the woodland path – snaking between gorse, bramble and tamarisk – was opening out to the salted airiness of the shore. Emma breathed in the goodness and strode on, confidently, hopping over the last of the stiles, pushing through thornbreaks, making her steepening way down to the lonely beach where almost no one came in late November.

Except today?

Today, in Zawn Dorlam, and for the first time this rainy week, Emma was not alone.

She gaped in surprise. Someone was . . . asleep. It seemed to be a child. Right by the pretty waterfall. But the child was fully clothed. Not about to dive in the sea. Just lying there.

In the cold. And the wet.

Emma grasped at her own confusion and shivered with the first tremor of fear. What was a small child doing lying on a beach in late autumn? In this dangerous spot? Instantly, it felt very wrong. Perhaps the child was sleeping – or something more sinister.

She had no choice. She had to check. She edged her way around the rocks to where she could see properly. It was not a child.

A petite young woman was laid out on the cold stones at the bottom of the waterfall, where the cascade became the stream. The woman was hooded, obscuring her face. And for that Emma was grateful. Because this was surely a body, a dead person: a corpse. No one alive, no one with a beating heart, would lie under the waterfall, unmoving, unblinking, soaking in the rain and the spate.

Emma inched closer. Now she could see inside the hood, and she could see that this was no ordinary corpse. This woman, that face, the horrific state of the flesh and the bone. Rotting, blooded, erased. And next to it, a little shoe, a single and forlorn baby's shoe, the leather likewise rotted, and greying, and split: like the woman's head.

Something worse than evil had happened here, maybe worse than murder. Something momentously wrong.

The rain hissed on the sea and the rocks, on the ferns and the slime, and Emma screamed out loud in her terror.

1

Now

I am gazing across this beautiful drawing room at my youngest and wealthiest client. Romilly Kelhelland, delicately refined in her dark jeans and ash-grey cashmere top. Who has paused in her monologue to take a languid sip of a clearish green drink, just delivered by a maid on a silver tray. I've not been offered any of this drink, which makes me wonder if it is alcoholic. Romilly occasionally has a glass of something stronger as our sessions naturally pause, like this. Or she will have one or two at the end, while I pack my stuff and think about going home, on the boat to Falmouth.

As Romilly sips, I take in the famous view from this place, Tamariz House. The view is surely the main reason a rich English sea captain and his Portuguese wife built this grand Regency house, right here, in the 1820s.

The bosomy bay window of Tamariz House oversees all of St Mawes, its fetching little harbour, and the green, wooded embrace of Place Manor, the Jesus Beach, and St Anthony's Head beyond. Even on a grey November day like today, this harbour offers a happy scene. Always busy, full of boats.

I look back, checking. Romilly is adrift in her own thoughts; I take the moment and gaze again at the town laid out before me.

Somewhere down there in St Mawes intrepid late-season tourists will be walking past the Tresanton, past the Victory pub, down to the posh Idle Rocks Hotel, and the wet-fish shop by the shuttered ice-cream place. Chatting and laughing, they will pass the post office and the ferry for Falmouth, where Jago Moyle, the boatman, loads all his customers.

And I wonder if one single person will even notice another neat, desirable, pink-painted Victorian terraced house where once a young forensic psychologist and her lawyer husband – Mr and Mrs Kyle Shapland – lived happily with their bonny daughter Minnie.

I doubt it. Why should they?

'You OK, Karenza?'

Reality returns: I revive. 'Yes, sorry, just a – you know. A memory . . .' I call myself to order. *Do the job*. Romilly Kelhelland is a private client, paying with her own money – or her family's money – for my time. I am no longer sitting in some bright, white, clinical interview room, with its furniture screwed down to the floor, as I interview another child-murderer about his fixation with stuffed toys. *That* is all over, which is as I wanted. This new job is different, a change, and I am – I believe – slowly building that new career, despite the current lack of clients. But this job needs an equal if different focus.

'What *are* you drinking, Rom?'

'Sbirulino. I'm *addicted*.'

'It's booze, right?'

Romilly giggles. 'OK, Professor Moriarty. You got me there, totally busted.'

'Isn't it a little early?'

'Is it? Oh well, can't help it, Karenza, they are so *delicious*. Tash and I discovered them last summer in Florence.'

'What on earth is it?'

'They make it at the Rivoire? The famous caff on the Piazza della Signoria? Think it's gin, finocchietto, champagne, syrup of alga sbirulina. Have you been recently? Florence? The Rivoire? You must try it!'

I chuckle. I like half a pint of Doom Bar at the Victory with Jago. 'Not exactly my local. Sounds nice though.'

Romilly smiles that seraphic smile which is used to being adorable. Cheekbones, blonde hair, mineral green-blue eyes, the desirable smile of a very lucky young woman: twenty-three and rich and splendidly educated. And entirely deceptive.

If you saw Romilly in a trendy bar in Brixton or Brooklyn – which is where she generally spends her time when she's not hiding away at home in Cornwall – you would never know that under those expensive jeans there are serrations of scars. The tell-tale pink ladders of self-harm.

Nor would you easily guess that there are dark bruises hidden beneath that cashmere pullover. The marks of drugs; the marks of trauma, abuse, danger. So much is hidden. These old aristo families with houses and boats and titled cousins all over Cornwall – who would guess there is so much sadness, even evil, concealed in these bloodlines, these revered lineages?

I know; Romilly knows. And this is what we are here to do, to deal with this, to ameliorate.

And so, leaning forward, I suggest we talk about it,

talk perhaps about *Mummy*. And, sighing, Romilly Kelhelland agrees, and thus we spend the second half of our allotted hour discussing her selfish, plastic-surgery-loving, coke-sniffing mother – a parent, who is, I believe, the main reason Romilly Kelhelland sometimes peels down her jeans and draws a sharp knife across her naked thigh. Exulting in the oozing blood and the welling pain.

Darling Mummy.

After thirty minutes of discussing her mother, Romilly Kelhelland looks drained, but maybe purified, a little, or so I hope. There is no point in this new job unless I can help; I want to do good.

The session is nearly over. In celebration, Romilly casually requests and receives another sbirulino. This time she offers one to me. I politely refuse.

As Romilly sips her glamorous drink, I sit like a poor relation, trying to remember if I have even *been* to Florence. All I can recall of Italy is one mad trip around the country as a twenty-two-year-old after my Psychology BSc at Bristol Uni, when Kyle and I attempted to squeeze everything possible into ten manic days, along with lots of great sex in cheap Italian hotels where the bath towels were like cotton napkins. Did we go to Florence? Maybe we did, for just one night, followed by a day in a horribly overcrowded art gallery . . .

Or was that Venice?

It was too much experience in too little time, that holiday. But it did not matter back then; we were always happy, *back then*. Our relationship was like an absurdly long honeymoon: from that first meeting at university – the rock-climbing club, of all places – to our first sex three days later, it was smooth and natural and seemed so right, and it carried on that cheerful path for so long, while I was a research assistant at the Maudsley, and Kyle was finishing his law studies, while we both enjoyed student hours allowing us to get away for the odd glorious week, often to go climbing together. Cliffs in the Pyrenees. The Old Man of Storr . . .

A village church bell tolls. The paid hour is nearly over. I look up, cough politely, very keen to do my job. 'Romilly? Do you want to finish here? We can overrun if you want?'

But Romilly is absorbed in her phone, smiling at some message or image; she sometimes does this, and I have learned to go with it, the flow of the session, let it end in its own way; and I am deep in my own memories now. I am wondering, did it ever go wrong, *before*? Did we *do* something *before*? Was there a misstep, some kind of foreshadowing?

I don't believe so. After the student years we had the urgent young professional years, along with an early marriage. Then I launched, full of ambition, into my doctorate at De Crespigny. And Kyle headed for prosecution as a career. Then Minnie came along, and the urge to nest: we moved home to Cornwall.

And then it happened.

Another polite cough. But this time it is Romilly. She is watching me, with a sympathetic but lazy smile. 'You know, Karenza, we don't always have to meet here, in Tamariz, if it . . . uh . . . if St Mawes is, like, sometimes, too intense?'

I nod, keeping my emotions tight. My client is clearly saying, in her languidly polite way: *if returning to the town upsets you, with all its associations, we can do it elsewhere.*

Summoning myself, I shake my head. 'It's fine.'

Because the offer is kind, but unnecessary. I normally

meet my new private clients in the spare room at my own flat, over the water in Falmouth, but Romilly pays well, and I want to please her and – despite the memories – getting the ferry over with Jago Moyle is fun, and St Mawes is usually an agreeable diversion. Coming here once a week means I get to go up to my grandmother's council flat above the town, full of love and gossip. I can cope with the *associations* – or exclude them.

Although they are unusually intrusive, this afternoon.

'Honestly, Romilly, it's all fine, so . . .'

We chat for another minute, but it is desultory; aimless, in a good way. 'Anyway, I think we *are* done for today. Excellent progress.'

Romilly returns my smile.

If only I had fifteen affluent Romilly Kelhellands to see every week! But as yet, I do not. I am struggling: the water of debt drags at me, yet I am refusing to concede that going private might have been a mistake. I refuse to concede this, because the alternative – going back to before – is so profoundly *awful*.

Going back will mean prisons and psych units and jangling keys – and listening to some apology of a human tell me how he sliced his girlfriend from navel to neck because he was being followed by the president of Russia. Painful bleak sessions which made me think, why do *you* get to survive? Why you? Not *her*? Why is the world so unjust?

'So, Rom, see you next Monday, same time?'

She smiles and agrees.

Collecting my years-old raincoat, I say goodbye and we do a brief sisterly hug, then I walk out of beautiful Tamariz House, past the antique portraits, past the marble and mahogany and well-chosen modern art – *Mummy* has *taste* – into the long, sloping garden, and into the fresh, sea-tanged Cornish air.

It is 2.35 p.m. I have a good hour before Jago steers the ferry back to Falmouth, the last boat of the ever-shortening November day.

So I have time and a nice present in my bag, for Betty Spargo.

2

It's a short walk up another hill – St Mawes is surrounded by steep green hills – to my grandmother's council flat, in the middle of the only council estate in the town. The only arguably poor district in all St Mawes. Everywhere else has been gentrified and refurbed and resold for several hundred grand, or several millions, and most of these council places have been bought by their occupiers – and resold, of course.

Now my maternal grandmother, Elizabeth May Spargo – Betty Spargo – lives here in splendid isolation. I like to speculate that she might be the last Cornishwoman left in St Mawes, save for transients like me, who come and go. Because no one who is actually Cornish *lives* in the beautiful Cornish sea-town of St Mawes any more. No one Cornish *lives* in the wider and beautiful Cornish peninsula of Roseland, not any more.

These days it is too expensive to be Cornish in the best bits of Cornwall. Nowadays, beautiful St Mawes, and the surrounding Roseland, is for the upcountry folk.

Climbing the grey steps to Granny's grey apartment block, I wonder, for the hundred and ninety-eighth time in my life, why Cornwall Council decided to make all their municipal housing as dreary as they possibly could. Was it meant to be some kind of punishment, to shame the occupants? If so, it has never worked on Granny. Granny Spargo has no shame, and no need for shame: she gave away her ancestral St Mawes house to us, to me and Kyle with our little baby. She ended up here, after a series of private flats. Climbing ever further up the hill.

She greets me at the door with her normal, vivid enthusiasm, and an enfolding hug.

'Karenzzzzzza! My darlin'! Well, well!'

As ever, she acts as if this visit is a wonderful surprise, as if we didn't have three separate conversations where I told her I was coming. Normally, with an old person, I'd worry this is dementia, but Betty is probably the least demented person I know. Also one of the shortest. About four foot ten, dyed red hair, sparkly hazel eyes. She mocks herself for it: she used to say, when tousling my hair, *You know when I was young I could run under a weasel!*

I vividly remember Betty telling me that when I was about six, when Mum was still alive, and I wondered if it was true, because Granny Spargo was so small. Then, when I asked Mum, 'Is it true Betty Spargo could run under a weasel?' and Mum burst out laughing, and said, 'Oh no, your granny's having you on, sweetie: she's a card, don't trust a word she says.'

It was my first introduction to human deception, but *good* deception. A complex thing. Perhaps that is when I began to get interested in human psychology. Including my own persona, much shyer and more awkward than Betty Spargo.

'Come in, come in! Karenza!'

'Granny, I'm already in.'

'So you are. That's lovely, take a seat, sooo lovely to see you, you're looking well.'

I snort, happily. 'I need to lose weight, Betty, I'm a big fat apple pasty.'

'Nonsense.' She chuckles, surging towards her tiny kitchen, which is all of three yards away. 'Men like a bit of puddin' on a woman. How is Jago anyway?'

'Oh, Betty, behave.'

She chuckles. I chuckle.

Betty Spargo is *always* trying to marry me off again – especially to Jago the Boatman. She thinks a Cornishwoman like me should marry a Cornishman like him. Kyle wasn't enough Cornish for her, more like Devonian or Essex-via-Bristol. Not a proper job.

As Betty busies herself in the kitchen, I gaze around her tiny flat, with its seashells and knick-knacks and Brontë books and her own wistful paintings of St Mawes harbour, really not bad for an amateur – and on the mantel I see her favourite photos. Me and my brother, nomadic Loic – where is he now? Algeria, Amsterdam? Antarctica?

After Loic, the grandkids. Then a nice pic of Mum – Betty's daughter – just before she died of cancer. Then Betty and her now-dead husband when he was an airman after the war: she stands beside him beaming proudly. She is notably pretty. My mum was equally pretty.

I was never as pretty. I look at the photo of me and Kyle on the mantel, taken when we first moved down here with baby Minnie. I am OK-looking on a good day, but definitely a little chubbier, round-faced, nice, sweet smile – so I am told – medium height, medium figure, medium everything. I have brown mousy hair unlike Mum and Granny's dark lustrous hair – before Betty's went grey and she dyed it flame red, becoming a four-foot-ten ball of energy with her hair on fire.

There is no photo of my only child on the mantel. I

think Granny keeps all of those in her bedroom, so they won't upset me, when I come visiting. Or maybe she can't bear to look at them, herself.

'There, now, what do you want? Up to you!'

She has brought a tea tray, and it has two choices. A little brown ceramic pot of tea . . . or a bottle of cheap brandy from Lidl.

'Betty, I always have tea.'

She chuckles, and pours us both mugs of tea, and herself a little glass of brandy. *To keep out the cold and wet, my lover.* I sometimes wonder if I am the only person over twenty-one in Cornwall who doesn't spend November to March half-cut.

'So.' Betty settles herself into the other armchair. 'Tell me everything, how is El Gruffalo?'

'He's good. Still quite aloof.'

'Is he still terrified of tiny dogs?'

'Yep.'

El Gruffalo is my beloved pet cat that Betty gave to me three years ago *just after it happened* when he was barely more than a kitten: a distraction for me, a rescue kitten with some obscure trauma. Hence his personality issues. The combination of his distant, gruff personality, and the fact he looked 'a bit like a Spaniard' according to Betty, gave him his special name: El Gruffalo.

Being called a Spaniard by Betty is a double-edged thing: on the one hand she thinks Spanish matadors are dashing – she likes brave masculine men, tin miners, wreckers, pirates, Jago the Boatman; on the other she thinks 'the Spaniards are always plunderin' Cornwall's fish', and she always uses that precise, delightful term: *plundering*. Not over-fishing or stealing. She's a talker, Betty, as was my mum; I am quieter, more pensive, observing rather than joining in.

A throb of sadness pierces me. I miss my upbeat chattering mum. I miss her, and I hate cancer.

'Ah, dear. You're thinking about Janet, aren't you?'

'How did you guess?'

'Because.'

'Sorry?'

'You know why!' She grins, cleverly steering us away from the sadder subjects.

'Betty . . .' I say, mock-stern. I know where this conversation is going. 'You really don't have a gift, you don't have a sixth sense, no one does. It's bollocks.'

She laughs, uninsulted, we must have had this dialogue a million times, and we both enjoy it.

'That's a lie now, isn't it, Karenza? Spargos had the gift for centuries. Spargo women, your mum had it as well; you're a Spargo as much as a Bray – you have it too. That's why you're good at your job, you can see into the other side, see through people, see them ghosts beyond.'

'No, Granny, I can detect ego dystonia, Twilight Syndrome, and, on a good day, incipient psychopathy. It's called forensic psychology.'

'Pff,' she says, knocking back her brandy, 'it's the Spargo talent, you should be thankin' your Celtic ancestors, we brought it over from Greenland when there was dinosaurs down at Loe Beach.'

Betty Spargo knows this is absolute nonsense, I know she knows: we both laugh, then she makes an excuse-me face which means she is going to have a cigarette. Betty Spargo officially gave up cigarettes ten years ago, but her version of giving up cigarettes is 'smoking cigarettes out of the window'.

As she smokes her cigarette out of the window, with her chin cupped on a feminine hand – looking oddly vampish, like a seductress – she asks me about my clients. Because she loves gossip even more than the average keen-witted, sassy old lady; and for my beloved nan, I deliver. I never talk in detail about clients to anyone else. Unprofessional. But for her, yes – what harm can it do?

As she puffs ferociously on her cigarette, I tell her about the Kelhellands. Romilly, the mother, the whole mad family, broken and sad but stupidly rich. She listens to it all, then she turns to me, and she says, casually, 'You know Romilly's grandmother was bisexual?'

'*What?*'

Betty has lived in St Mawes all her life, she knows virtually everyone here, and she knows virtually everything, all the history and the tittle tattle. And any blank spaces are often filled in by the postman, or Jago, or the butchers on the seafront. So I can quite believe this is reliable information, but I am surprised: this is *quite* a nugget.

'Really? Are you sure? The matriarch? Margaret Kelhelland? I thought she was all prim and proper, so . . . *bisexual*?'

Betty nods, extinguishing her cig, and returning to her armchair. 'Yep. It was the talk of the Victory. She had an affair with the nanny, they used to book rooms at that pub in Ruan Lanihorne for an hour, no wonder they are all so cracked, all that creeping about. You know I thought about being a lesbian once, but I didn't have the hair for it.'

Betty is making me laugh. She always makes me laugh. Sometimes I could stay here for hours laughing with Betty, but my time is over, and the last boat will be leaving soon. I make my I'm-going-now face and Betty nods and before I go I remember.

'Oh wait, I totally forgot. Should have had it with the tea!'

Diving into my bag I bring out, in its tin-foil wrapping, a homemade cake that I baked for Betty yesterday. A proper Victoria sponge. Betty loves cakes, used to make them herself, now her gnarled arthritic hands can't quite manage it – so I make them. She must have been expecting this, I normally bring her something, but her eyes are a bit spangly with tears as she takes it.

'Oh sweetheart, you didn't have to! Really. You're so busy, doing that mental work.'

'I wish I was that busy! I have too many free afternoons. It's a pleasure baking it for you . . .' I grin. 'Also you just gave me that *brilliant* gossip about Margaret Kelhelland.'

Betty smiles and sets the cake on a table, then she gives me a really *tight* hug as if she is never going to see me again, and I step out of the door and wave goodbye. I am going to be late.

Jago awaits. But not forever. November days are so brief.

Checking the time, I start jogging down the chilly road. Dusk is beginning to fall, sad low light on Carrick Roads. As I pace down, nervous about missing the boat, I think about what Granny Spargo said about the Spargo gift. There is no doubt Granny Spargo is insightful, like Mum: she is sharp, seeing things that others don't, but that's just feminine wiles and social skills: it has no evolutionary explanation and no scientific basis.

Indeed, it makes me a little angry, though I would never show my irritation to Betty. I file away the idea of a 'gift' alongside all the other woo-woo rubbish that surrounds 'Celtic Cornwall': the obsession with stone circles and fertility wells and the Men an Tol, the dreadlocked girls in St Agnes with their lacy wicca zodiacs and their tarot cards in Truro market – it is all ridiculous.

It is just another form of religion, except perhaps more vulgar. A tacky way of denying death. And death, as I have learned, cannot be denied. Death, which is unendurable, must be endured.

3

I've just made it. Jago is still here. Cheerful Jago Moyle, the boatman. His little ferry jogs on the spot, by the quay, as if even the waves are impatient to get going.

'Ahoy thar,' he says, speaking Pretend Pirate, which he does when he wants to tease me. I give him a smile, while trying not to smile too much. Betty Spargo is not wrong in sensing *something*. Jago has dark, dark hair, white, white teeth, and a handsome Cornish face. I am not immune to his charms.

'Ya nearly missed the boat, we can't be having that.'

He takes my hand to assist me on board. I like the way he does this, I like the fact his hand is strong and weathered and comes with a ready smile and a ribald story about his misbehaved family, fishing conger and sea bass out of Coverack these past seventy billion years. Jago Moyle is proper Cornish. Bachelor, still, at thirty-five. Too fond of the tourist girls at Portscatho beach in the summer, yet apparently fond of me, too. I do sometimes wonder . . .

But then I stifle the thought. I am thirty-eight, divorced, no kids – not now; I have two pets, a good if underpaying job, and that's it, I do not need a man, even if I want a man. Do I?

'How's the Kelhelland girl? Buying a superyacht?'

'You should chat her up. She probably likes inappropriate older men.'

Jago smiles. I chuckle. And I think: how easily we slip into this comfortable everyday banter. The Moyles have known the Brays – and the Spargos – for generations. The Old Tin-Mining Cornish: they are so interlinked, just as, in their way, the Rich Mine-*Owning* Cornish.

Jago disappears to steer the boat, we putter out of St Mawes, and I sit as usual at the front of the ferry and stick my airpods in and I uphold my phone to choose some music – I am wavering between two genres. One is minimalist music, music so beautifully simple and repetitive it is good for having new ideas. 'Rose Engine' by Spiro, or a shard of Philip Glass.

My other possible genre is overripe pagan neo-folk – and eventually I opt for the latter: Heilung. 'Krigsgaldr'. This is a twelve-minute song of constant, mesmerizing chanting repetition, a weaving heathen yodel of a song which sends me into my best mental state for carefully focusing on problems – how to help my next client tomorrow – and also it lasts right until the ferryboat docks in bustling Falmouth, which feels like London after St Mawes.

'Bye, Jago, see you again.'

'Come and have another pint in the Victory next time. No. What am I saying? Two pints!'

Smiling, waving, I pace along the high street of Falmouth, past the gnarly pubs and wind-chewed shops and semi-prosperous restaurants, all the way to the grand, newish Maritime Museum on the harbourfront, and then, at last, the door of my spartan, modern, wood-and-glass flat, with its spare room for clients and the splendid floor-to-ceiling view of Falmouth harbour.

Home.

Keying the door I step inside. Grateful to be back, because I cherish my cool, bare, soothing apartment. This place was my gift to myself when Kyle and I finally abandoned our horrible barter of blame and accepted that, like so many other couples who lose a child, we were going to get divorced. So I took back my old name – a Bray again! – and we sold the perfect, tragic, pretty little St Mawes house for plenty of money to rich Londoners.

I wanted to stay in the same area – near friends, father, Granny Spargo, work, memories, life – but I also wanted something defiantly different. Therefore I used all my money to put down the biggest deposit possible on this place, which means I have a small mortgage; this is probably the best decision I have ever made, because if I had a large or even medium mortgage right now, I would be going out of business.

I need more clients.

Stepping into the living room, dropping my keys on the glass table, I gaze out of the enormous windows at the autumn twilight. The view is not as perfect as the view of St Mawes from Tamariz, but it is exhilarating in its grittier way: the great sweep of busy water, the pleasure boats tootling out of Mylor, the bristling Royal Navy boats treading out to the ocean. The second largest harbour in the world. Or is it third?

I hear a mewl. I turn, and smile in greeting, at El Gruffalo. He looks distracted and aloof but then he generally looks distracted and aloof. And hungry. His other primary mood is overly happy and affectionate, purring like a loud machine which is possibly going wrong. He is quite the eccentric. I sometimes wonder if he is the first case of Feline Manic-Depressive Disorder.

Picking up El Gruffalo I give him a big huggy kiss and he starts the mad, loud, happy purring; then I go to the kitchen and squeeze him some food from a sachet. 'Here you go, Gruff. Try not to purr as you eat, you will choke.'

Now it's time to check on my other pet. Otto. A chameleon. I sometimes wonder why I bought a chameleon – was I actively trying to be the eccentric lonely grieving woman with quirky musical tastes who actually has a *chameleon*? I do not care. Otto is fun. He changes colour. Occasionally.

'Grey again? Otto, you're a chameleon. You're meant to change colour.'

Otto swivels one eye and regards me, sagaciously, but not unhappily. Maybe grey means 'Meh, life is OK'; if so, I can cope with that. I can also hear Gruffalo purring loudly as he eats.

All, it seems, is well; my modest chores are done. I make a mug of tea – enjoying the sense of being *alone* in my own place. With the oyster bar in the square below and the seagulls that steal chips from the tourists. *This is my place.* My castle, my lair, my fortress against an often cruel and frightening world, a place where I cannot be hurt, not any more, not if I don't love anyone *too* much so that when they die they break my heart.

Apart from Betty Spargo. And maybe Jago. And my brother. And a couple of my friends. Sometimes my father. Apart from all of them. But what can you do? No fortress is entirely invulnerable, there's always that forgotten tunnel under the eastern tower.

An interruption: my phone is making the glass table hum with the vibration.

The screen says *Kyle*.

Immediately – I hesitate. Do I want this call? I still

get on quite well with my remarried ex, but there is no denying the memories. And I am determined to move on, and he is still a busy lawyer in Truro, working with coppers every day, prosecuting wife beaters, drinking in the Wig & Pen, gossiping about hard judges and harder cases. I want none of that. Any of it. Coroners' courts. Parole assessments.

Verdicts of accidental death.

No.

The phone is still ringing. Persistently. I'll have to pick up.

'Kyle?'

There is a dash of unease in my voice. I really don't want to be mean but right now I don't want a long call or a languid chat.

Kyle, it seems, senses my mood. Over a decade of marriage can do that. Our chat is brisk, he moves to the point.

'Kaz, love, ever heard of a Natalie Tyack? Ring any bells?'

'Nope.'

He pauses.

'Really?'

'Yes. *Really*. Why?'

'Natalie Tyack. A young woman found dead in a cove, a year back, in West Penwith. The southern coast between Penzance and Land's—'

'Kyle! Twenty generations Cornish, remember? I know the coast like the back of my hand. Beautiful, remote . . . and?'

'How come you never heard of this case, though, Kaz? Was in the local papers, even made it on TV, and Cornwall is not exactly New York.'

I finish my mug of tea, watching an enormous herring

gull as it seeks out chips to steal. The orange-and-pewter dusk is falling over Falmouth, and the Roads.

'Dunno, Kyle. Last November I was in Australia, lecturing. Two terms. So I guess I missed it. Like when you go on holiday and a celebrity dies at home and you don't realize they are dead, unlike everyone else, until about six years later.' I persist: 'What's this got to do with me, anyway? I'm trying to get clients.'

'Well, that's it,' Kyle says. 'This could be a gig! New clients.'

At once, I switch off my distant mode; I am being unfair on Kyle, he is trying to help. 'OK, sorry, please: go on.'

His voice softens. 'It's the kids, the Tyack kids. They need help. And you were always so good with youngsters! CAMHS. Young offenders. You are *genius* with kids.'

'Thanks.'

I shun the obvious thought – I wasn't so good with one kid, was I? – and let him continue.

'You know you could walk into your old job tomorrow?'

'I don't want to come back, please stop asking!'

'OK, OK . . .'

'Anyway, why are you calling? I mean, if this is criminal, if there was a death, why is this not coming from DCI Ellis, or whoever?'

'Because they can't be arsed, and everyone lost interest, quite early . . .' He hesitates, apparently pondering, then says, 'OK, look: you need the backstory. Fact is, police drew a blank on the death; they tried – but got nothing. Couldn't find evidence of foul play. No motive for anyone to kill her, as far as we can tell. Yet no reason for her to die. Not suicidal. Yet it didn't look like an accident either: Natalie Tyack knew the cove well, it's a bit dicey, but she went there all the time. A local beauty spot, a waterfall by a beach.'

I'm gazing thoughtfully out of the window. The first spritz of a rain shower peppers the glass.

'It sounds like a nice puzzle, but I'm not a detective, and I'm not involved, not any more.'

Kyle interrupts, 'But you're *still* that brainiac psychologist I met in Bristol, right? A whizz at solving puzzles? And I bet you are still fascinated by bizarre, unusual psychologies, especially in children. You loved all that stuff at the Bethlem. Loved it.'

I can't deny it: I am still drawn to this stuff. One of my latest obsessions is Disinhibited Social Engagement Disorder, kids who don't know how to interact with adults, children who are too friendly, too sociable, who endanger themselves with overt affection; I have been listening to audiobooks about this for weeks, as I hike the Cornish coast, alone. Though generally not on that eerie and remote bit of coast between Land's End and Penzance; the long drive is quite annoying. That's *too* remote.

'All right, I'll bite. Tell me more. A young woman fell off a cliff. And?'

'As I said, she left behind two little kids,' Kyle says. 'I met them when it happened during the first investigation. Met them in hospital, Treliske. Broke my heart. When – if – you see the kids, you'll get it.'

'Tell me about these children?'

Kyle hurries on, sensing my interest. 'Solomon and Grace. They still live in the mad family farmhouse, with the father, Malcolm. Up there in the old woods by the sea. He's turned seven and she's nine or ten. He's talkative, she's withdrawn.'

'Go on.'

'They're quite wealthy, old mining money, blue blood. And the father desperately needs psych help, some intervention, and he is willing to pay for it.'

'Intervention in what way?'

'Well, this is it, Kaz. The kids have started behaving ... *strangely*.'

'That's not so odd, they are surely grieving. Their mother died, and they're very young.'

'Yes, but this is, I don't know – different, somehow. The kids are claiming they *know* what happened. To Mum.'

I stare at my mug of tea, now wishing it was full. Maybe with something tasty and a little intoxicating to go with this appealing puzzle.

'Anything else?'

'Not really. But that's enough, surely, it's a real mystery. How can these poor kids know what happened? No one was there, the children were tucked up in their jim-jams. How can they know *anything*? Yet they seem to know *something*. Everyone who talks to them comes away convinced of that.'

'Presumably people have actually asked the children?'

'Course. But they won't say any more. They clam up. That's why they are freaking everyone out – at school, everywhere – by claiming something bad happened to Mum, yet they won't spill the beans. Weird, huh? This needs a good psychologist, Kaz. Someone who can crack mysteries and who knows how kids work. It needs *you*.'

We chat a little more, and the call ends on an amiable note. It also ends with him giving me a number and me saying I will think about it.

With a new mug of tea in hand, I drift through my calm, quiet apartment, thinking about it. I text my best and oldest friend Dinah – funny, flirty, bright, the sociable opposite to me. I ask her opinion, has she heard of Natalie Tyack, this family, this case. She briskly texts back, *Yes, I vaguely remember that, why not, could be fascinating?* Then a thumbs-up emoji.

This is encouraging, but Dinah is always encouraging, always positive, so I still don't know. Grieving children is a bit close to home, but this conundrum is compelling. And I need the money.

One more circuit of my little flat, one more walk around my options. El Gruffalo is contentedly sleeping by the big window. No change there. But Otto has, abruptly, flushed into a new colour. Kind of greenish. A bit like the Sbirulino that Romilly was drinking. More importantly, it is surely green for *go*.

4

A faint, silvery drizzle falls on all the known world as I dawdle, impatiently, in my car, behind a farmyard lorry shedding wisps of hay. This is meant to be the main road from Falmouth to Helston, yet it can be blocked any time – like this – by fat tractors or lost tourists. Someone swinging a towed caravan into an old miner's terrace.

I hum with frustration. The further west you go in Cornwall, the more it is itself: the more Cornish – and intractable. The traffic slows, the roads narrow, the signals falter – everything gets bleaker and yet prettier. And I know that when I get beyond Penzance, and head along the Penwith coast, everything will be wilder *still*.

'Oh, God, hurry up!'

I am actually shouting at the infuriating lorry. It does not seem to help. And now, unbidden, I have a sudden memory of Minnie, laughing in the car, pointing at lorries and cows, and singing a song, and – no.

No. I don't want this memory, not here, not now. Switching to my music with fumbling hands I choose some Death Metal, any Death Metal, just do it quickly. Quickly quickly.

Here it is. 'The Dissolution of Mind' by Havoc Unit. The title could not be more apposite – 'Dissolution of Mind' – as this is what I am after. I like – consume – *devour* – quite a lot of Death Metal. Precisely because it is so dense and thunderous it blocks out *all* thoughts, especially ones I don't want. It makes my mind a pointless blank as the ugly, thrashing chords do their work. Halting the demons.

It takes a few minutes. My heart is slowed, the car is faster, the lorry is gone, I clock the clock. 1.30 p.m. Lunchtime?

I might as well use the time. I need more info. The ugly music done, I get a message from Dinah – *don't forget drinks tomorrow, the Kittiwake, 7 p.m.!*

I ask my phone to call Kyle. He answers quickly, his voice filling my rusty Hyundai. I can hear noises behind him – sounds like a pub.

'Let me guess, pint and a steakwich, in the Wig & Pen?'

He chuckles. 'Nah, Kaz, gone posh today. Greek salad and a glass of sauv blanc. Rocco's. Are you on the way to the Tyack fortress?'

'Yes.'

'It's all squared away then?'

'Yes. I called the father, Malcolm, yesterday. He's a bit wary, but I'm on the road. And thanks again for the intro.'

'No drama. I know you need the cash!'

'I do,' I say. 'But I also have some more questions?'

He says, 'Sure . . .'

And now I pause. Because I don't want to ask this question: it seems wrong. But it is unavoidable.

'Kyle, be honest, how much of a suspect is Malcolm Tyack? Older husband? Pretty young wife now suspiciously dead? He must have been top of the list.'

My ex sounds as if he is swallowing an olive – or wondering whether to reply. Then he says, 'Sure, yep, he was. But they got nothing. *Nada*. There are no suspects and there is no motive and there was no suicide note; all we have – all you have – is the kids gone doolally. Just focus on them, that's your job, right. How're you playing it? Did Malcolm Tyack invite you to stay?'

'God, no. Wouldn't expect him to. It's a longish drive but I can do it in a day, there and back. If I'm desperate I'll sleep at the Ship in Mousehole.'

He natters on about some time we stayed there – how one day he might take his new baby there, and I focus on the driving. I am in the humdrum outskirts of Helston – a Tesco's, a carwash, then I hit the old Helston waterside, the signs of ancient industry that no one quite understands.

'OK, Kyle, I'd better be going soon. One last thing, the mother, what was her name – Natalie? Tell me more about her. I've seen her photo, got your email, but I like to hear it in your *lawyerly* voice. You do such good summings up.'

He laughs, sardonically. 'Charmer. Let me eat my last chunk of feta.' He pauses. 'OK . . . She is – was – a looker. Right? Also smart, curious, inquisitive. Local girl. Life a real sob story: Mum from Redruth, druggy, alky, broken, Daddy apparently not much better – fled when she was born? Mum OD'd and died, and Natalie got taken into care in her teens. Crappy kids' home in Penzance. Anyway, yes, she was clever, funny – aced the A-levels, couldn't swing uni though – too much debt, I guess. Probably saw Malcolm as a safety net. He is pretty loaded, Tyacks are old dosh. He actually runs a couple of restaurants, one in St Ives, and one in Portloe, in the Roseland, actually you might know it, the Gunwale—'

'I do! Eaten there with Betty a couple of times. She took a funny turn after a cockle.'

'You mean she hit the vodka.'

'Perhaps. But Granny Spargo *always* take a funny turn after a cockle. I'm worried that one day she'll try a winkle.'

He chuckles. I smile, but then the smile vanishes – and again it hits me hard. And this time I do not have the chance to block it out, to slap on Morbid Angel or Brujeria. This is a memory so pure it won't be blocked out. Because for a moment we – we three – we are that happy young blessed family again, laughing in the kitchen in the little house in St Mawes, with Minnie dancing a tango by the fridge, showing off her new moves, and I am a mum – no, that's wrong, I am not a mum, I am *Mum* – stirring wine into herby mussels on the hob, and Dad is relaxing with a beer bottle after court work, and Minnie is beautiful and eight years old and blithely unaware of a world so full of horror, and everyone in that kitchen laughs – and now the darkness fills me, surges into me, a storm, so rough, so brutal I think I have to pull over or I will drive right over the sea-wall at Long Rock.

Minnie. Minnie Shapland.

Minnie.

'You all right there, Kaz?'

'Yes . . .' I slow the car. I am right on the seafront. I can see the dreamy aristo island-castle of St Michael's Mount, which is isolated by the advancing waves. The drizzle has stopped, and a blue sky shows. I stop. 'I . . . I . . . OK. Just . . . Cheers, Kyle. That's plenty. Enough now. Catch you later.'

The call ends, just in time that he can't hear me gasping with sadness – a sadness I know he shares, which he fends away with his sharp Essex-boy routine. And it is tough, this one, the surge of grief from nowhere.

I am used to these squalls, but they always hurt, so very badly, and I have learned that when they get through to me, when they enter the fortress via the tunnel, I have to allow them yet curtail them, almost ration them. So I will permit myself several tears for my dead daughter. Maybe ten.

Getting out of the car, I stare at Mount's Bay, the stiffening breeze drying my maximum permitted tears for Minnie, my daily limit.

Ah. My darling dead daughter. Sometimes I wonder if I look in the waves I will see her face, staring up, smiling, beckoning, *come and be with me*.

Taking out my phone, I lean back against the car, feeling the emotions ebb away like a wistful tide, and I scroll to my notes. I need to know where I am going. Baldhu House, five miles west of Penzance, another mile off the tiny winding Land's End road. Pronounced Bal-doo. I nod at this, at my own scrawly writing. I know enough Cornish to work out the etymology. Bal dhu. *Black mine*.

This is unsurprising. The whole of Penwith, like much of Cornwall – though more so in Penwith – is honeycombed with mines, some of them two thousand or even three thousand years old. Mines tunnelled by my Cornish forefathers, mines probably dug by Brays and Spargos, five hundred years back. Ten hundred.

And here it is on the map. And yes, it is close to the sea, close to the cove where that young woman fell, so mysteriously, leaving these kids who I need to help, who I am being paid to help, because I can help.

Back in the car, I steer around Penzance, then I take the road up-along, and the town dwindles and the road narrows, and soon I am praying I won't meet anyone coming the other way: steering in and out of minuscule hamlets and sudden turns past stone Celtic obelisks. Or the Merry Maidens: a stone circle representing girls mythically frozen into stone for dancing on the Sabbath. It's a legend that used to appal me as a child. Frozen into stone? Locked in forever?

I can sense the fierce Atlantic toiling away to my left, just over the rise, even as I drive through these arthritic old woods.

And now I have to stop, again: I really am lost. This last slice of far West Cornwall is so intricate it has defeated the map on my phone, and I haven't been so far west for many years. The sea wind buffets me as I climb out; the seagulls peer at me inquisitively, as they hover near-motionless in the scouring wind, now damp with a promise of drizzle.

There.

Baldhu House! I can see it from where I stand, that *must* be it, a large, rambling, ancient-looking, grey-gold building, alone in a slender, wooded valley, which leads down to the coast. I can see the distant wild ocean beyond.

At the wheel of my car I battle this last half-mile. The mud is thick under the tyres and cudding cattle are staring at me with vague resentment and the lane is so claustrophobic I can sense the dark, angry autumn brambles scratching all the remaining paint off my car.

Sheared trees with buzzcut branches speak of high winds, but the deep, dark woods also tinkle with a glimpse of idyllic streams, rushing to the sea. This is a forsaken place, even by the standards of wild Penwith, but it also has an enchantment. I can understand why you might choose to live here, far away from everything, yet in the centre of the only world that matters. Or, perhaps, a world you can't escape.

I am taking the final squelchy corner and now my mouth falls open, as I regard Baldhu House.

Because I've been here before.

I know it: this place is not new to me.

How? *How?* I do not know, yet it is giving me a sharp pang of recognition. But I have *not* been here before, I have no memory and there is no reason for me to have been here.

I feel faintly horrified.

This doesn't make sense, this is like waking up then realizing you are still dreaming, and this feels like a very *bad* dream. Like I know something approaches – and now I do want to turn around and quit. I can cope without the money, I will find other clients, this is a terrible error, surely this is a terrible error. Otto was wrong, or I misinterpreted him. Otto will be flashing red in my apartment. Go away, make good your escape, *flee*.

And yet this is ridiculous! This is the Spargo in me, yielding to silliness, to funny old stories told in seaside pubs, with cellars for wreckers and pirates. I will not flee. I am a professional, a qualified and respected forensic psychologist. I know all about child psychology, I have read Piaget, Blatz and Vygotsky. I know about the childhood stages of moral realism, and concrete operations. I know exactly how to do a Child Behaviour Checklist.

I am here to help some children, and I will Do My Job.

I park in the farmyard. This, it seems, is not a working farm, not any more. Some of the glassless windows in the outlying granite barns look medieval. Some of the big but grandly decaying house likewise looks medieval. With evil sharp windows, in places, like slits for arrows.

Yet it has also been modernized. Georgian, or perhaps Victorian?

Maybe I have seen it in a book, or online – that would explain the déjà vu. It is certainly a noble old farmhouse, however knackered: so perhaps it is known to historians? Or maybe it was pictured in some news report about the death of Natalie Tyack, something that didn't really register.

Yes, that must be it.

I pause, girding myself. Now I have to get out of the car and go to the door and meet this tragic family. A childless mother meeting a motherless child. A girl, and a boy. *She's withdrawn and he's talkative*. The weight of their loss seems to hang in the air.

Zipping my coat against a chilly wind, and the commencing rain, I scrunch across gravel to the big old door. Thick wooden thing, with impressive and defensive iron studs. Carved with gouges, like it has been hacked, or attacked. Sixteenth century? Seventeenth?

I clap the iron knocker. *Let me in, let me in.* The sound echoes.

Nothing. I knock again, and again, and I wait, for too long. Perhaps the house is empty? OK, that's it, I should go. No point waiting: just get going. There is no one here.

Or is there?

Beyond the house a large rambling garden begins, next to thickening woods. And now: I see movement. A figure. It looks female: a girl in a black anorak, black hoodie, shapeless clothes, walking away in the wet. She is a dark shape fading into the dark of the bushes, shrubs, paths. She looks as if she's clutching something: she is hunched, her stiffness broken over a package she holds.

'Hello?'

The figure pauses, her back to me. She is at a distance; I raise my voice. 'Hello? Can you help me? I'm Karenza Bray—'

The figure pauses, her back still facing me.

'Please, are you one of the family? Hello?'

Instead of turning, she crouches over herself harder, as if I terrify her, as if I will discover what she is hiding, in her package, something stolen.

One more go. 'Please? I've been invited. By the Tyacks. Are you a Tyack?'

At this, the figure pauses, perhaps preparing to turn, to show me what she's holding – and I get the overwhelming sense that I do not want to see her face, because it will be Minnie, or my mum, or someone else impossible. This is my guilt and grief returning. I feel cold salt water in my veins, ice and winter in my lungs. I cannot look. Cannot.

Must not. The figure turns. And I see.

5

The faintest glimpse of the whitest female face, drawn and strained. It is no one I know, and I am standing here in the drizzle, frightened for no reason. Now the figure hurries away, wordless in her hoodie, and I am left here outside the firmly closed door of Baldhu House with its sinister slitted windows.

'Hello.'

I jump. Someone has answered the door.

Gathering myself, I turn and see a soulful little boy with an unruly mop of red hair, who stares silently and questioningly up at me. This must be little Solomon Tyack.

Kyle's words return.

When you see the kids, you'll get it.

The boy smiles, shyly, yet impishly.

'Are you the lady come to talk?'

'I suppose I am.'

'Daddy said you were coming today. To speak to us. About Mummy.'

'Yes. All true.'

He steps back, and turns inwards, into the dark. Happy to get out of the wet, I follow as young Solomon Tyack leads me into the shadowy hallway. I can smell old wood, old leather, old mud, and a perfume that is sweetly overripe, or faintly decaying? Something not quite normal. The hall is chilly and sad, and it looms, but it also impresses. I am shunting the strange figure from my mind, focusing on this new job. My new clients.

'What's your name? I'm Solomon, but Grace calls me Sol or Solly.'

'Karenza. I'm Karenza Bray.'

'That's good. Karenza, did you know I'm going to have a lie-in tomorrow, Daddy said I can. I'm going to sleep until *seven*!'

Solomon Tyack smiles up at me. He is dressed in blue cords, a T-shirt with a picture of a Japanese anime octopus, and a little unzipped tracksuit top. He has a spray of saffron freckles over his little nose and forehead, which match his uncombed ginger hair. There is something feral about him; but also vulnerable. Beautiful and fragile, like the Penwith wilds.

Solomon proceeds, like a butler taking me to milord. He talks as he walks; I look about, seeing wood-panelled corridors, with hints of ominously large and darkened rooms beyond. Baldhu House is big, and apparently half empty. Solomon is still talking.

'Daddy said I got to bring you into the kitchen to meet everyone. I hope you like Grace, my sister, but I saw a *huge* black, black bird in my bedroom yesterday and she says I'm lying. Come this way. I hope there are snacks. Do you like snacks?'

'Yes. I do. All kinds of snacks.'

'Me too, they are my favourite things, with sausages.'

'I also like oysters.'

Solomon turns, his face bright with happy alarm. Shocked, giggling, 'No way! Oysters are horrid! You are amazing!'

'Thanks.'

I feel a surge of sadness as we walk, because little

Solomon inevitably and unwantedly reminds me of Minnie. The same innocent craziness, the same random adorability, even the same unworldly quality. That uneasy but beautiful feeling that kids of this age sometimes unwittingly possess. I know from my Piaget, my long studies of child psychology, that this age, seven, is right in the period of magical thinking, when kids don't just tell fairytales, they basically *are* fairytales. Granny Spargo would disagree. She would sip her brandy and speak of how kids are still close to that Other Place, whence they recently came.

Betty Spargo would definitely say 'whence'.

'The kitchen is over here . . . Karenza.'

He says my name carefully as if it is a special thing to be cherished. Then he pushes a door and everything changes. Unlike the rest of the house that I've seen, the kitchen is bright, warm, modern. Granite worktops, gleaming hobs, and a mighty oak island, around which there are three people gathered on high chairs.

A slender, pale, dark-haired girl of maybe ten stares solemnly ahead at nothing, with grey-blue eyes. I guess this is Grace Tyack. Does she have the striking looks of her mother? The russet-haired, russet-bearded man – sturdy, masculine, fortyish – will be the father, Malcolm. The man who warily asked for help.

And the angular, thin-lipped woman with multiple bangles and small tattoos on her hands, mid- or late-thirties.

Malcolm Tyack rises and offers me a pricey bespoke chair at the elegant kitchen island and a mug of tea.

I accept. I sit. Malcolm sits. I drink the hot tea, black. Feeling the tension and the awkwardness and the powerful quiet. How do I even begin this? *Oh hi, yes, I'm the forensic psychologist you hired, I hear your kids are reacting badly to the loss of their mother. Well, I can tell you that traumatic parental death has been linked to long-term deregulation of the hypothalamic pituitary adrenal axis in bereaved children and this can have multiple sequelae and and and . . .*

I stay quiet. This is not a formal interview in a formal interview room. It is not a prison or a hospital. I have to slowly feel my way and extemporize, let this grieving family guide me into itself. I know all about grieving families, so I should recognize the topography.

Small talk is made, with great effort, as the cold light begins to fade at the big kitchen windows. I do my best.

'I nearly got lost on those roads, even my phone gave up.'

Malcolm grunts.

'Yeah. Happens.'

Once again. 'And that last bit of lane, it's like a maze!'

'Mmm. 'Tis.'

Malcolm apparently doesn't want to say much at all. I am getting the same mixed emotions I sensed from him on the phone. He does not want me here; I am here at his invitation. He must *really* need help.

The small talks turns to the weather: the rain seems to have stopped again. Solomon fidgets. Grace Tyack stares resolutely ahead, as if she can see something compelling or even disturbing on the far kitchen wall yet is unwilling to alert anyone else. The angular woman is introduced as Molly, Malcolm's sister. She's 'helping with the kids'. I try once more to brighten things; I can detect *fear* in this family.

'Hello, Molly, I'm Karenza!'

'Hi.'

Molly offers me a limp fist-bump and a tiny smile which soon disappears, replaced by a discreet scowl.

Buoyant little Solomon is now bouncing impatiently up and down on his stool. 'Daddy, it's stopped raining, can I go play outside? There's a weasel! I want to see him. I'm calling him Noah.'

'Sure,' Malcolm grunts, but with the ghost of a smile. 'Off you go, lad. Find that weasel of yours.'

Solomon bolts from the kitchen, wrenching open the outside door. Cold autumn bustles in, bringing dead leaves and more tension. Molly rises and shuts the door and another heavy silence ensues.

At last Malcolm says, 'And, you two,' he looks meaningfully at Grace and Molly, 'give us the kitchen, will you? Please? Need to talk to Dr Bray here.'

He is obeyed. Grace gathers herself and walks proudly out of the kitchen; Molly shrugs and ambles away, pressing a vape to her mouth, still quietly scowling, at no one in particular.

Malcolm watches them go. I expect him to speak now that we're alone, but he just . . . *stares*. At me, or at nothing. This is clearly an intense battle for him.

I try to start conversations, but don't get anywhere. Eventually, I sit back, thinking: what is *my* impression? *Always assess your own impressions*: that is the forensic psych rule. And so far, despite his gruffness, he doesn't really feel, to me, like any kind of *murderer*. I have met enough murderers, and I can often get an initial sense in those first seconds: they say so much. But not this time.

And yet I know a woman died violently near here, and her children are apparently acting out. And I know, professionally, that the murder or suicide of a parent – a violent rather than a natural death – significantly raises the risk of depressive disorder in children for at least two years after the event. These kids are apparently disordered, one year after the event. Therefore this is prima facie evidence that something *bad* happened to Natalie Tyack.

Malcolm Tyack at last finds some more words. 'So, Dr Bray, how's this going to work then? What can you actually do for us?'

I seize on the opening. 'Well, first off, it's "Karenza", not "Doctor". Second, there are no rules here. Especially when dealing with kids, in their own home. We'll start with interviews, observations. Then if we're lucky we move on to, well . . . help. Therapy maybe. But I'll work around you and come and go as needed.'

A long pause.

'All right.' His eyes flick to the door, as if listening for something worrying, then back to me. 'And the money. We agreed all that. Yes?'

'Yes, of course, all settled.'

He nods. And falls again into wintry silence. The sky outside grows black and frigid and my mood edges towards pessimism, once more. How do I get inside this locked-in man, this locked-in family? What do I have in common with any of them? They are so rich, dynastic and strange, where do I truly start? Maybe with that unnerving encounter.

'I saw a young woman, in the garden, just as I arrived.'

Malcolm shrugs; I press on.

'Who was she? She was in a black hoodie, looked rather . . . nervous. Peculiar.'

'Black hoodie? That'll be Tricia. Cleaner. Doesn't like Baldhu, always got her hood up, lives over the way. Tied cottage.'

And that's that. The next silence is almost physically painful. We've already done the weather and the sorry state of the Penwith roads. Maybe I should try sport.

Does he like sport? Trouble is I know almost nothing about sport. Perhaps astronomy? Politics? Car repair?

Maybe I should just ask him, *Did you kill your wife?*

'How long?'

He has spoken, and after that prolonged silence it comes as a surprise.

'Sorry?'

Malcolm repeats, 'How long? Does it take? Till you're *done*.'

He says the word 'done' emphatically; he really wants this *done* and me out of here.

'It's hard to say. I'm sorry I can't be specific, until I know more.' I offer a slightly hapless shrug.

He grunts. 'OK.'

He tries to smile, but it is agonized.

I am refusing to be daunted. This may be a tough beginning, but I am reminding myself of prior difficult cases that initially felt as impervious as this. My rule was to treat them like a challenging rock-climb, take each movement in turn, don't think too far ahead. But I still need the initial foothold. I was good at rock-climbing. I can remember Kyle when he first stared up at me, moving from boulder to boulder; I recall that gratifying sparkle of desire, in his eyes.

And then I remember that me and Malcolm Tyack, we have an overlap.

'You know I've been to your restaurant, in Portloe? The Gunwale? I *love* the food there, that yellow Thai crab curry you do. Oh, my God!'

Malcolm's stony face relaxes. At last. A half-smile is proffered, then a little story about Newlyn fish market. I am in! For ten or fifteen minutes we chat about food, especially seafood. Turns out we share a love of oysters, langoustines, and even whelks, as long as they are doused in Tabasco; we admire the same famous seafood chef now working in Port Isaac.

'Yes!' Malcolm sighs, with a smile. 'Oh yes. I tried to recruit him! When he was twenty-five and doing mad stuff with scallops. He's on TV and everything now. Out of my league. For now, mind.'

His eyes gleam, and he tells me another story about crazy chefs, and I can't argue there; about 67 per cent of kitchen staff are neurodivergent, in my experience, and chefs might be over 98 per cent. And as we chat I take mental notes: Malcolm Tyack comes *alive* when he is talking about his job. He's ambitious. He's also successful. He has hopes and dreams, despite his evident grief.

Again: for me this does not add up to him being a wife-killer. But also, I know this means nothing. It is far too early to say, and domestic murders can come out of nowhere, or anywhere – like bad weather in West Cornwall. But this is my moment.

'Malcolm, why don't you tell me what's been going on here, in Baldhu House?' I smile in encouragement. 'Perhaps we can go from there.'

Malcolm Tyack spins the mug on the fine oak island, and nods to himself, and says, 'OK. OK. Well . . . there's been a lot. A hell of a lot.'

'Sure, but every journey: single step, you know.'

He takes a deep breath. 'All right – here's one for you. Yesterday, Grace said we are all in danger.'

'Sorry?'

He grimaces. 'My girl, she's not much of a talker. You'll see. But yesterday she went off on this . . . ah . . .' He scrubs his face with his hand. 'This bloody sermon. Saying we're all in terrible danger, all of us, *except her*. Except her? What's that about? I have no idea what's going on. It is like the kids are slowly going mad. Or they are hypnotized, by someone, something, some memory or place or whatever. Why? *What is happening in this house?*' Now he looks at me, with raw honesty. 'Please help us, Dr Bray. I have no choice left. Please help us before something really bad happens.'

He does not say the next word, but I sense it in the air. Before something really bad happens . . . *again*.

6

The tea mugs are diligently stacked in the dishwasher; Malcolm Tyack offers me a brisk tour of the house. He has work to do.

'It's big. And old. The house.'
'I noticed.'
'Let's go.'

We walk into the main hall, which seems to be the nerve centre of the place, along with the kitchen. I inhale that peculiar perfume again: age and varnish and leather . . . and dead roses. Like the smell of an old country church. Yet sweeter, sadder, stranger.

And disturbingly colder.

I shiver; he glances my way in the semi-gloom.

'Sorry about that,' he says. 'Can get bloody cold. Can't afford to heat the whole place: it'd bankrupt us. So we only heat and light a few rooms: the kitchen, kids' rooms, my rooms, spare room for Molly. A couple of living rooms. That's it. You may need a coat if you need the downstairs loo. And a torch after dark.'

I hesitate to ask the obvious question . . . but I remind myself I am here as a forensic psychologist; my *job* is to ask the obvious question. This family needs help, not politeness.

'Malcolm, have you ever considered something more

practical? This place is huge, it's cold. You have a young family, and you're miles from schools.'

He winces as if he has heard this many times. 'Course. And, course not. Baldhu has been in the Tyack family for centuries. Six hundred years? Eight hundred? No way we can sell. Or live anywhere else. Absurd.' He says this as if he means it, and he goes on, 'We've got mines out the back, beyond the garden, crap mines, barely turned a profit after 1800, closed in the 1880s. But we owned them. Our land. Our mines. We bloody *dug* them. This is where the Tyacks *live*.'

'And the farmland all around?'

'Nooo. Rent it to another farmer. Cows bore me, and they bored my dad, and his dad too. And I can't stand milk, it's basically cow mucus.'

'Never thought of it like that.'

He chuckles darkly. 'Fighting and mining are the Tyack thing. My ancestors put down the Rebellion, won a lot of land.' He looks marginally proud. 'Plus maybe we did a bit of wrecking. Y'know. Down at the zawn.'

'And the other Tyacks?'

'Dad's dead. Mum's disabled in Penzance. Wheelchair. Couldn't live here any more, gave the house to me. So this is where I live. With my kids. Not bloody moving.'

My professional mind is alerted. So the mother gave the house to Malcolm. Molly, the younger sister, did *not* inherit Baldhu. Did she inherit anything at all?

Perhaps I have found one source of the familial tension.

Malcolm continues, 'OK, down there's the cellar, dark, wet and cold. Medieval. Good for storing smuggled brandy in the 1700s, not much else. I put my motorbike parts there once, rusted in a week.'

'Upstairs?'

'Bedrooms. Seven. Ridiculous. Over there,' he waves a hand, 'we've got a breakfast room, never used, music room, never used, conservatory full of books – light keeps 'em dry. Then outhouses, greenhouses – it's endless – I could go on. You get the idea. House is all ages. Kitchen is the hearth. I have to do some work, restaurant deliveries tomorrow. Do you want to talk to Grace? Now's probably a good time; she has homework today and she *always* does her homework in the afternoon but if you hurry . . .'

The house tour, it seems, is already over. Not quite Hampton Court Palace. But I get the idea, and I do want to talk to Grace, alone, to start the job. Not a structured interview, that can wait – merely a chat for now. And the meagre day is already dying, and the journey home could last eighty minutes, in the autumn murk.

'She'll be in her room.' He gestures to some modestly grand, crooked wooden stairs. 'Third door on the left. Just knock.'

And with that he departs.

The stairs are almost invisible as the light retires. The lazy rain has returned: it is hissing on the windows as a wet November continues its tedious theme into winter. Finding a light switch, I flick it on, and the stairs are made just about visible. A weak, money-saving bulb casts a yellow glow on the hall and the balustrades.

Climbing the stairs to an equally shadowy landing, I pause. There is an arched window here: Gothic. It overlooks the surrounding woods and fields. The sea, nearly black in the twilight, is visible between the silhouetted cliffs. The lights of a distant ship sparkle wetly on the horizon. So far away the ship does not seem to move.

I approach the third door on the left. All the doors

are old, all the floorboards creak, the antiquarian decay is evident, and yet the wooden floor is laid with exquisite Turkish carpets. Tyack money is not nothing, I surmise, and it has been around a long while.

Softly, I rap on the door. A quiet, lonely voice replies. 'Yes?'

'Hello, Grace. It's Karenza. Can I come in?'

A long pause. Then, 'No.'

'Sorry?'

Nothing.

'Grace?'

The girl within sighs audibly, and answers: 'Why do you have to come in?'

'Well . . . if you want me to help.'

The next pause is even longer. Then Grace says, 'Fine.'

I turn the squealing doorknob. Inside it is, thankfully, brighter. A pleasant, large, green-painted bedroom with big Georgian sash windows, one of them half open, overlooks rustling twilit gardens. The old mines must be just beyond, if Malcolm, that big brusque man, is not lying; and why would he lie?

As I think this, I realize the danger I could be in in, *simply being here*. The only man in the house might be a wife-killer, and I am investigating his family. And he knows I might uncover things, so he does not want me here; at the same time, he has no choice: his kids need help.

Fear flutters in my stomach. I ignore it. Kyle would never send me into danger. We got divorced, but it was tragic, not bitter. We share too much.

Grace sits cross-legged on her bed with a book on her lap. Charles Dickens. *Bleak House*. At the age of ten? Clearly a bright girl. Scholarly. *Always does her homework in the afternoon.*

Grace is dressed in black leggings and a black T-shirt, but she has swapped her hoodie for an oversized white cardigan that is oddly aged for a little girl. Instinctively, I assess the room; it is part of the job – read the scene as if it is psychological Braille.

Her room is decorated with antique maps of Cornwall, pictures of sailing ships, and oddments. Big shells, conches, gathered from the zawn, maybe. Two globes – also antique? Then a mangy old stuffed polecat poised in a glass box, its sharp, ugly, yellow teeth bared forever.

Lots of books ranged across two walls. More Dickens, *Dracula*, Shakespeare sonnets, Harry Potter, books about whales and Antarctica. Brass instruments. Nautical. Something like a sextant. A small old silver hand mirror. It could almost be the room of a naval historian.

'Can I sit on this chair, Grace?'

Grace says, with a shrugging voice, 'Fine.'

I add the evidence of these monosyllables, and the lack of eye contact, to what I have already noticed about Grace. A possible, tentative diagnosis of Autism Spectrum Disorder is clearly knocking on the door, but I do not especially care. It does not matter *at the moment*. I want to help this little girl, who is in some mental distress far beyond the implications of neurodivergence. And grief is not a syndrome. Neither, for that matter, is fear – especially if there really is something to scare you.

And little Grace Tyack thinks they are all in danger. This girl is fearful – of what?

'I'm here to help, but we need to talk, Grace. Could you please put down your book?'

A sigh of defiance, then, '*Fine.*'

The book is dropped, Grace looks up and to the side, and her pretty, pale face is outlined. She regards the window, which is now rattling in the blustery dark weather, and says, 'Rain. Again. Always raining.'

'Do you dislike the rain?'

'Yes.'

This is said with some venom, followed by silence. The chilly wet wind is gusting through the window. I let the silence continue until Grace gets uncomfortable. I imagine she could go a long time without talking. But it does not take so long: after a minute, Grace speaks.

'But . . . I like the wind. I love the wind here in Baldhu. Last week I read about a sailing boat that went so far in the wind it turned into a raven, a beautiful raven, and then it died. It drowned in the sea in the night.'

She looks right at me, a flashing glimpse of grey-blue eyes, then averts her face again.

I take this opportunity. 'Grace, I'd like to talk about . . . some things you've said.'

'Like what?'

I wish she would look at me properly so I can read her expressions, her body language. But Grace Tyack does not oblige.

She is staring fixedly at the window, as if she can see a face out there, or a fascinating view of old whaling boats.

The room is silent apart from the wind and rain. The dead, stuffed polecat – or is it a mink? – glares at me. Yellow fangs ready, a killer of the woods.

I have to start somewhere. 'You said to your father that the family is in danger.'

The next reply is swift.

'No, I didn't.'

'He says you did.'

'No, I didn't.'

'But . . .'

The cold Penwith wind ruffles the curtains. I start to frame a new question, but Grace turns and flashes a long, fierce glance just over my shoulder. 'My father is a *liar*.'

'Sorry?'

'Don't trust him. Anything he says. Don't. He brought that mirror in. That one, there, there, said it was Mummy's and I might like it. He lied. I despise that thing. Horrible. Ever since.'

The anger is jarring from a ten-year-old. Confused, I look at the hand mirror. It is small, pretty and silvery, lying demurely in the shadows of a shelf. Rather fine-looking, obviously antique.

I reach out to examine it and Grace yells. 'No! *Don't touch it!*'

'Why not?'

She frowns. 'It's Mummy's. You might see her face. Solly says he did.'

I grasp at my own unease. Grace is ten: she should be beyond magical thinking. Is this regression? Some latency, perhaps, part of her stuck at the age of seven?

'When, Grace, when did Solly see your mummy? In the mirror?'

'Then.'

'When?'

'Not saying. Ask Solly. He did it to her, did those awful things.'

'Grace?'

Silence again. The wind, the polecat. Hunting rabbits.

Grace mutters, 'I have to do my homework now. I always do my homework now.'

'Just a few more questions. Who is "he", Grace? Solomon?'

'Not saying.'

'OK. What do you mean when you say, "he did awful things"?'

'Didn't say Solly, said *things*. THINGS!'

'Grace?'

'Things!' She is yelling now. 'Things! Things! Things! Them! Why don't you listen? Why doesn't anyone ever *listen* to me?'

The loud words jar. Grace is so young and troubled, and so angry, and maybe on the brink of something worse. As if she is about to break into hysterical sobs.

I have pushed this far enough. Kids are often the hardest cases of all.

'All right, Grace, I'm sorry if I upset you.'

Grace talks to the wall behind me. 'You didn't.'

'That's good.'

A silence.

'I wonder if we should call it a day, Grace.'

Silence.

'I'm going back to Falmouth now, it's a long drive.'

Silence.

'OK, I'll go.'

Grace speaks to the wall again: 'Bye.'

I rise and walk to the door, expecting nothing more from this stilted, angry, peculiar conversation.

The polecat grins in victory. The rain that Grace hates, the breeze that she likes: they fill the room. But then, as I near the door, Grace Tyack suddenly says, 'Are you not . . . coming back?'

I turn. 'Sorry?'

'You. Not coming back. Again?'

'Well, it's kind of – up to you guys.' I am almost stammering, I am so strangely unnerved by Grace. How can that be? I was unfazed by that serial killer in HMP

Belmarsh who dismembered both his victims. This is a ten-year-old girl somewhere on the spectrum, a ten-year-old with unresolved grief.

Grace says, 'You're really, truly going now? To Falmouth? Past Mousehole?'

She pronounces it right. Mowzl. Not Mouse-hole. A local lass.

Grace adds: 'I knew it. Everyone goes. Everyone *goes* in the end. Like a cannibal running to his cave by the sea.'

'Sorry?'

'I read it in a book. About cannibals. They always live by the sea.'

I do not know whether to answer.

Now Grace looks yearningly, straight at me, not at something over my shoulder. Finally, she is holding my gaze. Eye to eye.

'Karenza.'

'Yes?'

'I'm scared. Please come back. *Please.*'

Is that a rolling tear? I believe it is. And my natural urge is to rush over and hug this disturbed child. But I know that is wrong: you must maintain a distance, and already Grace has swiped the tear and turned off her emotions and buried herself in her book. *Always do my homework*.

So I murmur, loud enough for Grace to hear, 'I will be back. I promise.'

I go out onto the softly lit landing of ancient Baldhu House. And realize, with some disquiet, that my heart is pounding.

7

Malcolm

People are shouting at him about halibut. Malcolm thinks: *My God, I can do without this.*

Halibut.

'Malcolm, how many? How many halibut do we need?'

'Fuck knows. Seven hundred thousand?'

The sous-chef looks at Malcolm, unhappily. 'Malc?'

'Sorry. Sorry, sorry. Got stuff at home. Y'know. Please ask Chef, I have to sort out the VAT.'

Anders the sous-chef gives him a sympathetic glance. *Stuff at home?* Malcolm winces, inwardly, at the implications – *stuff at home*. His dead wife, Natalie. His strange, motherless kids. The questions unanswered in the sad, beautiful house he cannot ever leave. The house he shared with Natalie, now dead. Yes, he, Malcolm, definitely has *stuff at home*.

Malcolm stalks back to his office, away from the clattering chaos of the kitchen, thinking about Natalie, trying not to think about Natalie.

At the top of the stairs he pushes the door and sits at the desk, which overlooks St Ives harbour, from Smeaton's Pier to Porthgwidden beach. The view is one of the best in town: Malcolm sometimes likes to speculate how much money he would make if he sold the place and let it, inevitably, be converted into flats. He would make way more money than he does running it as a restaurant.

But that would be selling off another little chunk of Cornwall, to the *incomers*.

Malcolm takes in the view, with a vestigial feeling of satisfaction: of ancestral ownership. When the mines and the farms were exhausted his clever forefathers bought this property, and similar in Newlyn and Fowey, and they became fish wholesalers: sending pilchards to London, by the barrel, by the billion.

And yet, most of those properties have slowly been sold and *turned into flats* to keep the main house going, and now Malcolm, from the last line of the Tyacks, sells sea bass poached in lemongrass and green chilli to hungry Londoners.

But the income, so varying, gives him more migraines. The only reliable thing is the rent from the farm, but that is not much. So every day, like today, he stares at numbers wondering if this year they might go under, and then he will have to sell. They could live off the money for years, but he cannot ever sell, and they must absolutely never sell Baldhu – no one else would understand it; they would know the reputation, they would learn the truth, they might actually sue.

And now the world crowds around him again. Texts, emails, kitchen chatter percolating up to the office, a shouted question from the other office next door.

'Malcolm, we've got a problem with the veggies, lorry broke down on the A30.'

'That waitress, called off sick again – who can we ask—'

'Hey Malc, about that halibut—'

'*Yes*, I am calling the wholesalers about the bloody halibut!'

The hours pass, fast and yet slow. This is not the enjoyable side of the biz. The creative stuff, working on menus with the chefs, changing the décor by season, planning a new gastropub in Porthleven, he likes that, loves it sometimes.

For the first time in ninety minutes, he looks up from the books. A rare sunny November day is decaying, he can take a break, go back home and see the kids: it is Saturday. The restaurants will survive without him for one afternoon, maybe an entire evening; all these questions can be answered by others.

Grabbing his phone, coat, keys, he makes his way down the stairs – handing the restaurant, the Halyard, *in toto*, to Anders, thanking God as he does it that he found Anders, because he is clever and capable. A manager in the making. Then Malcolm sprints across the backyard and jumps in the big, dented Toyota, and checks the road conditions online; and he sighs. The map tells him the only main road out of St Ives, to Carbis Bay, is blocked by a traffic accident, meaning it could take him an hour – two hours – to cross the ten miles of Penwith, north to south, if he uses the A roads.

B roads it is. He will have to go the other way, to St Just, then cross the granite crest of Penwith, slowly stealing through the farms and moors.

Even as he looks at the map, the messages ping. One of them is about the halibut. Malcolm laughs, a little bleakly. He switches his phone off, and then he keys the engine, leaving St Ives behind.

Soon enough he is in St Just. The granite buildings in the little square. And for a moment he idles the car, by the clocktower, immersed in memory.

Because this is where he met Natalie. This is where he stumbled over her, like coming across a lovely flower, a rock of gleaming pyrites. She was just standing there. A primrose of the spring that he found in the May-time sun in this humble yet pretty little square of St Just-in-Penwith. And she was smiling at him, beautiful and dark-haired and sadly lovely and so entirely radiant. And holding a new pasty in a brown-paper wrapper from Warrens.

Natalie.

The sadness hits him, with the thundering guilt, and it makes Malcolm close his remembering eyes.

He recalls how he told her that the pasties were better from McFadden's. She looked at him like he was a clown. But then she laughed, and it was like the sound of the stream that flows down Bathsheba Valley, and he asked her if she wanted a drink at 12.15 p.m., not knowing how else to ask her out. He was thirty-one and she was twenty. She told him he was clearly an alcoholic; he probably loved her from that moment on.

In his own way. Which no one understood and no one understands, and which many do not believe.

Malcolm revs the old motor, and races on, heading south now, over Penwith, meandering through the past. Towards Cripplesease and Madron, into all the places she loved. As the car takes the dips and curves of the B roads, he looks up: he can actually see the outline of Ding Dong mine, with its sweet, soft meadows, overlooking Mount's Bay. And that is more than a memory, that is an icon to be revered. Because that is where he first made love to Natalie – on those meadows, in bright warm sun, his body next to her lovely body, her shy and lovely smile. That first time was so sweet it nearly made him cry and he had never felt that way with a woman until he met her, it actually unmanned him, and he didn't mind, from then on he wanted to be unmanned.

Onwards, and backwards. The battered car speeds past stone hedges and gnarly ash, and ever more memories. Here, near Nancledra – this is where she found a fox's skull, light as a blown eggshell, its jawbone still there, still marvellously hinged. There, over at Trezelah, that's where she tried to teach him the names of the moorland plants, star moss and cloudberry, bog asphodel and cotton-grass, and as soon as she said them he half forgot them – yet he looked at her with dazzled delight, he never forgot the way she said the words, the old Cornish words she had learned; primrose is *briallen*, and that's what she was, his *briallen*, his primrose. Natalie Skuse.

The car speeds on, down the nightmare tiny roads, around these beautiful tiny lanes: he rumbles through puddles, swerves around a hiker, startles a fine young horse, which canters away, jumping for joy in the last chilly autumn sun, the sun, which is fast disappearing, as he reaches the highest hill of all, with the grand view to Cape Cornwall and the oceans. And again he *remembers*.

He remembers standing here, once, early on, with Natalie; both of them were looking west, hand in hand, and content, quietly and entirely in love. But then she dropped his hand and she made some notes; she was always making notes. She told him on their first proper date that one day she wanted to be a writer, but she was so secretive about this writing, shy, maybe ashamed it was no good. She seldom let him read the things she wrote, and he never pried too much.

But that time he asked her, *what are you writing*, and she pointed at the horizon, at Cape Cornwall, Sennen Cove, the mighty blue seas beyond, and she said, 'You know every Celtic nation has a legend of the west, of the other place, close to heaven. *Lyonesse*. The beautiful land of the dead.' She smiled, in that sad, happy way. 'And I wonder if that is why we came here. We weren't chased here, we weren't *pushed* here. We *came* here, to find it.'

And when she said this, he looked at her, this girl from the kids' home, this check-out girl from the Spar in St Just – and he reached out and held her hand, and he was happy.

And now he is unhappy. And he is maybe getting nearer to the source of the unhappiness. The fields and moors descend to Gulval. Veering left, he takes the quickest and narrowest route. Past thrashed dark hedges and flailed grey bushes. It is all cowering, shivering, brutalized.

Natalie may have loved all this landscape, including its scars, but all his life Malcom has been more ambivalent, perhaps because, for so long, the Tyacks *owned* so much of the land – and abused it. Mined it, blasted it, scraped it, soured its lovely streams, made them run red with metal ore. They all did it, all the old families, they gored the land and made it bleed: Bassets and Killigrews and Vyvyans, Williamses and Boscawens and Rashleighs. And the Tyacks, too. Here, in the far southwest, the Tyacks definitely did their best, digging and breaking, smashing and looting, so they could build Baldhu House, and fill it with *things*.

He is close enough now, he needs to make calls.

Picking up his phone he turns it on – and immediately it rings, like it has been waiting, building its own tension. The screen says Molly: his sister.

He takes the call, his sister speaks. 'Malcolm, please, Malc – now – you must *come now*!'

He stares out of the car window, bewildered. Molly sounds strange, breathless. He can hear noises behind her. Something smashing? 'What the hell? What's going on?'

'The kids! Malcolm!'

'But I thought you were taking them to Truro, the movies – I was heading back to spend some ti—'

'Just come now!'

His sister is never like this. Molly can be waspish and snappish, and also funny and laconic, but he never hears her *panicked*.

'OK – I'm coming!'

And here he is, the last mile then the last hundred yards of mud; he swerves dangerously fast, parks up by the barns, and leaps from the car. Running into the house, he calls for Solomon or Grace, Molly, but as he crosses the hall he sees.

The floor of the hall is scattered – with ceramic shards. A vase must be broken. He does not recognize it but then Baldhu is full of all these *things*, in rooms used and unused. Probably it is old, Chinese or Indian or English. Anyway it is just a thing, it does not matter; what matters is that Malcolm can hear *screaming*.

It sounds like Grace, and it sounds as if she is in the living room, yelling, time and again, as if she is being tortured. Her howls are interrupted by softer, older words: his sister, trying to calm her.

And now it gets worse. He can hear Solly, upstairs: shrieking, similarly. Solomon is just seven, but who is comforting *him*?

Sprinting upstairs, he nearly trips on the rucked, fading old Turkey carpet and the shouting gets louder; halfway down the landing he pushes the creaking door, and he is met with the sight of Solomon, in his Chelsea shirt and shorts, in this innocent boy's bedroom, with the Chelsea duvet and the Lego dinosaurs. Solly is sitting on the floor with the neighbour, Sam, sitting right behind him.

Why? Because Sam has his legs either side of Solomon and this is because Sam is *holding on to Solomon*, with his arms wrapped around Solomon: the neighbour is caging him, straitjacketing him, as if the boy is a madman, as if worried that if he lets go Solly will do terrible things, to himself, to the house, to the world.

The room is blasting cold. Malcolm looks across – the main window, with its view of the woods, is shattered. Sharp fangs of glass are glittering on the sill, showing that the window must have been punched *out*. Malcolm is guessing Solomon did it.

He gazes at Sam, his expression saying, *What?* But Sam's tanned and anxious face is focused on the small boy in his grasp.

'Jesus, Sam, what happened?'

Sam looks up at Malcolm, but as he does, Solomon struggles and kicks, pushing and scrapping. 'Daddy, make him let me go! Make him *let me go*!'

'Sam, what the hell?'

Sam looks exhausted, a grown man holding a seven-year-old boy. 'Thank God you're here.'

'What's been going on? Molly rang me, but—'

Sam exhales, shaking his head. 'Yeah. She rang me too, buddy. I came straight over. It's been going on for an hour, apparently – the window – the kitchen – Christ—'

'*Daddy!* She did it!'

'What, Solomon, what?'

Solly shakes his head. He shouts but the words are meaningless. Just yells. Yips like a feral dog, like a fox in the winter fog, in the garden. The image is beyond distressing.

Once more Solomon fights to be free, pushing and pulling at Sam's arms, a beast controlled, and Sam gives Malcolm a stare that says: this is your kid, your son, your terrible mess. I can do my best, but *you* need to sort it out.

Malcolm nods, and kneels down on the carpet opposite his boy and Sam.

'OK, Solomon, OK. Sam will let you go – if you promise to calm down.'

The boy's sweet face contorts. It is an anguished face, full of unfallen tears, about to roll. A brave boy fighting terror and grief. As if he is listening to the news about his mummy all over again, the morning after that discovery at the zawn. Malcolm cannot ever forget it: the neat stripe of blood on her face, as if she was an Apache brave, prepared for death. Did she know in that last moment? Know who did it, and why?

'Please, Solomon, can you promise not to act up if Sam lets you go?'

The awful yapping has stopped: the boy is quieter. The wind flutes through the broken window, and Malcolm wonders what else is broken.

Solomon looks directly at his father, imploring, seeking reassurance. Malcolm smiles, as best he can, then he nods in Sam's direction.

'OK, Solomon, OK . . . Sam will let you go.'

Slowly, Sam unfurls his arms, opening the cage. Solomon is free. Free to run around the house, smashing the place to bits. Instead, he crawls across the carpet and sinks into Malcolm's arms.

Solomon is quiet. Malcolm can feel his boy's little heart galloping away, but the boy is quiet. Malcolm can smell Solly's clean hair: grass and straw and vanilla. He thinks, *the sweet smell of your children: it is maybe all there is, in the end: the only good thing*. Especially when the mother has gone.

Malcolm rocks Solomon, back and forth. 'It's OK, mate, it's OK. You're good now. Good now. Dad is here now. Everything is good.'

Solomon nods and mumbles. Sam says, 'They were fighting so bad. We had to separate them.'

'Jesus.'

Malcolm talks down to his seven-year-old, cradled as if he is two. 'What happened, kiddo?'

Solomon speaks, quietly now, almost tearful. 'Her. She. Grace. She . . . put it back in here.'

'What?'

'The mirror. The stupid thing that shows things.'

'What?'

'I found it on my bed, and I hate it, and she laughed and said I am stupid, and I threw it out of the window and then we had a fight all over and broke things and then and then—'

'What?'

The boy goes silent. Solly climbs out of his father's arms and moves away, suddenly looking a lot older. He sits on the floor like an older person. Arms draped over knees, hands flopping, fiery red hair hanging low over his forehead, staring at the floor.

'Daddy, she said I killed Mummy. That I pushed her over because she liked Grace more. That's not – not true, is it? She's lyin' again.'

Malcolm gazes at Solomon, and then at Sam, and then at his boy, at his tousled russet hair, peppery red freckles. What can a guilty father say to this? What can anyone say to this? Sam Berenson is flushed; he looks mortified, or horrified.

Solomon lifts his eyes and gazes at the window he broke. Then he speaks, wordless no longer. His voice is deeper, serious, adult.

'Grace knows. You do know that, Daddy, don't you? Grace knows because she did it.'

8

'Can't believe you're on that case. Wow. That weird family.'

'Natalie Tyack, I remember that.'

'You could become a famous detective. Mrs Karenza Holmes of 221B Maritime Parade.'

I groan quietly, in the middle of the cocktailing crowd, then I look in despair and, with a hint of irritation, at Dinah. Walking into this birthday party at the airy, glassy Kittiwake Café – organized by her – I was instantly surrounded by people who already seem to know that I've been hired by the Tyacks of Baldhu House, up there by old Penberth Cove. The ancient family with the young, dead mother.

How? It must have been Dinah. Only she knows, apart from Kyle, and Kyle is a lawyer, a pro: he would never reveal this.

Dinah makes an apologetic face. 'Sorry,' she whispers. 'Sorry, sorry. I only told one person, the new owner, Ed. He loves gossip, you know, and we're hoping he might fund a scholarship. It's so frustrating having to ask for everything from Exeter . . .' She sees my angry glare and mutters, 'And he's nice. He's moved down to be nearer his kids, he told me. Better than the last owner – remember those awful pad Thais?'

I don't care: I am fuming. The new owner of our

favourite beach café is like Jago Moyle – just as charming, ten years older and a lot posher, and with way more money – and even more indiscreet. Of all the people to tell! He'll have spread it instantly: working the room, smile as bright as his signet ring.

I turn back to the expectant people, drinks in hand, looking at me. I will have to ride this out. I can't deny what I'm doing; but I can be quite opaque about it.

'Well . . . maybe a bit of me always wanted to be a detective. I used to devour Agatha Christie by the shedload.'

'She totally wrote them by the shedload.'

I turn and see Priya Hardwicke sipping from her flute of Camel Valley fizz. She's a friend of Dinah's. I've never quite befriended Priya, never quite found the time. Dinah always makes time for everyone: she collects people. I wish I had that social gift.

Priya asks, 'There are two kids, right?'

'I can't say: they are clients now. But I guess that's public knowledge.' I shrug and sip my own fizz. 'So, well – yes.'

'Poor children, and the mum so young.'

'I simply want to help them.'

'Is that all you can tell us? Really?'

Another voice, male, and yes, of course, it is Ed Hartley, the down-from-London owner. Handsome, dark-haired, generous smile, grey-blue eyes sparkling, funny.

'You have to tell us more! There's a dead body!'

'Sorry?'

'Oh, come on.' He grins. 'Indulge us! What's your hunch? It's like a TV drama, and we are absolutely *famished* down here when it comes to gossip. Cornwall needs gossip!'

I can see Dinah looking at him, admiringly. And now I suddenly realize that she *fancies* him, hence the tattle: she was trying to charm him. I wonder if she realizes he's probably gay, despite the kids. I know the signals. Cheerily, I respond, 'Well, there's a really freaky polecat, definitely looks like a killer. But he's stuffed in a vitrine. So I'm ruling him out. For now.'

Ed Hartley sighs in a good-natured way and says, 'I've met the family a couple of times, lovely children; but Malcolm Tyack, he's a tough businessman, and the brother, the *enfant terrible*?' He regards me with a meaningful nod of sympathy – but then he is summoned by his wait-staff, and his nod becomes apologetic. The manager steps briskly away to check on his other guests, to work the room.

I take the moment to grab a canapé from a tray that is being expertly ferried around by a white-shirted girl. Probably a student from Falmouth University, just two miles up the road, in Penryn.

My guess is that at least two-thirds of the guests at this fiftieth birthday party are from, or linked to, the university. Some are lecturers, some older students doing PhDs, plus the birthday boy himself, who is a full-on Head of English, with a sideline in Cornish history: Noel Oswell. Bumptious, funny, full of himself.

I turn to the birthday celebrant. 'Noel. Happy birthday!'

Noel chortles. 'Thank you. *Fifty?* How did it come to this? How did I make fifty?'

Dinah says, 'I guess you were forty-nine?'

Noel forces a chuckle and turns to me, with an inquisitive look. 'So you're working for the Tyacks? That's quite a family, even without the murder. All that history!'

He reaches out and puts a hand on my arm. It could

be simply friendliness, yet it irks. Patronizing. Or maybe I am being over-sensitive, annoyed at this unwanted scrutiny. Noel chuckles, spitting flecks of canapé.

'That coast is quite notorious. Don't go wandering at night! And the infamous zawns!'

This is intensely awkward. I make another note to scold Dinah. Then I cover my uneasy silence by filching another canapé – good, salty, tapenade – as Noel expounds to the room on wider Cornish history. He is a specialist and makes sure everyone knows it. He has written books on copper mines and mackerel boats and Cornish ghosts and bal maidens – girls employed aged nine to break rocks in the mines, until the early 1930s. I wonder if he knows my great-grandmother, Betty Spargo's mum, was an actual bal maiden. Probably not.

Noel is lecturing. 'Like I say, they have quite a history, the Tyacks of Baldhu. Rumoured to be wreckers, in the seventeenth and eighteenth centuries. Even up to the nineteenth. Along with the Killigrews and the Coppingers – the cruel Coppingers! And the Tyack mines ran out early, yet they stayed mysteriously wealthy. So . . . one has to wonder.'

Priya interrupts, 'But I thought that was all a myth. For tourists. Wreckers?'

Noel shakes his head. 'Nope. The usual revisionism – anything exciting gets filed as nonsense. Well, in this case it's true, they really did lure ships onto rocks, and whole families specialized in it, especially in Penwith and the Lizard. Running down the cliffs to crack a few skulls, women stealing away with rum in their kettles, the men with hatchets, and crates of Chinese silver!' He pops a canapé and repeats a rhyme: 'God keep us from rocks and shelving sands and save us from Breage and

Penberth men's hands.' A pause. 'And Baldhu House is about a mile from Penberth?'

Noel Oswell knows how to tell a story. He has half of crowded Kitty Café listening in. Except me, because Noel is irritating me, he is so *confident* of his knowledge, and because I can't help remembering Malcolm Tyack admitting the family might have been wreckers. But then, what does it matter? Evil genes, over many generations? *Really?*

At last Noel brings his theatrical little lecture to a close with some gruesome story about a steamer, the *Ana* out of Bilbao, wrecked in fog on the Three Stone Oar rocks, off Morvah, and how maybe a dozen shipwrecked sailors made it to the beach, only to be hacked to death on the sands. And all that rum, indigo and coffee beans were stolen and hidden in Penwith cellars. And silver. Lots of silver.

'The wreckers waited in Morvah church till it was one minute past midnight. They wouldn't murder anyone on the Sabbath, but Monday was fine.' He chuckles and eats another canapé. And now someone else butts in with memories of Natalie Tyack: the news story, the discovery of her body on the beach, the beautiful young woman on the TV, the suspicions of the family, of murder, then the way it all dribbled to nothing – and all the time I am squirming in discomfort.

At last, Dinah intervenes. 'OK, guys, enough. I've been totally indiscreet.'

'You certainly have,' says Noel. 'Tell us, Priya, why *are* people so obsessed with beautiful dead women? Such a cliché!'

I can't take a minute more. Stepping away, I loot a final flute of bubbles, down it in two, and make for the exit, on the way cornering Dinah, who is suitably contrite.

'Oh, my God, I'm so sorry. I shouldn't have told anyone. I literally mentioned it in passing to Ed. Can you forgive me? And bloody Noel Oswell, he's insufferable! How does his wife cope?'

I glare at her. She is my best friend, we go back ages: she knows I will forgive her, and she probably did just pass it along without thinking, because she was flirting.

'You owe me a few days' pet-sitting.'

She agrees, hurriedly. 'Yes, yes. Of course. Anything!'

I frown, then offer a forgiving smile. 'Please don't say any more.'

'I will take a vow of silence, and I'll feed El Gruffalo for a week!'

We have a brief and reconciling hug.

I grab my coat, call my taxi, pause for a glance at lovely, starlit Gyllyngvase Beach, where the sea is becalmed on the first dry, quiet night in weeks. I see Noel Oswell staring at me from inside the café: squinting, puzzled. He notices my returning gaze and smiles briskly, somehow rudely, then turns away.

My cab arrives, and I scoot home to my silent, pristine and welcoming apartment. I pay honour to El Gruffalo, who loftily ignores me, as if he is waiting for a more important video call; I say a smiley hello to Otto – grey, with a hint of black? – then sit at my desk with my laptop, the distracting windows firmly curtained, going over my notes and tasks for tomorrow. Two clients are lined up: that's pretty good.

And yet, I am looking at my calendar with a hint of frustration. I need all the clients I can get, and I like the intricate, difficult, funny, challenging humans I meet, I like all of it.

But now?

Now, despite this evening, maybe because of this evening, all I can think of is that house in the beautiful woods of Penwith. And those two children in their lonely rooms along that gloomy dark-panelled landing. And the rain and the moon on the rocky waters of the zawn, where the wreckers lured the boats, and the sailors, to their doom.

9

I watch as Malcolm drains his tea, and as he eats another biscuit. Briskly brushing crumbs away.

Malcolm is finishing his description of Recent Events. When he came home to find his house in chaos, broken plates here in the gleaming kitchen, a smashed vase on the floor of the hall, a window shattered in Solomon's bedroom.

'Anything else?'

Malcolm half-shrugs: stroking that red beard, musing. 'Not really. Lots of things tipped over but no one burned the family bible.'

He sweeps more crumbs off the kitchen table, onto the floor. I take a mental note: he is a man who expects things to be cleaned for him.

He goes on, 'Maybe Grace chipped some furniture in the living room. She was rampaging around but she's not exactly, y'know, a sumo wrestler, it was more . . . things knocked over. Molly calmed her. Eventually.'

'And they really didn't say why they were arguing, apart from that mirror?'

'No. That was it. The mirror. Caused this huge ruckus. Idiotic. A bloody hand mirror.'

But as Malcolm Tyack says this his confident eyes slide – unusually, and for the tiniest moment – to the side. What I observe is a *tell*. This evasive moment, however fragmentary, says Malcolm Tyack may be lying.

My own memory nags: Grace, near shrieking, in her room. *My father is a liar!*

'This mirror,' I say. 'Do you have any idea why it bothers your children so much? Grace was also extremely agitated by it.'

'Honestly don't know.' And this time his eyes remain fixed on me. 'It was their mother's, Natalie's. God knows where she got it from, probably found it in some chest around the house, after the wedding.' He gestures, expansive, the owner. 'There are so many rooms, so much stuff, random antiques. I think it's Indian maybe, Japanese? Anyway she always kept it close, in her special drawer, with her notebook, a few mementoes, old photos; she never had much. Tough childhood.'

His eyes are misting over. This gruff and masculine man: is he missing his dead wife, or is he suffused with guilt?

'So how did the kids get it? The mirror?'

'I gave it to Grace, when she was really distraught, after the, you know, the accident. It was something of her mum's, something precious to keep. Thought it might console her.' He sighs, profoundly. 'That was a mistake. Solly thought I was favouring her, so he stole it, then she stole it back. Then they both claimed they hated it, yet they won't let me touch it. Now I'd throw it down a mine if I could, but then they would hate me even more.'

He looks at me, from his kitchen chair, firm now.

'I've brought it in here. Kitchen. Neutral space. Feel free to examine it for magic spells.'

I swivel: the mirror sits innocently on a kitchen shelf. Delicate and bright, yet apparently suffused with some power over these kids.

'You can examine anything, that's why you're here. The psychiatrist. To sort it all out!'

'Psychologist. Forensic.'

'Just sort it out,' he says, then he softens. 'Please help us. This cannot go on.'

He stands up, scraping his chair. I do the same, out of politeness, yet I am confused. Is this it? I drove all the way over from Falmouth, for a brief half-hour chat of an afternoon? Then I am sent away again?

Perhaps not.

Malcolm reaches in a pocket of his Barbour and retrieves a set of keys. He drops them onto the dark, fine-grained kitchen island, towards me. They briefly jingle in the quiet of the echoing and near-empty house.

'There,' he says, sombrely, heavily. 'These are the keys to Baldhu.'

I hesitate. 'Really?'

His sigh is profound. 'We need a lot of help from *someone*. And . . . the kids are grateful. Solly told me he *really* likes you yesterday. Told me we have to get you a present for Christmas. Says we should tame an owl from Trevaylor woods, and you'd like it.' Malcolm allows himself to laugh drily, sadly – then back to business. 'I work long hours, kids come and go from school, football, Grace does flute, there are playdates – sometimes. Molly also comes and goes, helping out. And I can't be here all the time when you visit, and you will need to visit. So, you'll need keys.'

I lift the keys, unsurely, contemplating them. Wondering if I should accept; wondering what Otto would think: flashing orange for careful?

'Silver key's for front door. Chunky one's for back door, in here, kitchen. You'll work out the rest. What else?' Malcolm frowns, asking himself this question. 'You may meet Miles, my younger brother. Drifts in occasionally, lost in his own world. You'll know him when you see him. Tricia the cleaner comes in – the one you saw – but she whips around quick, airpods on, hood up, couple times a week. That's it.' He shrugs, more businesslike. Zips up the Barbour. 'OK, I gotta nip back to the Halyard. Crisis with a prep fridge. Mutton blood everywhere. The house is yours till the kids get back from school, with Molly, should be soon. She's looking after 'em.'

He rewards me with a final cold smile, and paces past. Then I hear the door slam, and an old but powerful car revving in the yard by the eyeless barns.

Gone.

I am, for the first time, alone in Baldhu House. Malcolm has trusted me with the entire place. Not the act of a guilty man with things to hide. So maybe he is not lying after all, and the kids are reacting in the floridly irrational way kids sometimes do, in the stages of childhood grief.

I have been taking notes about childhood grief, reviving my training. Lifting my phone I read:

> *Grief symptoms normally attenuate four months after the death – stomach pains, head pains, bad insomnia are frequent, in these first months. Only one in five children will show symptoms of clinical severity, 10 per cent show impaired functioning three years after the death . . .*
>
> *Boys react – externally – worse than girls. Aggressive, sleep disturbance, bed wetting – pre-existent disorders in parents make it worse; parental warmth, authority, and consistent discipline promote resilience . . .*

Seven-year-olds have nightmares and dream of the deceased, headaches appear, argumentation, perhaps hallucinations in severe cases . . .

There is much more. It tells me that the Tyack children are behaving abnormally, they are disordered. But it is not entirely off the dial. I need to go deeper.

And I can start here: Baldhu House. Therefore I gaze about, deciding. I could explore the many empty rooms, or the gardens, the woods, the dark old barns, but right now there are two things I want to see above all else. The mirror, of course. And then I will go to the waterfall, where Natalie Tyack died.

I walk to the shelf and pick up the antique mirror. And look at it closely.

It is elegant, bright silver, surprisingly heavy for its ladylike size: real solid metal. Quite precious. It has sweet filigree metalwork around the glass, representing flowers or vines. The handle is plainer, and – as I look closely – it has writing, and a very faded indented square – there was surely once an escutcheon here, or a crest.

The mirror feels European, and yet it has faded Chinese writing on one side. Taking out my phone I snap some pics, close up; I want this translated, the mirror assessed, but already I can speculate. An antique Chinese mirror, how did that arrive in Baldhu House, to be taken up and cherished by Natalie Tyack?

Turning the mirror in my hand, my thoughts run colder as I see the other inscription, delicate and well formed.

For his beloved daughter Frances, Willyam Tyack
   PENZANCE, Cornwall, 1832

In 1832? It is not hard to work out how this mirror arrived in Cornwall, in Penwith, in Baldhu. A valuable Chinese object, probably on some boat returning from Asia, and blown wildly off course.

Then wrecked at Penberth Cove, with all its treasures scattered among the seaweed and the rocks. I see the exhausted sailors crying out in pain, dragging themselves to safety; even as the eager wreckers come down the cliffs with staves and axes, to crush their heads. And then they cart off the crates of tea and shots of silk – and a box of Chinese wonders, including a dainty lady's mirror. Noel Oswell even spoke of 'Chinese silver'.

And then it ends up here, a gift from father to daughter, always handed down at Baldhu.

Another, darker idea intrudes. The woman who owned this precious thing might have been on that boat, survived the wreck, and brought it ashore, only to be stabbed in the moonlight, her body defiled and robbed of this treasure.

The mirror feels quite poisonous now. I look for half a second in the ancient glass, see my own pale, round face reflected there, full of anxiety. The mirror does feel like a haunted thing, even as I know this is absurd. There is only history, good, bad and unbearable.

Replacing this problematic object, I head off outside, to the waterfall.

The air is cold, the sky is grey, and the world is stilled; it doesn't take me long to find the route Natalie must have taken a hundred times, out of the house, around the granite kitchen wall, to a modest clearing in the writhing oakwoods, and an old, eroded sign. *To The Beach*.

Noises delay me. I can hear car doors slamming, the voice of Molly, Solly, Grace: they are back. I wonder if

I should greet them – but no. I want to see the waterfall: it seems important. I also remember Noel Oswell's pompous words: *the coast is quite notorious.*

I begin confidently. The path, threading between yellow flowered gorse and stunted coastal oaks, follows narrow green Bathsheba Valley. The path doesn't have much choice: on either side, there are thickets of thorns and nettles on steep rocky slopes, hemming me in.

Even in overcast late autumn it is, I realize, quite an idyllic walk. The fern-strewn beauty of the valley matches its lyrical, biblical name. The stream at the bottom of the valley runs in glorious spate, singing and joyous, enriched by all the recent rains. In spring, I imagine, this place must be Edenic. Quietly riotous with wildflowers.

There is no litter, no evidence of careless tourists; we are so far away from anything. There is one burst grey football left in the grass which speaks of kids – probably Solomon. It leaks red oily water into the stream.

And now I pause, because now there is a choice, a different route, the obvious path becomes less obvious. The shadowy lane divides, as the stream splits, or braids further down the hill. For a second, I hesitate, and turn right and follow along for a few minutes – and then I realize: I am not alone.

10

A man stands there halfway down the path; he turns at my footfall.

He is tall, youngish, good-looking. A confident stance: square face, sandy-haired. He wears pricey wellington boots which make him look soldierly. And an expensive green waxed jacket: much newer than Malcolm's.

'Hello,' he says, and without my asking, goes on, 'Sam Berenson.' He offers his hand to shake. I can hear the trace of an accent, American, but not very American. He drawls a question.

'Have you come from the house? Baldhu?'

Hesitant, I answer, 'I guess, um—'

'You're Karenza Bray? The psychologist? From Falmouth?'

How does he know?

'Er . . .'

'Sorry to freak you out! I'm the neighbour, live with my wife, in Anjarden Farm, up the hill there. I was just heading back, been for a hike – now the rain has passed. Malc told me about you.'

He shrugs, and smiles sadly, says a few more words of welcome. We chat, and the minutes pass. I feel frustrated, but then he asks, 'Were you going down to the waterfall?'

'Yes.'

Sam says, 'Ah. That place. It's a known danger spot. The rocks are unstable, especially when wet.'

'I heard.'

He sighs, mournfully.

'Every time I go there, I think the same. So sad.'

I am zeroing in on that accent. New York?

He goes on, 'Such a *stupid* thing. So random, and those poor kids. And she was so young, and pretty, and so . . . *likeable*.'

'Of course, it is tragic.'

I'm not sure what else to say. I am also shivering, slightly. I point up to a distant house, just visible through the trees, which must be Anjarden.

'Have you lived here long, you and your wife?'

'If this was New York or London I'd say we've been here forever. Six years at least.' He laughs. 'In Cornwall, as I have *belatedly* come to grasp, you can only say you really live here if your great-grandpa lived here from birth. Half a mile down a mine. Eating turnips in pastry.'

I smile. 'Swedes. Pasties contain swede. Yes, it can be like that. The Cornish are quite insular.'

'No kiddin'.'

'I mean, they migrated here in 3,000 BC and haven't moved much since. And even if they go away they tend to come back. I did.'

'Hah.'

I ask, 'How on earth did you end up here? It's a long way from Manhattan.'

'I moved to London young – for college, LSE. That's why I've lost at least *half* the accent. My wife is very British – and she's always lived in London, but her family have a holiday home here, near – whatizzit – Carbis Bay?' He puts confident hands on hips, like the landowner he is. 'I'm in finance, she's a designer. We had your regular London townhouse, but she told me she always wanted to live on this coast, and she said she'd found this perfect house, Anjarden. It's a bit like Baldhu but smaller and . . . Well . . . There ain't so many rats in the loft. If you know what I mean.'

'I do.'

'To be honest I thought I might hate it and we'd be back in London in months, but I've come to love it. As long as you can escape every week or two – and most of the winter – it's *grrreat*. We're the nearest neighbours to Baldhu, so we became good friends with Natalie and Malcolm. The kids used to come over a lot. Solly loved playing soccer on our lawn, Natalie would come over too . . .' He turns up the collar of his waxed jacket, as if warding off questions as much as the wind. 'And now they don't come at all really. It's so freaking *sad*. And my wife doesn't like to intrude, not any more.' His sigh is heartfelt, then he goes on, 'Those kids. I was there for the meltdown, the other day—'

'You were?'

'God, yeah. Molly needed help. Called me at once. I was right there in that room when Solomon said it. When he said that about his sister, Jeez, it was horrible. And he was growling, like a damn hound. And the way he sees those black birds all the time. Why did Solomon say Grace killed her? Why *that*?'

I am shocked into silence for a few seconds. I struggle to say, 'Solomon said *what*?'

Sam looks at me, uncertainly. 'He said, or at least implied . . . Grace killed her. Killed Natalie. After Grace tried to blame Solom . . .' He is open-mouthed. 'Ah. Dammit. Malc didn't tell you all this, did he?'

'No. He certainly didn't.'

Sam shakes his head.

'Shizzle. I've way overstepped. *Sorry.*'

'It's OK. I just—'

'Listen, I really have to go. I'm sorry – I'm way out of line here. I . . . I was simply heading home. It was nice to meet you. Hope we meet again.'

He gives me a quick, half-hearted fist-bump, like he doesn't have time to shake hands. And with that he scurries away – almost running, disappearing into the black cages of the densely knotted winter trees, threading his way home to Anjarden.

Irritated and perturbed, I stamp back to the main path, then turn right, heading down to the falls. Malcolm Tyack had every chance to tell me this crucial information earlier. And he did not: so I was correct, he was lying, or being evasive; he hid this. In which case, what is the point? In my driving all the way, day after day? If I get fed untruths?

There is almost nothing I can do to assist his children if he is going to lie about something this fundamental. If the children are feeling guilt to the point of culpability, no matter how illogical, that explains a lot of their peculiar behaviour.

It also speaks of a deeper story. Why would the children feel responsible for their mother's death?

A billion alternative possibilities occur to me, as I march down the proper path, the right way, the true route. In my muddy trainers I climb over two stiles, as the vastness of the sea emerges between the thorns. The third stile brings me into the open: Zawn Dorlam. I can hear the waterfall, see its spray. This is it. Where the Bathsheba stream rushes past us and hurtles itself at the little cliff, and leaps, giddily, into the air. Like an act of misplaced faith.

It is a dainty waterfall, pretty, sweet, poignant. I find

myself wondering if the cliffs would be a good climb. There are plenty of footholds, but the water on the granite would make it insanely dangerous. I miss the climbing.

And if you fell from the top? Sixty foot, and sheer, onto the rocks below: extremely easy to die.

I sniff the air, wet and cool. It is refreshing, yet there is something else. Rotting seaweed? I wipe dampness from my eyes: the wind is kicking the wetness back up the cliff, salting me and spraying me, even as I wonder what Natalie Skuse thought on the night she stood here, and was pushed, or jumped, or fell. Did she not think of her beautiful children? Did she think of them and sob?

And even as I think this, I see another small figure, down there on the beach.

It is little Solomon Tyack, all alone. He is right by the waves, dangerously close, on this *notorious coast*. He seems to be hurling something into the waves, a small object. I cannot see what it is.

And then he begins to walk into the ocean. Like my own daughter, sleepwalking to her death in the Roseland.

11

'Solomon!'

I am screaming, as loudly as I can, above the roar of the waves and the crash of the waterfall. 'Solomon! Solly! Stop!'

The boy does not respond. He is in his school uniform: shorts, white shirt, pullover, blazer. He must be cold – the wintry day is biting – and now he is ankle-deep in the water, hypnotized, it seems, by the sight of the waves. Is he *sleepwalking*?

'Solomon! Please!'

Again, no response, not a flinch. He is up to his calves in the waves: a big one could easily seize and drown him. I must get down: there must be a path. I have to stop him. What is he doing?

The misty spray veils him from my sight. Scrambling left, I see a muddy, treacherous path, zigzagging down. I have to go down on my bum and slide. I will be covered with mud; it doesn't matter.

Now I am near the beach, and I can see Solly clearly. He is calf-deep, staring fixedly at the waves, and then at last he turns at my shout and his eyes are dark, burning, angry, as if I've done something terrible, and yet I also see desperate sadness there, as I race towards him: to grab him. The way I could not save Minnie, my own daughter; this time I am awake – this time is *different*.

'Solly!'

He barely knows me, he is nothing to do with me – yet I feel a strange almost-love inside me, burning, fierce. Urgent, I reach out and snatch him up wildly, wrap him in my arms, hard, fast, protective – and then I haul him back from the waters. He is so small, smaller than Minnie was: it is so much easier to save him.

'Oh God. Solomon!'

When he is safe in my arms, and we are back up the beach, I sense him soften. Then he shudders: he is crying into my chest, this poor grieving boy.

'Solly, what were you *doing*?'

He struggles to speak, slurs a reply, 'Shhhhhoe.'

'Sorry?'

The boy turns his sweet face up to mine, hoping and yearning, yet frightened, trembly; I can smell his sweet, childish breath. His red fiery hair is tousled and salted, his socks and shoes soaking. I need to get him back to Baldhu. But first he needs to calm down.

'Solomon, what do you mean, "shoe"?'

He takes gulps of cold air. 'They say – they say – they said she had one shoe, when they found her, on the beach, so . . . You always have two shoes, don't you, so I gave her a shoe.'

This means nothing to me. 'Who found a shoe?'

'A baby shoe, a tiny little baby shoe, so I gave it to the sea so maybe Mummy will come back from the sea, like they did.'

'Who?'

'Will she . . . Karenza? Will Mummy come back from the sea? Will she be washed up here again? Her body?'

'Oh, Solly!' I clutch the boy close to my heart. 'I don't think that is possible. I'm sorry, I'm so sorry, but we need to get you home – you're drenched. Your Auntie Molly is there, yes?'

'Yes, she's with Grace so I ran down here.'

'Do you often do this?'

He shivers. 'I'm not allowed to go far from the garden, but it doesn't matter. I sometimes come here to find Mummy. One day, one day maybe the sea will give her back . . .'

I would phone for someone to come and help us but of course there is no signal. I look up at the brink of the cliff, the grassy heights, the cold grey rocks, where the waterfall tumbles.

I fancy for a moment I see that woman again, the woman in the hood, Tricia the mysterious cleaner, staring down, hunched and burdened and angry, white-faced and scared, but I do not. No, I do not. There is no one here to help.

We begin the long walk back up Bathsheba, the way the boy must have come. Solomon is so tired that by the end I am practically carrying him. This would be a fine time to bump into Sam Berenson, but I have to do this alone, with the child I saved from the sea. But did I save him? What was he doing? Was he actually trying to kill himself?

With a chill from within, I realize this is not impossible.

Riemann & Yang, New York, 2017: childhood bereavement is linked to suicidal ideation in children as young as five . . .

We have reached the front door to Baldhu. Molly's car is here, so she must be inside. Aren't they worried about little Solomon? Do they just let him wander off?

The door behind us swings shut, on its ancient hinges. The house surrounds me and little Solomon, who is now almost asleep, slumping in my arms, this precious boy.

The enclosing silence is oppressive, and strange. It is of a piece with the odd, enclosing smell in the hall, fragrant yet forgotten things, left to themselves in a loft or a cellar. Old perfumed fur coats, or rotting barrels of brandy. Or something else.

Solomon stirs and pushes me away. 'I'm all wet, want some dry clothes—'

'Of course.'

He is staring at something, across the hall. The little cellar door. Tiny, dwarfish – and firmly shut.

'She's down there,' he says. 'She's always down there.'

'Solomon! Where have you been?'

I turn and see Molly running from the kitchen. She stares at Solly, then at me.

'What happened to him?'

'I was down at the zawn. I just found him there – he was—'

'Oh, Solly.' Molly doesn't let me finish. She shakes her head: half angry, half exasperated. 'Solomon, sweetheart, you've *got* to stop going there.' She looks at me. 'He's *always* doing this, says he's going to play football, but then goes down the zawn, to paddle in the sea. Come on, you.' She takes him by the hand. 'You're wet through.'

As she passes, Molly gives me a hard look which seems to say that this is my fault in multiple ways: because I found him, and he's only turned seven, and I am meant to fix all this, and what am I doing here anyway.

Molly has her nephew by the hand and is pulling him

upstairs. 'You need a bath and some new clothes – look at you!'

Then they are gone, and I am alone in the hall. Solomon is not the only one who needs a bath and a change of clothes, but there's not much I can do about that. I am lost for words, and purpose. What should I do now – go home?

Stepping into the kitchen, I wash the mud off my hands and face and dry myself on tea towels as best I can. New clothes will have to wait for now. I stare out of the kitchen window, trying to decipher what I have witnessed; then I go back into the hall and gaze at the little oak door leading to the cellar.

I cannot resist, it has been mentioned too often: and Solomon seems scared of it, as if it is part of his grief. I pull and push, twice. It is firmly locked, but I have keys. Did Malcolm put the right key on my keyring? This is as good as moment as any. Molly and Solomon are upstairs. Grace must be in her room doing her homework.

Quickly, I try my keys. None of them fits.

Resentment rises. If Malcolm Tyack is going to hide things from me, I want to know what else he is hiding. I try one last key.

And then I am halted by a girlish voice.

'I'm going to tell Daddy about this.'

12

Flushed with idiotic guilt, as if I am doing something wrong or even *terrible*, I turn.

Grace Tyack is standing at the foot of the stairs. Neat and formal in a blue and white school uniform.

'Grace, how long have you been there?'

'Long enough. Watching you.'

'Watching me?'

'For long enough to see. What you were doing.'

'But . . . I just wanted the key.' Ludicrously, I feel as if I am the miscreant child – and quiet, cerebral, ten-year-old Grace Tyack is the accusing adult. 'I want to open the cellar door.'

'I will have to tell Father.'

I remind myself: this is just a child.

'Tell him! It's fine, he gave me all the keys. I just don't have keys for the cellar, and I want to look.' I push on, firmly: I will not be bossed. 'How come I didn't hear you come down the stairs, Grace?'

'I wasn't upstairs, I was in the conservatory, I heard all the noise. Solomon was down at the zawn again, yes?'

'Yes. I found him, he was . . . very upset.'

Grace shrugs. 'He keeps doing that, like somehow he can find Mummy again. Does he even realize she's dead? I don't know.'

'Ah—'

'*I* know she's dead, dead as a dodo, don't you worry. It's just everyone else that's *weird*.'

'Well, that will change, Grace, when things calm down. It really will.'

Grace scowls. 'It's *fine*. It's all mad anyway.' I stare at her, but she goes on, 'Why were you trying to get into the cellar?'

'I just want to understand the house, your environment, the history, that's part of my job.'

'But we're not supposed to go in the cellar, *that's* why it's *locked*.'

'Why is it always locked?'

'Stairs are steep, and it's wet down there, sometimes dangerous. Daddy calls it *dank*.'

She tails off. Her eyes wander the hallway, looking for something, up in the ceiling, in the high corners, something I cannot see.

I need to get proactive; I need to take the advantage of this – Grace, virtually alone, in Baldhu, with her brother and auntie occupied, and father absent. Maybe 80 per cent of psychology is simply talking: interacting, observing. And I haven't really done that yet: not professionally.

'Grace, do you fancy a real chat?'

'What kind of chat?'

'A proper one. We haven't really talked yet, have we?'

'Suppose not . . .' She pouts, assessing me. 'But you'll have to be quick.'

'Why?'

'Soon they'll *all* be back. All the grown-ups. Having a drink.' Her sigh is vehement. 'I *never* want to drink. Why don't adults just drink *water*, like normal people?'

This is quite emotional for normally reticent Grace;

again it tells me to seize the day. 'Then I suggest we use this time.'

She eyes me warily, yet her voice is hopeful. 'It will really help?'

'Yes, I think so.'

Grace sighs, half acceptant. 'All right, but not for ages. I didn't approve of the interview with the horrid policewoman. DC thingy. Curtis.'

'OK. An hour, max.'

She fixes me with a stare. 'Thirty minutes,' she says. '*Max*.'

'Fair enough. We can do it in your room, Grace. Wherever you feel comfortable.'

Grace yields and turns, and now for the first time I try to see her with clinical eyes. I am also dredging up training: in my metaphorical left hand I am holding Julia Pym's *Interview with the Child,* fourth edition, that battered old book I had at the Bethlem, scrawled with a trillion annotations and feathered with Post-it notes; in my actual right hand I have my phone – camera, notebook, search engine.

As Grace slowly ascends the stairs, I observe her gait. It seems quite normal, maybe a little languid, evincing sadness. She carries herself with dignity, however: with the air of a wronged princess at court.

In her room she sits in her pink socks, cross-legged on the bed, and I sit on the chair, and the polecat hisses at me, soundless and timeless. I glance around, taking in the naval knick-knacks and melancholy seashells, beautiful and pale.

For the first time I notice a photo of Grace's mother, Natalie, on her own. She looks like she is standing at the top of the waterfall where she died, Zawn Dorlam, where I was standing an hour ago, rescuing her little boy. Natalie, predictably, looks beautiful, but her smile is distracted, troubled, wistful.

I clear my throat. Grace already looks bored, time is passing. 'Grace, could you write something for me, on that exercise book?'

A puzzled frown. 'Such as?'

'Could be anything. How about . . . your name and address?'

Obediently, she picks up a pen and the notebook, and begins to write, carefully and neatly. I watch the fine motor movements, the precise way she makes letters. No problems there, apart from, again, that unplaceable but definite sense of sadness. But that is to be expected in a child of ten who is mourning her mother.

She holds up the book and shows me:

Grace Jacinta Trevezah Tyack. Written in this my father's house of Baldhu: Penberth Cove, West Penwith, in the Parish of St Buryan, in the Duchy of Cornwall, on the last Friday before the Feast Day of St Brendan of Birr

I stare at her.

She bursts out laughing. 'I sometimes write it like that. Freaks people out.'

This is the first time I have heard her laugh. Her laugh is charming, all the more infectious and bubbly from someone normally quite withdrawn, or tense.

'You like to surprise people?'

'I don't like being bored.'

'I see.'

She is staring at my phone, where I am summoning an app. I say, 'I'd like to record this this, if you don't mind?'

She shrugs. But her arms are crossed: a picture of defensiveness.

'I wondered if you might do that, but . . . I s'pose it's all right, you can record, because you know I'm not going to tell you everything.'

'I see.'

'And anyway you really shouldn't ask too many personal questions, not at this time.'

'What do you mean, not at this time?'

She shrugs and doesn't answer. This is not going very far: I can see she is eccentric, intelligent, quite articulate, surely on the spectrum, also sad, perceptive, and often shy or quiet to the point of muteness, but I have to press on – and go further. *Twenty-two minutes left.* I ask questions quickly now, rapid-fire, hoping she will open up. I ask questions about school, friends, interests, passions, the past, which elicit the one-word responses: Yes, No, Fine, No. Sometimes, No, No, No, No, Maybe, No.

Occasionally, however, she says something which I hurry to note down. When she talks of her friends at school she describes, unasked, the various ways people can cheat at games.

'Some of my friends at school, they cheat all the time, but I am used to it.'

'Why? How come you are used to it?'

'Because my family cheats, especially my brother and father. I have to be careful of them, they're not like . . . Mummy. My mother played by the rules.'

'How do your brother and father cheat?'

She blushes, and looks over my shoulder again, as if someone looms behind me. 'Solomon says he sees things, these big black birds; I think he does it to frighten me, to frighten everyone.'

She has leaned over to the little bedside table and now she picks up a toy, for comfort perhaps. A little plastic house, far too young for her. I get the sense of regression once more: she is scared and sad, and this is a toy from a happier time, when she was younger.

'Tell me more about this? The birds?'

She gazes down at the tiny doll's house. 'Solomon says there are these birds outside, or sometimes in here, and sometimes they would prefer to talk to Daddy. He claims he can't hear them, that they don't make any noise, but I can see him moving his head like he is listening, to the birds, always listening.'

'And you don't see them or hear them?'

'No, Mummy would say it is silly. They won't ever talk to me, I won't see them, and besides, I really wouldn't listen.'

I notice that Grace is opening and shutting the door of the little doll's house, again and again. This, I think, is Grace *perseverating* – repeating an action beyond any sense, for her own psychological purpose. By opening a door, and shutting, and opening, she reveals something of her mindset, themes of escape and closeness, dependency and separation. Where is Mummy: not in here, not in there, she can't come in, she's not inside.

This brief interview is more rewarding than I expected. I ask some more, final questions, I get the terse answers again, and then she scolds me for being like the policewoman. I apologize. The room is quiet; only the stuffed dead polecat screams without a sound, into the void, yellow teeth locked in a grimace – of menace, or fear. Abruptly I realize the polecat could actually be terrified, hissing at a predator, caught forever at the moment of its impending death, by some macabre Victorian taxidermist.

A chilly draught comes from somewhere, but old Baldhu is full of creaking, chilly draughts.

And now as I am about to bring the structured interview to a close, as I can hear the rest of the family stirring – doors, chatter, stairs – Grace Jacinta Trevezah Tyack, of Baldhu House, in the Parish of St Buryan, launches into a long speech.

'You know, when I was really little, on sunny days Mummy would take me down to Zawn Dorlam, you know – the waterfall, where you were with Solly. You know it's called Dorlam Brialli? That means the falls of the primrose . . .'

'I didn't know that. Dorlam Brialli, that's pretty.'

'And whenever we did that, Mummy would make us ham and mustard sandwiches, our favourites, and we'd unwrap the sandwiches on the zawn, looking at the sea, playing games about the next ship we'd see. We'd get points for a white boat, and points for a red boat, and we'd sit there for hours, and she hugged me so tight, it . . . was just me and Mummy.' A sharp, emotive breath: this is a struggle for Grace, talking so much, revealing these emotions. 'Mummy loved the zawn. She told me she loved it even before she met Dad, she used to – used to go there when she was smaller with her friends, they'd go on the bus; she loved going there when she was sad, and she wanted me to love it too. And I did, but not now. Not now.' I detect a stifled sob, as she goes on. 'And then once when we were down there, she and me – she said, she said, she said she loved me more than anything in the world – and I asked if she *really* loved me just as much as Solomon, and she said *of course* she loved me just as much as Solomon. And that's the only time she said that. And I told her I loved her back anyhow and I didn't care if she loved Solomon more and then that did make her cry, really truly cry, so I didn't ever say it again.'

She raises her tearful gaze, and fixes it on mine. 'I wish I had.'

13

The rest of the family is definitely stirring around me. Leaving Grace alone, apparently contented with a book of Nordic myths, I head downstairs and aim for the kitchen where I find noisy Solomon, in dry clothes, with a glass of juice, who grins as if nothing has happened and then runs off 'to play'. Molly is also here. She eyes me silently, then ambles off as well. I am alone in the kitchen.

My social instinct is to leave, immediately. I've seen and done enough for more than one day. Yet I need to speak to Malcolm. I *must* talk to Malcolm Tyack.

The problem is solved by the ancient low rumble of Malcolm's big old car.

I quell my emotions and listen as Malcolm pushes open the front door, and comes into the hall. Seeing me in the kitchen he looks at me, half surprised. 'Still here?'

I take a deep breath. 'Still here, Malcolm. Had a long day.'

'OK . . . And?'

'I might be making progress with Grace. But there are other things we must discuss. Something else happened.'

His dark face shows hope or worry. 'Like what?'

I don't hold back. I describe exactly what happened

at the zawn: Solomon knee-deep in the sea, doing some childish magic, to make his mummy return. As I speak I scrutinize Malcolm, intently, for his reaction. He appears sad, distressed – yet not surprised. He hears me out with an unfocused gaze, then says, 'He keeps doing this. We've told him to stop. He's all right now?'

'I was worried, those cliffs, the sea!'

'We try to stop him wandering, but he's like me, as a kid, always drawn to the zawn. Where's he now?'

'Molly gave him a bath, it seems that he's . . . fine.'

'Ahh.'

'When he was down there, in the sea by the zawn, he had a tiny kid's shoe. He was throwing it in.'

Malcolm's gaze sharpens. Is this another tell? Is he about to lie? He gives me an explanation.

'Probably one of his own, when he was a tot. He makes these offerings. Like he can win Natalie back. Sometimes he gathers rocks and shells, says Mummy left them for him. On the beach.'

'Why a shoe?'

Malcolm shrugs irritably. 'Lord knows, isn't that your job?'

'Yes, it is, but I can only do this job if I'm given the entire truth.'

Malcolm ignores this; instead, he goes to the fridge and grabs a half-drunk bottle of white wine. The bottle looks subtly expensive. Drinking at five? He offers me a glass and I wave it away.

'No, thank you. Driving. Listen, Malcolm, before I go I want you – I need you – to answer something else. Because, if I don't get a satisfactory answer, I can't come back.'

His expression changes from defensive, or uncaring, to anxious-but-trying-to-hide-it.

'Sounds dramatic. OK.' He grabs a high chair, sips at the wine. Meets my gaze with his gaze. 'Tell me.'

'Earlier on I met your neighbour, Sam. On my way to the zawn.'

A glint in his green eyes tells me he might know what is coming. His gaze is, however, steely. There is anger in there, and maybe a deeper threat – a menace of some kind? He says, gruffly, 'Sam, eh?'

'Yes, Sam. And, thing is, he explained to me about the meltdown. When things got smashed. He was here, right?'

Malcolm Tyack is staring into his chunky wineglass. I see no need to put this nicely. 'He explained what Solomon said, when Solomon was acting out. He explained to me that Solomon claimed, or implied, that Grace is somehow responsible for the death of Natalie.'

Malcolm Tyack says nothing.

I push on: there is no turning back. 'Why didn't you tell me this, Malcolm? Sibling rivalry. Accusations between the kids. Surely you realize the importance of this? If you want me to help your kids – and they *really* need help – I have to know everything you know. Otherwise,' I lift my hands, expressing the pointlessness of it all, 'pff!'

The kitchen is nearly quiet. Just the patter of persistent rain on panes, in the dark of an early evening. Across the island, Malcolm takes a deep swallow of wine, swipes his wet lips with a meaty hand, and meets my enquiring gaze. 'All right . . .'

He hesitates for a long time, but then seems to decide something. 'I'll tell ya something I have not told anyone. I'm going to have to trust you, because I don't exactly have much choice. You're already here, in the family, and the kids are desperate, and Solly is acting out so bad – we want you to fix things, otherwise this is all going to get a lot worse.'

I say nothing.

Malcolm exhales, as if he has been saving his breath, and says, 'The night . . . when Natalie died, I remember waking up, long before dawn, maybe 4 a.m., and realizing she was not in bed with me. Felt odd. Don't know why. Just odd. Out of the ordinary. Saw that she'd put on clothes. Drawers half open. You know how sometimes you just get the sense when something has gone, and the sense something is awry. Natalie often kept strange hours, wandering the moors, down at the cliffs, but normally she'd kiss me goodbye, I'd half wake up . . . Not this time.'

I am saying nothing: let him speak.

'I felt this sudden deep anxiety. My first thought was naturally: the kids. That's always your first thought. Right? D'you have kids, Karenza?'

'Did. I understand.'

He does not notice, he goes on.

'So, I ran into Solly's room. He was fast asleep, or so it looked. Then I went into Grace's room. And – she was in her *warm clothes*. There was a full moon. She was simply sitting there, in a chair, staring hard at nothing. Staring like she could see someone or something. At the window maybe. Her clothes looked damp, like she'd been out. It'd been raining earlier. I mean. Why? What happened? Then Grace seemed to realize I was standing there. She turned to me and said, in that flat, emotionless way: "I just saw Mummy, by the waterfall. It's my fault. Because now Mummy's *gone*." And the way she said *gone* it wasn't like she'd gone for coffee, it was . . .' Malcolm Tyack closes his eyes, pained by the memory. 'Like it was gone forever. And it was.'

I am bristling with questions. I ask one: 'But the police said you presumed Natalie had driven off – her car was gone?'

'It was. And sometimes Natalie *would* do that. She used to get insomnia, nightmares – she had that rough childhood, it preyed on her – sometimes she would deal with it by driving away, sitting in her car, calming herself down. She didn't like the kids seeing her *that way*.'

I watch as he drains the rest of the wineglass; I ask, 'And then the police found her car next day?'

'Yup. Parked by the road at Penberth. Must've walked along the coast to Zawn Dorlam. Where her body was found.'

'And you didn't tell the police any of this?'

Malcolm sighs. 'No. Because maybe it does implicate Grace. Fully clothed, wet from rain, been outside, says her mum is dead, and she saw her at Zawn Dorlam and it's her fault? Doesn't take a genius TV detective. Grace knew Natalie was dead at the zawn before anyone else. And she maybe told Solomon. Or somethin' else? Tries to shift the blame? Who knows?'

'But Grace was, what, nine years old? She's probably making it all up.'

'You think?'

'Yes!'

'That's what I believed at first. Wanted to believe. Put the coincidence to the back of my mind. But when Solly said that the other day – came right back and—'

I interrupt, 'But why didn't you tell the police? Nothing would have happened to her. Even if she was involved, which I don't believe, she was below the age of criminal responsibility.'

He draws an apparently painful breath. 'Grace has also said strange things. Other times.'

'Like what?'

His eyes are downcast as he murmurs, 'Occasionally she says things like: *I'm not one of you. Not like the rest of you.*' He shakes his head with great sadness. 'Maybe, I don't know, maybe she's felt, and she feels, eh, different, awkward, unloved?' An anxious pause. 'And sometimes she . . . blamed her mum for this. They argued, very badly.'

I let this settle, for a moment. An accusing child, that is a new context. But it may just be her neurodivergence; she *is* different. And, of course, we all diverge in one way or another.

Malcolm looks hard at me. 'Do you see now? Grace had bad feelings about her mum sometimes, really grim, they rowed so fierce, Grace shouting *I wish you were dead*, all that, all that kid stuff, almost teen stuff, and yet other times their bond was intense. I don't know! What would *you* do if you suspected your child might've killed someone? Or was somehow implicated in a death? What would *you* have done?'

Malcolm sits there, glaring at me, knocking down wine. And I say nothing. Maybe I accept Malcolm's explanation. The reflexive natural thing is to protect the child: forget the suspicion, even bin it. If Minnie had somehow said something as bad as this, as self-incriminating as this, my maternal urge might well have been to pretend it never happened, and that could easily have overcome my moral unease, forever.

The kitchen is truly quiet.

Malcolm broods, morose. I gaze out of the kitchen window, looking at some blackbirds on a garden fence. They are all there, in a row, silhouetted by the moonlight, by the clearer night skies beyond. As if they have been watching. For the second time I refuse a glass of wine, and instead I get in my car and drive home, from Penzance to Helston to Falmouth, and now of course the night skies cloud and the endless rain begins again, and I turn on the wipers, listening to their repetitive querying thumps, as if they are saying: What *is this* Why *is this* What *is this* Why.

14

'Just a ginger ale, please. The posh one. That one.'
'No worries.'
The nice young Welsh guy behind the bar smiles cheerily and cracks the top of some tiny artisanal bottle with a florid faux-Victorian label.

'Anything else?'

I do not know what Dad wants, so I say, 'No, that's it, thanks. Thanks so much. Ta. Thank you.'

Why am I over-thanking? Because maybe I feel guilty at just ordering a ginger beer, nothing alcoholic. My boozy upbringing – Dad, drunken uncles, Granny Spargo – told me you're not meant to do that. And then I remember Grace's words. *Why can't adults drink water like normal people.*

Taking out my phone I tap notes about Grace Tyack. Her aloofness, her precociousness, and her apparent isolation in the family. As I type, I realize that part of me feels a distinct *affinity* with Grace.

Because I was not unlike Grace as a little girl: bookish, withdrawn, distant, and definitely lonely at times, but also smart, resilient, and eloquent when needed. We are probably in a similar space. This is not a huge surprise. All my adult life I have resisted taking a diagnostic test for Autism Spectrum Disorder – not because I am scared I might pass but because I am fairly sure I *will* pass, at least in a mild way. So it is pointless: I do not need proof. I self-diagnosed long ago, using my own history.

The proof is in the backstory: when other girls at school automatically knew how to interact and socialize, as if they had some magic potion they drank before meeting people, I had to diligently learn – by copying others, or watching drama, or reading clever novels – how to talk, how to stop talking, how to read complex facial expressions as if they are ancient Sanskrit and can be interpreted with an applied and delicate skill. All the stuff that came instinctively to other people came from hard work for me, although – as Kyle often pointed out, in our happier days – this is possibly what makes me good at my job. I have learned to carefully read faces, minds, expressions, lips, eyes, and also carefully remember conversations, intimations and situations, because I *have* to; and I am now better at it – he would say, flatteringly – than nearly anyone.

A text pings from Dad.

Just finishing up love, give me ten

A sigh: typical Dad. I taste more of the ginger beer, and gaze around. This is his choice of venue: the Old Tun House. They have proper dartboards on the wall and folk nights where hairy men play fiddles, so it does feel like a proper old man's pub, the kind of pub where you would expect to meet a seventy-four-year-old widower with a fondness for a drop.

And Stuart Bray is certainly fond of a drop. Dad has been a pubgoer all of my life; I can't remember a time when he wasn't *down the boozer* or *having a jar* or *sinking a few with the lads*.

It was like that way back, when Mum was still alive,

before the cancer, when we were a fairly normal family, when Dad ran the kayak business between stints in the Old Quay Inn, and Mum did the books in the cosy kitchen of an evening, and me and my younger brother Loic watched ancient reruns of Charlie Brown cartoons in the lounge because he really liked Snoopy, and I was in love with the surprisingly beautiful soundtrack, that jazz piano, Vince Guaraldi, the music simultaneously jaunty, cheerful and sophisticated in a way I was yet to understand but which I already knew I liked. *Particular kinds of music.*

It was maybe then I realized I have a voracious appetite for unusual, new, provocative music, no matter where it comes from, the stranger the better sometimes: and also giving me definite genres of music for particular emotional moods. Like Arvo Pärt's Vespers on a bad day; Mozart's Vespers on a jubilant day.

And *Hatred Anger and Disgust* by Pyrexia when I need to keep the demons at bay.

My ginger beer is nearly finished. The chapter of my audiobook, *On Psychopathologies* – Chapter 26, 'Epigenetics: New Theories' – is over. I text:

Dad! Can't wait all day. Where are you??

'Karenza. Sweetheart.'

As ever – with impeccable timing, just before it gets genuinely annoying – Dad shows up. He has a foaming brown pint of Tinners to hand and, taking a chair, he starts to natter away, as he always does. His new thing is planes and how they are all fake.

I suppress a giggle. 'How can planes be fake, Dad? People fly on holiday.'

'Not saying they don't fly, just saying they *can't* fly.

Technically. Think about the fuel. How can you store all that fuel in a plane, enough fuel for it to take off – it don't make sense. Think about it! You're a bright girl!'

'Dad, we went to Malaga on holiday, remember? When Mum was alive? How did we get there if planes can't really fly?'

Dad completely ignores this, as he always does with awkward *facts*. And so – even though I know it is hopeless – I try something else. 'Why would they fake plane fuel anyway? What's the point?'

'Who knows? And *that's* the point. They do something with Nikola Tesla energy, I reckon. It's like the way they inject us with microchips when we are five months old. It's child abuse!'

My sigh is lengthy, amiable, and defeated. Dad chuckles healthily. I note that he is looking sprightly, as he nearly always does. He has a big red nose from the booze, veins crackling in the face, but otherwise a good head of grey hair, all his very own teeth; Dad looks better at seventy-four than some men at sixty-four, and now as Dad downs his Tinners and moves on to another story about some weird dinner he went to, I wonder, not for the first time, if all the mad conspiracy theories keep Dad young, in some ironic way – the same way religious faith, however ludicrous, seems to offer health benefits.

'So there was at least ten of us and there were carol singers at the door . . .'

I let my eyes glaze. So I can think.

I have no religious faith. None at all. If anything, I have anti-faith. I have been exultantly Darwinian since I was a nerdy, scholarly sixth former devouring Richard Dawkins, and yet sometimes I accept it might be *nice* to have faith, the same way it might be nice to be like Dad and happily believe Princess Diana was slain by North Korean assassins.

It is all a cop-out. But a consoling cop-out, and one I sometimes yearn for, when I am missing Minnie, or missing Mum. Ghosts of them would be better than what I have of them, which is memories, and nothing else. But it must be accepted, or you go mad. There really is nothing.

'Are you even listening?'

Dad is still banging on about this weird dinner. Now I feel guilty, and I pay attention, realizing this is a story I haven't heard. It is a story from my childhood, when Mum was alive. I say, 'Sorry, start again, sorry, Dad.'

He looks unexpectedly sad: this apparently is a maudlin story. 'I just remembered it this morning. I was walking here seeing the first Christmas decorations go up outside the Pannier Market. Reminded me.'

'OK, and—'

'You were with a friend. You must have been eleven, Loic just seven, it was Christmas Eve, and it was when I finally understood about the elite paedophile rings, remember?'

'Yes. Haven't forgotten that one, Dad.'

'So me and your mum were invited around to friends for supper, with Loic, Christmas Eve supper, and we had a few drinks, I was on the Baileys.'

'Tell me a lie.'

'And the host, Colin Jones, you remember, back then in Devoran?'

I nod, a little intrigued now.

'Colin and Wendy, yes, nice couple, ran the corner shop. They had a boy, Andy, think he got me into rock-climbing.'

'Yes. Them. So . . . So anyway, Colin told me I was totally mad and I was well sauced by then and,' Dad looks actually guilty, almost devastated, 'I went into this uncontrollable rage, pointing and shouting, red in the face and all that, shouting at Colin, and also Wendy, *"You're worse than the blood-drinking paedophiles, you fucking zombie sheep"*, and all the kids got frightened, and Loic – you know how sensitive he is – he was crying, I was storming around the living room, and your mum was also crying, and they dragged me out to the car, and Loic refused to get in with me so they drove off and I had to walk home alone, and all the time, all the time I was doing this I was,' Dad winces, *'Dressed as Jesus.* Your mum bought me the costume – loincloth and crown of thorns – that morning, and I'd put it on, and I basically forgot I was wearing it and—'

I can't help it. I burst into peals of laughter. Joyous laughter. Choking out the words, 'Oh, my God, Dad. You were dressed as Jesus when you shouted *"You're worse than the blood-drinking paedophiles, you fucking zombie sheep"*?'

Dad looks mortified. 'Yes. And I'm not proud of it.'

I have to force myself to stop laughing, as Dad is so clearly uncomfortable. But I am unable to stop laughing so I go to the bar and get him another pint of Tinners.

As I tap the money I think Dad has certainly earned it. Best laugh all week. We always used to laugh as a family, too, when we were together. Never really rowed like the Tyacks, no one ever felt left out, or apparently unloved: like Grace. Who loved her mother and, moreover, actually looks so much like her mother. So why would she fall out with her mother who was so close to her, who took her down to the zawn to eat sandwiches? Why did Grace ask if she really loved her as much as Solomon? What would make a child feel alienated from her own family to this extent?

And now, abruptly, I think about her age. Ten years old. And the length of time the Tyacks were married, before Natalie died.

Ten years.

Could it be?

Is Malcolm *really* the father? She doesn't especially look like him, but she does look like her mother. But then again that often happens, randomly, and he clearly loves her . . .

I carry the drinks back to Dad – but I am wilfully lost in the puzzle now. Maybe more than lost. As I go deeper into this, it sometimes feels as if I am drowning in the sad, seductive mysteries of ancient Baldhu and the Tyacks; and yet I do not care. Perhaps I am one of those drowners who finds the process peaceful, reposeful, even euphoric: because the cerebral anoxia of the flooding airways invokes the neuroprotective activity of the brain's serotonergic system, which subjectively makes dying easier, due to the mood-enhancing function of this neurotransmitter.

Or so I have read, and told myself, many times, while crying.

15

Molly Tyack answers the door at Baldhu House. I have the key to the door in my bag, but it does not feel remotely right using it without trying the knocker first. Not yet anyway. Perhaps one day it will. I cannot work out whether that would be a good thing or a bad thing.

'Oh, it's you,' says Molly, adding a belated and blasé, 'Hi' – as if she is surprised that I have shown up, but really doesn't give a hoot either way. I step over the threshold. Molly has her light-brown hair tied tightly back, emphasizing her fine, gaunt cheekbones, and also a pair of smallish tattoos on her slender but sun-punished neck.

Molly traipses through the hall in her long dark skirt and white linen shirt, heading towards the kitchen, putting a vape to her mouth and exhaling exuberant phantoms of steam, every fourth step. The scent of the vape-steam is apple or cinnamon and something else. Weed? Stronger than weed?

As we enter, inevitably, the kitchen, I note the tranquillity of the house. When I called, to warn Malcolm that I wanted to go round and talk to Solomon, he agreed, hurriedly, then complained of a super-busy restaurant, then said, *I'll be working, till late. But Molly will be there, she's doin' the school run.*

But there is no noise of children, and that is hard to hide even in a house as big as Baldhu, especially with a child as boisterous as Solomon.

Sitting at the island I accept a handle-less cup of green tea and Molly languidly says, 'The kids will be back soon, if that's who you're after.'

'Well, yes.'

'Tricia's doing it today.'

'The cleaner?

'Uh-huh. She is picking up the kids, as a favour to me. She said she was in Penzance and Grace has got some dental check-up, or whatever . . .' Her eyes slide across mine, either stoned or indifferent or both. Probably stoned. 'I thought I'd get some time here alone, for once. In my *lovely childhood home*. Ah well.'

This barb is obvious and aimed at me. I find myself bridling at Molly's attitude: *your niece and nephew desperately need help. I am trying my best to help*. I am also confused by her stance: on the one hand she apparently loves the house, at other times she has a cool indifference to Baldhu. Even an aversion?

I also find myself professionally counting Molly's tattoos. Four, five, six, some maybe hidden? I have seen enough tats in my professional past, I've learned the arcane language of prison tattoos – quincunx tats, Borstal dots, Jamaican sleeves – and I know the unspoken Forensic Psych rule of tattoos and piercings: more than six means the tattooed or pierced person has a significantly elevated risk of suicide. Every new nipple ring or random tat is, after a certain juncture, a likely stepping stone of self-harm all the way to self-destruction. Especially hand and face tattoos, and piercings in unusual places: eyebrows, genitals, cheeks. Markers leading to death, like tell-tale footprints in the mud in an old-fashioned police procedural, devoured by my puzzle-solving mind.

'I like your hand tattoo,' I say, pointing to an obviously misguided smear of a tat on Molly's left hand, above the thumb. Like a tiny dolphin – but it could be a dead ant.

'Oh,' says Molly, faintly blushing. Bingo. 'That. Yeah. Fucked up on Es in Ibiza. Wasn't my best moment.'

I feel guilty for my tiny lapse into cruelty. But then, Molly is not exactly co-operative, or friendly, and I am here to help.

I strive to be nicer.

'What do you do, Molly? I mean, when you're not here?'

A shrug, a vape. 'I own a little shop in St Ives. Sells Celtic jewellery to tourists. Celtic crosses and shit. I tell them the metal comes from sunken ships off the Scillies and they lap it up. Actually it comes from Guangdong.'

I smile and chuckle, politely. I am yearning to ask Molly questions about inheritance, money, Malcolm, sibling jealousy, Grace's alienation, and of course, at the very back of my mind, the potent possibility that Grace has a different father. But for now all that is too brutal, and the last question is *far* too brutal – so I attempt something else.

'Can I ask you some family questions? About the past?'

Molly is distractedly tapping her vape as if she has run out of whatever-it-is. 'Shit.' She lifts the top and says 'Shit' again. Then, as if she is vaguely aware of someone else in the room, 'You what?'

'I said, I have questions. Sorry if they seem intrusive, but your brother did ask me to help, and that inevitably involves the whole family.'

'Sure. Shit. Why not . . . *Questions*.'

'OK. Can you tell me how did you get on with Natalie? Because, a sister whose brother suddenly marries a much younger wife, that can be a challenge?'

Now Molly stares, direct and suddenly a lot less stoned, right at me, and her brown-grey eyes positively gleam. Like she has been waiting for someone to ask this for a long time.

'You really wanna know about me and Natalie Skuse?'

'Yes.'

'My oh-so-beautiful, oh-so-fertile sister-in-law. Me and the sainted Natalie?'

The words toll out like the bells of St Buryan: *oh-so-fertile*.

'Erm, yes. Please elaborate?'

Molly proffers a sly smile. 'Nah. If I tell you the truth they'll say, Oh she's the jealous bitch, and put me down as a suspect. Again.' A throaty laugh. 'Can't have that . . . *Can we?*'

I suppress the urge to take out my phone and record this conversation. 'But what does all that mean, Molly? You don't have to tell me anything. However, I really do want to help.'

The noise of a car interrupts, distant voices, kids. Molly rolls her eyes. And smiles at me.

'Bad timing, babe.'

'We can try again later?'

'Yeah . . . maybe,' she drawls. Then, bizarrely, she leans forward, very close, and she takes my hand, clasping it between her own. 'You know, Karenza, you don't seem like a bad person.'

'I hope I'm not. I'm a professional, and I am here to assist the family. I don't . . .'

She nods curtly. 'So, just . . . go away is my advice.'

I stare. 'What?'

'This house has always been freaky and draughty and shit, so what, we can cope, we always cope. The Tyacks. What we don't need is some dope making it even worse, digging up the past, not for those poor kids, poor Grace.'

This is bewildering. The strangeness of the words does not have time to sort itself, because Molly is heading for the hall to meet the children, and I am obliged to follow.

Tricia the cleaner is just taking her key from the latch and turning to talk to the children. 'Come on, Solly, Grace, it's raining again.'

Tricia is about forty, and with the hood of her dark blue hoodie let down, I see has dyed-blonde hair and a kindly demeanour; she smiles pleasantly at me. But I am struck by the half-hidden emotion in Tricia's eyes.

It is fear.

She is staring around the hall as if she is scared, as if the idea of taking a further step into the house is an abomination. Even though she cleans here twice a week. Then I recall what Malcolm said of her: 'Cleaner comes in . . . but she whips around quick, airpods on, hood up.' She doesn't linger any more than she has to.

Molly asks, 'How are they, Trish?'

Tricia glances at me, then at Molly, nervily. 'Oh, OK. Um. A bit, uh, distracted. OK, I have to go now.'

Tricia steps from the door, backing into the twilit November rain, putting her dark hood up, as the kids come into the house.

Solomon runs in first, of course. He says, 'Molly Molly Mollymo!' and she grins – a sincere, natural grin – and then he turns and smiles at me, his red hair wild as ever. 'Karenza, you're back! You know I worked out what I want for Christmas! I want n'exoskeleton!'

But there is something strange about him. He keeps pausing, and turning, and twisting his head, looking everywhere, this way and that, as if he can hear things we cannot. Something loud. It is odd, painful to watch.

'Solomon . . .'

Grace comes in, following her brother. She looks at everyone in turn and says calmly, 'He's doing it again, Auntie Molly. *The thing*. Like he can see the birds.'

Tricia says, brightly and falsely, 'OK, bye!'

She is gone, as quickly as she came. I can hear her car screeching in hurried reverse, even as the kids steer past the adults for the kitchen.

Now Molly turns to me and says, gesturing at her vape, 'Can you mind the castle? I really need to stock up. Won't be more than an hour.'

Before I can object, Molly too has gone. Slamming doors, starting her car, heading down the lane for the brightness and dryness of civilization, as if she seizes any opportunity to escape.

The door to the kitchen swings open. Grace comes out with a plate of two precisely arranged biscuits and a glass of pink juice. She brushes past me, saying, 'He's in there. You'll be all alone with him.'

Standing here, I fight the sudden, unprofessional urge *not to* go in the kitchen.

Not to be all alone with Solomon Tyack.

16

The kitchen at Baldhu. All alone with Solomon Tyack. I wait at the open door, observing. The best tools of a forensic psychologist are her eyes and ears. But it is so much harder to observe in the random, foreign, domestic context of a living old house like Baldhu.

I seldom miss my old job, but I miss aspects of it. The ability to decide the environment of an interview, for instance. For a structured or semi-structured interview with children as young as Solomon, I would always try to ensure I had a waiting room, maybe a playroom, along with the interview room. I needed places where I could quietly harvest *capsules*, observable moments, moments where I could secretly watch parents interact with children, or children bored on their own, or children interacting with toys. They can tell you so much.

All I can do here is peer through the doorway, like the household voyeur. At Solomon.

The boy sits at the island, on his wood and black-metal chair, kicking his heels and munching on a piece of dark cake, or gingerbread, perhaps. Next to his plate is a glass of milk. He is intently focused on some reading: it looks like a book of cartoons. Anime.

With his cute, scruffy, half-tucked-in uniform of white shirt and grey jumper, grey flannel shorts, blue socks, polished shoes – a uniform I do not recognize, so it is probably a little private primary school – he looks absolutely benign. At first glance, the perfect image of a freckle-faced, seven-year-old boy in all his innocence. Not a boy who hurls baby shoes into the sea to magic his dead mother back to life. The boy I hauled from the waters.

He clearly has not heard me at the door. He slurps the milk hungrily, gnaws at the cake as if he is famished, turns another page of the comic, eyes devouring images. Next to the plate I see a couple of toys. A half-finished Lego dinosaur – T. Rex – and some kind of plastic toy gun. A pretend space-fiction laser gun, maybe.

I watch as he eats, the way he acts. Because at times the innocent normality disappears, and his behaviour is again disquieting. Every so often Solomon Tyack does not look normal or benign: as in the hallway, he twists his head, up and around, and his eyes widen, like he can see things or hear things, over there, by the fridge, or above the windows. Perhaps they are frightening things, because he occasionally looks scared; other times he merely seems surprised, or perplexed.

Yet there is nothing to be seen or heard. The kitchen is quiet.

What is he seeing?

I know from my revisions that childhood grief at his tender age can get so severe, especially when it stems from a violent sudden death, as with Natalie Tyack, that it can, rarely, cause hallucinations. These are normally auditory hallucinations, which are always more common. Is this it then? Is that what I am witnessing, second hand?

I also know that childhood grief – and its attendant maladies – is best dealt with directly. The child should always be told the truth and given the full experience: the child must go to the funeral, understand the process. The child should not be fed euphemisms and evasions. The child must not be told the parent has 'passed', or 'gone to sleep', as that leads to confusion. They must be told the parent is 'dead', however brutal.

And I do wonder how brutal Malcolm has been with Solomon. Perhaps not so much: especially if he feels guilty?

'Hello, Karenza!'

Solomon Tyack is looking my way. I have been so focused on my own thoughts, I have not noticed the simple fact that Solomon has finished his cake.

He chirrups, brightly, 'Can you answer me a question, Karenza, please?'

His voice is lively and normal. He wrinkles a freckled nose as I enter the kitchen properly.

'Uh, sure. What is it?'

'Well, this comic I got from Grace, she lent it me, and it has noctopus under the sea deep down with ten arms and it eats kids that go to the seaside and it's a bit scary but . . . Do you know if this story could happen in real life? Are there, like, octopuses like that in the sea? Eating children like me and Grace and my friends?'

I step closer. Relieved that the strange behaviour has stopped. I pull out a high kitchen chair opposite Solomon and sit down. 'No, there aren't monsters like that. It's just a comic, Solomon, just a bit of fun.'

He laughs, showing pretty white teeth. 'Yes, I was thinking like that, but the sea is deep deep like the mines and it's just a comic. Yes. Anyway, I've read it now and it's finished. Mummy takes us to the zawn for picnics in the summer, I don't think she would do that if there were *real* octopus monsters. Not *real* ones that eat people.'

He pauses. A flash of sadness in his eyes. Mummy is not here any more: the present tense is painfully incorrect. Solomon's eyes cloud.

'Mummy wouldn't do that, would she? Even now? Karenza?'

I give him a blank-faced smile, not saying too much but trying to reassure. Then I ask, 'Shall we have a proper chat, Solomon? A good proper chat about things?'

He frowns; he wipes silvery milk from his lips with a sleeve. He says, 'Hmm, a chat, yes, all right. What do we have the chat thing about?'

I take a breath. 'You . . . do know your mother is dead, don't you, Solomon?'

I hate asking this, but I have to. His comments have opened this door, I must step through. I see the stir of deep sadness in his eyes.

He tilts a determined chin and replies, 'Daddy told me she's dead, I know.'

'I see, I see. And . . . did you go to the funeral, Solly?'

He nods and then he shakes his head, struggling with emotions, then he nods again. 'Yes.'

'What was that like? The funeral?'

He gazes at me yearningly, with a face that asks why I am opening up all this pain. I hate this part of the job, being like a surgeon cutting tender flesh.

He mumbles. I cannot hear him. I ask him to repeat it, and he says, 'They put her in the ground. Slevven.'

'Sorry?'

'Church, ground, they put her *down there. Slevven.*'

I realize he means St Levan, that old, old church on the coast near here.

'And how did you feel when you saw that?'

Solomon fidgets, he picks up his toy raygun and points it at the wall, sadly. Then he says, 'It was ages ago, and I was, I were, I saw them put her into the ground and I thought she will come back, she will grow back when it gets to summer time; I think she might come back as a flower, because Mummy loves flowers and roses and all green things and she loves garden time, and roses come from seeds that are put in the ground. But I don't think this any more. Sometimes I think it is my fault she is dead.'

He shoots the raygun, making little noises.

'Why did you think that, Solomon? Why is it your fault?'

'Cos I didn't brush my teeth.'

'What does that mean?'

'Mummy always tells me I must always brush my teeth and that night I didn't, I just didn't, I wasn't even trying and then the next day she was dead, Daddy told me, so I did it. Didn't brush my teeth then she was pushed off the cliff.'

'Do you still think that? Do you still think she is dead because you didn't brush your teeth?'

'No.'

'So what do you think now?'

'I don't know. She is alive or dead. I don't know.'

He points the raygun at me. *Bang bang bang. Zap zap zap.* A phallic object, taking revenge. He makes little noises with his mouth, killing me dead.

'Why did you say your sister killed her, Solomon?'

'Didn't.'

'I believe you did, people told me. You certainly suggested this.'

His face is fixed, and defiant, then it is not. He looks

downcast yet angry and he says, 'I was lying. I know it's bad. I wanted to hurt her: she is mean.'

'How is she mean to you?'

'She says I am lying, lying, lying all the time, about the birds and the noises and Mummy and the people in the cellar.'

'There are people in the cellar?'

'Not always, but sometimes, sometimes yes. Sometimes it's an animal. Big darkshape thing, come up from cellar, into my room. But when I want to see her, darkshape goes away then comes back, and now it is locked again – Daddy locked it away, hanging the key, hanging it, hanging there – you know we were wreckers in olden times? We would stove in heads, my uncle Miles told me. We dropped stove things on their heads, ha ha. Splat.'

He is grinning now, abruptly. Saying *splat* and enjoying the word. Ha ha. Ha ha. *Zap zap zap dead.*

SPLAT.

This isn't going anywhere helpful. To switch things up I take out my notebook and rip a large blank page, and then I hand the page to Solomon, along with a pen. 'Solomon, could you write your name and address, and then maybe do a drawing?'

He seems to relish the chance not to talk about his dead mother; I do not blame him.

Eagerly he takes the page and does his task and, as with Grace, I watch him, closely, as he writes and draws. Once more, I see nothing wrong in the motor movements. He writes letters quite well for his age, though he writes nothing flamboyantly strange like Grace. Just *Solomon Tyack, Baldhu House.*

'And a drawing?'

'What will I draw?'

'Anything you like, maybe Baldhu. Yes, draw Baldhu House.'

His tongue sticks out slightly between his lips, as he does all this. I note it down: the tongue thing is generally called the Babkin Reflex, a primitive reflex associated with tasks requiring mental concentration, physical co-ordination and fine motor skills. It is also, as I diligently learned in my training, possibly a vestigial glimpse of that moment in human evolution when we moved from the spoken word to the written word: the tongue expects to form the words being written.

Generally all this is integrated and disappears as children mature. Solomon is only just seven; I do not think this semi-integration is an especially bad sign. He sometimes appears and talks much younger than his years, but he is grieving for a mother. And deeply grieving children sometimes regress to an earlier age, deliberately. As if they can reinvent the old world, before the bad thing happened.

However, the Babkin Reflex is also, occasionally, associated with memory troubles, deeper emotional problems. I shall not ignore it either.

'Finished!'

Solomon proudly turns the page around and shows me. He has done a fairly simple drawing of the house, four-square and solid, not especially detailed, as if he does not care. Much more detailed are the big squiggly birds flying around the house, and the trees next to it. I was so absorbed in my thoughts of his mental integration I did not notice he was adding all these *birds*.

They are forbidding-looking things. There is a stick woman next to the house and the birds are as big as the woman.

'Solomon, do you keep seeing birds, inside and outside the house? Is that why you've drawn them here?'

He scowls, and asks, 'Do you *like* my drawin'?'

'Yes. But why all the birds?'

He scowls again, and completely ignores the question. He picks up the gun and points it at the dinosaur, *zap zap zap*.

'Solly, tell me about these birds – are they like the people in the cellar? Tell me about "darkshape" – what is that?'

Zap.

Now he turns back, and he shrugs, perhaps from boredom as much as evasiveness. For a troubled seven-year-old, I am pushing it, and on so many sensitive issues. One more go.

'Please just tell me about the birds. You talk of them a lot, you've drawn them here, but I don't understand. No one else can see them.'

'I can. Can can can. Everywhere anyway anyway anyway why do I have to tell you anythink, you're like her. Like Grace.'

'Sorry?'

'Don't believe me what's the point what's the point what's the poinnnt?'

'All right, Solly, all right, we are nearly done. Just one more—'

'No. No. *No no no*. All these chats about Mummy she is dead Daddy told me. Dead!'

'OK, we're done. I'm sorry—'

'*Dead!*'

'Solly—'

'She is so *dead* so dead dead she is *dead and buried* and someone stoved her, they did splat with her head, smashed on the beach, we wrecked her, they wrecked her, that is what we do, Uncle told me, Daddy does this, we all do this in here, we all drop stoves on the lady's head, and they splat and there's blood and there's brains and it's horrid.'

He is shaking now. I have pushed way too far.

'*Splat splat splat*, wrecking her head. Daddy and Mummy and *splat*!'

Now, inevitably, he bursts into tears. I have strayed way over the line. This is always a risk, with kids as young as Solomon. Pushing back the chair, I get up to leave – then I don't.

Abruptly, Solomon has stopped crying. He is now frozen, white-faced, staring at something behind me. And nodding. As if he is actually interacting with whatever he can see. And what he can see seems to terrify him yet control him.

He speaks to something – some object – something – right behind me. Behind my left shoulder. He is trembling with fright, now; his hands shake as if they are palsied; his knees wobble. This is more than a bird or a shadow or a brief auditory hallucination. This is clearly visual and profound.

He speaks obediently, deeply frightened, shivering, sad. 'Yes. Yes, I will. I am – I – I am sorry.'

This is profoundly discomforting, way worse than his tantrum.

'Solomon, who are you talking to? Who are you seeing?'

He entirely ignores me.

'Yes,' he says to this spectre about three feet behind me, 'I'm sorry about the mirror. I will – will find it again. I'm sorry for what I did.' He nods. 'I'm sorry, Mummy.'

And then, he starts from his dream, his reverie,

whatever it was, and he looks at me as if he has no idea who I am, and it is me that is the ghost, and then he runs from the kitchen. Leaving me alone with a raygun, a Lego dinosaur, and a tremor in my frightened fingers. Those fine motor movements.

17

I listen to his running footsteps, taking stairs, then silence. He must have returned to his bedroom, to sulk. I have endured worse, though this is perturbing; making a child cry is always painful. And yet, at the same time, it can be necessary. I will remain *forensic*.

For a long while I sit there, staying calm. I make some more notes, assessing Solomon's significant confabulation and hallucinations, then, rising, I step out into the big echoey hall, lit dimly by that yellowy bulb. The sweet-odd scent of decay is stronger, this dying autumn afternoon. Winter is palpably near, and closing in.

Then I notice. The little door that presumably leads to the cellar. It is wide open and inviting. The same cellar that Grace said was so *dangerous* for the kids, which is why the door is usually locked. But then, why unlock it? *Who* unlocked it?

I stare at the black void of the doorway, leading down to the cellar. What if Solomon ran down there? Into the dangerous cellar, roiled with emotion, caused by me?

I surely have to go down. I have no choice. He could be in danger, sunk down here in his anger and sadness. *There are people in the cellar.*

Darkshape.

Crouching under the low stone lintel, I make my descent, gingerly, heading down the slippery stone steps.

The air is musty and claustrophobic, and it gets darker as I go down; the hallway light does not pierce too far. There is just enough light for me to make it safely to the bottom, which is a long way under the house. And here the cellar is so intensely dark I have to turn on my phone torch, a phone – I realize – that I have been using all day, recording and writing. A phone, therefore, with a battery of questionable strength, right when I need it.

'Solomon?'

No response. The air is deader than dead; the floor seems slippery, maybe just accumulated dampness. And this space is not sweet-scented like the hall; it is muskier, fetid. I turn the beam of my torch to the murk at the end of the cellar, and I suppress a gasp.

The cellar is *huge*, it is more like cellars: plural. There is a wall of ancient stonework at the end, glistening with damp, but a crumbled hole in the wall shows further black chambers beyond. Multiple chambers, maybe even tunnels.

'Solomon? Are you down here? Solly?'

Nothing, again.

'Solomon, please, are you down here? Please let me see you.'

I swivel and check the rest of the chamber. My phone-light – which might be about to die – shows various objects, all unpleasing. A few bolts of rotting cloth. Darkly soaked rugs. A shattered wine-barrel, a piece of obscure metalwork, tormented in shape, rusting bones of some old machine. Another arched stone vault. There is no one here, in the enormous swallowing cellars. How far do they go, what is behind me?

'Hello? Solly?'

Nothing. I got it wrong, he didn't come down here.

I sense I am entirely alone, there is no one else in these vaults, and that is not surprising: this is not a place to linger. No wonder Malcolm keeps it locked.

I try one last time, always try one last time. 'Hello?'

Silence. It is so quiet, I can hear my own laboured breathing, as if I am scuba diving. My breath is also visible, a faint clammy mist, as I turn my phone torch onto the other wall behind me.

This wall looks even older. The damp, medieval stones glisten, as if they are covered with something silvery and organic. Like a thin placenta. As if something is beyond them, struggling to be born.

And now I do hear a noise. And it is the slam of the little door up the steps. And the turn of a lock.

18

For a few moments, perhaps a minute, I pause, in the gloom. A childish prank has been played; I do not need to play up to it, to give these mischievous children any satisfaction.

Yet the panic is beginning to rise. A glance at my phone says I have minutes left of light, then I will be thrust into absolute blackness. Immersed in a drowning and total dark, with the medieval stones, and the writhing machine. And the sound of my own hard breathing, which makes shapes in the cold, down here. Under Baldhu.

Is this how Minnie felt, when it happened?

I panic, properly. For twenty seconds. And then I stop myself. I am trapped in a dank, ancient cellar, with no way out, but it is merely a childish stunt, and no more than that. Three, four seconds.

Get a grip.

Crouching, almost on hands and knees, I climb the slippery stone steps to the locked cellar door that should open to the hall. On the top step I stand and slap the woodwork.

'Grace, Solomon, *open the door.*'

No response. Not even whispers of childish glee, at a successful joke, an adult humiliated. Just . . . nothing. Maybe no one is out there giggling? Maybe the kids have dispersed, leaving me trapped.

I slap, again, more urgently. 'Grace. Solly. I know this is one of you, both of you. Please open the door. This is not especially funny.'

Again: nothing. The silence is emphatic. I step back. I can, somehow, sense the house breathing in and out, in the cold autumn night. Breathing through leaky old windows. Through hanging doors in forgotten rooms. Through tunnels barely known, to ice houses, and beyond.

No wonder it is a struggle to keep it all warm. No wonder Malcolm does not even bother. It would be impossible. Just do the necessary minimum, just bring light and warmth to a few chosen rooms. Don't bother about this musty old cellar: no one comes here from one week to the next . . .

I bang again on the ancient door, with its wormholes and rusty nailheads.

'Guys, for the last time. Open the bloody door!'

I am about to say, *Or I will tell your father*, but then that makes me sound like a hostile adult, a bad stepmother, not professional.

Part of my professionalism is, surely, accepting what cannot be altered, for now.

Turning around I go back down the steps and then, with great reluctance, I switch my phone off, to save the battery, thus dousing the torchlight. Now I sit with a shudder on the cold, slimy cellar floor with my back against the cold, hard wall and I let the blackness come. I allow it, let myself drown in it; I cannot fight it, so I must accept it. But it is hard: total darkness is a hard thing, it presses on your eyes the way extreme silence presses on your ears.

Perhaps it will be better if I close my eyes.

I close my eyes. And as soon as I do the colours

explode, and the memories. I have no music to keep them away, no 'Edifice of Tyranny' by Ouroboros.

Therefore, I let the memories come. I know what they will be; they will be *the* memories. A flickering montage of my tragedies.

And here comes the primary and guilty memory. Beautiful, dreamy, blonde-haired Minnie. Sleepwalking. Always sleepwalking. At the age of four or five, right up until that night. And the memory arrives with the same lacerating questions. Should we have done something? Should we have moved sooner, away from open water?

The cellar is dark, my mind is bright with sadness.

We always locked the front door at night: the easiest route to St Mawes harbour, and its clear and swallowing depths.

Yet that night, for whatever reason, no one locked the front door and that night, of all nights, Minnie went seriously sleepwalking out of her bedroom and down the stairs and – why? as if she was lured? – straight out of the front door and – step by awful step, in the unseen hours – she walked eyeless and unconscious to the harbour wall and she must have stumbled into the waters, ten feet from her own home. From Kyle. From *me*. From her own mother, who should have been there, to protect her, to save her.

I was not there.

No one was there. All this time Kyle and me, we slept on, unawares, until that terrible following morning, that coldest of clear April mornings, when I called to Minnie, *School, darling, you need to get up!* And no bright voice returned, there was no moaning funny girl saying, *All right, Mummy* – and then I went, with the first nagging anxiety, into the bedroom and it was empty and yet the bedclothes were disturbed, and the house was urgently searched, and no sign was found and even as the awful possibility dawned, the phone in my pocket trilled. With a friendly voice that said the worst thing ever.

Jago Moyle.

'Night fishing boat coming back to Penryn, they – I'm sorry – they saw a body, in the water, they recognized her, they brought . . . her on board, I'm so sorry, so sorry – my God – Karenza—'

A small girl floating, face up, serenely, in her Primark patterned pyjamas, in the cold, calm waters of the harbour. Not far from the Jesus Beach, and St Anthony's Head. The coves with the willows; the stands of the cedars, and the ashes.

Floating face up, with her arms out. Maybe smiling with the acceptance of death.

Here, now, entombed in the darkness, I breathe the clammy air of the locked-up cellar in Baldhu. Trying to slow my heart and dull the pain. The grief can still punch me, physically, if allowed. Level me. Over the years since the loss, I've learned to cope. The same way I learned to cope with my likely ASD. Strategies. Mechanisms. Therapies. Yet it doesn't mean *the thing* goes away; it never goes away. The limb is always lost, no matter how good your crutch, your prosthesis, your fake-it-to-make-it – you are still faking it.

Opening my eyes, I look into the blackness of the cellar.

And I blink, in fear; and I rise, warily, sliding up the wall.

There is a noise in here. Like a quiet but intense breathing, or maybe it is more of a rushing sound. Like water, or maybe something moving rhythmically. Backwards and forwards, to and then fro. Could be the breathing of a big, stealthy animal. Down here in the dark – but that makes no sense.

Standing up, fumbling for my phone – lost in my pockets – I gaze into the absolute blackness, defiant, absolutely not afraid. I have seen worse. Where is my damn phone? It is so lightless I cannot see my own hands.

Too late.

The noise becomes a wild flapping sound, and it comes nearer, and then – then it is right in my face. Some bird or bat, flapping urgently, with desperate wings, leather yet feathery, rancid and pungent. This *thing* is slapping wildly at my eyes. I can just feel and smell this hideous flying thing, this animal, scratching at my eyes.

'Stop it!'

The creature flaps. It must be desperate to get at me, or get through me and somehow escape, like I am barring the way.

'Help!'

And then, at last, a voice. There. Yes.

'Hello?'

The thing is still flapping, but less so, *less so*.

'Help!'

The voice, again, louder.

'Karenza?'

It is Malcolm. And now there is light angling into the gloom, I look up, my eyes wide. The creature is abruptly gone. Is that the sound of it winging away? Was it an owl? A raven? More likely, just some trapped pigeon. The shadows skitter; it is definitely gone.

'I'm down here. Please. *Let me out!*'

'Just come up!'

I don't need to be told. Stumbling to the foot of the stairs, I scramble up the slimy cold steps, and emerge into the yellow light of the hall, which feels positively dazzling.

Malcolm Tyack stares at me. Astonished. 'What on earth—'

Brushing myself down, I meet his gaze: I shall not be humiliated.

I say to him, 'Your house is haunted.'

19

We sit in the kitchen. My phone sits there, recharging. I sit here, recharging myself, regaining composure.

'Must have been bats,' Malcolm says, shrugging.

'Probably.'

'There are bats down there, I think, I so seldom go down. The cellars go on and on. Maybe as far as the mines.'

'I saw.'

He shakes his head. 'But run it by me again, haunted? What d'you mean? You're a scientist, a doctor, a psychologist: *what* are you saying?'

I keep my voice steady. 'I mean that this is what is being perceived, by Solomon at least. I saw him talking to his mother, his dead mother, in a state of . . . almost . . . automatism.'

'What does *that* mean?'

'He was not himself. He was transfixed. He is clearly enduring auditory and visual hallucinations, perhaps from childhood grief, but these percepts are quite particular, pareidoliac perhaps. And—'

'In English?'

'He is seeing the ghost of his mother, so this is a haunting. You don't have to believe in ghosts – I certainly do not – to accept that a lot of people see *something*.

And I'm afraid he is seeing something, and that may well be Natalie.'

He gazes my way as if I am half mad and shakes his head. 'OK, whatever. We have to find out who pulled that prank on you, gotta be one of 'em. No one else in the house. And it's so typical of Molly, sloping off to buy weed.'

He goes to the door of the kitchen, and shouts as loud as I have heard a man shout.

'Grace! Solomon! *Get down here.*'

I can sense Baldhu quaking: that voice must reach every corner. Even the barns.

Three minutes later the kids are assembled in the kitchen. Malcolm makes them stand, like they are in a dock in a court, because they are, for now, for their father, *the accused*.

'Grace, Solomon, did you lock Karenza in the cellar?'

They shake their heads; they are perfectly mute. I assess Grace, professionally. Sweet and sometimes beautiful, *yet clearly lying*. I wonder if Malcolm can tell. He must know his own kids.

'I'll ask this one more time, Solomon. Tell me. Did you lock Karenza in the cellar?'

He mutters, seems shamefaced. Eyes down. 'No, Daddy. No. Please.'

'So who was it? Was it your sister? Karenza thinks maybe it was your sister. Grace. *Tell me.*'

Grace shoots a quick glance at me, then at her father. 'Why should I answer?'

'Because,' Malcolm growls, 'I am your father, and I am asking you, and you will tell me.'

She pouts, shrugs, says, 'Yes, I did it.'

Malcolm sighs, profoundly. 'Great.' He looks my way,

his face saying *Sorry*, then turns back to his errant daughter. 'OK, Grace. You did it. *Why?*'

Again she slips a glance my way, before answering. 'Because it was a good joke. Clever lady in the scary cellar, woooooo. I knew she wanted to see the cellar, so I deliberately left it open, to tempt her. Then I shut it after her—'

Her father interrupts, 'But why? Why play this *terrible* prank?'

Grace comes right back. 'Because she made Solomon cry. About Mummy.'

A silence. I feel deeply uncomfortable. I did make Solomon cry; I am also slightly in awe of Grace, her cool, mischievous revenge. I cannot prevent the thought: a girl this clever and scheming? *Could* she? Could she actually be involved in her mother's death? But why? Perhaps if she senses, even subconsciously, that she might not be Malcolm's child, she would hate her mother for betraying her father, and for this lifelong deception. So that may be a motive; yet there is no proof.

Malcolm says, 'Grace, stop. This is serious. Why did you do it?'

She makes a protesting gesture. 'I'm not joking. I did it. And that's why. Trapped her like a mouse, using bait. Cos she made Solly cry.'

Malcolm gazes hard and bewildered at his daughter, and then he concludes, 'All right, I'll deal with you later. Please, both of you, go to your rooms. But first, Grace, you must say sorry to Karenza.'

Grace looks my way. She smiles coldly. 'Sorry, Karenza.'

'It's fine.' I rather want to say: *Well done you, you clever girl*.

With a handwave, Malcolm dismisses them. Solomon

runs away as if he is sprinting up the wing for his football team or running for his life. Grace stalks out, dignified. With a last, tiny, triumphant smirk.

Once they are gone, Malcolm looks at me, as if he needs to speak, but so do I.

'Malcolm, why do you keep the cellar locked?'

'Because it's dangerous, slippery, you've seen it now.'

'Nothing else?'

'Course not. Barely use it. My mum and dad never used it. Too damp. They always kept it locked.'

'But there's a key?'

'Yep, usually hanging on the corkboard, just there, right by the door to the kitchen. You can see it from here.'

I crane: yes, there is a corkboard in the hall, right by the kitchen door. I say, 'Grace could easily reach that, standing on a chair. That is presumably what she did.'

'Sure she could. When they were toddlers, they couldn't reach the key. *That's* when it was a risk. Solly still couldn't make it.'

I accept the explanation; I am tired now, I just want to go home. 'Listen, Mr Tyack. I have to go soon, but I need to say this again.'

He sits back, waiting.

'Solomon can be helped. But I'm not going to lie, this is quite serious. The hallucinations are profound.'

'What can you do?'

'Well, for a start I can ask friends who have more expertise in parapsychology. And then I can arm myself, if you like. That is to say: I can help, and I will help, but this is not going to take a week.'

He exhales, like a defeated man. The chuckle that follows is dark. 'It's been going on for months. If it's sorted by next spring I'll be bloody grateful.'

I rise, he rises.

He says, 'I am really sorry about Grace. She can be like this, like her mum: there's a devilment in her.'

'It's OK. I somewhat admire her enterprise.'

He smiles bleakly and leads me to the front door. As he opens it, to let me escape Baldhu, he says, 'Bats, eh?'

20

The menu of tthe Oyster Shack is a big but friendly thing. It's actually handwritten on a big card, describing the local mussels, Dorset crab, and wild line-caught sea bass – probably hauled in by Jago Moyle's brother two days ago, fishing out of Coverack. I know from experience that it is all good, I wish I could eat here daily. It's only the money from Malcolm Tyack that makes it feasible today.

The idea of this makes me feel obscurely guilty, eating because of their suffering, but then I remember I actually do have to eat, and I also notice the oysters, and I read

Helford Natives (Oct–March only)
Camel Estuary Rocks (all year)

Simple and effective. I am definitely having oysters, with some nice crunchy sourdough. Lemon and Tabasco. With perhaps some chips and mayo. And maybe a big bowl of the lobster bisque? Diet starts tomorrow.

'Sorry I'm late!'

Priya Hardwicke is here, looking a little hassled, and hanging her puffer jacket over the back of her chair.

'Traffic sooo bad. Got a cab in the end.' She is gazing about the restaurant. 'Pretty busy for Tuesday lunchtime?'

'The food is seriously good. I can totally recommend the fish soup.'

Priya makes a happy face, which she generally does. I've long admired her from afar, the way she is always smart and professional, always turned out nicely. As she is today: dark rollneck pullover, stylish jeans.

'Ladies?'

The waiter, timing it perfectly. We order, only dithering as we wonder whether we should demand a *whole* bottle of Spanish wine to share. We decide, with happy concord, that yes, we can cope with a whole bottle of Albariño.

And then, for a while, as the wine arrives, followed by the oysters, chips, soup, salad, we get reacquainted. I ask about home – her pleasant Penryn house; I've been there a couple of times, met her frantic husband Felix, the exuberant kids, Leo and Tilly. The kids were noisy, but fun. Too much fun maybe, because the last social encounter at their house happened way too close to Minnie's death. The unselfconscious laughter of a young, growing family was notably painful, at the time, for me. I avoided families – especially happy families with children – for many, many months. But now it is easier.

'So Felix is good. And the kids?'

'Oh yeah, all fine. Well: *almost*. Leo wants a drum kit for Christmas.'

We roll our eyes at each other. Concurring on the scale of this horror.

Priya offers a low chuckle. 'Felix says we could compromise and buy him a leopard.'

I laugh, thinking of Priya, at that birthday party. And Dinah's indiscretion, and Noel Oswell's annoying pomposity, and everyone's interest in the Tyacks. Cornwall is starved of gossip!

'So.' Priya leans in, with perfect timing. 'Tell me about the Tyacks! You said you had *stories,* and *questions*!'

'I do,' I say. 'But, truth be told, I am highly uncomfortable using real names. I know you know who I am referring to, Priya, but I'd rather call them Family T, Child A, Child B, and so forth. It's the only way I can do this.'

Priya nods, sombre, acceptant. 'I'm sorry, of course, you're right. We mustn't treat this as gossip. Family T it is. Ask away, I am eager to help. *Professionally.* And whatever we say won't go beyond this table – promise.'

'Thanks.'

I've made my point, it is time to talk – but I am not *entirely* immune to the theatre of it all. So I eat one fresh and excellent oyster rather slowly, adding a dab of Tabasco, tipping it down my throat. Swallowing, making Priya wait a few seconds, then I sip water, and I say, 'I think the house is haunted.'

The surprise, as promised, is real. Priya's soup spoon is halfway to her mouth, and the spoon stays there, for a moment. Poised. '*Serious?*'

'Yes. I mean, I don't actually think there are phantoms floating up from the mines, but yes, there is activity which I would file under haunting. As in, hallucinations which appear as dead people, dead women. To members of Family T.'

'Wow.' Priya devours her spoonful. 'Do go on.'

The oysters nearly finished, I turn to the copper mug of big, fat, salty skin-on chips as I recount, in anonymized terms, most of what I have learned. Of the Tyacks of Baldhu. Family T. The strange and disturbed behaviour of Child A, the youngest, the detached eccentricity of Child B, the oldest, the alienated one. And the father, Parent X, who lost his wife, Parent Y.

Priya says, sipping at her Albariño, 'None of that necessarily says haunted.'

'I'm coming to that . . .'

I conclude my story, focusing on the hated weirdness of the mirror lying on a shelf, and the threats of Child B, and the story of Child B sitting in her bedroom, envisaging her mother *at the exact time of her death* – her accident or suicide or murder, and then, finally, the sadness of Child A, throwing gifts into the sea, grimacing and hallucinating in the kitchen. I don't mention the cellar and my own terror. Am I embarrassed? Perhaps, but also it seems irrelevant.

Priya has been silenced. She is obviously intrigued. 'Quite a case. You know, of course, that I lectured in all this last year.'

'Yes, naturally. Parapsychology. Paranormality. The invisible made visible. That's one reason I asked you for lunch.'

'And thank you for that.' Priya drains the last of her wineglass. It is swiftly refilled, as she adopts a more teacherly voice. 'So, my turn?'

'Please.'

She closes her eyes, thinking, then she gazes at me and says, 'This is a *really* good example. Of a haunting. If you study these things, this case stands out, immediately.'

'Why?'

'Because,' Priya sips the renewed wine, 'most hauntings – whatever they really are – tend to be subtle. Smells, bells and whistles. Objects moving. Or appearing. Or just disturbing people. Apports.' She goes on, 'The mirror, for instance, is what we call a trigger object. It's classic. An everyday item that achieves early emotional significance in a case, and which sometimes leads to greater paranormal activity later on.'

'But,' I am puzzled, 'if that's true, what makes this case, Family T, stand out?'

'For a start: the girl, Child B, in the room, seeing her mother.'

'Why?'

'Because it is *rare*.' Priya's expression is quite intense. 'In the literature, it's called a crisis apparition. People get a vision of someone distant, a loved one, a friend, a brother, supposedly at the moment that something bad happens. You hear of them a lot, but in reality they are unusual. And you have a perfect example.'

I feel suddenly uneasy.

'And there is a logical, non-spooky explanation for these . . . apparitions?'

Priya nods, firmly. 'For sure. I'm a scientist, like you. It is all in the brain. The latest theory about crisis apparitions is that people who are intimately linked can subconsciously sense trouble ahead: you can sense when a mother, a child, or faraway friend, is endangered, simply because you know them so well, and you can accurately guess something bad might happen to them. Sickness, drugs, risk. This can evidence itself as a dream, or a daydream. It's the same way people subconsciously know their own anatomies.'

'Explain?'

'Look at it this way. A friend of mine once had a *terrible* nightmare: that she had a nest of mice, hiding in her breast. Mice gnawing away at her flesh. Six months later, she was diagnosed by an oncologist. Her subconscious knew before her conscious self, and before the doctor.'

'Breast cancer?'

'Exactly.'

'But what about the precise timing, Priya? Child B in her room. How can anyone explain that?'

'A mixture of coincidence and a form of wishful thinking. Who knows exactly when the mother died? No one. The mother was found later, and the timing of death was estimated.'

I nod, agree, and consider all this as the coffees arrive. I sip my dark and bitter espresso. And I say, as if talking to myself, 'Unless of course the haunting stuff is all a diversion . . .'

Priya nods, frowns, not quite understanding me; but now my own mind races on. Could the entire family, all of the Tyacks, be somehow faking it *together*? Perhaps it is all a distraction: because one or two of them *are* guilty. Maybe *all of them*. The entire family? And they cover for each other.

I am, in that scenario, enabling a huge deception, and I am the useful idiot. But the weirdness is *surely* too much, too far-fetched. I look up. Priya is speaking.

'It's a compelling example of a haunting, I rather envy you.'

'You're welcome to help, and the ghost stuff is *definitely* more your field.'

'I will help all I can! But we still haven't talked about Child A. Actually seeing a figure, a ghost? Again, that is genuinely rare. What is happening to *him*?'

I nod. 'I know. It is concerning. And his reckless behaviour at the beach, the magical thinking. At some point he might need formal psychiatric assessment. If the hallucination continues – or, God forbid, if it worsens, into long-term delusion, even psychosis. But I don't want to drag the poor kid to hospital unless it's totally unavoidable. They're all suffering enough as it is.'

'He definitely saw his mother? In the kitchen?'

'He actually used the word *Mummy*. So, yes, in his

head, yes.' I sigh, heartily. 'I feel so sorry for him. Protective. Because he's otherwise charming. Lovable. And so is the girl, in her own way.'

Priya is musing, then she says, 'Have you researched the family? Family T?' Priya sets her espresso cup down, continues. 'Researched the house itself?'

'No . . .'

'You should.'

'Why?'

'Because that house is old, isn't it? House R. Some old places get an historic reputation for hauntings, and if you dig deep enough, you'll find the logical explanation. For *everything*. It's a form of psychogeography.'

'How does that work?'

Priya finishes her final wine and explains. 'Let's say there's a street with a particular house – House H – where someone is brutally murdered. At first people will react to that house in a negative way, because they know the facts, the recent history, the killing.'

'I see.'

'But eventually the memories of the murder fade away; initially the details, then all the facts. It's human nature.' Priya half smiles, enjoying her lecture. 'But people over generations will still make negative associations with House H, as that is what adults handed on, perhaps unwittingly. And so the negativity endures down the years, the bad vibe; people act differently around House H. They may avoid it, or act weirdly going into it, giving it a jarring atmosphere and reputation, even though the circumstances that created this negativity are totally forgotten.'

'Ah. I think I get it.'

Priya offers her soft smile again. 'It's a neat explanation for haunted houses, right? And you can see psychogeography in action. There's a place called Gin Lane in London. Famously painted by Hogarth.'

'Pretty sure I know the image – the one with mothers dropping dead from booze?'

'Exactly! It was a genuinely notorious spot, in central London, between Soho and Covent Garden.' Priya puts her neatly manicured hands together, as if she is praying, and leans forward. 'And here's the kicker – even now, the area of Gin Lane is weirdly down-at-heel. Properties there can be noticeably cheaper than somewhere two streets away, for no rational reason. It's the reputation enduring, subconsciously.'

'So House B of Family T might have the same historical aura? From something lost in the past?'

Priya shrugs, amicably. 'Could be!'

I smile. 'Thanks, Priya, this is properly helpful.'

'My pleasure, seriously. All very intriguing.'

The bill arrives. I want to pay it all, but Priya insists on splitting it. Perhaps she knows I am not the richest woman in Falmouth. The bill is halved, the waiter pulls back our chairs, we make our way out.

Slipping on her puffer jacket, Priya says, hesitantly, 'Ah, Karenza, I really want to ask something else.'

'Sure.'

She looks uncomfortable. 'You are being careful, aren't you?'

'What?'

'Well . . .'

She goes quiet as we press the door of the restaurant, exiting into the chilly afternoon. The Falmouth waterfront beckons. Cold, jostling, salty, and naval. Grey and whipped by a near-winter wind. The last bleak shreds of November.

'What do you mean, careful?'

'As you know, I've studied all this. And there's a pattern to hauntings, and one theory as to how they arise.'

'OK. And it is?'

'The contemporary idea is that hauntings are psychic symptoms of wild grief or guilt, or terrible anger, buried deeply – hidden – within families. Family histories. So you could unearth something pretty bad, worse than what you already know, and it may cause severe reactions.'

'Really?'

'Yes. Really.' Her face is sombre to the point of darkness now. 'Fact is, some hauntings lead to madness, violence, death. I investigated a case in Dorset, rich family, bit like yours, big, sad country house. The case ended with at least two gruesome suicides, possibly a third, years later. *Horrific.*'

She pauses, then goes on.

'I'm serious. If you ever meet a *truly* haunted family – and it sounds like you have that – all they ever say is they never want it to happen again, and they wouldn't wish it on their worst enemies.' A wan smile. 'Please just be careful? If you are in the middle of a haunting, don't tell people they are delusional, don't argue with them, play along with it. And whatever you do, *don't* get emotionally involved, don't dig into their inner terrors, don't dig up the bones.'

'I hear you.' I grin. 'Jeez, Priya, I'll be fine! I used to hang out with psychopaths who cut people into cubes! I think I can cope with a spooky farmhouse and some disturbed kids.'

Priya nods, and sort of laughs. 'Of course you will. You're the eminent Karenza Bray! You did ten years at Exeter Jail!' She waves as she walks away. 'Let's talk again soon. OK?'

I wave back, in a manner that says, *Thanks, but I really won't need help!* Then I turn. The wind is bringing a new and bitter sharpness. Standing on the harbourfront I tighten my scarf, and I watch as a brave little fishing boat tootles along Carrick Roads. Probably heading off to sea for the long cold night.

Still the wind stiffens. And still the gulls mewl in complaint. As if, with their lamentations, they can prevent winter.

21

'OK, thank you, Karenza. As ever!'

My possibly favourite, and certainly least-perplexing client, Dilyth Gilchrist – affluent, middle class, yachtie family, neglectful husband – is at the door, saying goodbye. I smile as she slips on her nice winter coat.

'It's my job, Dilyth, and it's a pleasure to help. Do please read that book I recommended.'

Dilyth nods politely, and in the way she nods I know she *won't* read it. She will order it online, read half a chapter, then drop it with a bored little sigh and return to her prosecco. And I can't do much about that, I can only suggest, and nudge. Most of my job is this: an hour of hopeful nudging, once a week. Few clients – probably no clients – are like the Tyacks. So compelling, so fascinating: so utterly immersive.

I smile again at Dilyth as she exits. 'It was a good session, good progress. See you next week?'

Client departed, I walk back into my living room. On the way I notice El Gruffalo. All morning he's been in one of his lofty moods, like he is deep into a podcast on quantum physics that I could not possibly understand. But now suddenly he is acting up, hissing, hackles raised, standing at the lovely windows, staring out, sometimes tapping the window with a paw, sometimes mewling in horror.

It must be a tiny dog. He always acts like this – entirely mad – when he sees a tiny dog. Not big dogs, as you might expect, not medium dogs, as would perhaps be understandable, but the little, tiny yappy ones. It makes no sense as they are zero threat to him – he's a big, fat, imposing cat, El Gruffalo, and yet he freaks at these miniature hounds – and now, as I go to the windows, look down into the piazza, yes, there it is. A tiny little dog is being walked by a middle-aged lady, a dog with a tartan jacket. When did people start putting their dogs in human clothes?

Picking up El Gruffalo I squeeze him tight, crooning a cat lullaby.

'C'mon, Gruff. It's just a tiny dog, you can cope. It's not even big enough for dinner, you could have that dog for elevenses.'

Nuzzling and hugging him, I hold him close to my heart: soothing and loving. This usually calms him down. For a second he struggles, and as he does I note that his concern has made Otto turn a kind of livid yellow, as if the madness is spreading around my flat, then at last Gruff does calm down. His struggles cease, he reverts to the loud motoring purr, like a freezer engine about to blow.

'There,' I say, giving him a final kiss and dropping him to the floor. 'You can have some more treats later, OK?'

I glance out of the window as I set down my cat, to make sure the annoying dog has gone. It has gone. But I can see something else that also interests me. Noel Oswell. He is pushing the door to the Oyster Shack, with his wife beside him. He is greeted at the door by the owner, as a regular customer, an effusive embrace. Not something I ever get.

I guess this is not surprising. Noel is affluent and a bon viveur – he likes his food, I recall the way he scoffed those canapés. I didn't know he liked my favourite seafood place, but then I hardly go there because I can't afford it. He can.

Now I flash a glance at Otto. His yellow is also fading to his usual calm grey. All is well again?

Maybe. Apart from that rather ominous warning from Pryia Hardwicke. Be wary. *Severe reactions.*

Sitting at the table in front of the big seaward windows, trying not to be distracted by the impressive winter waves rolling into Carrick Roads, I think about House B, and Family T. Right now just about everything makes me think about Baldhu, and right now I am thinking of Molly, and her strange words: *oh-so-fertile.*

If Molly does suspect Grace is not Malcolm's daughter, that would grievously deepen her resentment. Natalie becomes the pretty young wife from nowhere – who somehow stole the dynastic house, handing it on to her two kids, and one of these kids isn't even a Tyack. That gives *Molly* a motive, a reason to resent Natalie, and a reason to abhor the house even as she desires it. And also a reason to want me to push off, as she does.

The whole thing compels me even further. Even deeper.

For the third time in two days I open my laptop to do as instructed by Priya. Research the history of Baldhu and its denizens. And for the third time I get nothing much.

The Tyacks are old Cornish. I've known that all along. But the wife, Malcolm's mother Davina Tyack, née Kenworthy, is from London – and is now disabled in a home in Penzance. Not Cornish at all.

I must, however, focus on the Tyacks. That's the more interesting stuff, the old stuff, the ancient, haunted stuff. For generations, the Tyacks, and various Cornish families they married into – Bassetts, Southcotts, Nankivells – have been mining and farming, and maybe wrecking. Even a spot of piracy? I note there is at least one marriage with the Coppingers, the 'cruel Coppingers'. They were wreckers, murderous, known for it.

At other times the Tyacks married first cousins. I am not surprised or shocked by this. I know that historic families in Cornwall – especially West Cornwall, *especially* remote Penwith – have been intermarrying, in truly complicated ways, for centuries. Because there simply wasn't much choice.

Perhaps that is why Malcolm Tyack went so notably off-piste. Natalie Skuse. A girl from a kids' home in Penzance. Poor. Pretty. Pert. Penniless. And maybe pregnant by someone else?

And, also, precisely not the kind of girl a Tyack would normally marry. That might have been the evolutionary reason that drove him, without his even knowing, towards some genetic variation.

So what about House B?

Again, for the third time, my research largely draws a blank. Baldhu is, as I have already guessed, moderately celebrated by niche local historians: 'a classic Cornish manorial farmhouse, with early medieval foundations, and subsequent additions in the seventeenth, eighteenth and nineteenth centuries'. This historic exterior was, it seems, briefly used as a location in a minor TV drama series, years back.

This is surely where I have seen the house before, what gave me that déjà vu when I first showed up. Baldhu has been on TV. Probably with women in Regency dresses alighting from a brougham in front of that grand front door. The TV guys must have carefully edited out the cowpats.

I press on, I need more, but more is not forthcoming. Despite its long history, Baldhu seems, if anything, to have lived a boring life. There is a lack of interesting *psychogeography*. This is no Cornish Gin Lane. Several people died in its bedrooms over the many decades, as people do in venerable dynastic homes. And the area around the house – around Penberth – has witnessed some deaths, nasty accidents, maybe suicides, in the nineteenth century, even eighteenth. And a couple of miners died in the Tyack family mines.

And this is all.

For a rambling house that has sat in the middle of those gnarling woods by that growling sea and those plunging cliffs, that is really not much. Eight centuries should produce more than *that*. No murders, no wartime battles on the cliffs, no Barbary raids for Cornish slaves. And not much about the wrecking either, like it was all hidden away, down there in West Penwith.

I sit back, thwarted, staring at Otto for inspiration. He eyes me with one eye, sardonically, and stays resolutely grey. *Sorry, Karenza.*

Is there anything else I can try?

Deep in my irritation, I politely swear, apologize to Otto and El Gruff, then pull the laptop shut. Looking at stuff online is not going to cut it. I have to go and find out for myself. And I have three whole days before my next client: a precious window of a long weekend. I've done the interviews with the kids, and I still have work to do with Malcolm and his siblings, but now I need to look at this case as a whole, observe the entire family, in context.

I gaze once more at Otto in his cage.

'Sorry, Otto. I'll get Dinah to feed you.'

He seems to shrug and turn a pale pink. For permission?

Picking up my phone, I call Malcolm. He is his usual brisk, brusque, at-the-restaurant self, but he is not resistant to the idea that I come for an extended period. Several days in a row. Friday and the weekend.

Distractedly, as is his manner, he says, 'You might as well stay in the house. We have about five hundred bedrooms.' He snaps some order, to some chef, then comes back on the line. 'Try not to strangle Molly, I know she can be annoying. See you this evening.'

The call ends. I go into my bedroom to pack a small suitcase. I feel like a diver on a ridiculously high board, about to take the plunge. I could possibly cripple myself, or I could win a medal. More importantly, I could really help those kids, and that is pretty much all I care about now.

Three nights at Baldhu.

22

I have now done this last winding, tortuous leg of the journey, from Falmouth to Baldhu, so very often – in reality, and online – I have begun to learn the place names down to the actual *farms*. Not just villages and hamlets. I know the names of meadows. Or carns. I can probably name each shivering tumulus of gorse, quailing from the cold December wind.

Trungle. Trevithal. *Tregiffian.*
Trungle. Trevithal. *Tregiffian.*

It is a bit like a Buddhist mantra, or a plea to the ancient gods that I won't meet an intractable farm truck loaded with silage coming the other way, forcing me to reverse for half a mile, at 1 mph.

Trungle. Trevithal. Tregiffian.
Halwyn, Bosava, Rosemodress Cliff.
Rosemodress Cliff?

As I steer around yet another standing stone, I wonder where a name like that comes from. I know some Cornish, and many of these names do not seem particularly Cornish, but nor do they sound purely English.

Perhaps they come from somewhere else entirely. The idea is fanciful, but it appeals to me: that this last, distant, untouched, mutilated, bleak, lush, wind-scoured, salt-seeded, wood-daled, teetering, pagan cliff-edge of the world is deeply lost in an uncanny valley all its own, where something even older – older than the Cornish *or* the English – can still, especially on freezing winter afternoons, or misty spring mornings, be discerned. A deeper seam of the world is revealed.

Choone. Tol Toft. Zawn Gamper.
Baldhu. 1/3 mile.

I am gaping, in mild surprise. There is an actual sign: a melancholy wooden Victorian fingerpost, hiding slantwise in the hedge. Presumably I have not seen it before because it has been hidden by autumn foliage. Now winter is here it is exposed.

Coaxing my weary car along the mud-crunching lane – it is cold enough for a deep frost in Penwith, today – I make a final turn into the farmyard outside Baldhu House and step out into the wind. The beautiful, ocean-perfumed wind that cleans the sky to freezing blue.

Apart from the urgent breeze in the near-leafless trees, all is silent. There are no other cars in the yard. There aren't even any cows in the nearby field, philosophically chewing the cud. No one is watching me. No birds. No people. No sheep.

I flip open my car boot and haul out my case. It is a satisfying weight, containing enough for three nights in Baldhu, with practical clothes for wintry clifftop walks. A couple of nice pullovers if we are to eat in any formal way. Will the Tyacks do that? How does this family work? Do people come over?

That is why I am here. To look under the hood and examine the engine: the emotions that drive the drama. It is a challenge I relish, as I key the door – though I wish I wasn't so obviously alone.

The house is empty: I am sure of that as soon as I inhale the dying scent of the echoey hallway.

'Hello?'

Quietness. No Molly, no kids, no Tricia, no family.

Hoisting my bag, I go into the kitchen. There is enough winter light to see, and it is certainly quiet enough to hear my signalless phone *ping* as it eagerly connects with the Baldhu Wi-Fi. I lift it up and read: a message from Malcolm Tyack.

Kids at party. Late. Molly away for day. All yours till about 7.

So the house is empty for quite a while: this gives me all the time I need. To explore Baldhu properly.

I do downstairs first. I certainly do not need to see the cellar.

The drawing room contains a big new TV, ancient stone fireplace, antiquarian books, specimens of rock and tin, and a few scattered toys: a spaceman made of weird green jelly, and another biggish Lego dinosaur, its face casually smashed off.

And on a wooden stand in the far corner I find a huge, ancient book. The faded, gold-tooled letters on the front say Holy Bible. I remember Malcolm mentioning this. *No one burned the family bible.*

The book is too heavy to pick up comfortably. I open it on its lectern and flick the fragrant pages. Genesis, Ecclesiastes, Revelations. The type is venerable, and there are elaborate monochrome illustrations. The divine shafts of God striking the Israelites.

Right at the end I spy something a little more intriguing. The Tyack family tree, from the late seventeenth century, carefully handwritten, first and elegantly in quill pen, then black fountain pen, then modern pens. Noting birth dates, marriages, deaths. A notable decline in penmanship runs through the pages, mirroring the decline in the Tyack mining fortunes.

Someone – Malcolm, Molly? – has kept the family tree up to date. *Natalie Tyack née Skuse* is written, in biro, as the wife of Malcolm. Her kids are also here, with absolutely no question over their parentage: Grace Jacinta Trevezah Tyack. Solomon Andrew Trewortha Tyack. But the year of Natalie's death is *not* written in. Was it too painful? Too early?

Too guilt-inducing?

I close the bible, turn away, and drift through further rooms. Shrouded, quiet, dusty. One is full of tatty musical instruments and ancient porcelain; the next is entirely bare. Then I come to the dining room. It, too, is eccentric – a strange mix of classy mahogany dining furniture, a plastic seaside bucket, smiley wedding photos of Natalie and Malcolm – she really was pretty; he looks like a lottery winner – and drawers of tarnished silverware.

There is not much else. I aim for the stairs.

The upper storey reveals even less than the ground floor. I find a series of bedrooms, box rooms and old bathrooms, all as expected. Antiques, dust, a microwave and fridge in one bizarre corner, as if someone tried to live in one room.

There is just one bedroom that truly interests me.

Malcolm's bedroom. What must have been Malcolm's and Natalie's.

Quietly pressing the door open, fearful for a tiny moment, as if the angry ghost of Natalie Skuse waits at my shoulder, I enter and look around.

Any immediate sign of the dead wife has gone. No lingering perfume or make-up: no hoarded clothes, nothing identifiably female.

There is an ensuite bathroom – clean, luxe, modern.

And at the far end, one further room leads off the bedroom. It says 'Office' on the door, in kids' crayon written on taped paper, something done by Solomon or Grace, years back. Maybe as a warning to themselves: to wandering infants, or to anyone. *Don't come in here: Dad works here.*

This door is firmly locked. And Malcolm certainly has not given me the key. I have used up all the keys.

This is maybe sufficient for now. The guilt encroaches, like the congealing chilliness: I have almost finished, but not quite. Standing by a dressing table I notice the hand mirror.

The trigger object.

It has moved again; presumably Malcolm brought it here. Or maybe the mirror is following me. Of course, this is absurd.

For a while I simply look at it: silvery and delicate, with its glass blindly reflecting the ceiling. It is giving me another idiotic shiver of nerves, like it is toxic, or explosive, trip-wired to the dangerous past. I tut at myself: it is merely a mirror, albeit antique and stolen from some wretched shipwreck. And now, as I gaze at it, I remember I have a friend who might help me here. An old friend from uni, an antiques expert, now a rich auctioneer in London.

Taking up my phone I send him an email.

Hey, Ben, long time! Too long. Hope all is well. I know this is a bit abrupt, but I wonder: can you help with something? I've found an old mirror, Chinese, any idea what it is, what the writing means, what any of it means . . .

I attach a dozen photos and end the email with a desire to meet in London, soon.

London! The idea of London feels intoxicatingly superb and alluring down here in Penwith; it feels as if I will never see a big city again, let alone *London*.

A minute after I press send, he replies. Excitedly, I open the email:

Hi, I'm away on holiday, I will be back at my desk . . .

Dammit. I feel cheated, but I can hardly blame some old friend for going on holiday. Until he's back I will have to work out the mirror for myself. Setting down the phone, and suppressing my tingling nerves, I pick up the mirror. I closely read the engraving, I gaze at the all-too-faded little square, I examine the beautiful, sadly dented handle for secret compartments, like it will have some concealed note inside, with the verdict on Natalie's death. Unsurprisingly, there is no secret compartment.

Now I hold the mirror properly, turn its glass towards me, and see again my round face and my brown hair and my slightly disappointing nose, the anxious face of a pensive but professional woman, in the gloom of the room on this December afternoon. As I regard myself I also see something behind me.

Suddenly. In the trees. Trees that scratch their bare twigs at the window, moving oddly, like a significant animal was just there, but has fled – a big dark bird, or something else, a child?

What was it?

I whirl around. There is nothing there. The trees have stopped moving, they are still and bony-black against the harsh blue winter sky, which gazes down at the gardens where I have not been. And now, I realize: the gardens! These gardens feel important. Solomon told me how much his mother *loved the flowers*, in her garden time.

Dropping the mirror with relief, I head downstairs for the warmer kitchen and the back door. It is locked, but this time I have the key.

Stepping outside, I quickly discover that the gardens are large, green, unkempt – and properly beautiful, even in early winter. A tinkling fountain of ancient stone concludes an alley of dense hedges. A little pond seems to harbour roiling fish; the water is beginning to ice over. The gardens are obviously too big to be maintained properly, but the unkemptness makes them lovelier.

At the very end of the gardens, wild Penwith begins. Not even farmland. A mix of proper moorland and dense black woods. Yet there is a rusty gate, and a path. Leading where?

I check the time: 3.40 p.m. Probably half an hour of winter light remaining. Twenty minutes. Surely enough. Why have a path here? Did Natalie take this path? Swinging the gate, I march out, but the paths of gorse and stone go this way, then split, they go another way, then split three ways, until I realize, about ten minutes too late, as the grey December shadows fall upon the world, that I am foolishly lost. The light is almost gone.

Stars are appearing in the clear night sky.

I reel around. There is no light to guide me. No other houses anywhere. I didn't turn on any of the lights in Baldhu. How stupid. There is no moonlight. I am out in the wilds. But I can use my phone as a torch, I pat my pocket as I recall.

I set down the phone, by the poisonous mirror.

No phone. No torch.

The fear is the faintest tingling. But I can ignore it. I am only twenty minutes from the house. Can't be much more. But where is Baldhu House? In this dense dark I might walk the wrong way. But would that be so dangerous? In the end I will surely find a farmhouse or a road, even in the turgid blackness: this is not the Amazon jungle.

But it is jungly enough. And the notion rises: maybe this is what happened to Natalie? It was a dark night. She was upset from a bad dream or a childhood memory. The care home in Penzance. She got a bit lost. She panicked and fell over the cliff at Zawn Dorlam – and died.

No. That is nonsense. Natalie Tyack must have known that path better than almost anyone. Even in the dark. Also, she apparently drove the other way. Drove as close as you can to the zawn then walked from the road at Penberth? Maybe it *was* a simple but terrible accident.

There. In the murk, in the trace light from the wintry stars, I can see a shape I recognize. A clump of ancient Penwith boulders. A small carn. I saw it before as I strode out. That is surely the path back to Baldhu House.

It is terribly cold, a clear night with a quite fierce winter wind. I yearn to be inside. Slowly I jog down the path. Yes. Yes. Surely this is it.

'Stop!'

A voice. A very loud and masculine voice. A voice I do not recognize. Now the fear is urgent, and deeply real: the primal fear of a woman alone in the dark and a man shouting, and pursuing, right behind her.

I begin to run. *Fast.*

'Stop!'

I will not stop. Why should I stop? Stop so I can be *raped*? I need to get to Baldhu. I am sure I am on the way to Baldhu. Once I am in Baldhu I can sprint inside and slam the door behind me, turning the key, making myself safe. What kind of man walks these stupid moors, in the dark, then finds a solo woman, and shouts at her? Only a bad man: and I have met enough of them, and I know what they can do.

'Don't do it, don't run, *stop*!'

I ignore the scary shouting. I sense the flash of a torch. I run faster, but then I stumble on a thorny arm of bramble. It snares me, half twists my ankle, and I yelp; I am half falling, and the man is going to catch me.

No, I will not be caught. Hauling myself up, scrabbling on rocks, I push myself on, but even as I run I can sense this monster behind me, so close. And now he has me, he is rugby-tackling me, from behind, and he is saying, 'Got you got you got you!'

I struggle in his grasp, but he has me pinned down. He is tall, strong, angry. This is it. A horrible nightmare is coming true here, in the dark and the cold, among the rocks of old Penwith.

'You stupid woman,' he says. 'Look down. Look there. Stop struggling.'

What does he mean? I strain and lift my head a few inches. I gaze fearfully ahead. And then my brain blanks to whiteness at the sight. I am less than a foot away from a dark swallowing void, which plunges deeper into the earth.

It is the lip of a disused mine shaft. I was about to run right into it. And now the soil and rocks beneath begin to sag; this is not over, I am close to falling in, even now. I am going to fall, I am slipping.

The words resound in my head.

Black mine.

Bal dhu.

23

'Jesus fucking Christ.'

I am still slipping. The grass is icy-wet, and the bricks are unstable, and gravity is tugging me down towards the lip of the pit.

A yell.

'Don't move, don't move a damn inch, you're slipping!'

It's no good, it is inevitable that I will fall, I cannot stop this. I stare ahead and down in blind, whitened fear. How far down does it go? A disused tin mine? Certainly enough to kill me. To smash me. My rock-climbing skills won't help; this yawning hole is ten foot wide, and I have no purchase on the icy rocks and dewy wet grass. I am already falling in.

'Help!'

'I am!'

'Please!'

'Stay perfectly still – you're sliding close – I can pull you back.'

I wait. Eyes now firmly closed with prayerful horror. This is it, this is how I die, a stupid woman in a stupid panic on a stupid task, running around a wilderness known for tin mines. I will slide and fall into this hole and spin down the void, smashing myself and my bones on one rock wall then another . . . But even as I yield to despair I feel surprisingly strong arms – as he pulls me, tugs me away, drags me, bodily, from the horrific gaping mouth. And now, as I am scraped away from my own idiocy, I begin to feel it beneath me. Harder earth and drier rocks, and then actual proper solid ground.

Saved.

I look up, as the swearing man lifts himself away from me. As I push myself back, further from the danger.

Slowly, slowly.

The torchlight blinds me.

The man averts the torch beam; I shift myself, and slump down on a chunk of mossy boulder.

Breathing the cold night air.

Alive.

This man sits next to me, places the bright torch on the ground but angled so that it throws light on us both, without dazzling.

I feel like retching. The aftertaste of fear. I spit, instead: not very feminine.

He says, affably, 'You probably wouldn't have died.'

His voice is mild, and slurred. He sounds young, and also a little drunk. I spit again, dust from the rocks from my stumbling fall. I am humiliated: I have just been saved by a wandering drunk. Though it is better than dying. At last I say, 'Why the hell is there an open mine shaft?'

The man chuckles, and now I can see his face. He is a younger, thinner, softer, blonde-haired version of Malcolm. So this must be the brother? The *enfant terrible*?

'This is Cornwall: there are ten thousand mines, especially in Penwith. They've been mining since year zero—'

'I'm Cornish. I know there are mines. But they get capped off.'

He gazes my way. 'Not all of them, hundreds left.'
'But so close to the house?'
He asks me, 'You must be Karenza Bray? I did wonder. Trace of an *echt* Cornish accent?'
'And you must be Miles. The brother.'
Tilting towards each other, we do the most bizarre and awkward handshake in Cornish history. I say, slightly more composed now, 'Thanks for saving my life.'
'You're welcome. But like I said, ya probably wouldn't have died: mine is flooded about twenty foot down, I'd guess. It's all flooded around here if you go down far enough. Not far at all. So you'd have dropped in the water. Like a stone. Plop.'
I think about this, still panting the cold night air. I say, 'But that would be icy water, with no way out, and how long would it take firemen to get all the way out here, and how would they haul me out of the shaft, even if they got here in time?'
Miles Tyack shrugs amiably, the sweet scent of beer on his breath. 'Yeah. You'd still be in the chutney. So you might have died in the end? That's true. I am a hero after all!'
'So why isn't it capped? I know they cap mines close to houses, they are so dangerous.'
'Ahhh. This shaft was only exposed last year, in all the rains, last November. A little landslip. Shafts everywhere around here. They didn't map 'em precisely in the fourteenth century, didn't leave schematics of the adits. And besides,' he sways the torch beam, flashing it so I can see, 'there are signs everywhere. Till they can cap it off properly.'
He's right, I can see now. The bright torch beam shows them.

Keep Out.
Danger.
Open Mine Shaft.
Keep Out.
I simply didn't see them in the dark.

'And you tripped quite flamboyantly over some barbed wire that was also meant to warn you.'

Of course, I remember the bramble that snagged me, sending me sprawling. I look again. He's right. It was not a trailing bramble: there are a few low strings of barbed wire blocking the path, enough to warn any sensible person, halt any dog walkers, and stop any wandering sheep. I ran into the low-slung wires and went flying. I feel the pang of my own stupidity.

'I'm an idiot. Jesus. Please don't tell anyone. I'm meant to be the sober forensic person.'

'Don't worry, promise won't tell. And, let's face it, I probably didn't help much, scaring the bollocks out of you, shouting *stop*, a strange guy lurking by the Stone Age tombs!' He shakes his head, laughs the scented, beery breath again. 'We really need to do something about it, get it capped properly. And I could see you heading directly here, didn't know what to do.' He sighs animatedly. 'Shall we go to the house now? I have a torch to guide us, and I am experienced at fighting wolverines.'

'Oh God, please. Yes.'

Having been already saved from a probable slow death by drowning, I am quite happy to feel Miles Tyack take my arm again, steering me around the last of the boulders. When we reach the gardens proper, he lets go.

As we approach the brooding silhouette of Baldhu, I turn to my drunken saviour. 'Why *are* you walking the moors at night?'

He gives me a slurred smile. I can see he is handsome in a quiet, fair way. Mid-thirties. Less macho than the red-haired Malcolm Tyack.

'Just down for a couple of nights.'

'Sorry?'

'I mean, I'm staying at the Saracen, the pub, over the hill. I've had a few already so I can't drive, and anyway I like the walk. If you know the way and you have a torch, it's bracing. Not *necessarily* fatal.'

I allow myself to laugh. Mainly in abject relief as we step into the warm kitchen, a kitchen which Miles brightens with light, and then hot coffee.

'So, my brother said you are staying here?'

'Yes, apparently. Don't know where yet.'

'Ah, then you must be in the main guest room. An honoured spot! Second on the right on the first storey, if you, um, need to freshen up. There's a nice big bath in there.'

The idea is beyond appealing.

'Thank you, thank you.'

'Come down for drinks! Weissbier and schnapps . . . Or gin. Around seven.'

I am too tired, for now, to talk any more; I go to the stairs. Then I wonder, in my befuddlement, if I have forgotten anything: I turn. I can see into the bright kitchen, the door framed by darkness. I can see Miles on his phone, talking, animatedly, frowning, scowling even. Still, a stray woman nearly died in a mine owned by his family. That would not be good for the Tyacks. He is surely calling to let people know – 'we have to get it capped' – I just hope he doesn't use my name.

Moving on, I furtively retrieve my own phone, then find the second door. I missed this room on my tour, and I am worried what lies beyond might be some cobwebby Gothic nightmare. It is not. It is smart, even chic, with well-chosen modern furniture and nice abstract paintings that hint at the sea, and the bathroom gleams as expensively as the kitchen. I feel slightly guilty as I take it all in. It feels too posh for me, I feel like a guest in a hotel I can't afford, trying not to think about the bill.

I run myself a bath and soak in the luxuriously scented bathwater, letting the horrible memories of the day float away, driving them from my mind. Then I wrap myself in big soft towels and go to lie on the bed for just a minute. One lamplight glows. The glowing fades . . .

I wake abruptly in the semi-dark. Feeling the mild panic of someone who has slept at a strange time. Disoriented. What time is it? I might have slept for six hours. Ten. It could be 3 a.m. What woke me?

Voices. This is it. I can hear low, murmuring voices. Like ghosts, wondering whether to wake me.

Then I hear the clink of glasses. Drinks.

24

Drinks are stiff. The atmosphere is obvious as I enter the drawing room and take the offered seat. Everyone is gathered here, yet somehow scattered, isolated in themselves. Sam the neighbour smiles brightly from across the large room at me.

Next to him, alone on the grandest sofa, is Malcolm, mute, maybe bored. Then Molly, in the saggiest armchair. She looks as if she would rather be on heroin. She looks as if she might *be* on heroin.

Miles is in the chair nearest to me, next to the drinks tray. He seems to be in charge of the drinks. He is certainly in charge of his own drink, which appears to be gin and tonic with no tonic; he is topping it up liberally with pure gin. As I settle into the last leather chair, Miles leans across to me and murmurs, with the air of someone who shares a dark secret, 'Guess you might fancy a largeish one?'

'Please.'

'I'll do you a French 75. *Unfeasibly* potent.'

'I've no idea what that is.'

'It'll be just the ticket, Dr Bray. Tickety fucking boo.'

'Anything will do! Thank you.'

I almost add for *saving my life* and for *not telling anyone about me and the mine* and the latter, if I said it, would be as sincere as the former. The last thing I want, in this tense room with this apparently misfitted group of people, is to be the centre of attention. I am getting old playground vibes, from Devoran Primary. Before I laboriously learned to be social, to please, to read intentions and distract the bullies.

And I do not quite know how to read everyone here, yet. Although I definitely sense bridled aggression.

Except maybe from Miles, the amiable drunk. Who is handing me a flute of champagne: apparently the 'French 75'.

I sip; it is delicious. Champagne maybe mixed with something stronger. Gin or vodka? I have an urge to gulp it in one go and demand a replacement. Numb the needling pain of the social anxiety in the room. I recall Priya's words: *One theory is that hauntings are psychic symptoms of violent grief or guilt, or wild anger, buried deeply – hidden – within families.*

There is certainly emotion buried here, but it isn't buried very deep. The stilted chat continues, ludicrous in its superficiality. They talk about nothing at all. Weather, the recent rains, the derivation of the word zawn from Cornish *sawan*: chasm. More drinks are distributed by Miles. Then Miles mentions Natalie, how she liked the winds and storms of Penwith. He says it as if he is trying to get a reaction, but no one responds, no one at all, not with words – but I clock the expressions. Sam fiddles guiltily with his drink, Molly glares angrily at Miles, Malcolm has his face to the floor – from sadness, shame, worse?

Miles is motioning. I willingly accept another French 75. I am a little out of my depth. Not so much in a social way. I'm not cowed, I've seen the lunacy of the posh as much as the poor and I feel pity for both, but I just do not *understand* the social interplay here. The undercurrents are so complex: whirlpools of resentment, backwaters of remorse, maybe eddies of loathing, yet also love, perhaps. The conversation idles along, then Miles says, 'OK, I'd better be going, back to the Saracen.'

I ask the obvious question. 'Why aren't you staying here, Miles? In Baldhu?'

A frigid pause settles over the drawing room. Molly breaks it. 'My baby brother prefers his teenage friends.'

Miles smiles acidly, shoots back at his sister.

'At least I have friends: you mainly have Tramadol.'

She smiles, benignly. 'How old is she this time, seventeen? Do you help with her homework?'

Miles chortles. 'Seriously. Try *more* Tramadol. Maybe thirty at once? Give it a real go.'

Malcolm says, wearily, 'Guys, please. I got us all here so we could meet Karenza. She's trying to help. With the kids.'

'Karenza and I have already met,' Miles says, slurring again. 'She was exploring the grounds. I told her about our lovely mines. How we sent men naked underground to toil for threepence a shift, twelve hours a day, and then they died of black lung aged twenty-seven.'

'We did allow them to eat pasties,' Molly says. 'If you ask me, we were overgenerous.'

Miles laughs, loudly. 'Put down the fucking pasty, you shirker. Get back to the rockface!'

'My great-granny worked in the mines,' I say, interrupting the room. 'She was a bal maiden, aged nine. Sent to break rocks in all weathers. Barefoot.'

The room is completely silent. I have imposed myself. I smile at everyone. 'In the end she went deaf, because of the noise of the mining stamps. Crushing the ore. So,

I just want to say: thanks for the work. We needed the money.'

The room is still silent – then Miles and Molly both laugh. Sam titters nervously. Malcolm looks at me, intrigued. And now Miles is slipping on his coat, heading out. He flashes a sympathetic smile at me, and says, 'Nicely done. And it really *was* a pleasure to meet you. Ignore my sister. She's just like my mother. *Sorry.*'

And with that he is gone, wobbling towards the kitchen; in seconds he is followed by Molly, who barely says goodbye to anyone. Talks about sleeping in her flat in St Ives. Her fast car is heard in the silent drawing room. Then Sam seizes his moment and departs with words about his absent wife. And then *drinks* are over almost as soon as they commenced, and it is just Malcolm and me.

'So . . .' he says, heavily. 'That went well.'

I laugh.

Malcolm gives me a rueful smile. 'Sorry 'bout my siblings. We're not always *quite* this bad. Thought you handled it pretty well.'

'Don't worry, I've encountered hundreds of families, in my job – they are nearly all cracked in their own way.'

He flashes me a grateful glance. Warming to me?

I have to ask, 'What was all that about Miles? And the pub? The Saracen.'

Malcolm yawns, and fights to hide it. 'He's sleeping with a bar girl there. She's barely nineteen.' Another, smaller yawn. 'He likes the girls.'

'But why can't *she* stay over here?'

He shrugs. 'The bar girl? Apparently she flatly refuses.

To stay over in Baldhu. At night.' He checks his watch. 'Kids'll be home soon.'

With that he rises and starts clearing the drinks. I go to help him, but as I collect the glasses, I am thinking. I am not like the bar girl from the Saracen: I can't refuse to sleep over in Baldhu. It is too late now.

25

As promised, the kids return – delivered by Tricia, who nervously waits at the door again – but they do not linger long with the adults. Solomon is not quite his ebullient self. He tries to tell us enthusiastically about the party and the man who could make *massive* dinosaurs out of *purple* balloons and *orange ones too*, but he almost falls asleep as he does, and Malcolm packs him off to bed.

Grace stays in the kitchen a little longer, nursing some apple juice. I engage her, as best I can. 'How was the party? Did you have fun?'

Grace looks older than her years and quite swish in black, matching her black hair, setting off her cool blue-grey eyes. There is a glimpse of her mother here, and the young woman she will become. She says, 'They only invited me because they had to.'

'I'm sure that's not true.'

Grace's smile is chilly. 'Of course it's true. Everyone likes Solomon. No one likes me.'

'Grace—'

'It's *fine*.'

With that, she takes her glass and goes to exit the room, giving her father the driest peck on the cheek, saying, 'Goodnight, Papi. Don't forget to fix the window.'

He cups her cheek, paternally, 'Of course, sweetheart.'

Grace exits; her footsteps recede down the hall, up the stairs. Heading to bed. Malcolm exhales ruefully.

'Ah, my daughter. What are we going to do?' He winces. 'And now we've got Christmas coming. The first proper Christmas since . . . You know.'

My sympathy surges. I too have had the shredding anguish of the First Christmas After. I could try to reassure Malcolm – but there is no reassurance here, and he is not a man for sentimental nonsense. I move the conversation on. 'What's that about a window? Fixing it?'

'Solly's window. You remember he's been banging on about black birds, seeing them in his room?

'Well. Yes.'

His frowns. 'Of course he imagines some of them, probably he does – but not *all* of them.'

'Sorry?'

'The other night, I went to his room, to check on him. And I actually saw one. Bird. Desperate little thing, fluttering in the corner, the way daddy-long-legs flit about. Panicking.' His frown softens. 'Anyway, then I realized the window in his room falls open in the right breeze, and it directly faces Trevaylor woods. That's where they come from. Might be why he then sees them everywhere else, it triggers him. And then he scares Grace.'

'It's a nicer explanation than actual ghosts.'

He nods, and yawns.

I say, 'You do look shattered. You should probably go to bed, as well.'

His eyes seek mine. 'Thank you. It is. I mean: it's draining. The grief and the chaos and now the kids, acting out, and the restaurants are *exhausting*. Going OK, but exhausting. Can't afford to screw 'em up.' He exhales. 'Look, Karenza, I meant to feed you a proper supper, nice risotto, but do you mind if we just picnic? Forage in the fridge?'

'Of course.'

I do not mind this at all. This gives me a chance to observe Malcolm Tyack, alone, at home, how he lives. And also I am hungry, and it turns out the promised humble 'picnic' is all delicious: the big steely fridge has a purpose. The Tyacks live well, they live in a way I have not experienced. As we polish off the *jamón ibérico* and heritage tomatoes, Malcolm sloshes full glasses of good Rioja, to chase the stilton and the brie, the ripped baguettes and the succulent apricots.

This is the moment. Malcolm needs to know. And I know the psychological value of opening up, of telling secrets; it is key to establishing mutual trust. It is a trick, but a wholesome trick. If I want to know the truth of the Tyacks, they need to see something of me.

Between sips of wine, and stabs of cheese, and sweet, sharp slices of apricot, I unfurl my sadly tapestried story, and I tell him about Minnie. The sleepwalking *that fateful night*. The drowning. The desolation. The divorce. I do it quickly, so I do not stumble, let alone cry; I don't want that.

'And now I live with a schizo cat with weird issues, and an inscrutable chameleon, and it's . . . OK. Sort of.'

Malcolm gazes at me, mouth open, sad-faced. 'It's never OK. Losing a child. I'm so sorry. What can I say?'

'We are not entirely dissimilar, you and me.'

His shrug is melancholic. 'Thank you for, well, all this. And being honest.'

'And you? I don't know much about your extended family. Beyond what I've seen.'

He obliges. Yawning again, drinking again, he gives me the basics. He tell me of his 'boozy reprobate father', who 'died in a yachting accident, racing around Brittany – that's probably where Miles gets his alcoholic gene'. He expounds on his waspish, fastidious mother, who never liked Baldhu, who obviously preferred Molly to her noisy, annoying boys, 'We were always in scraps, or fightin' each other, she got bored of us.' He tells me she now lives in Penzance, in a home, with disabilities. He makes it sound like his mother *wanted* to go into a home, and into dementia, so as to escape, after handing over the estate.

Malcolm says, straight out, 'Molly was outraged when I got Baldhu.'

'I did wonder. Yet you say she preferred Molly?'

'Molly is too angry to understand.'

'I don't get it.'

Malcolm devours his wine. 'Mummy thought Baldhu was nightmarish – dirty, old, creepy – the kind of place with birds in the bedroom, because we can't keep anything out. She gave it to me because I have kids, but also as a black joke, I think.' His smile is sardonic, maybe bitter. 'Forcing me to look after it, the Tyack legacy. A curse of sorts. The house we must never sell or quit. And she probably thought she was saving Molly – allowing her to live somewhere else, though all Molly has done is seethe, ever since. Mummy did give Molly a chunk of cash, but she's spent most of it on epic holidays. Unsuitable young men. And cocaine. At least she didn't waste it.'

He drains the wine, then adds, 'Molly always *hated* Natalie. My sister is a terrible snob, felt I was marrying down, can't ever accept that I really loved Natalie.' His eyes cloud with sadness, which seems to embarrass him.

'OK, you're right enough, I'm wallowing, need to go to bed.'

He gathers plates and slots them in the dishwasher; I help. I am, of course, thinking of the other reason Molly would hate Natalie: if she suspected Natalie of bringing a bastard child into the family, and pretending Grace is a Tyack. Deceiving her brother.

Just as we finish, ready to ascend the stairs, we are interrupted by a yell from Solomon.

'Daaa*aaaad*.'

He rolls his eyes at me, as if he is saying, *parenting never stops!* I feel like saying to him: make the most of it. Because sometimes it actually *stops*.

Malcolm calls out, loudly, up the stairs, 'Yes, Solly, what is it now?'

'Daddy, there really is a bird here. Another big bird in the room again! Can you get the bird out?'

Malcolm grimaces. 'Christ, this place, I should've fixed the damn window!' He raises his voice. 'OK, Solly, I'm coming. I'll brick up the bloody window.'

He offers me another rueful smile, says goodnight and quits the kitchen; for a minute I loiter, then I wonder why on earth I am loitering. I am exhausted. I nearly died today, falling down a tin mine. So insane I do not want to think about it.

Climbing the stairs, I pass that moody sequence of arched Gothic windows with the view of the distant and troubled sea. The night sky is cloudy, the moon obscured. I can hear Malcolm and his son talking loudly in his room as they chase the bird. Their voices are high-pitched, as if this is amusing, but in some warped way: they do not sound quite normal.

Malcolm's voice is particularly strained: a rasping tone. 'Solly!'

'Dad, you're not getting even close!'

He shouts, his words meant to be reassuring, yet somehow fearful. 'All right, give me a break, Solly. It's not easy. Wait!'

'It's moving again! Dad!'

Solomon sounds truly animated, over-excited. Puzzled, perturbed. I walk down the landing: the door to Solomon's room is wide open. I can see Malcolm standing on a chair. Trying to catch this mad, fluttering bird with careful hands, trying not to kill it. A good man, caring, loving, looking after his children.

But now I gaze, appalled, at the scene, and I understand it all too well.

There is no bird. There is nothing. There is a boy and his father in a room yapping at a trapped bird that does not exist.

Malcolm turns and rolls his eyes, in exasperation, at me.

'Has to be the woods, keep getting in. They must be from Trevaylor. OK, Solly, I'll get him, we can let him go together!'

Solomon shouts, 'S'moving again!'

I check, and check again, as if this is going to make any difference. It makes no difference. *There is no bird.*

Ducking back into the shadows, I walk on. Feeling quite *perfectly* sick. I push my door and lie on my bed. Then I urgently slip off my clothes and get into bed like I can sleep but of course I cannot. Instantly I pick up my phone to take notes.

These are maybe the most disturbing notes I have made on this case to date. Perhaps some of the more peculiarly disturbing notes I have made in a career of forensic psychology, of homicides and rapes and terrorists in Belmarsh.

The father is also haunted. They are all seeing ghosts. The entire family.

I do not know what to add to that. Also, it is hard for me to type, as my fingers are faintly trembling. Death and ghosts loom close in Baldhu. And they are beginning to surround me. I will and I must talk to Malcolm about this, because it has to be confronted: in the morning. Tomorrow.

For a while I stare up at nothing, mouth open but voiceless, like I am just under the sea and trying to speak to someone above the surface, then I realize this is really no good. I cannot sleep, and I need to sleep, I must accept my need. So I lean over to my bag, and I take a strip, and I pop a Valium to help me sleep as soon as possible.

Two Valium.

26

'So you got the bird out in the end?'

Malcolm smiles wanly. And yet his eyes evade mine, perhaps. 'Yes. Got it out. Think it was just frightened.'

'You reckon they get in from the woods?'

'Trevaylor. Yeah.'

His eyes are indeed evading mine, as if he is lying, but it might just be indifference.

I swallow my toast, take a hit of the Colombian coffee, which is welcomingly strong. Malcolm is holding his breakfast mug aloft, draining the last. The mug is decorated with the flag of St Piran, the flag and cross of Cornwall, black for dark rock and white cross for raw tin. Black mine. *Bal dhu.*

I am pondering my course of action, the pro way to go about this. Hitherto, my focus has been almost entirely on the children. I was going to do more interviews with the kids, then perhaps consider therapies, even if I got no further working out what happened to their mother. But now the scope is wider, because it has to be.

The father is also deeply invested in the delusions. So what else is he seeing? What else is awry? He may or may not be self-aware; perhaps he does sometimes realize he is seeing things, the way demented patients get moments of painful awareness, near the end of life:

this phenomenon is called *terminal lucidity*. Or maybe last night was not any kind of end, maybe it was the beginning of something new and even darker.

Do I confront him? Now? If so I must circle there, draw him into the subject without him even realizing. I will have to do so, this weekend, I cannot let it pass, but maybe not right now.

'Talking about Solomon.' I put two hands around my own mug, carefully, like it is sustaining soup, and I am in a flimsy tent in the Antarctic. 'I don't want to get outsiders in, not yet. But if all of this worsens, then an intervention might well become necessary. We can at least get him in the system, CAMHS, for official assessment, as a start. Also Grace, perhaps. But this weekend I can just observe.'

I want to add: and maybe get some assessment *for you*. I do not.

Malcolm says, 'We did do something with that thing, CAMHS, but it's so . . . slow.'

'I know, but I might be able to speed things up.'

'Thank you.'

'No need. It's my job.'

I look down. My toast and jam is finished, my fresh-brewed coffee is beginning to cool. Malcolm actually seems somewhat refreshed by sleep, ready to get on with things. He is looking about his space: for car keys, phone, stuff that shows he must be about his business. I am possibly losing my chance. I say, 'So, about last night—'

But he says, 'I'm really late, got to get going. Right now. Sorry.'

Inwardly, I curse; I say, 'But just a quick—'

'Nope. Sorry! Got to go. There's an open mine shaft about half a mile beyond the gardens, we *really* need to put some kind of wire over it. Listening to you last night, talking about your daughter's sleepwalking, got me thinking. Should have done it months back. But everyone's been so distracted!'

I wonder: has Miles told Malcolm, about my stupid accident? Does it even matter?

'Good luck with yer observations, Karenza.'

He departs speedily, with the jingle of keys and a workmanlike stride. I am left alone and frustrated in the kitchen. I stack the plates and mugs in the dishwasher, I sweep the crumbs from the kitchen island. And then, as promised, as planned, I spend the morning *observing*.

I do not observe much. I shift from room to room and back to the kitchen. Then I spot Solomon, wandering in the hall, in Chelsea top and jeans, his eyes fixed on a little screen: a video game, which he holds in front of his enraptured eyes like it is a sacred text in his own secret religion.

As the boy ambles through the hall and I say good morning, he notices me just enough to smile brightly. 'Hello, Karenza, sorry I'm not really listening to what you're saying. But I still like the sound of your voice!'

And then he wanders off. Eyes focused on the screen.

Grace is similarly dismissive, in her cooler fashion. I discover her in the conservatory. She is sitting with her knees up in a cosy armchair, utterly absorbed in a book. The conservatory is filled with bookshelves and ancient nautical maps and Victorian cross sections of tin-mine tunnels – and more pretty rocks and shells. A lovely space, making the most of any sunshine, winter or summer; it looks across the smaller southern gardens to Bathsheba Valley.

I say hello, Grace says a quiet and formal hi, as if

she does not want to be disturbed. Fair enough, yet I feel a need to interact.

'You enjoy spending time in here?'

Grace's gaze does not leave her book. 'It's quiet. No one bothers me.'

'It's a beautiful room. Your mother must have loved this space.'

Now I see a flicker of sadness across her face.

'She did. She used to read here all the time.'

The sadness passes. Grace loudly turns a page of her book. Saying nothing. I check the cover. It is *The Greek Myths*, by Robert Graves.

'You like mythology, Grace?'

The girl gives me a low, sardonic look. 'I can see why they call you *forensic*.'

I smile, undeterred.

'What do you like about Greek mythology?'

Grace does her favourite deep sigh. 'Oh, lots of things.'

'Tell me.'

Her shrug is subtle. 'I like the way people change. *Metamorphosize*. Boys becoming flowers, or girls dissolving into water, becoming rivers, lakes, harbours . . .'

It is another one of those mental leaps, where Grace can feel or sound like a literate adult, where at other times she feels like an infant. Grace lobs a final glance at me, a glance which clearly demands that I leave.

So be it. I retreat to the kitchen, and a big cup of tea, and I watch out of the window as Malcolm and some male assistant march down the garden. They have toolbags and rolls of chicken wire. Off to cover the open mine shaft.

And after that I do: nothing. Worse than nothing. I feel spare and pointless. The family continues its life around me. I've got three precious days in Baldhu – and this is the second, and yet I observe little. Nothing more than I know already: the haunting, such as it is, whatever it is, which has spread to the father. I wonder if Molly sees anything? Drunken Miles? And what about Natalie, could she have also been embroiled in the madness?

Yes. This is my purpose for the day. Natalie Tyack. I need to know more about the dead woman who materializes in the kitchen, to terrify her son.

27

The inland road is under maintenance. I have to take the even wilder, narrower sea-side road, which winds along above Mousehole, between twisted little woods, edging above delicate coves, all the way down to the fishing port of Newlyn with its busy fishmongers, peeling walls of fish dealers, the odd trendy new fish restaurant made out of a converted pilchard warehouse; all of which gazes at the fishing harbour, bristling with spiny white masts. Then the road divides – one fork heading along the seafront into Penzance, the other bending left into low hills and bigger houses.

I turn left, and then quickly pull over, the faint Cornish mizzle speckling my windscreen. A blue sky to the west says clearer weather is on its way.

I check the online map: I am near – there it is.

St Petroc's Children's Home.

I know this must be it because I have seen online images of this big, churchy, impressive, granite-stone Victorian villa. I checked the history. It closed as a kids' home years ago, not long after Natalie must have left, and then it was used as cheap accommodation for local workers – a long-term budget hotel for seasonal staff.

But there are few obvious signs outside, just a wooden plaque which is so weathered you can see the layers of that same history. Under the peeling hard paper saying

'Petroc's Hotel', you can see more peeling paper with 'Petroc's Home', with a cheery picture of a happy child playing hopscotch, and a widely beaming adult, and a tiny posh crest as if this is all some noble charity – and everything about it screams sadness.

I gaze about.

Several of the grander windows are boarded. A loud builder's sign announces impending development. *Eight Stunning Luxury New Apartments.* It seems the old St Petroc's, like so much of seaside Cornwall, is being turned into upscale housing. *Desirable* holiday homes. From its position, I imagine the top-floor flats, at least, will have lovely views of Newlyn Harbour. Million-quid views to go with sixty-thousand-pound kitchens and standalone baths and maybe a nice shared gym and cedary sauna.

Picking up my phone, I check all the notes from Kyle: on Natalie.

'Father abandoned Natalie and her mum when Natalie was tiny, no record of him. No name, no surname, nothing. Mother – Jacqueline Skuse – brought up Natalie alone for a while, but she got into money trouble, and drugs. She died of a heroin overdose when Natalie was nine. No close relatives known in the area, and after some dodgy fostering – she was troubled and rebellious, who can blame her? – she went into St Petroc's.'

The words are bald, but the emotions are profound. I stare ahead: poor Natalie Skuse. I am not entirely surprised by the story; Penzance, like too many Cornish towns, is simultaneously blighted with unemployment, penury, drugs, even as the rich keep flooding in, buying up the nice places. But even in this web of stories, fraught with unhappiness, Natalie Skuse stands out. Fatherless, then abandoned, and essentially orphaned, then stuck in a home. A rebellious and intelligent girl socially tossed away.

Kyle's notes conclude in his pithy manner: 'She got great A-levels. But there was no one to encourage her into uni. Ended up in a cheap flat-share in St Just, working behind a till at the Spar. No wonder she fell for Malcolm Tyack, or pretended to fall for him? Fleeting chance of escape.'

Putting the phone on the dash, I look out. A couple of guys are walking into St Petroc's. One in a suit, one in richer casual clothes: puffer gilet, posh cloth cap.

Jumping out of the car, I approach them. 'Uh, excuse me.'

The men turn, surprised.

Quickly, I explain my quest: to know more about St Petroc's of the past. The men smile, apologetic; the man in the suit says, 'Ah, sorry, I'm with the developers. Just taken on the job.'

The other guy has even less of a Cornish accent. Very much London. 'And I'm a buyer.' He shares a grin with his companion. '*Maybe!*'

The men laugh, and turn, ready to go into the building. I have one more question, for the developer. 'Can you tell me when you bought the place?'

'Sure! A few months ago. Right after the crappy hotel closed. It's a great location, so we snapped it up. Marvellous ocean views, as I am about to show my friend.'

The two men give me a final smile.

Gone.

Thwarted, I pace to the car. I need more. Perhaps locals will be more forthcoming. The old home is surrounded by small grey houses and blocks, the same dull colour as Betty Spargo's place. Council flats? People might have lived in them for ages, yet I also know the wariness of local Cornish to intrusive questioning, especially from strange faces. *Incomers.* And there is no one casually passing, and I can't knock on doors like I am a policeman. I will be rebuffed.

My eyes alight on an old corner store. Verran's. Sounds local Cornish; looks as if it has been around for several decades, now making a humble living from UHT milk and lottery tickets. I really need to luck out with an older, bored shopkeeper, who has long known the area.

The door opens with a jingling bell, and a sweet-faced lady, early sixties, greets me with a smile, and a thick Penzance accent. Local for sure. Maybe this is my luck, arriving right on time, like the chuffing little train from St Erth to St Ives. Minnie used to love that train, the heart-shaped punch in the tickets.

'Hello, my dear. How can I help you?'

'Hi,' I say. 'I'm Karenza Bray.'

I use my classically Cornish name quite shamelessly. Establish trust and connection at the start.

The woman's cheery face brightens further. 'Bray, eh? Got cousins called Bray. Over in Hayle. I'm Julie.'

The two of us exchange smiles; Julie gestures merrily at the window.

'Looks like it's brightening up out there, don't it? Enough blue to patch a sailor's trousers!'

The woman is clearly bored, and keen to chat. I have properly lucked out. Now it is time to lie: another lesson I learned in the Bethlem. Build an emotional story, get people psychologically invested, so that they will open up; then you fake it.

Whipping out my phone I show the woman a photo of Natalie Skuse.

'I'm doing some research . . .'

Julie takes out some glasses and looks at the photo of Natalie. And her face drops into sadness.

'Oh my, the poor girl that died up the coast. Porthcurno way. Horrible accident, wasn't it? How did you know her? Can I help?'

I can see the face of my professor tutoring me at the Bethlem. *Lie!* 'She is – or was – my best friend. But we lost contact years ago. I'm trying to find out what happened.'

Julie puts a hand to her mouth.

'I'm sorry.'

For a few seconds I feel some shame, and then, as Julie sits us down for a proper chat, I don't. Because I am doing the right thing. What happened to poor Natalie Skuse needs to be unearthed, and her kids and her widower need to be saved from their delusional grief. And maybe a murderer needs to be arrested.

Julie is full of information. Garrulous, even. I discreetly press the *record* button on my phone as Julie talks.

'Saw Natalie Skuse a lot. Sharp as a tack, that girl. Popular. Leader of her little gang, they used to buy sweets in here, then cigs . . . chattering away.'

'Anything else?'

Julie muses, looking into the middle distance. 'She was quite wild, I heard. Clever but . . . untamed. Yes. She liked the moors, used to go off to find flowers, rocks, shells, a wanderer. I heard she married a rich man, at the end? Not surprising, she was a flower, that girl: a rose that lovely was bound to be plucked.'

Plucked. I file the word away. *Plucked.*

'Anything else?'

'Not much, no, my dear, sorry. There was rumour and scandal about the home. Owners sometimes came down from upcountry, posh men, big cars, did wonder if they were, ah, you know, getting involved with the girls. Heard there were abortions. Girls were easy meat. Sad job.'

I file this away. 'When Natalie – my friend,' I make a mournful face, 'when she died, was there much of a fuss? Like, you know, lots of police?'

Julie frowns. 'Come to think of it, not so much.'

'So you're saying the police didn't come round? Asking people?'

'Maybe once? Certainly didn't seem too interested. But it was an accident, so I suppose that explains it.' Julie's smile is sorrowful. 'I'm so sorry for your loss. I wish I could help properly.'

'You've helped a great deal.'

'I hope you find the answers you need, my sweet.'

'Me too. I'll take a Diet Coke and leave you alone.'

Cracking open the Coke, I climb back in the car and drive the thin roads back to Baldhu. The rain has entirely cleared, but the wind has replaced it. Big rolling waves crash and spume on the rocks of the zawns. I feel renewed, and not just by fizzy caffeine. I feel like I am rolling back a carpet to reveal an historic mosaic, and a tiny portion can now definitely be seen. The flukes of a dolphin. Turns out the kids' home was badly run, full of quite wild girls, and possibly there was child abuse – and then it briskly closes, becomes a bad hotel? And years later the police were not interested, even after an unexplained death?

As I park at Baldhu, I resolve to ring Kyle, very soon. Why did he really put me onto this mystery? Was he dissatisfied with the police investigation?

Key in the door, I prepare myself for the claustrophobia of Baldhu, the big rooms with confining moods and clashing souls. But the sweet-scented hall leads only to peace. Solomon is smiley and tired in his muddy football kit, with Tricia leading him off to a bath. Grace is reading in the conservatory. She has swapped the Greek myths and is onto *Beowulf*. Has she moved all day? Malcolm is in the kitchen chatting business – stocktaking, new menus, a possible cocktail hour. He waves at me vaguely as I wander in.

The evening is equally peaceable. Tricia goes, putting up her hood; supper comes. I am waiting for the moment to confront Malcolm about his delusions, but it never quite arrives – this is the problem of being immersed in a domestic scenario, I now realize. I have to go with the flow, I can't be suddenly shining harsh lights as if I'm the secret police.

And so we chat, we eat: grilled fish and noodles. Solomon pesters his dad with questions about the Christmas tree, and where 'all the Christmas trees go in the end'. Malcolm answers each one with loving fondness. The noodles are delicious. Malaysian with a well-judged hit of tamarind. Even Grace seems in an emollient mood, teasing her brother, but sweetly, then precisely coiling noodles on her fork, and delicately eating the morsel, as she gazes at me, and says nothing.

After supper the kids disperse to bed. Finally, Malcolm and I are sitting alone in the living room, half-heartedly watching a movie. Sipping wine, but not too much. It is almost as if he and I are a couple. He asks about my day; I lie and say I walked the moors, to help me think.

Malcolm smiles, poignant and pensive. 'Just like Natalie, she loved to walk. Knew the names of everything, insects and birds, right down to the lichen on the Merry Maidens. Taking notes. Writing poems.'

We return to the movie; the frustration rises. Abruptly, I lean forward and turn off the TV.

Malcolm looks at me; I launch into it.

'Malcolm, about last night.'

'What?'

'You, and Solomon, and the bird in the room.'

He sits back, apparently puzzled. 'Yes?'

'Malcolm, there . . . well, there's no easy way of saying this.'

'Say it.'

I brace myself. 'There was no bird.'

The room is silenced. It was already quiet, but it is as if the wind outside has stopped, theatrically and sympathetically. Yet now it picks up again, a patter of rain on the glazing.

'What the fuck are you talking about?'

This is a reaction I have seen before. Some people react *extremely* badly to being told: you are suffering hallucinations, delusions, figments.

'I was there, in the door, I saw. There was no bird. You are . . .' I can't say it, I can't say, *you are seeing things*. 'It was imaginary. Malcolm, it was imaginary, and . . . that's it.' I want to go on and say, *this is not unknown, human groups can share delusions and they can share psychoses, it is called the madness of many*, 'folie à plusieurs', *and hey, maybe we could start with family therapy and then move on to MRI* – but Malcolm gazes at me with deep anger. He is a big man: his anger, alone with me, is not comfortable.

'Don't be absurd. *There was a damn bird.*'

What can I do with this? 'No, Malcolm—'

'*No!*' He is actually shouting. 'Don't be fucking stupid. I'm not hallucinating! There was a bird, in the room, what would you say that for?'

'Because—'

'Because you're determined to blame me? I'm the mad father? So I must have killed Nat?'

'No, no, no no no—'

He picks up his wineglass, and for a second I am sure he is going to hurl it at the wall, or in my face. Stoving my head in. *Splat*. He does neither. He gulps down the wine and sneers, 'Who's the mad one, Karenza? Really?'

'Sorry?'

'It's you, isn't it? Down in the cellar? Bats in your bloody face? Why did you go down there anyway? There are no fucking bats down there, I was trying to be nice. You made it up, or you are – what was it? – *delusional*.'

This gives me pause. No bats? But then it was a pigeon. It was something, it was not nothing. This is gaslighting and I've been here before, and I thank God for my long experience with clever psychopaths in prison. I also, however, know I must not push this, not tonight. I flutter a gaze at him. Be the submissive, yielding female.

'OK, I'm sorry. Probably I am wrong. I'm sure there was no bird but perhaps I didn't see it, I jumped to conclusions.'

His expression is a mixture of intense relief, and dwindling anger. 'Well, exactly.'

'I am really very sorry.'

He exhales, sharply, but no longer furious. 'Hmm.'

'Please accept my apology.'

Another sigh. 'It's . . . all right, I do understand. This family. This house. It can get to you.' He rolls his eyes. 'Shall we finish the movie?'

I nod, meek and acceptant. 'Of course.'

And so we sit here, the two of us. Like a long-married couple getting over a row, as if I am not a forensic psychologist who has just accused him of being delusional, possibly haunted, as if I am not envisaging, just down the line, a call to the police liaison psychiatric nurse, and the possibility of civil commitment, to avoid Serious Untoward Incidents.

The movie drains away. I am barely aware of its theme. And now again like a couple we clean the drawing room and stack the glasses and turn off the lights and ascend the stairs – and there are no birds this time, thank God. The kids are quiet and asleep, the house is quiet and asleep. I bid Malcolm goodnight then go to my room, and stare for five minutes into the bathroom mirror.

The wrinkles around my eyes have grown deeper: I look tired, and no wonder. And yet my round face is reassuring enough. I have been through worse. I picture irrepressible Betty Spargo, Lidl brandy in her hand, toasting me: *C'mon, Karenza, you are your mother's girl, don't give up. And never be scared.* I picture El Gruffalo, leaping away from little dogs for no apparent reason. Why does he do this? Is he seeing his own version of ghosts?

Ideas stir, but formless and nameless; yet hope is maybe kindled.

Tucked up in bed I try to read for ten minutes to get the right brainwaves but then my eyes droop anyway. I don't need a Valium, sleep is coming hard and dark like a fall of black snow. I shall let it bury me – but just as I am about to be entombed I am stirred by a knock on my door.

'Who is it?'

'It's me.'

Malcolm. I really do not want to talk to Malcolm. I am blurry from near-sleep. I want him to go away.

'What is it?'

'I want to say sorry.'

I frown, staring at the grey, vague shape of the door. I am praying he won't open it. Is he going to confess he imagined the bird? That would be progress, but I cannot handle it now.

'It's all right, Malcolm, not tonight – there's no need—'

'I just want to say sorry. Natalie, I'm so sorry.'

My blood runs as cold as the Bathsheba stream. 'Malc . . .'

He thinks I am Natalie?

'Come back to our bedroom, Natalie. I'm sorry. I shouldn't have done that. It's . . . it was wrong. I got so angry. Shouldn't have done what I did. Come back. Please.'

I hear the doorknob turning. He is going to come in. I am *terrified*.

The door begins to open. A squeal of hinges.

The horror is real.

'No. Go. Go back to bed. Malcolm!'

'Natalieeeee . . . You know I love you. I shouldn't have done any of that, not to you.'

I realize that I will have to *be* Natalie. Or he will come in.

'Malcolm, please, we can talk tomorrow? Let me alone, tonight. *Go away.*'

'I love you, Natalie.'

'I understand, of course, we'll talk, but please, let me sleep for now.'

A dreadful pause.

But it works.

The door was ajar, and now it softly closes again. I hear Malcolm walking away. The creak of the historic, polished floorboards. And I am left here, heart sprinting, mouth dry, prickled with fear.

Help.

28

'You all right, Karenza?'

Malcolm is smiling as he offers me some more buttery carrots.

I take more carrots, and I smile back, and mumble thank you, and apologize for my quietness, mutter that maybe I had too much wine last night.

Malcolm eyes me sceptically. But I am at a loss to deduce what he is thinking. He might be entirely lucid right now, or maybe half of him thinks I am Natalie.

What can I do?

I can look down at my roast chicken Sunday lunch in Baldhu. In the dining room. My hands are trembling a little. I notice Molly has spotted my hands, I see a tiny, knowing smile. With an effort, I remind myself: I am the professional here.

And they are all delusional.

'You're not hungry, Karenza?'

Molly is now gazing at me as if she is a bored doctor who senses an interesting cancer case. I mumble again, awkwardly. Molly maybe has a non-insane reason to be bitchy. She came over this morning and she and Grace carefully made this lunch – a roasted free-range chicken, proper red-wined gravy, the Tyacks definitely eat well – and I am pushing her excellent food about the plate, trying to hide uneaten meat under garlicky cabbage. As if I am six.

'It's all right, I hate roast chicken too, it's *boring*,' says Solomon.

'That's enough, Solomon. Your sister and your aunt spent the whole morning cooking this—'

'That's why it's *boring*,' Solomon says. 'Grace made it. Everything she does is boring. All she does is read stupid *books*.'

'Solomon!'

Grace looks unfazed.

Solomon growls and says, 'Why do you always stay in the 'servatry, where Mummy reads?'

Grace offers up an adult sigh, and says to her brother, 'Do you want to go down to the cellar again, Solomon? We can always go down to the *cellar*.'

Malcolm snaps, 'Grace!'

Grace smirks decorously. Solomon does not reply but his distraction is back, in force. He looks around, as if he can sense things.

Grace looks at Solomon and says, 'Why *do* you do that? All that twisting and grimacing? It's *creepy*.'

There may not be birds in the room, but things hidden are now seen. The father is as cursed as his accursed kids. Maybe Molly as well. Grace turns and smiles at her father, then she rises and says, 'I've finished, Papi. I've had enough. I'm going off to my room, if that is permissible.'

Her father's exhalation is pained. 'Sure.'

Solomon kicks off again. 'If Grace can go, I can go! I only wanned ice creams anyway, Mummy always gives us ice creams, not like Auntie Molly—'

'*All right, enough*. God's *sake*.'

Solomon's face twitches: he looks at his shouting father. Then the boy bursts into a sudden urgent sob and he too runs from the room. Stamping footsteps on the stairs.

Malcolm stares imploringly at the ceiling, as if seeking solace from God.

Molly calmly takes out her vape. She sits back and sighs with studied indifference, and then she flamboyantly blows vapour at the ceiling. The tension is too much; I hide it by pushing back my chair and clearing the dishes. Molly and Malcolm sit there, as I busy myself. I do not care.

Chores done, like I am a servant, a new version of Tricia, I lace up my walking boots and step urgently out of Baldhu, and I take a long, calming, determined walk to Zawn Dorlam, until I reach the bubbling waterfall where Natalie died. Then I climb a modest carn, wobbling on the boulders, and I find a decent shred of signal and I text Priya.

Been some developments. Would love another chat. K

Then I email my old friend, the antiques expert:

Hey, Ben, sorry to bombard, but I'd LOVE your feedback on my mad Chinese mirror . . .

Now I text Kyle in Truro:

Hey. Need to speak if poss. Tyacks – mystery on mystery, can only really talk in person. Also, can you do me a fave, look into who owned St Petroc's Kids' Home? You're great at this. The legal stuff, thank you

I wait. And wait. And none of them replies. But this does not surprise me. It is Sunday. Priya has a young family, Kyle has a new wife and that tiny baby. Ben also has a bouncy brood.

I am the odd one out, the loner, the solitary bookish girl on the playground with no friends.

The ocean churns, indifferent and oppressive. I turn, look inland, at the eternal gorse with its eternal yellow flowers, timorously shivering in the breeze. The yellow is the only colour apart from the grey of rock, and the dreary green of the winter grass. Dark thorns maybe hide dead hares. Sheep's wool is snagged on barbed wire, with traces of blood.

The day has become as foul as the night before. I trudge dutifully back to Baldhu as a winter mist congeals along Bathsheba Valley; the old house looms out of the murk like an abandoned black ship in a nightmare.

Unlatching the door, I go straight to my bedroom and lie on my bed trying to take notes and wondering vaguely if Natalie simply killed herself out of too much paralysed anxiety, flavoured with peculiar fear, because this is what I am feeling, and I have never felt anything quite like it before.

Lying back on the bed, I get to thinking about Minnie, and this is not good. So I stand up and go to the window, throw it open to the twilit December fog. Welcoming in all the strange black birds of Trevaylor, the birds that do not exist. I cannot bear to join the family for supper, for what fresh horror will emerge? I need to get away from here first thing tomorrow and get a cool head and take a fresh look.

I message Malcolm from my room.

Feeling a bit tired, will skip supper. See you a.m.

He replies briskly.

Understood. See you for breakfast before you go?

As if this is all perfectly normal. It is not perfectly normal – but I try and make it so by watching five straight episodes of my favourite ancient sitcom on my phone, to blot out the world.

It is nearly 11 p.m. when I hear Malcolm shouting in terror.

29

I am still in my clothes; I step outside.

The rest of the house is silent. Molly must be in her room, Solomon is in his room, Grace in her room; only I have stirred, and I stand here on the landing in the yellowy shadows.

Malcolm's shouting is so loud and so obviously fearful. Why has no one else responded?

Maybe they are used to it, maybe they are genuinely fast asleep; maybe only I can hear this.

Abruptly, Malcolm emerges from his bedroom. He is putting on a thick coat, he is dressing to leave. He looks at me, startled. And also frightened. I have not seen *this* expression on his face before. It is deep fear. Even in the gloom of the feeble bulb I can see he looks pale, perhaps trembling.

'Karenza!'

'Malcolm! Are you OK? I heard you shouting.'

His eyes give it away: he is about to lie. 'No, no, no. Just – uh – just—' His eyes are *desperate*. 'Look, I just got a call. There's some problem at the restaurant, burst water pipes. This bloody cold. They freeze. That's probably what you heard, lost my temper, that's all—'

This is an obvious, pitiful lie. I have not seen many worse liars than Malcolm Tyack right now. And he is babbling.

'Gotta go, roads will be dark, it's twelve miles or more, and there's diversions, uh, please tell Molly. She will look after the kids. School. Doubt I'll be back tonight. OK. OK. Burst pipes, what a nightmare.'

He is hurrying down the stairs, leaving me alone on the landing. And I am looking at the open door of Malcolm's bedroom: wondering what made him cry out in terror and flee his own house.

With just a second of hesitant fear, I cross the threshold into Malcolm's bedroom. Inside, I survey. It is basically the same as I last saw it. A little more despoiled: bedclothes in some disarray, a book – military history – lying open by the pillow, like someone was reading and then maybe climbed from the bed.

Now I look up, and across. The 'office'. This time the door is slightly ajar. For the first and only time since I have been visiting here – as far as I know – Malcolm has left the office door unlocked.

First, I turn off the bedroom light, to hide my presence, then I push open the office door.

The office has a big, moonlit bay window which gazes down Bathsheba Valley, now dark as death. In the far distance a tiny light moves from right to left: surely a big container ship. Sailing from faraway to anywhere, and unafraid of wreckers.

A creak of the house makes me look up, back, sideways – but no, just a noise. The house exhaling. Settling in its ancient cold, the sigh in the sleep of eight-hundred-year-old dreams.

In the office I flick the sturdy switch of a brass lamp on the big hardwood desk, with its patriarchal view of everything, through that proud stone window. Malcolm must like to sit here and look at this. The wintry view of barely moonlit Bathsheba. Where the black winter trees reach up, with bare-boned fingers, to rip away the white mask of the moon.

This is my job. Ripping off the mask that hides everything in Baldhu. And my urgent investigation does not take long. The office is small, a masculine den. Hunting and fishing and fighting. It has pictures of Malcolm as captain of his school rugby team: big, laddish, even thuggish. A rugby ball at his feet. A silver rugby trophy sits on a shelf; a noble wooden cupboard contains two shotguns and boxes of shotgun cartridges. A good reason to lock the door?

Books adorn another shelf: history, politics, geology. Then a photo of the kids, looking happier, older, with Natalie smiling and squinting against the sun. They are having a picnic somewhere green and bright, the sea distant, a Penwith cliff probably.

A pricey-looking filing cabinet is unlocked, and its metal drawers slide open. It is full of dull business documents, bills for the restaurants, bills for the house, water, gas, car, bonds, shares. I am getting the full ponderous sense of Malcolm's heavy responsibilities. His tiredness, carrying all this, and now doing it alone while haunted by his troubled family. And his dead wife.

On the desk I find a laptop. Shut. Surely password protected. I don't bother opening it, I don't need to; fallen on the floor, between the tidy big desk and the black metal swivel chair, is a brown paper folder, with a word handwritten on the front in firm, manly capitals. I lean down, pick it up, and read:

Natalie

The thought strikes me: I wonder if this is how the Tyacks felt, when they found a rich seam of tin or copper, by the glow of tallow candlelight, down in the Black Mine.

Here be riches.

Opening the folder, I see yes, it is a rich seam, gleaming in the light of my thoughts. There are photos, some old, some new, most of them phone-camera snaps printed out, in quite high resolution. My forensic instincts come alive as I sort, quickly, through the images. *This is it*: here at long last are the *clues*.

A photo of Natalie by some big marina. Boat masts behind her. Looe? Mylor? St Mawes, even? It is too generic to be identifiable. Another photo, also quite recent, shows Natalie seen through a large window, in a pub, maybe. It seems as if it may have been taken with a telescopic lens. She is talking to a man. I gaze close.

Miles?

And more photos. An older one of a younger Natalie in what looks like St Just. A younger Natalie on a quayside: that's Falmouth, I recognize it immediately. My own apartment is visible in the corner of the image. Surely a coincidence. Around the time I moved there. And yet an unsettling coincidence.

At a noise, I stiffen. The soft wind whirrs its way up Bathsheba.

Is that all I heard? Or was it someone entering the bedroom, beyond the office, about to discover my illicit detective work?

I wait, alone. There is no point in hiding: I am in the always-locked office that belongs to the possibly wife-killing father – I can't explain it away.

And . . . nothing. No one is out there.

The relief surges once more. I glance up and out, as the breeze tousles the gorse in the moonlight. The tiny light of the container ship is gone. The light in my churning mind is bright enough: Malcolm Tyack was spying on his beloved wife, even when she met his own brother. These are not photos taken for fun, or with Natalie's knowledge. In none of them is she looking directly at the camera, in not one of them is there a sense of her posing, the stiffness of someone being photographed. These are the images taken by a spy.

The fact Malcolm was stalking Natalie sends up several hundred red flags. It *really* implicates him in her death. I know from my laborious years in the prison-psychology world that stalker behaviour is commonly observed in murders of women. Indeed, stalking is such a warning flag, there is a protocol that can be invoked, and I have sometimes invoked it. If a therapist learns that her client is stalking someone, and making menaces, they have to inform the potential victim. This is called the Tarasoff Warning.

Malcolm looms ever larger as the potential killer. And I am temporarily sharing a house with him, and it appears he sometimes believes I *am* Natalie. And yet now is there also a question mark over Miles?

Taking out my own phone camera, I photograph the photos. I will have to leave the folder here; I do not want anyone to know that I found it. And I wonder if the police found this folder. Surely, if they had done so, they would have taken a much greater interest in the guilt-ridden husband.

As I photograph the images and store them for later, I consider the words of the woman in the shop, in Penzance, by the care home. *The police certainly didn't seem too interested.*

Two more photos, much older, give me pause. One is of Natalie aged about fifteen or sixteen, standing on a Cornish beach in bright spring sunshine, with St Michael's Mount blurry in the background. Her beauty is already evident, maybe a knowing beauty for one so young. She has a bad haircut, and a dazzling smile. Who took this photo? Maybe Natalie had it, and her husband got a copy.

I apply the same logic to the last image. It's a group photo of the residents of the children's home. The Gothic Victorian architecture of the building renders it unmistakable. The photo is taken in the garden at the back; the girls are all in rows, in summer dresses. They look like a big sports squad: the adults stand at the rear, the kids neatly arrayed in front of them.

St Petroc's. The house of scandals and rumours, and men who came down from upcountry, to the place where the girls were 'easy meat'.

Young Natalie Skuse – top row, second from the left, aged sixteen or seventeen – does not look traumatized, or beaten down. But she does look wary. The dark hair frames the pale face and the eyes gaze ahead. Frozen. She obviously does not want to be there. But who would want to be stuck in a children's home at such an age?

Click.

This last photo is stored.

The rest of the contents of the folder comprises a few documents. A scan of Natalie's birth certificate. Natalie Marina Skuse. Mother: Jacqueline Mary Skuse. It says Father Unknown but someone – surely Malcolm – has handwritten a firm black question mark in this unfilled space.

So Malcolm was researching his wife *that* deeply. Tracing the unknown father?

Beneath the birth certificate I find a few of images of Natalie's bank statements from random years – a few months before she died, a year before, five years before, ages ago. Clearly Malcolm wanted to know where and when Natalie was spending money. On herself? On someone else?

But the spendings are random. *Penzance. Falmouth. Truro.* Shops, bars, pubs, restaurants. Then Exeter University: twice. Also a couple of restaurants. One is the Oyster Shack, again near me, and I feel a subtle tightness in my chest. Then a more obscure café in Falmouth, the Morgat. These two transactions are on the same days as the payments to Exeter Uni. How did that work? She went to Exeter then drove, as fast as possible, back to Cornwall for a meal? *A lunch?* It's probably a two-hour drive. You could do it, but why? It is a puzzle, but it doesn't add up to much. Wherever they are, these are all places you *would* go if you wanted any kind of life away from isolated Baldhu.

And here, on a later statement, yet another visit to the Morgat? Not long before she died?

Again, I take photos. Speedily, now. I have been in this room long enough. Even the laggard winter dawn will arrive in time, I mustn't be discovered here.

The folder is finished. With care, I put everything back in place, as best I remember. On the floor. Wondering why Malcolm was looking at it a few hours back: for it to be here, and out. Is he still researching his dead wife, looking for some clue about her death? That suggests he is *not* guilty. Or maybe he was just looking at these images of the woman he stalked and killed. *Wallowing* in his guilt. And then he saw her ghost, conjured by his remorseful mind, in this haunted house, with its cellarful of secrets, and he fled.

I rise, about to switch off the masculine brass lamp – and then I notice a final photo that must have slipped from the file onto the floor. Or perhaps Malcolm dropped it.

Bending down, I pick it up. The image flushes me, instantly, with a ghastly clamminess. Another long-distance photo of Natalie Skuse. I recognize the setting: the little square in front of Truro Cathedral, in the summer sun, with baskets full of flowers hanging from cast-iron lamp posts. Natalie is a few years younger, and she is smiling broadly and talking to a youngish man, who smiles right back, as if they are falling in love.

It is my ex-husband. It is Kyle.

30

Breakfast is brisk in Baldhu, mainly because I want it to last fifteen seconds and get the hell out. Molly listens to me as I explain that Malcolm had to leave late last night.

'Frozen pipes, or something. In the restaurant, the Halyard?'

Molly shrugs. The kids eat buttered toast, gently bicker before leaving for school. Apparently unfazed by the absence of Dad.

Do they simply not care, or are they inured, because this happens a lot? I have not time for deeper queries. After a few apologetic sips of coffee I grab my things and leave Baldhu, and after driving half a cloudy mile, onto proper roads, I feel such a gasp of relief I pull over. Stop. Gasp, hard, again.

The winter wind is welcome. Buzzing down the window, I inhale the sweet country dampness, scented with cattle dung and wild oceans and pungently rotting seaweed, and it is beautiful.

Only now that I am out of Baldhu do I realize that I have been in deep, stiffening stress for my entire time in the house, like someone crouching, awaiting the next blow.

Someone killed Natalie Skuse, I am increasingly sure of it. But who? Malcolm, Miles, Molly?

Turning the wheel, I speed on, escaping Baldhu, this coast, Penwith, the danger, and now as signal returns my phone *pings* right on time. Stronger signal here. I pull over.

It's Priya.

Hey Kaz sorry only just saw this, sorry. Want to have a proper chat, call at 4ish?

I reply with an urgent '*Yes thank you*', then I text Kyle again, keeping it neutral, giving nothing away, and again he does not reply. There is less excuse this time – Monday morning, my second text? He must be at work, he will be looking at his phone; perhaps he suspects something?

Yet this doesn't remotely make sense. The photo of him and Natalie was taken at a distance. He would be unaware of it, and if he knew of it, and any implications, why hook me up with this case? Maybe he really is just busy.

But I will catch up with him. I must know what he was doing with the lovely Natalie Skuse. And now I consider that smile shared between them, in the photo, and it stings. It looked like desire, certainly flirtation. This would have been before Minnie died.

Angrily I start the car; angrily I speed on with the rest of my day.

I drive fast to Falmouth, I park; I bump into Dinah descending the steps from my own front door, and her pet-sitting.

Dinah laughs as I press her with questions; her laughter feels inappropriate, but of course she knows nothing. I must fake normality.

'Chill out, Kaz. It's all good. Otto went a sort of

tangerine, think he misses you. El Gruffalo is still acting like I am some annoying servant.'

'I'm sorry about my cat. He's got issues. Inherited weirdness.'

'Reminds me of my ex.' She giggles again and I try to join in, perhaps unconvincingly, because Dinah now says, 'You all right, Kaz? Bit stressed?'

I wave away the question as politely as I can; but Dinah persists.

'That weird old place. Penwith. Hm.'

All I can offer is a pleasantry. I know my best friend deserves better but my mind is full of ideas, fears, dilemmas: what if I *do* prove that Malcolm is the killer, what then? He goes to prison, and the kids are left without a father and a mother, an awful fate. Poor little Solomon and Grace: it would finally destroy them.

And I cannot abide that thought. They would probably have to live with feckless Molly, but she is surely incapable, or maybe with boozy Miles, but he is possibly worse. Malcolm is actually a good dad, if you ignore the fact he might have brutally killed his wife and is maybe going mad.

Apart from that, he's great.

Dinah offers me a puzzled glance and I respond with a promise of coffees this week, and then with relief, I key my flat. Once inside, I give El Gruffalo an official five-minute hug to soothe him. Once we are both solaced, I turn to Otto and take him carefully out of his cage and sit him on my outstretched palm and I stare deep into his superb eyes. I know he really likes doing this, I have no idea why.

'Hello, Otto.'

He regards me with the unfathomable wisdom of a reptile. Otto is indeed, as Dinah warned, a faint yellow-tangerine, which I have never seen before. It is like a warning light that comes on in a hire car, and you don't know what it means. The oil is half gone; the carburettor needs servicing; something obscure is *wrong*. Could be something dangerous.

I place him back in the cage, make sure he is watered and content, because I have to get on. The rest of the day is dense with commitments. I get the boat over to the Roseland. No Jago to banter with, not on this shift. I keep checking my phone for messages from Kyle, no reply from Kyle. I do a good session with Romilly Kelhelland, who eschews green cocktails this time and talks divertingly about her mother, who is now microdosing psychedelics and claims to have achieved a Kundalini orgasm with her new younger lover, 'she says it made her head wobble like a Hindu shopkeeper in a racist sitcom'.

Then even Romilly Kelhelland says, 'Are you OK, Karenza? You look stressed.'

I reassure her; the session ends. I stride further up the hill to Granny Spargo's council flat – *Last Spargo in Roseland*, it could be a movie – and Betty Spargo is as wry and salty as ever. She smokes out of the window, and drinks Lidl brandy and then – finally – I can't help it, this is all so comforting. My beloved granny: what will I do if anything happens to her?

Finally the stress gets to me. Out of nowhere, I burst into tears, on Granny Spargo's sofa.

31

'Jesus, darling, my lover, what is it?'

She sits next to me. Puts a comforting and cardiganed arm around me. I realize I have not had a human hug for a few days, maybe since I was last here with Betty Spargo. It helps. She hands me a perfumed paper tissue. I dry my eyes, and I say, 'I think, Betty, for the first time ever, I will actually have some brandy.'

Betty laughs and pours me a generous glass. As I sip the harsh yet comforting warmth, I confess I have not brought a home-made cake and she tells me to stop being an idiot, and she asks me what exactly is wrong, and I wonder if I should tell her, and then I think: *why not?* I trust Granny Spargo more than anyone, probably love her more than anyone, and she is a great judge of character.

I also know she was never mad keen on Kyle, liked him well enough, but felt I could have done better, or at least done *differently*. Should have gone for Jago the Boatman! Funnier, more manly, more Cornish. She will be neutral and perceptive if I broach this.

'Granny,' I say, sipping more brandy for courage, 'I know you had doubts about Kyle . . .'

She frowns, confused.

I hurry on. 'Do you – did you – ever think he might have been unfaithful to me?'

She looks shocked, then whips right back, 'Nope.'
'Seriously?'

'*Definitely*. He's not that type. I know it! I know the unfaithful type; it's not Kyle – he loved you, for sure, I saw it – and remember, I have the Spargo gift. I can spot a wrong 'un in St Agnes from the top of Carn Brea.'

I manage a chuckle, a sniffle, my tears are dried. She says, 'Why in heaven are you asking this?'

I say it can wait, maybe forever – the tiny ferry is leaving. We have another deep hug, and she begs me to come back soon – as if I need begging: I love hanging out with Betty – then I say goodbye and I jog down the hill to the quay, where the winter light is failing, but the jolly Christmas lights are shining.

Only now do I realize Christmas is truly coming. The shops are playing Christmas tunes, soon there will be spangly Christmas trees in every house. And where will I spend Christmas Day this year? With Dinah and her kids, like last year? With Betty and her elderly friends, like the year before?

Every Christmas it is the same: I am the odd one out, the divorced and childless woman, the loner. I get several Christmas invites, but I always feel spare. It is the only time in the year when I dislike my freedom, my solo status, my decision to have brief liaisons and nothing more serious, despite the protestations of Betty and Dad. Don't you need a regular man? *No*. Don't you want to marry again? *No*. But maybe at Christmas . . .

Perhaps I will spend Christmas at Baldhu. The idea is simultaneously horrifying, and weirdly mesmerizing.

On the boat back to Falmouth I am happy to see Jago Moyle but before he can offer a handsome hello

I say, 'Please don't say I look stressed! Jago, if you say I look stressed I will push you in the Fal.'

Jago grins, as if he was indeed about to say that but has now changed his mind. He goes and steers the boat, puttering out into the Roads, into the winter twilight, heading for the sparkle-shore of Falmouth, but as we near the quay he comes over again.

'Hey. I forgot to ask. How's Granny Spargo, still on the sherry?'

'Yes.'

'Good woman, your nan.'

'She really is.' I hesitate, then add, 'You know she thinks I should have married *you*.'

There. I've said it. Blurted it out, after all this time. Why the heck did I say that? Slurping brandy at 3 p.m. What was I thinking?

Jago gives me a long, soft, peculiar look that I cannot quite decipher. He says nothing.

He takes my hand as the boat reaches Falmouth, to help me off the boat. He squeezes my hand warmly. 'Karenza Bray,' he says, 'whenever you slow down, let's have that drink, in the Victory.'

Is this it? Is this him saying some kind of yes? Yes to what? I do not know my own mind. I am too deep in Baldhu.

I reply, 'I'd love to, soon.'

And even as I say this I can see Otto flashing vermillion for *you stupid woman*. Vermillion for *just say yes. Respond*. This is an offer. *You like him!*

But Otto is not a thirty-seven-year-old forensic psychologist with a tremendously difficult and potentially dangerous case, which is nonetheless the most compelling she has encountered in her career. He is a chameleon.

Walking away from the quay, without looking back at Jago – not easy – I climb in my car, and I race through Falmouth and then as soon as it hits 4 p.m. I pull over, a few yards from my flat, and call Priya Hardwicke.

She is keen to listen, I am keen to talk. I describe the evidence that Parent X is also now being plagued by hallucinations, and not just auditory, not just voices but actual human figures. I do not mention that Malcolm apparently thinks I am Natalie, because I am not yet sure how to say this without breaking protocol.

But what I have said is enough.

'Wow. Even the *father*? I mean, Parent X?'

'Yep. And I am starting to wonder about others, ah, let's call them Auntie F, and Uncle G. All of them might be afflicted.'

'Do you have theories?'

'The obvious one is contagion: it begins with one family member, and the delusions spread. But there is a particular phenomenon, called *folie à quatre*, which is particular to families, especially remote, religious. Could be that, not sure it fits.'

Priya's voice sounds puzzled.

'*Folie* à *quatre*? Don't know it. Must be rare?'

'Very. Therefore, I don't know.'

Priya says, 'I have another idea.'

'Please tell me.'

She takes a breath, and says, 'I believe it is the *house*. Infrasounds. That explains pretty much everything.'

I am out of my depth here. 'What is infrasound? Like infra-red, or something?'

'Infrasounds are sounds just beneath the threshold of our perception, *deep* sounds. Low throbs, say. And they are *known* to cause unease, distress, and auditory and visual hallucinations.'

'Really?'

Her phone voice is confident in my car.

'Trust me. And this is a classic example. The *cellar* is the key. Hence the manifestations there. The echoes coming up through the house, the long historic corridors, open doors, attics, all acting like a flute, vibrating the air. For *everyone*. Hence the entire family being affected.'

'Wouldn't I have been affected as well?'

'You don't live there, you haven't been there long enough. It is a subtle phenomenon, and it often takes time. But I believe,' Priya sounds pleased, 'that I *may* have solved your haunting.'

'Can we test this? Empirically?'

'Yes – we totally can! And I've got a PhD student who can run the tests. Ollie Towey. We've done it before, and I can tell him of your case, but he won't hear any details, just the paranormal element.' She pauses, then adds, 'If I'm right, and I am sure I am, that's it. Case solved: remove the sounds, the distressing delusions will disappear. And that means you never have to go back to House B and . . . that might be for the best?'

This is a peculiar remark. 'Sorry. Why might it be "for the best"?'

Priya's tone is uncomfortable, as she explains.

'Well, I know you are a very . . . private person.'

I murmur a yes, and she continues, 'You should know, there is a ton of gossip about your case. In the uni, in Falmouth, all over. People like Noel Oswell. Journalists.'

I squirm. I have certainly not forgotten Noel Oswell and the drinks at the Kittiwake. Foolish Dinah, spilling the beans, then everyone feasting on the spooky beans.

'Yes. I remember.'

'Noel came up to me in Tesco, in town – I was shopping! Started asking questions, what's going on, is the case reopened. Of course he loves that, the old family, mad Cornish history – maybe he senses another book? But what he asked was . . . intrusive. I didn't say a word and told him to shove off.'

'Thanks.'

'But you see my point, Karenza; people are *seriously* interested. This could be a big news story – there was a death – and if it all explodes, do you want to be at the centre of it? On TV?'

'No.'

'So I reckon my PhD student could help. If it is infrasounds, you have the answer, and you can check out of House B.'

'OK, thanks. Thank you so much.'

Even as I finish the call, my phone pings with another message.

Kyle.

Hey sorry been madly busy, want to meet tomorrow, am in Falmouth, Kittiwake Caff, can grab half an hour around lunch, major meets. 2 p.m.?

Slipping the phone in my pocket, I think: Oh yes, Kyle Shapland, oh *yes*, I really want to meet tomorrow. Even if you are *madly busy*.

32

'Not indulging, Kaz?'

Kyle's question comes with that cheeky Essex-boy grin of his. I want to slap him. I don't slap him, I don't smile, I say, 'Just a Diet Coke. It's fine. We're on the clock, right?'

'Yeah, big day, big clients. Reckon I'll skip the grub too.'

Kyle pulls a face, mock-apologetic, and takes a swig from his half pint. We're tucked away in a corner of the Kittiwake. The place is abuzz. I spot Ed Hartley, the owner, working his charm on the customers. He gives us a wave. I wave back, praying I don't bump into anyone who really knows me. This place is too exposed – all glass, the great view of Gyllyngvase Beach. Anyone could see us. I don't want to waste time on pleasantries, for a start, and Kyle insisted he only had thirty minutes.

So I get straight to the point. 'Kyle. I've got a question.'

He swallows the beer. 'And I thought you just wanted my company!'

Again: I have the urge to slap him. Instead I hit him with the bluntest of questions. 'Did you have a thing with Natalie Tyack?'

He blinks. He blinks way too much, but he says, after an overlong pause, 'Have you lost the plot?'

'No. And I want a straight answer.'

'What are you actually on about?'

He realizes I am serious, or at least he pretends to realize. Then he says, 'No, I did not have a bloody affair with Natalie Tyack. Christ on a tricycle, why would you believe *that*?'

I keep my voice icy. 'Because, *in that light*, I'd like you to explain this sweet little snapshot?'

I pick up my phone and show the photo of the photo. It is beyond clear. Him and Natalie, smiling and flirting in the little piazza in front of Truro Cathedral. Where the British Legion sells poppies in November.

My ex is atypically speechless. He downs some beer, gawks at the photo again, then he mutters, 'Bloody hell. Where'd you dig that up?'

'Malcolm Tyack's office. Baldhu House.'

'Can I?'

He wants my phone. For a moment I have an image of him stealing it, throwing it in the river at Tresillian, then going to live in Algiers.

I let him take the phone so he can look closer. He says, 'Long-range job, this. Looks like someone was playing private eye?'

My ex is not stupid. He is a successful lawyer and prosecutor, he uses his working-class Essex accent and demeanour so people underestimate him.

I say, 'Spot on.'

Kyle exhales. 'That makes him much dodgier. Why the hell didn't the police—'

'Kyle!' I won't let him distract me, this is not a court where he can cleverly pivot away. 'Kyle, explain the photo. You. Her. Now.'

He hands back my phone, face blushing red. Finally, he meets my eye. 'Look, I'm sorry. Yeah, I knew her, briefly. Met her a couple of times. This is one of those times. Afterwards, we nipped round to my office.'

'For a quick one?'

'No. For Christ's sake, *no*!' His voice is pathetic and imploring, but honest. After so many years of marriage, I know him.

'Then explain!'

He swills more beer and gives me another honest look. 'She wanted legal help. Don't know who pointed her my way, she rang out of the blue.'

'Help with what?'

'Wanted to sue that kids' home she was in. Petroc's.'

'Why?'

'Never said. I got the impression something nasty went down there, but she wasn't specific. Never got that far, we only met twice—'

'Really?'

'Cross my bloody heart! I told her the truth, that it would be tough, cost two arms and a leg. I gave her some names, lawyers in London, but I don't think she followed through.'

I sit back, take a tiny hit of Coke. Do I buy this? Perhaps. But he's got more explaining to do. 'OK, what about the lovey-dovey smiles? Looks like you're about to kiss. With tongues.'

He runs fingers through his hair, and I see, with a mean little thrill, that it is thinning. He was always proud of his hair. Am I being unfair?

He says, 'All right, I fancied her. Nothing happened but yeah, I fancied her. She is – was – gorgeous. Funny. Sharp as a pin.'

'How nice.'

'Oh, come on. I am flesh and blood!' He is louder now; defiant. The barman at the Kittiwake momentarily looks over as my ex, the proud prosecutor, pleads his case. 'Are you saying, Karenza, that in all our years of marriage, you never fancied anyone else? Seriously?' He flexes me with a look. 'Jago the Boatman?'

Bullseye. My ex is observant. Also: he's not wrong.

I regroup. 'OK, so let's say you're right, and nothing happened. But you liked her and fancied her.'

'Yeah, I did. Shoot me.'

'And you met up.'

'Twice. That's it.'

'Is this why you put me on this case?'

My turn to score: I see it in his face.

'Partly, yeah. When I heard, years later, that she was dead, it came flooding back. That funny, clever girl, with the tough background. I was livid, for her sake. And then I met the kids, after she died, during that joke of a police investigation. That made it ten times worse. Such sweet kids, and Grace Tyack is the spit of her mum.'

I absorb all of this. A lot of info. I ask the next obvious question. 'Why keep quiet about all this?'

He hesitates, like he's working it out for himself.

At last, he says, 'Thought you might jump to conclusions – like you have. You'd suspect something went on – *which it didn't* – and then you'd reject the clients. And I *really* wanted you on this. Because you're bloody good at psychology, and at solving mysteries. And Natalie Tyack deserves the truth. Her kids deserve the truth.'

'You should have come clean from the start.'

He nods, grim-faced. 'Yeah. Probably should've. Sorry. Cock-up on my part. Anyway, now you know the lot.'

'Not quite. What's with this "joke of a police investigation"? I've heard this from others. You need to elaborate.'

He checks his watch, which is infuriating. 'I'm seriously pushed for time.'

'Tough, you've been economical with the truth, and you have ten minutes. Tell me. Why didn't they make more effort?'

'Dunno, but it kinda stinks.'

'Meaning?'

'Think about it. West Penwith, November, juicy murder? That's catnip. Beats nicking shoplifters and smackheads. Could make a career. It attracted some glory hunters, from Exeter as well as Truro.' Kyle lowers his voice; we are in a well-frequented café, with a gossipy owner. 'Then suddenly: oh, just an accident. Nothing to see. Move along there.'

'What were their names? The detectives?'

He looks at me, surprised and wary. 'You're having a laugh?'

'Dead serious. You owe me this.'

'Christ, all right. But I don't want you fucking up my network in Truro, or my relationship with the police.'

'Names. Now.'

He sighs, and yields. He gives me three names. I jot them down. One I recognize, a Truro veteran. Sound. The other two are blanks.

He's clock-watching again. I seize my remaining time. 'Kyle, I want your pro opinion, as well.'

'Fire away, I'm telling you everything now.'

'*Do* you suspect the husband? Malcolm? We have evidence he was stalking her. Would that be enough for an arrest?'

He exhales, thoughtfully. 'Maybe, maybe not. Husbands get jealous, hardly a smoking gun.'

'You know the stats on stalking and femicide.'

'Course I do. But . . . you're after my gut feeling?'

'If that's all you've got.'

My ex shakes his head. 'I don't reckon it's Malcolm Tyack. When I met Natalie, yeah, she was flirty, but she made it crystal clear how much she loved him, and how much he doted on her. The marriage sounded, to me, very happy. Then I met him, after she died, with the kids, and he just didn't strike me as a wife-killer.' He looks up at me. 'What's your take, Kaz? You always used to say you can often tell in the first ten seconds.'

I come straight back. 'Same as you: Malcolm Tyack is not the type. But that was before I found all the evidence of his stalking, and now he is showing evidence of mental disorder.'

Kyle looks alarmed.

I say, 'I'll tell you another day.'

'All right, OK, but – Jesus – watch yourself. What if we're both barking up the wrong cliff and it *is* him? Are you going back there? Into that house?'

'Yes.'

'You sure? You know you could just walk away, and I'll take all this to the coppers, try and get the case reopened.'

'The same police that failed to properly investigate the first time?'

He finishes his beer, grimly. 'Fair point.'

'I can't just leave it now. I'm involved.'

'Solomon and Grace?'

'Yes.'

A heavy silence. Unspoken between us is the thought of our own kid, our little girl we lost. Maybe this is my attempt to right the world after that terrible wrong. If so, there are worse crusades. I press on.

'I can't just leave them there, Kyle, in that madhouse.

I have to crack this and help them. I've got to go back. To Baldhu.'

He nods, acceptingly. I have one more question for my ex-husband.

'Any joy with St Petroc's? The kids' home? It's clearly important.'

Kyle sighs. 'Not really. It's a rat's nest of holding companies. All in London. Could be dodgy, could be bog-standard legal stuff.' A shrug. 'Weird thing is, my firm handled the sale of the property, recently.'

'So? You're the biggest legal office in Cornwall, what's odd about that?'

Kyle shrugs and looks genuinely puzzled.

'Well, I went digging for the deeds of sale. Should be on file. They're not. Might be nothing, could be something. That's all I've got.' He nods, ruefully. 'I know it's not much. Right, I've *got* to scarper.'

And with that, he goes. I linger to finish my drink, frustrated, hooked, staring at the wrapped-up families on windy Gylly Beach, the kids and the parents, the dogs chasing sticks, the pangs in my heart: Minnie. Then I turn to my phone and seek out photos of the two detectives. Diana Curtis and Gideon Bryant. Both early middle-aged. Both unknown to me. Both look utterly unremarkable.

'Hello?'

I look up. It's Ed Hartley, beaming almost flirtatiously, though I still think he's gay.

'Just wanted to say hi, and thanks for the biz.'

I chuckle. 'We barely spent ten pounds.'

'All adds up! Times are tough!' He lingers, a hand on the empty chair opposite. The signet ring and excellent manicure suggest he will somehow manage to get through a slow season. 'Can I say something more personal, Ms Bray? Karenza?'

'Karenza. Yes, of course.'

He sits down in the chair Kyle has vacated. He leans across and talks with unexpected passion. 'It's probably not my place, but I hinted before, about that family you're . . . assisting.'

There is no point in my hiding, as he already knows.

'The Tyacks. You said you knew them.'

His expression lacks its usual happy charm: he is sombre, concerned. 'Just be careful of the younger brother, Miles. I had some business dealings with him, a few years ago, when I first came down to Cornwall. He is . . .' A very long pause. Ed shakes his head. '*Volatile.*'

'Are you suggesting what I think you're suggesting?'

He looks even more serious, then stands up. 'I've probably said more than I should already. Just be careful. Please. I want you to come back to the café.' He smiles. 'And maybe spend over ten pounds?'

He laughs, I smile, the tension eases. But as he goes back to work, I am left with two pressing thoughts. Why is everyone warning me off this case, and why am I suddenly focused on *Miles*?

33

Baldhu is cold today, even in the kitchen.

Oliver Towey doesn't seem to care. He is tall, gangly, young, with a hint of brown stubble.

Malcolm stares at the kitchen island, which is covered with Ollie's kit. His expression is sceptical. 'That's it? An app? A couple of tiny microphones?'

'Ah, yes.'

The student blushes. I squirm, feeling responsible for the arrangement of all this – *we can test for infrasounds in Baldhu, it could be the answer*.

I say, 'My friend Priya, at Falmouth Uni, says Ollie's an expert. Swears that this works.'

Malcolm gazes again at the modest array of gadgets. 'I could buy these on Amazon for a tenner.'

Ollie's voice is unfortunately reedy, but his young opinion is forthright. 'Honestly, it *works*, Mr Tyack. On a small scale. Of course, if you're assessing low-frequency sounds *professionally* – earthquakes, disaster zones, power stations – there are special barometric devices, highly technical and expensive, but in a house we only need this. Yes, it looks amateur, but it has surprising functionality.'

'And the clever theory again?'

Malcolm's sarcasm is heavy. And yet I can also see uncertainty in his eyes. Because Malcolm, of course, ran from Baldhu at midnight, terrified by *something*. My guess is that Malcolm wants this to work, is probably *desperate* for this to work. To provide a neat explanation for all the madness, and a means to move on. The sarcasm is a defence, hiding his neediness, and his fear.

Ollie runs through the theory of infrasounds and their psychological effect on humans. His language is dense, scientific. Malcolm appears attentive; my mind wanders, I have already heard all of this from Priya.

The damp, late-afternoon light is greying to black at the kitchen window. I can hear Miles and the kids in the drawing room. They are decorating the impressive Christmas tree which Malcolm and Miles ceremonially unloaded an hour ago. The tree is stupidly big: maybe Malcolm bought a tree that big in the hope it would blot out the grief of the absent mother.

If she can really be described as *absent*.

Now I tune back in to Ollie. Who has gained in passion, explaining the supernatural with science.

'There was a case in Liverpool, um, 1990s, a half-empty student residence with multiple reports of hauntings. It was finally sourced to a rusty lift shaft. Emitting infrasounds – big machines can do this. The infrasounds were amplified down the, ah, long corridors, like air vibrating in a flute.' Ollie Towey gestures around. 'Big old houses can have a similar topography. Corridors, cellars, attics. Hence the commonality of hauntings in such places.'

Malcolm asks the obvious question. 'And why would that create terror? Of ghosts? Hallucinations?'

'No one is entirely sure. But tests have been done. Infrasounds definitely induce discomfort, fear, visual distortions, and of course you don't know why you experience this, because, ah, you can't hear the noises! Classically like haunting! And, well . . .'

Malcolm's face says, *Go on*.

Encouraged, Ollie goes on. 'There is one brilliant theory which says we have an evolved fear of infrasounds. Why? Because apex predators emit them – lions, tigers, and leopards – when they are about to attack. That low, blood-curdling growl. They do it probably to terrify the prey into paralysis. So when we hear infrasounds, we are blind and back in the African bush at night, hearing our own ancient nameless evolutionary dread, the sound of oncoming death. In the jaws of the predator.'

I stare at Oliver. The lanky twenty-two-year-old who has almost silenced Malcolm Tyack.

Malcolm lifts a hand of acknowledgement. 'Nice story.'

'Thanks.'

'Please find the tiger in Baldhu.'

'Thank you. I'm sure I will. Then you can all go back to normal.'

The student stuffs his kit in his bag and disappears.

Malcolm gives me a look. We are alone in the kitchen, sitting at the island. Does he right now think I am Natalie? He has appeared entirely sane ever since I arrived earlier today, so I believe not. He says, 'I don't know what frightens me more. The nameless evolutionary dread that stalks the halls of ancient Baldhu. Or Christmas.'

I laugh softly, even as I examine my own laughter. How can I laugh along with a potential wife-killer? Yet I know you can. I have laughed with psychopathic serial murderers.

He rises and walks out into the hall, heading for the

drawing room. I follow him, mentally assessing his gait, demeanour, all normal – and then I can't help smiling.

Because the Christmas tree looks splendid. Magnificently festive. Big, tall, green, silvery, gold-orbed, lavishly tinselled, decorated with posh Victorian baubles, china and crystal and coloured glass, no doubt some Tyack heirlooms.

'Wow!'

Miles gives a small bow and a lopsided smile. I study him, trying not to show it. He drawls, 'S'nice, *right*? I think it looks *fabulous*, totally Yule. But the kids, ah, they aren't so sure—'

'Cos of the fairy!' says Solomon, apparently distressed, jumping up and down in his blue school uniform, white shirt untucked. 'Where's the fairy? We *always* have the fairy!'

Grace is pouting, adult, quieter; she turns to her father. 'Papi, where *is* the fairy?'

Miles offers an apologetic gesture to his older brother. 'I searched all the Christmas boxes. Sorry, bro.'

Solly yelps, 'Where is the *fairy*? Mummy's *fairy*. Where is it?'

'Oh God,' Malcolm mutters, retreating from Solomon's anguished yells and Grace's withering glance. He says, whisperingly, to me, low enough that the kids can't hear, 'Natalie had a special fairy. She would put it on the top, saying this is Mummy's fairy, like *she* was the fairy. Bollocks if it's lost.'

Solomon is now howling, a proper tantrum, regressive, too young for his age. Miles is apparently abandoning the cause – turning to a little table and knocking back yet more liquor. Grace looks as if she is silently cursing the world with her superior intellect. Arms folded.

Solomon shouts, Malcolm shouts louder.

'*All right! Kids, shut the hell up. Please. Solomon, stop your damn whining.*'

His anger is too much: even Miles flinches. Solomon stops whining, but now he is intently looking over my shoulder, staring at the wall behind me. And then *Miles* does the same and – despite myself – I turn, half expecting to see Natalie Tyack in a lovely long dress, right behind me, blood on her cheek, the water of Dorlam Brialli in her lustrous dark hair.

There is, of course, nothing there. A wall, with a painting. A ruddy Cornish ship in a wild winter storm.

This family.

Malcolm lowers his dark tone. 'Kids. *Stop*. I'll go get a frigging great Christmas fairy right now. The shops will still be open in Penzance.' He addresses me. 'Mind the castle, with Miles, please? Don't let him attack the Armagnac.'

He doesn't give me time to disagree. He grabs coat, keys, phone, and storms out. His car noise dwindles in the dark and the rain, and the quietened kids slope away, waiting for Papi to return with the promised *fairy*.

Miles says: '*Gimlet?*'

I presume it is another cocktail, and I am not wrong. He leads me into the kitchen and whisks it up.

'Deliciously simple. Just Plymouth gin, naval strength, natch. Bash of lime juice, dollop of sugar – gimlet!'

He hands me the glass. I take it, guiltily. Drinking means I am staying the night, not driving. The option of staying has already been offered: it seems to be an open invitation now.

The two of us sip the gimlets. I assess my drinking partner with a lot more diligence than before. Fair-haired Miles is dressed languidly. Leather jacket, unbuttoned, chest hair, *he likes the girls* . . .

'You know the shaft is still open?'
'Sorry?'

Miles shrugs, eyes blurring. I wonder how many *gimlets* he's had.

'I saw it today, strolling over from the Saracen. The deadly mine!'

'But I thought Malcolm had capped it, with chicken wire.'

'Think they tried, him and some carpenter, but the chippie insisted it was too hard. He wants to wait. Supposedly it needs proper rude mechanicals from the council. They're coming after the New Year.'

The fear stirs inside me. I am not scared of ghosts, they do not exist; I *am* cautious of people who *are* scared of ghosts, what they might do in their madness. I am definitely *scared* of big open mine shafts.

'Try not to go wandering out there at night? Natalie used to do that, wander around at night, look what happened to her!' He guzzles his drink, eyeing me laconically. 'Ah God, I shouldn't jest, it is so sad. She was so sweet. The little Christmas fairy, with the wand. Casting her spell on all the men.'

I set down my gimlet. However delicious it is, however tempting it is to yield to the anaesthesia, I need to be proactive. Miles is loquaciously drunk – yet again – and I've got him on his own. I can make the most of this.

'Miles, can I ask you something?'

'Only if it is interesting, and possibly obscene.'

'Do you think Baldhu is haunted?'

It works. This query stops his boozy sardonic drawl. Completely. He hesitates. This is what I want: Miles off balance.

Suddenly he looks more sober, as he puts down his cocktail and says, 'Well now. That is an interesting question.'

'And?'

He pauses. 'You know, I feel sorry for you, getting involved in all this. Us. This fucking family! All the ancient curses.' He leans forward, hand briefly on mine, the experienced flirt. 'I like you, Karenza, you're nice. Something sad happened to you, didn't it? I can tell.' He tuts expressively. 'So you don't need all this, you should just leave. Flee into the night! Before it gets worse.'

Yet another man saying, go away.

He guzzles the gimlet, as if that is an answer.

But I won't be dissuaded; Malcolm will be back soon and I have another psych technique I learned at the Bethlem. Calm repetition, until it gets annoyingly irresistible. Do not be deterred by social awkwardness. *Repeat, repeat, repeat.*

'Miles. Do you think Baldhu is haunted?'

He grimaces, rather like Solomon. And I can see the strong family resemblance in the eyes and mouth. Uncle and nephew. He sploshes more gin in his gimlet, offers the same to me. I cover my glass with a hand. We gaze at each other.

He says, 'You know I'm a scientist, like you?'

My reaction must be sharp because he laughs, sourly.

'Why does everyone act so surprised? Just because I inhale Talisker at 10 a.m.? Yes, I studied chemistry at Cambridge. Then metallurgy, at Heidelberg. Lived in Berlin for a decade, still have a flat there. Hence the German.' His smile is both drunk and modest. 'Guess the metal is still in the Tyack blood – tin and copper, always tin and copper. Anyway, that's how I made my money. That's why I have time to drift across the moors rescuing *mädchen* in distress. Dealing raw metals with Russians.' He swallows gin, lime, sugar, and winces at the bittersweetness. And goes on, fervently, 'Those oligarchs – my God. You think *I'm* bad? *They* drink. They taught me how to really drink vodka. In Verkhoyansk.' He chuckles. 'Always press your nose to a slice of bread after you down a shot. Or you will puke like the possessed.'

I let him run on. Then I ask again, 'Do you think Baldhu is haunted?'

This time he pretends not to hear, looks out of the kitchen window, mutters about the endless rain. 'It was like this last winter. Never stopped. I swear I'm off to Thailand soon as Christmas is done.'

'I hear you. But do you think Baldhu is haunted?'

His sigh is melodramatic, but his frown is sincere. 'Please. I'm a metallurgist! And a businessman. I know the price of lithium hydroxide monohydrate, in Singapore dollars.'

'Excellent. So . . .' I smile, calmly. 'Miles, do you believe Baldhu is haunted?'

His eyes meet mine. He takes a deep breath; he takes yet another hit of the gimlet. Then smiles brightly and yet with great sadness, and he says, 'Yes. Of course it is. Natalie hated it.'

34

I hide my surprise, and say, 'You've seen things?'
'Sometimes, yes.'
'Like what?'
'I don't know. Just vibrations mainly. Or black shapes. Solomon calls them darkshape, it's a good word, *darkshape*. Like the shape of a woman and deformed, yet not quite human – or sometimes just a void of ominous darkness. But sometimes no more than a mood.'
'Of what?'
'Murder. Anguish. Death. Ancient sadness in the winter. Not fun.'
'And Natalie? She saw things too?'
'Not directly, I don't think, but a few years ago she told me something. She said, this place is evil, and it's affecting *the kids*. Never got more specific than that. Then last autumn, she said it again, how *the kids* were acting out, Solomon seeing her, seeing darkshape.'
I remember Grace's words: the clever lady in the cellar.
'OK, OK.'
I have my phone out. Typing notes. Fast. Can this be *folie à quatre*? If so, why did it not apparently affect Natalie? Same goes for the infrasounds. The strange pattern of haunting – some family members, not all – is problematic from any angle. If it is classic psychological contagion, the fears of the most credulous

slowly affecting everyone, why do some resist, and not others?

My mind is riffling through the pages of my training, the pathologies of perception, the variety of hallucinations, Charles Bonnet Syndrome, perceptual misinterpretation, Capgras Syndrome, epileptic twilight states, anything and everything – and nothing really fits.

I look up at Miles. He offers a sorry smile as he leans and pours more gin, lime, sweetness. I allow him. I think: if only it was just boozy Miles having these visions I could blame hepatic failure – known to cause delusions – and also delirium tremens. But it isn't just Miles.

'Has anyone else witnessed things?'

He answers, drawling. 'Not sure Mummy saw much, but she said Daddy did. He used to hate the cellar. Some months he used to run away to his yacht, like he preferred the sea to Baldhu.'

'And Molly?'

'Yes, a little. One time, I remember Molly screaming in the middle of the night. She must have been about thirteen, said she saw something. God knows why she was so keen to inherit this damned place. Mummy gave it to Malcolm as a big fuck you to Daddy. I got money, which is *much* better, much easier to turn into *more* money. Palladium, nickel, and molybdenum.' Miles gazes up, looking over my shoulder.

But this time it is no ghost. Someone is at the door, saying, 'So, um, uh . . . I've finished and I've got the results.'

Ollie Towey has returned, his rucksack of gadgets in his hands. I had forgotten he was still here. I ask, keenly, because this could be it, finally my answer, 'And? What did you find?'

The lad looks confused. 'Shouldn't I tell Malcolm?'

Miles intervenes. 'My esteemed brother has gone Christmas shopping. You can tell me. I'm Miles Tyack.'

Ollie stammers, 'W-well, OK. Um.'

'Spit it out, dude.'

'There are no infrasounds. Nothing significant. I've checked everywhere.'

Miles laughs triumphantly. 'The ghosts survive to fight again! Huzzah.' He takes another hit of booze. 'Good old Baldhu. Never lets you down! We've probably got an Assyrian fire demon, under the fridge.'

Ollie says, 'But there are other things. It's complicated.'

Miles sniffs. 'How is it complicated? If there are no infrasounds?'

'Well . . . There are anomalous sounds in the cellar.'

I look at him, remembering that bird in my face; I will never forget *that*. 'Sounds like what?'

'A rushing noise, water perhaps? Whispering away. I picked it up with the mic, but if you lie down you can physically hear it, if you try.'

I also recall the noise I heard when I was locked down there. Something rhythmic, could be water. But how?

Miles looks drunkenly exultant. 'Congrats, you've discovered the well.'

I look at Miles. 'What?'

'Yeah, under the house. Another Baldhu *secret*.'

I am intrigued, yet annoyed.

He detects my irritation. 'Malcolm didn't tell you? It's true. We have a well right under the house. Hidden away. Could be a thousand years old, or more.' He laughs, darkly. 'Goes verrrry deep. I'll show you.'

He stands, lifts a follow-me arm, as if he is a tour guide. I follow him and Ollie comes too, into the hall, through the nasty little door, and down the clammy steps. Into the dankness of the cellar. Unexpectedly, a light is on. There is a bare bulb swinging softly in a non-existent breeze, emitting a bitter yellow light so feeble it leaves corners entirely in the dark. The light switch is hidden in a recess, that's why I didn't find it before, and now I see it, far too late.

Miles is on his knees, pulling at a damp old rug. We stoop to help him; the job is quickly done. Beneath the rug, there are more flagstones. No sign of a well. Then I notice that one of the flagstones looks like wood and is much bigger: ancient hardwood, glistening in a different way to the stone. And a small metal ring is embedded deep in the time-polished gnarliness.

Miles already has two fingers hooking the ring. He pulls, and gasps, and pulls again, and the thick, heavy wooden cover flips up, and over. Loudly. *Bang*. And there it is.

'Jesus,' says Ollie.

The shaft of the well is wide enough to fall down. Another swallowing void, like the Black Mine beyond the garden. I lean closer, using my phone torch to illuminate the deep black shaft, but it is so dark the light gives up after a few yards. I say, 'What's that noise? The rushing sound?'

Miles explains, with a slur. 'A stream, running deep under the house. Sometimes it almost dries up in the summer.' He peers down, grimacing. 'Not now, though. Not with this heavy rain. Eventually it joins Bathsheba and runs down to the zawn.'

Ollie says, placidly, 'That would explain the anomalies, the sounds. Vibrations down here.'

Miles strains and lifts and slams shut the great wooden cap over the well, then pulls the rug back, covering it, as if he never wants to see it again.

He squares up to Ollie. 'It explains how the cellar is

so damp. And maybe more? *Dieses Haus ist voller Geister und Hexen.*' He shakes his head. 'You don't want to dig too deep. I'd stop here if I were you.'

Ollie senses he is not needed any more. In the hall, he gathers his stuff and departs, hastily, with a warm thank you from me. Even as his car disappears into the nocturnal drizzle, I can see Malcolm returning.

He stomps into Baldhu, holding a small plastic fairy like a sporting trophy. He yells for the kids, they descend from their rooms, they watch as he climbs on a chair and tapes the fairy to the top of the tree, then he gives everyone a glare which says: *if anyone dares to complain I will throw them off the cliffs*.

No one dares to complain, his glare is too frightening. Malcolm makes the kids supper, they get up to retire again. But as Grace rises from her chair, she comes silently over to me.

I can sense the family around us. Grace looks shy and apologetic and then she seems to gain courage. She leans close and gives me a tiny, meaningful hug. 'Goodnight, Karenza.'

I am a little shocked. I am not sure I have ever seen Grace hug anyone apart from her beloved Papi.

Malcolm watches this, half smiling, half frowning as his daughter turns and leaves the room.

Miles is obliviously drunk as he takes up his coat and torch. Heading back to the Saracen, over the moors.

As he goes out the back door, I belatedly realize that it's not the girlfriend who doesn't want to sleep in Baldhu.

It's *Miles*.

I am alone with Malcolm again, in the big bright kitchen, risking so much, yet wholly consumed by this puzzle, as well as the need to save Grace and Solomon, sleeping innocently upstairs. They do not deserve to be left here, orphaned.

I find I urgently want Malcolm to be innocent. This is bad. I am emotionally involved, over-invested, but Grace *gave me a hug*; that lonely child *gave me a hug*. She reminds me of me; she reminds me of Minnie. I cannot help it.

I clear my throat and broach the topic of the day: the lack of infrasounds.

Malcolm blankly gazes at me, as if he expected this, says nothing.

I ask, 'Malcolm, why didn't you tell me about the well?'

He seems unruffled. 'Is it relevant?'

'I don't know. Is it? Miles made it out to be a big family secret.'

He shrugs. 'More of a pain than anything, that well. Spreads damp and rot. Big reason my mother hated the house.'

Is he lying? I estimate, possibly not. Perhaps just being evasive.

I watch as Malcolm rustles up pasta. Excellent spaghetti vongole with sweet little clams, and a green salad, perfectly dressed. Plus luscious wine. A cold Portuguese white, 'from Alentejano, by the sea, the Costa Vicentina'.

We eat, and drink, in relative silence.

He yawns with exhaustion and says, 'I should be more entertaining. I'm sorry for everything.'

I remember how *entertaining* he can be, trying to get in my bedroom, believing I am Natalie. I say, 'It's fine. I know you're hard pressed, what with the frozen pipes at the restaurant.'

Giving me a glance, he adds, 'And I'm sorry for my drunken brother. Did he keep you amused?'

'In his own way.'

'Do you think you're getting somewhere?'

'Yes. It's a complex case, but yes, slowly.'

He lifts a hand. 'Good. Please, please carry on. OK, I'm going to bed – at nine. Like an old person. Thank you.' This time his gaze meets mine and lingers. 'Thank you for staying. For helping us. Really. You know, when you first came here, I was antagonistic. It was stupid. I'm sorry.'

And then he rises and quits the kitchen, leaving me with another flip-flop of emotions. Maybe Malcolm is innocent, and the instincts shared by me and Kyle are right? He loves his kids. He's not an obvious killer. He seems weary and sad – and frightened of ghosts, or memories. But if he is not guilty, then who is? Someone killed Natalie Tyack, it was no accident, I am sure. And now the siblings rise into the picture.

Left alone in the kitchen, I fill a big glass with water, and I retreat to my bedroom, thinking: yes, I might as well leave a toothbrush here now. Clothes. I have practically moved in.

I take out my bag; I drop spare underwear in a drawer, toothbrush and toothpaste in the lovely bathroom. I am now a guest who stays for a while. Or more like a distant but welcome relative.

Night falls hard over Penwith. Cloudy. No moon, no stars, no sky really. Everything is surrounded by nothing; there is nothing out there. Except a small quiet voice – and a little girl knocking at the door. Saying, timorously, 'Karenza?'

I stir from semi-sleep, get out of bed. Grab my gown and open the door. At least it is not Malcolm.

It is Grace. Barefoot, in zodiac pyjamas, alone in the chilly, echoing dark of ancient Baldhu. Holding a plastic bag.

I kneel so I am face to face with the girl. Grace Tyack looks as if she has been crying. This sometimes-emotionless girl is not lacking emotions now. She is red-eyed, and grief-struck. I throb with sympathy. Losing a mother at this age?

'Grace, darling, what is it?'

Grace lets tears fall. She rubs them away, embarrassed, with the heel of a pale little hand. 'I know you want to help us . . .'

'Of course, that's why I'm here.'

Grace whispers – she does not want to be heard? 'Karenza, do you really think you can make all this better?'

'Yes, I absolutely can.' I say this with more conviction than I feel.

Grace nods, her tears drying.

'All right then, maybe you could see this. Maybe it will help.' The girl gulps. 'In the last days, before . . . before it happened, I found Mummy looking at this. In her bedroom. Staring at it for hours and hours like it was weird. Staring!'

'What, Grace? What?'

She says, 'One night Mummy was drunk like Uncle Miles always is and she kept saying to me, when she saw me at the door, *This is it. He knows, I am sure. He knows. No one will know. They mustn't know who Daddy was. Must never know.*' Grace's last gasp is painfully sharp. 'What does that mean, Karenza? How could this tell her anything about Daddy? And then she said more things but . . . but . . . Just make it better. Please.'

Her hands are in shadow, holding the bag. Then she thrusts the bag at me, and she turns and scampers away, into the receding and ancient darkness. Swallowed up in the black, like she was never here.

I retreat into the light of my bedroom. I look down at the bag. There is something heavy inside it, something with a certain shape. I know exactly what it will be. I take it out of the bag.

It is the silver hand mirror, and it glitters malevolently in the meagre light.

35

I wake hours before first light. It is nearly midwinter: the dark pit of the year.

Switching on the lamp, I lean across and pick up the mirror. I want to call my auctioneering friend and beg for an answer. He must be back from holiday. But it is barely 6.20 a.m., so it's a terrible time to call. Instead, I send a message, hoping it won't ping too loud on his phone.

I focus on the clues I do have.

Natalie was obsessed by the mirror. And it became important in her final days. So the mirror must have told her something or revealed something. But it has no secret compartment with a handy note inside. I know that.

My mind races: I won't sleep now. I have stuff to do at home, clients to see, pets to cherish. However much I am fixated on the intensity of Baldhu, life continues elsewhere, I may as well get on.

Showered and dressed, I pack my bag – and for a moment I pause, like a guilty thief, and then I think, to hell with it. I pop the mirror in my bag and hurry down the creaking old wooden stairs in the murk, where I am surprised by the pre-dawn light in the kitchen. Someone is in there.

Malcolm. Dressed. Yawning. Staring at me, appalled.

The kitchen is chilly, the windows are dark, the grey dawn faintly rises, and I see the dark birds on the fence, outside, watching us, again.

He says, 'Why have you come back?'

'What?'

'Why? Why now? It wasn't my fault. None of it.'

For a moment I am thrown. Then I look into his eyes – and I see. Malcolm believes, again, that he is talking to his dead wife. He is being haunted: right here, right now. And as I stand in this chilly kitchen, I remember the advice from Priya – don't deny people their illusions. Do not dispute or interrupt. I have to act as if I am Natalie. Maybe I can *learn* something.

'I had to come back.'

He gazes at me, frowning, puzzled. Or something else. As if he really is half asleep, or drugged. His voice is slurred. 'No, you don't . . . He did it. Not me. Not me. But I got so angry about the man. What did you expect?'

'Nothing.'

'You did that to me. No wonder I was angry. I *could* kill you. *Could*. Now and here.'

He is half rising. I realize, abruptly, that I am in a kitchen that is *full of knives*. If this state of haunting is akin to sleepwalking, I know there are serious dangers. People have been strangled by loving partners, fast asleep. Sleepmurder. It happens. Kyle once handled a prosecution.

'All right, Malcolm, I'll go.'

'Go. Go go go. Or I will. I will.'

'Goodbye, Malcolm.'

I turn to leave, but I am too late. His expression is changed. As if he has woken up – but angry. Flushed, bewildered, furious. Breathing deeply, he steps away from the chair, and stares at me, pale-faced. And then he comes for me, fast and aggressive, and I cower, and wait for him to strike me – with a knife, a hammer, anything, and I think, *I was so stupid, so stupid, hauntings are dangerous, they can end in death.*

I am about to be killed as he killed his wife . . .

And then, wordless, Malcolm pushes past me, into the hall; then upstairs, away. Escaping.

Gone.

I stand here for a long, silent moment. I breathe deep, calming myself.

Time to go.

Hurrying to the grand front door, I step out into December air, damp with near-rain. The windows of the barns stare at me. Eyes darkly gouged out, making me recall the words of Miles, describing the hauntings. *The void of ominous darkness.* I race the car too loud as I exit. Desperately grinding the gears. The thick squirting mud is trying to stop me. My heartbeat is still painful, the tension, fear, terror, is only slowly ebbing.

At last the car pulls onto the bigger road – and my mind feels freer. Released from the web. I see the weathered road signs for Newlyn, Penzance, St Ives, escape. I slow the car to a halt. Then I decide: go to St Ives, why not? It is such a pretty town, Minnie always loved it: our visits made us all happy. St Ives might soothe me now. Also, I have started so early, I have time to spare before my normal, more boring jobs.

Thirty minutes later I am parked and walking down Downalong, in the middle of dainty, overpriced, seaside St Ives: the labyrinth of plush granite cottages, chichi art galleries and upmarket cafés. I notice, as I have never noticed before, *Tyack Crafts and Jewellery*. That must be Molly Tyack's shop, which will be open soon, awaiting customers for its pretty Celtic crosses made of fake Scillonian wreck-metal.

Actually it comes from Guangdong.

I avoid the shop – I really don't want to bump into waspish Molly – and instead I walk on to the seafront near the church and the lifeboats, staring at the ocean. Here I pause at the cast-iron railings, and I lift my phone, hoping for a reply from Kyle – but no.

And yet, I *do* have a significant email, which has just arrived. It is the one I want: my message has worked. It is from Ben, my old uni friend, now an auctioneer in London.

As is typical, Ben Clarke is articulate and wry, but also richly informative, full of stories. Keenly, I read his apology for his late reply, and his usual pleasantries, and then I get to the substance:

What you have here is a fascinating object. I hope you don't mind but I shared it with colleagues. Our conclusion: this is an example of Chinese Export Silver. That means silver fashioned in China for the Western market, generally from the mid-eighteenth century to the early twentieth century. That said, the glass might be much older, it is hard to discern from the photo; they used to do this, fit ancient glass in new metal.

Why is it called Chinese Export Silver? China does not have much gold or silver of its own (hence perhaps their obsession with jade &c). However, when Western traders penetrated China they realized they could exploit Chinese metal workmanship, which was superb, and much cheaper than the Western equivalent. As a consequence, the Western powers imported gold and silver into China, had it worked to Western tastes, then reimported it to Europe. So this would be a hand mirror designed to sell to a Western woman, or explicitly ordered – bespoke, as it were.

The silver on your mirror is hallmarked. On one of the photos we see the symbols for the Cumshing workshop. They operated from about 1780 to 1820, in Canton; most of their silver was reimported by the Portuguese – they predominated in Canton at that time: Macau &c.

What may be of particular interest to you – down there in Celtic fairyland – is that a famous shipment of Cumshing silver was lost off the West Cornish coast in 1803. On a boat called the Santo Gonsalo. *There were even allegations of wrecking! Many died and corpses were found on the beach, dragoons were sent from Truro, but they came too late.*

Could this be part of that notorious shipment? Who knows. The mention of Penzance in the other inscription is suggestive, so my guess is it is pretty likely, but that brutal provenance will never be proved. We often have this problem, I remember a Chinese vase, sold in Munich . . .

He digresses, as he occasionally does.

I lower the phone. The provenance may not be proved to Ben, but it is proved to me. I stare out at the sea, watching the gulls patrolling the beaches in their random formation in the grey sky. I am getting ever closer. The mirror was in that shipment, it was looted by the Tyacks, even as they maybe butchered people on the beach. It was handed down the Tyack family line, yet maybe forgotten over time, as hand mirrors went out of fashion. And then one bright summer day, Natalie Tyack found it, neglected and unloved and dusty, in some ancient chest in a forgotten room in the deeps of old Baldhu, and she took it up and cherished it for her own, seeing her own pretty face in this lovely looking glass. Why not? It is a beautiful thing, and she would not have known the blood-soaked source, the way it found its way up the cliffs and along the lane to Baldhu.

I lift the phone again, expecting Ben to continue in the same vein as he began.

He does not; his digression ends, and he changes course.

> Back to your mirror, and the English inscription, 'For his beloved daughter Frances, Willyam Tyack'. We have looked into this, too. It turns out the Tyacks are a very old Cornish family, from near Penzance, and linked to wrecking (there it is again!). More piquantly, the mirror, here, appears to be a wedding present. Willyam Tyack's daughter Frances married one Isaac Coppinger, in 1832 – hence the date in the inscription, so the mirror passed out of Tyack possession, into that of the Coppingers. And the Coppingers are definitely associated with wrecking, and also piracy. A suitable gift, one might say.
>
> There is a postscript to this rather dramatic story. Your mirror is not unknown to the world. Indeed, it has been up for auction here, in our house on Bond Street. This of course is no coincidence: there are only two famous auction houses in London, and your object is quite valuable. A seller would come to London to find the wealthiest buyers. We also have detailed records of all auctions going back to the 1770s: we are quite proud of them. A colleague has looked at our history of antique Chinese silver auctions and he believes he has found your mirror. Twice.
>
> It first came up for auction in 1905, for sale by 'the

Coppinger family, of Helston, Cornwall'. So, they still owned it, in their old family house, by Prussia Cove, near Helston. The description exactly fits your mirror, the filigree work, the Cumshing hallmark. Indeed the faded crest on the mirror, now apparently illegible, worn away by time, was still legible back then. It is recorded as 'two dolphins on either side of a stylized sword: the Coppinger crest'. Rather lovely. And yet, the mirror did not sell, because the Coppinger family withdrew it from auction at the last moment. Who knows why? It's as if they wanted to get rid of it, or make the money, but they also had some attachment to it. And in the end this emotional attachment prevailed.

Nor is this the end of the tale. The same mirror came up again(!), in the late 1950s, again it was to be sold by the 'Coppingers of Helston'. And again they withdrew it, at the last moment. This time there is a photograph in our records, and it is unquestionably your mirror. There is no explanation for their vacillation over the sale. One might imagine sentimental value overriding avarice. Your guess is as good as ours. We are mystified but intrigued.

I have a colleague, Charlie Graydon, who is the Chinese Export Silver guru, and he is fascinated. He missed a free Korean BBQ lunch to research your mirror; if you ever meet Charlie, you will acknowledge the significance of this self-denial. He's looked into the fate of the barbarous Coppinger family, but they seem to have vanished now. No one is left in Helston: the dynastic home was sold many decades ago. Perhaps it was the last of the line who tried to sell the mirror, then balked?

What a story! I'd love to know how you got hold of it.

> *Remember how we used to get free lunches in Bristol? That place in Clifton with the cellist . . .*

Ben goes on, reminiscing about our student days. I skip the words, not because I do not care, but because my mind is now surging onwards. The mirror was apparently *not* in Baldhu: *it left the possession of the Tyacks*. Natalie did *not* find it in Baldhu, so how did she get hold of it? This precious yet cursed thing that terrifies the children. Which now throbs in my bag.

Avidly, I read the rest of Ben's email, desperate for more clues. He talks about us meeting for drinks in London soon, or he may come down to Cornwall.

Then he signs off, unexpectedly.

> *Before I go, one more thing about the Chinese mirror. Charlie tells me that historically the Chinese have a peculiar, intense, and rather foreboding attitude to mirrors, as in, darkly superstitious. For instance, as with the Victorians, if there was a death in a Chinese house, all mirrors would be covered: they believed that if the mirror 'saw' the dead person, or the coffin, further deaths would follow.*
>
> *There is an even older, creepier Chinese traditional belief, or mythic perception, as you prefer, which is particular to personal mirrors – hand mirrors like yours. This legend attests that when you look in your hand mirror, you are not seeing yourself, you are looking at a demonic being that is merely pretending to be you, while plotting your death.*
>
> *Isn't that fantastic? It's also true, in a tangential way, when you think about it. Because when you look in a mirror you do see death, in that you see your own ageing face, and death at the end.*

Brrr! I think I may go on a diet.

I do hope I haven't freaked you out. Thank you for this brilliant distraction, it has brightened up grey London days! Let's have that negroni soon

Ben xx

I put down the phone and walk on down the harbourside, past the Moomaid of Zennor ice cream parlour, and the Porthminster Rum and Crab Kitchen, and then I stop again, and gaze out at the ocean. Across the windy bay the lighthouse blinks at me.

As if it is surprised to see me.

And now it sends out a warning.

36

Baldhu Baldhu Baldhu.

All I want is to go back there. I can't help it. If I was drowning in Baldhu, now I am drowned, turned into a mermaid. Wild and sacred Baldhu. Where the stream tumbles down Bathsheba Valley to the waterfall of the primrose. A place of purity. Pure beauty. Pure intrigue and magic: innocence and death, ghosts and moons, a beautiful corpse on a beach, somehow possessing a haunted Chinese hand mirror, which showed the demon of her own face, plotting her own death.

It is dark, yet it is richly dark: all so noble, superior, aristocratic. So *not-suburban*. So much greater and grander than humdrum reality.

Which is where I am now, sitting in my flat, with the seagulls eating chips on the balcony. El Gruffalo is lying sprawled, in a self-satisfied way, across my laptop, like a fat sultan on opioids. Otto is as grey as I have seen him. Expressionless and clueless, both front claws tightly clutched on his favourite fat twig. Motionless, too. Apart from one globular left eye which revolves like a surveillance camera, observing me as I slump on the sofa.

I stare at my big, stupid, beloved cat, at my quirky and likeable lizard, at the big windows where the rollers sometimes barrel across the bay towards St Mawes.

Darkness is coming.

'Gruff. Help me. I'm stuck. It's a brilliant maze, but it's going nowhere. I'm usually good at this.'

El Gruffalo vaguely opens his eyes to dark liquid slits. Then my cat closes his eyes again and sprawls more expansively. As if he is demonstrating his superior social standing.

I turn to the cage. 'Otto, please – give me something, anything. I'll feed you another mealworm. Think of all that calcium.'

Otto's bulging right eye joins in the surveillance, revolving like some superb gyroscopic technology. But still his skin displays the greyness of ignorance, to match the neutral grey waters of the River Fal. All out of ideas.

I yelp into the quiet, 'Come on, Karenza, think!'

I am talking to myself. Again. Living alone I have got used to talking to myself these last years; though maybe now I am chattering with the ghost of Natalie Tyack, who lives inside me, according to Malcolm Tyack.

I say to the room, 'Why would Natalie obsess over the mirror? Why did little Solomon throw a shoe in the water? Why does Grace feel estranged from the family – does she know she might not be a Tyack?'

Unsurprisingly, the room does not answer my absurdly tangled and various questions. Perhaps music will help, for thinking. Hitting my sound system, I choose Spiro: 'Yellow Noise', 'Burning Bridge', 'Rose Engine'. The repetitive yet tuneful automatism, the mix of folk and maths. Perfect for focusing my emotional mind.

Maybe I should call someone. Maybe Dinah, or the Hardwickes, or maybe my brother Loic in Cambodia, or wherever he is; maybe I could even ask Dad. Sometimes Dad, in his Weird Lost World of Conspiracy, will have an unexpected and invigorating angle, something beyond normality, but surprisingly useful as a result.

Have you considered it could be the CIA? Think of those sub-Atlantic cables, what are they really *for?*

No, maybe not Dad, not this time.

Deep inside, I am increasingly worried that I *can't* solve this. Which will hurt, appallingly, because it means failing those kids. But it will also hurt me, professionally, my self-esteem. I am a forensic psychologist: this is my allotted role in life, the one thing I can do successfully on this earth. Save the kids as I could not save my own kid. Solve the mystery and rescue this shipwrecked family. If I can do anything in this life, it *must* be this. And if I can't do this? The night comes closer.

Because it is getting late. The winter evening is stealing over West Cornwall. That darkness is creeping from Nanquidno to Nanjizal, from Joppa up to Zennor, the darkness is shrouding Carbis Bay and Crows-an-Wra, as I sense the Tyacks slipping ever deeper, towards chaos, into the pit.

'No!'

I say this out loud. El Gruffalo opens a slow, single eye, and observes me. And now my phone rings.

Granny Spargo!

Happily, I pick it up, turning down the music. Betty often rings at odd moments, and I am always happy to swap gossip with her.

As usual she has gossip. Quite a variety of it, eccentric and very Betty. She tells me she ran into someone who knows someone who told her, over scones and jam, that the Cornish barman of the Victory is possibly having an affair with Romilly Kelhelland. I file this away, kind of hoping it is true, a nice sensible local boyfriend for

Romilly. If it is the barman I think it is, also a good choice. Handsome and funny.

Now, seamlessly, as is her wont, Betty segues her gossip on to my cat, El Gruffalo. She says she just met 'someone who knew him as a kitten, they got on really well' – which makes me laugh, and we laugh together.

'Anyway,' she adds, 'she explained why the Gruff has those issues. Apparently his mum cat was mauled by a tiny dog, lost an eye. Yet El Gruffalo never witnessed it, given that it happened before he was born. How in the world does that work? You're the scientist, my darlin'.'

I chuckle, slightly sadly. I have no answer. Poor Gruff. Hard start in life. Like Natalie Tyack. In a way she was like a rescue cat, and Malcolm Tyack was the rescuer.

And now Granny moves, finally, on to Kyle. As of course she would: last time I saw her I suggested he had possibly been unfaithful. Now I reassure her I was wrong. 'I was just upset, that's all, Granny. This case, in Penwith, it's getting to me.'

Betty croons soothing words. 'Well now, sweetie, you just be careful. These posh people, they like to kill animals for fun.'

I wonder if Betty is being sarcastic. I am pretty sure the Spargos and Brays did plenty of poaching, rabbiting, and ferreting. I nevertheless reassure her I will not let the Tyacks kill me for fun.

We say goodbye, I promise Betty I will be over soon.

Picking up my phone once more, I flick to the photos, and the photos of photos. The photos of the birth certificate: father unknown, big question mark. The photos of the bank statements, but they all look meaninglessly random. Now I look at the photo of the girls at the St Petroc's Children's Home. That photo of Natalie looking agitated yet frozen. Frightened somehow. Certainly stiff, and awkward.

It is clear Natalie hated something about St Petroc's. Men coming down from London? And if Natalie did not want to be there at Petroc's she would surely have had friends near her, that bright sunny morning, friends as a guard and a consolation, as support. That's what you do in school photos. You are told to gather, and your friends get close, especially if you are unhappy.

I recall the words of Julie the shopkeeper. *She was sharp as a tack, that girl, leader of her little gang.*

Natalie's friends must be in this photo. But who are they?

Urgent, I remove Gruffalo and boot up the laptop.

Here. I am on the case: Natalie Tyack's social media; Natalie *Skuse*'s social media. Seems she preferred to use her maiden name online, if she used it at all.

Which she rarely did, *Natalie Tyack née Skuse* was not very active online. But maybe her old friends will still be linked?

Hurriedly, I sift through Natalie's friends and followers. There are not many. A few boys – old boyfriends?, a couple of mums in mums' groups. Where are the girls of Natalie's age? They would still only be about twenty-nine or thirty now.

And then I find a likely friend, from way back.

Maisy Harrington, thirty.

But Maisy is now living in Epping in London, been in London for ages. She is not close now and was not close to Natalie a year ago.

How about this one: Lara Hicks? She is also thirty. Yet she is now in Scotland, and she's been in Scotland for a while.

Another blank.

These girls, if they really were Natalie's gang – they scattered. They didn't want to hang around Penzance and St Petroc's, with its scandals and abortions and men down from London.

One more.

Bethany Merwin. Same age. Seemingly an online friend of Natalie's for many years, even if their visible social media contacts are near-zero. As if they wanted to keep it private.

The placidly pretty face of a darkly blonde, thirty-year-old woman gazes at me, and – yes – it is a face I recognize. I pick up my phone and the photo, of the girls of St Petroc's. Standing directly on Natalie's right is a blonde girl with a placidly pretty face. The face is thinner, fresher, but this is surely her. Bethany Merwin.

One of Natalie's gang.

I feel excited and a little nervous. If this lead runs into dust where do I go next?

I seek out Bethany's own social media. It is not striking; she is also low key. But here she is.

Bethany Merwin.

And she still lives in St Just-in-Penwith. Where Malcolm met Natalie. Where Natalie worked as a check-out girl at the Spar, before the wild moorland rose was *plucked*.

And in one of the photos she is in the white clothes of a pharmacy assistant, standing outside the Day Lewis Pharmacy.

I check the website. Day Lewis. St Just. Open until seven on Mondays, Wednesdays, Fridays. If I absolutely race the moors and the backroads, I can be there before it shuts.

Tonight.

Otto is looking at me, swivelling both eyes. Then he

flicks a lurid red tongue, and he sticks his tongue onto an unfortunate moth, which has just flown in his cage. And now he eats the moth, alive, with great pleasure. Its dusty wings crumbling to nothing in his green and smiling mouth.

Even Otto, I think, is a killer.

Given the chance.

37

The rain finally gives up in its determined bid to prevent me reaching St Just, about a mile outside the little town. The Atlantic wind is less easily defeated. I have to forcibly shunt at the door so as to open it – and the wind contemptuously slaps it shut as soon as I am out.

I am trying to recall the last time I was here. Perhaps as a teen? Before?

A long time ago, anyway. The St Just Christmas lights kick and swing in the gale, but no one is around to enjoy them, not on a nasty wet Monday night, in this very last little Cornish town, at the end of the end of Cornwall. The last town before the raging seas entirely win out, a mile away, at the dark eroded roots of the plunging Penwith cliffs.

In the humble, windswept town square, surrounding the war memorial, just two premises glow with apparent life, the Admiral Bolitho pub, and the pharmacy, and it looks as if the pharmacy is about to close: lights are being turned off.

There are two young women inside, and one of them certainly appears to me, as I squint from the darkness, to be Bethany Merwin.

How am I going to approach an absolute stranger? I can't rely on Cornish names and a friendly old Cornish lady. This is much more intimate, personal, intrusive. Explosive, even.

Nor can I rely on this girl being happy to betray Natalie's secrets, or to betray Natalie. This is a good *friend* of Natalie.

Bethany Merwin is at the door of the pharmacy, bidding goodbye to her workmate.

'All right, see ya, Jen, I'll lock up. Won't be any more customers tonight – look at it!'

The workmate hurries off into the dismal night, speedily zippering her puffer coat, and giving me – sheltering under a bus stop – barely a glance. Bethany Merwin is alone in the pharmacy. For a few minutes. This is my chance. The mirror.

Words won't cut it, but the mirror, *that* might shock. It won't be pretty, I will have to be horribly aggressive, but I know from experience it can work in interviews, interrogations, cross-examination. I have seen Kyle do it – and he is an excellent prosecution counsel. Produce striking evidence from the off. Flourish it. Attack and destabilize the witness, or the accused. Like throwing the first unexpected punch in a street fight.

The door makes a jingle as I step out of the weather. Bethany, who is locking glass cupboards, turns in surprise.

'Bethany Merwin?'

The young woman cocks an inquisitive glance my way. Intrigued more than shocked. 'Yes?'

'Hello, I'm Karenza Bray. A forensic psychologist.'

Before Bethany can register surprise, I chuck a grenade.

'Bethany, did Natalie Tyack ever talk about the father of her daughter Grace, her paternity, or anything like that, when she was alive?'

The hesitation is so brief it is almost negligible.

Bethany replies, 'No.'

'You sure? I've heard people saying she did.'

Bethany looks at me, pauses, then shrugs. 'Who the heck are you anyway? What have you got to do with Natalie?'

Now's the moment. I step closer, open my bag, and take out the lovely, glittering, antique Chinese hand mirror, with its long-gone crest of the Coppingers.

'I know she owned this mirror, loved it, and it meant a lot to her. Why?'

And this works. There is another tiny but more telling hesitation. Bethany does not seem outraged or perplexed by the evidence. Just surprised, curious – and saddened.

'Who are you really? Police?'

'No. Like I said, I'm a forensic psychologist. I'm trying to help Natalie's kids, in Baldhu House.'

Bethany's face relaxes slightly, in a mournful way. 'Ahh. God. Solomon, Grace? How are they?'

'Not brilliant. They are grieving, badly. And showing evidence of disturbance. They need to know what really happened to their mother. They need closure.'

Bethany stands at the counter in her smart white-and-blue coat. Shakes her head. 'Oh *God*. Those poor kids. I'm not surprised they're messed up.' Another meaningful hesitation. 'So you're *definitely* not police?'

'No. Would that be a problem? If I was?'

'No.' Bethany frowns, and her frown is angry. 'That would not be a problem.'

'Sorry?'

'Police would be a nice *surprise*.'

'Because?'

Bethany exhales. 'Cos police have *never* been here, never asked anyone about Natalie, even though we all lived together!' The anger rises. 'We were good friends for years. Forever. From the bloody home. Then she dies in a weird accident. Or murder. Yet nothing?'

'No one ever came here?'

'Nope, and it's not right, is it?' Bethany gazes past me, at the darkened streets of her little town. Where the feeble Christmas lights dance mournfully in the wind. 'It's like the coppers didn't give a toss. A young woman dies and it's all quite mysterious and she could've been killed, but the reaction is *meh*. And we're her old gang from Petroc's.' Another angry shake of her head. 'Like they *never* wanted to know how or why she died. I dunno. I dunno.' Bethany calms herself and gives me a level gaze. 'But you *are* trying to find out, finally? Someone is finally taking an interest?'

'Yes, I am.'

'How did you know about us?'

'Social media. Random photos. Those kids need your help!'

Bethany nods. Seems to think. Then she says, 'Let me finish up here.'

'Sure . . . but . . . because?'

'Because I wasn't her very best friend.' Bethany's frown is sad again. 'That's Katya. And she works in the pub. Bolitho. It'll be the end of her shift as well. She's probably in there right now. Can you wait two minutes?'

I reassure Bethany that I can wait two hundred minutes, if it helps find out the truth. In the event it takes less than two minutes – Bethany has obviously done this chore many times – then we are out of the door, and into the pub.

It, too, is nearly empty. West Cornwall is being deserted, everyone fleeing the midwinter weather.

Katya is shorter, darker, shyer. And another young mum, eager to get home.

Bethany persuades her to pause and sit down on one of the many empty leather banquettes.

Katya complains, 'Jake's looking after the kids. He's helpless on his own.'

'Just ten minutes, Kat. Because this woman, Karenza, is trying to find out what *really* happened to Nat. She's actually got the mirror – remember Nat's mirror?'

'Hmm.'

'She knows Natalie and was wondering about Grace and her dad.'

'What?'

'Yes. And you know what all *that* means.'

Katya looks at her friend. Appalled. 'But what's the point in going over it *now*, Beth? Why get into all this? We'll all get into trouble.'

Bethany persists. 'Don't you want to know what really happened? Apparently her kids have gone *bananas*.'

Katya's expression softens. She glances my way, nervously. 'Are they all right? Solly and Grace?'

I answer, 'They're not doing great. I think they would really benefit if they could find out what happened to their mother.'

Katya pauses, then shakes her head. 'I've no idea about anything else, no mirror, nothing. Sorry.' She glares at her friend Bethany, and adds, 'Don't say any more, Beth.'

'But—'

'No! We don't need this, it's all *over*, it's not going to bring Natalie back, is it? It's closed, it's history. *Christ*. You want all that back? Let it bloody *go*. Don't be a fucking idiot, Beth.'

Katya is up, and out of the pub. The door opens to a blur of wind and drizzle, followed by silence. Bethany shrugs, awkwardly. But she does not leave. The pub is still virtually deserted. A bored barman scrolls his phone. Two young guys drink lager as they talk about football.

I press on, before the road runs out entirely. 'Can you tell me anything more? About Petroc's? Or maybe the mirror?'

Bethany Merwin scowls, wrestling with conscience, perhaps. Or fear.

'Anything about her history? Background? Anything?'

She snaps, 'I'm not gonna destroy her family – or what's left of her family. Kat's right. She's dead. And it won't help her kids. Probably make it all worse.'

I am headbutting a wall of frustration,

'Anything? Please?'

Bethany takes a deep sigh.

'Let's just say we were all happy when she met Malcolm Tyack.'

'Why?'

'She proper fell in love. She was besotted with him. Malcolm! She always liked older guys – and Malcolm was good and kind, protective. And rich. A rescue party! Natalie adored him. And he was the same to her. Loved her right back.'

I muse on this. I ask, 'OK. And so – so they were faithful, do you think?'

Bethany says, quite firmly, 'Yes.'

'Are you sure? I think her husband, Malcolm, suspected something.'

Bethany scowls. 'Then he was an idiot. Nats was flirty, sure, she liked being pretty, liked men admiring her, but no, she loved him. Stupid man.'

This is going nowhere. At last Bethany says, 'Look, I'm probably done here. Kat's right. What's the point?'

'Because your friend was probably murdered?'

This is effective. Bethany looks at me in silence. She

half shakes her head and says, 'I know she was freaked about life at home. That mad old house. Baldhu? Years ago. Something strange was happening there. Weird, or scary, some creepy well, some cellar, some story down there. That's all she'd say. She was seeing some man then, maybe, but just for advice, I reckon. And a few months before she died, she got strange again—'

'How?'

'Nothing in particular. But, we were in here, having a drink, didn't happen often . . . and . . . and she asked me how you get a birth certificate. I figured she was trying to find her long-lost father. Daddy. Maybe to sort the mess in her head.'

'And? Did she?' I am eager, leaning forward. 'Did she find her father?'

'As far as I'm aware . . . no.' Bethany tuts at herself. 'And maybe that's for the best.'

Bethany Merwin is looking for her phone, ready to quit. Desperate, I chuck one last question. 'What about the mirror? It seemed to shock you, surprise you?'

Bethany gives me an inscrutable stare. There is a long hesitation. Then she relents, and says, 'All I know is, that mirror was precious to her. She kept it hidden, like a secret, in the home. Once, she actually told me how her mum gave it to her, before her mum died. You know her mum died when Nat was young? Like, nine, dunno. It was an overdose, I heard.'

I hide my surprise, thinking: the mirror did not come from Baldhu? It always belonged to Natalie Skuse?

Beth sighs with great sadness and goes on.

'So, like, eh, the mirror was Natalie's only evidence of her parents even existing. That beautiful thing. That silver mirror.' Beth shakes her head. 'Nat was obsessed with it, kept it in a box, so rarely showed it, wouldn't let people touch it. Kept it close. I always found it a bit peculiar, unsettling, those Chinese words.'

She stands up, leaving me with these final words: 'Natalie was always the prettiest and the funniest. Out of the whole gang at Petroc's.'

'Meaning?'

'The one you would go for. If you were rich, and came down from London occasionally, and you were looking for prey. Not that I ever saw anything, but I heard . . .'

And then Bethany Merwin shoves at the door and exits the pub. The two boys laugh at some ribald joke. I look at the time, and think about the weather, and I wonder who Natalie's *mother* was, how she came to possess this haunted mirror once owned by the cruel Coppingers, and then I think again of the wind and the rain, and the long, treacherous drive to Falmouth. And I realize where I am inevitably going to be sleeping.

Rich men came down from London . . .

One word tolls in my mind as I drive the last forbidding miles.

Natalie Tyack was *prey*.

38

Grace greets me at the big dark door of Baldhu as if I am, indeed, now part of the family. A Tyack. I hurry to explain, 'I texted your dad. Told him I was a bit stuck – so I might need to stay over, again—'

Grace shrugs airily. 'Yeah. He said.' And she wanders off down the hall towards the kitchen.

After a bit I follow her, and find her alone, reading a large hardback book of Egyptian mythology at the kitchen island.

'Where is everyone else?'

Grace turns a page, barely acknowledging me.

'Grace. Where's Dad, Solly, Molly?'

A vague half-shrug. At last, she says, 'Solly's asleep. School tomorrow. Molly, dunno.'

'Your dad?'

'In his office.' She jerks an eyebrow upwards, indicating the office upstairs.

I nod, suppressing my minor guilt. The office where I sneaked in and found the photos, the birth certificate, and the bank statements; all of it. These pieces of the puzzle maybe fit a little better. Natalie was searching for some personal truth connected with her childhood, her parents, her kids' home. Yet she loved Malcolm: she was faithful. So maybe Grace is Malcolm's after all? If so that will be an intense relief, even as everything else tightens painfully.

But if Natalie wasn't *straying*, why was Malcolm was engaged in his marital espionage?

Then I remember what Grace said. *He knows, I am sure he knows, he mustn't know, they mustn't know who Daddy was . . .*

And my mind does another backflip, as Grace turns another page. A dry sound in an almost soundless house.

The wind has died. The rain has given up. Baldhu is curiously warm. Taking a chair, I ask, 'Everything OK here?'

Grace rewards me with a brief glance. 'What?'

'Everything fine here in Baldhu?'

Grace glances over again, smiles distantly. She says, 'You mean have there been any strange wooooooo noises? In the cellar?'

'Well, er . . .'

'You mean is Solomon talking to Mummy again? Even though she is dead?'

I force a chuckle.

Grace slaps her book shut. 'Enough 'gyptians! All they do is talk about wheat harvests. And the Nile.'

'It was quite a static civilization.'

Grace turns suddenly voluble. 'They mummified cats. And insects! I like that. Tiny, mummified beetles. And if your dog died you had to shave your eyebrows off. And the brothers would sleep with the sisters, if they were . . .' She looks at me. 'You know. *Posh.*'

'Pharaohs?'

'Yeah. Like pharaohs. Like *us*. Not like you.'

'Fair enough.'

'All right, I am going to bed! Tricia takes us to school tomorrow.'

With that Grace marches off, leaving me alone.

A message pings. It is from Malcolm.

Sorry v tired. Hard at work up here. Gonna sleep. Please forage for food it's all yours. I trust you with kids! See you in a.m.

I open the fridge and find eggs, cheese and ham. Good eggs, good cheese, good ham. Of course. I make myself an omelette, pouring one glass of wine from the half-opened bottle. There is always a half-opened bottle of respectable wine in Baldhu. Then I clear up and yawn from the weariness of the day, the puzzles and the driving, and make my way upstairs. Pleased that, last time I was here, I had the good sense to leave a change of underwear, and T-shirts, plus toothbrush and toothpaste.

But sleep is evasive. Baldhu is still thankfully quiet, but my brain is not. I am getting nearer to the heart of the dead dark rose of Baldhu. The roses Natalie loved to grow.

The mystery is being unpetalled, until only thorns remain, perhaps.

Because, as I get closer, so does the sense of danger. That dark devouring well, down here; the black devouring mine, out there.

I am all too awake. And thinking, hard. About what Bethany said: Natalie being freaked out by the cellar, the well, *some story down there*.

What story?

My mind speeds. Why would a family hide away – literally and psychologically – a well like the one in the cellar? Hide it so diligently, so assiduously? Always locking the door that leads down there? So that it took a determined student complete with special equipment to find it?

You would only hide a well that desperately if

something bad happened there, something that might become a sad or scary story.

What could it be?

The light of the phone is blue and unhealthy on my silent face as my brain switches into its highest gear, and I go back through the history of my prior searches into Baldhu.

Here. The mines. The dead miners. The hints of wrecking. Nothing. And that slightly mysterious death in the eighteenth century? Also nothing: or, rather, nothing that could link to the well. But here – yes, here! That random death in the nineteenth century, down at Penberth.

Now I dig deeper: into news reports, microfilmed, digitally scanned, whatever. There is not much but there is *just enough* online to get the sense – but it looks as if I missed the crucial connection.

A young woman, 'her sad remains unidentifiable, found on a beach at Zawn Dorlam, in St Buryan's Parish, Penberth, in November 1865, by a visitor from London, Emma Macintosh. It is thought the body was washed down to the coast by one of the many converging streams, engorged by winter rains, which lead to the zawn. Suicide is suspected. A baby's shoe was found near the corpse.'

A shoe.

And that date, November 1865, it triggers me. Here is a trigger object in words. Because I can remember that date written down in this house. And as for the 'converging streams', they trigger me, likewise, because I know where at least one of them comes from, where it runs under: Baldhu House. And via the bottom of that well in the cellar.

Up up up I get, phone torch ready. I put on warm socks, a dressing gown, and creep from the bedroom, stealthy and silent, tiptoe along the silent yet creaking landing, down the grand yet creaking stairs, turn on the greasy yellow hall light, slip into the living room. Turn on just one lamp.

The family bible sits proudly on its lectern, barely opened from one year to the next.

I open it. The perfumed pages of the ages are flicking past. The last verses of Revelations.

Write the things which thou hast seen, and the things which are, and the things which shall be hereafter . . .

It is here, right at the end:

Behold, I come quickly: blessed is he that keepeth the sayings of the prophecy . . .

After the Gothic type concludes, it is followed by handwriting. Quill, pen, ballpoint. The Tyack family tree. And here is Eliza Tyack.

Born 14th August 1841

There is no mention of a marriage, a husband, anything like that – nor of a death. Whereas these are all carefully added to all the other names. And yet, in a different hand, but also inscribed in beautiful, careful Victorian ink, someone has remembranced Eliza Tyack's children, therefore illegitimate? Shamefully born to an unmarried woman?

Lucinda Ariel Rosemodress Tyack
Born 2nd February 1865

and

Daniel Lowell Trevedra Tyack
Born 2nd February 1865

And then these names, these twin babies, they *also* disappear entirely. Their marriages, their deaths, their lives: they are likewise not mentioned. They vanish like smoke.

Like something precious thrown into deep water.

Standing in the cold, barely lit living room of Baldhu, with its old curtains and medieval fireplace and its tin samples and its smashed Lego dinosaurs, I half-expect the ghosts of tiny Daniel and Lucinda to appear, carried in the arms of their doomed, suicidal mother, dark hair dripping wet.

Surely, Eliza Tyack must be the 'lady in the cellar', as the children call her. The darkshape, like a woman. If the denizens of Baldhu House are being haunted, they are being haunted not just by Natalie Tyack, but by this peculiarly similar case more than a century ago.

The young woman found on the beach in 1865 was probably – surely – Eliza Tyack. But her body may have stayed lodged, rotting at the bottom in the well, for weeks, or months, before the strength of the rains washed her out from under, and she was carried to the zawn. And I am guessing she took her two babes to their deaths as well.

I have seen this in my forensic psych career, mothers driven to suicide, who take their children with them, so they won't be neglected and motherless, so they might even meet in the hereafter. They are always the worst cases, because I can discern the absurd logic. For weeks after Minnie's death, I got suicidal thoughts: simply because I wanted to be with her, with Minnie. If there is an afterlife, I mused, then I can go to her.

But in the end my atheism and rationalism prevailed. There is no afterlife. If only.

Now I glance at the bible again. Those twins.

I wonder, if the engorging winter rains carried poor Eliza Tyack down those converging streams, scattering her remains, maybe it did the same for the two little babies. Scattering their drowned and putrefying bodies down Bathsheba, to the zawn, towards the waterfall of the primrose. Or maybe the little babies were too small, and they are still down the bottom of the well, or what is left of their bones. But at least one tiny shoe *was* washed down there, with Mummy.

This is a truly horrific story. And this is quite enough of a tragedy to stay with a family for generations. You can't get rid of a well; you can't get rid of the house. It is yours, it is ours, it is *us*. We are the Tyacks of Baldhu. But what to do about the well? Where the shamed mother killed herself and her kids? Hide it away under a heavy wooden lid, cap it off like a mine, then cover it with an ancient heavy rug, and perpetually lock the cellar door. Pretend it is not there. Do not mention it.

Except, obviously, it does get mentioned from time to time, and even little children overhear things, and young Solomon Tyack has got hold of some garbled version of this ancient haunting story, this family shame, and he has – quite understandably – blurred two dead young women, two lovely young mothers, into one. Eliza Tyack and Natalie Skuse, united across the centuries. One with a baby's shoe beside her rotting remains.

The living room rustles. A mellow susurrus. I am so exultant in my discovery, I do not care. *Come, ghosts, come*. Because now I have confirmed there are no ghosts, as I always knew – there are just awful, evil memories, and black ripples that have disturbed the dark waters of this family for many decades. *Psychogeography*. And one of the old leaded windows of Baldhu is loose, allowing in the winter breeze.

That is all.

I rise, shut the window tight, then I escape upstairs, to the safety of my room, hugging the secret to myself. Like I stole it. A successful thief. The cracker of safes. I am even closer to the truth now. I *can* solve this puzzle, because I am good at puzzles. I can save this family; I can save the children *and* stop them falling any further into the dark. Can't I?

39

When I wake, bright winter sun streams through the windows. I forgot to pull the curtains. Checking the time, I am mildly shocked.

Is it 9.20 a.m.?

I've slept way beyond my normal waking time because it took me so long to get to sleep, I was so excited by my discovery. The big old house seems quiet, but that is no wonder. They have presumably all left. I feel a fierce sting of guilt. Tricia has taken the kids to school; Malcolm has surely gone to work.

In the kitchen I cut some sourdough, make toast, brew tea. I glance at my phone and check my emails as I munch the toast.

Then I start looking for Coppingers, owners of the Coppinger mirror.

I need to find a link from the Coppingers down the years to today, which might lead me to the deeper truth. I also need to find Natalie's father. Increasingly, whoever he might be, he seems pivotal to this aspect of the tale. Natalie Tyack went searching for him. Perhaps she *found* Dad, and the finding was not what she hoped. I have experienced this in my career, adoptees hunting for biological parents, and encountering something bad, so bad it can destabilize lives, families, minds.

But I am not getting far with the Coppingers. As Ben

said in his email, they once owned a biggish dynastic house in Prussia Cove – *the* cove for wreckers and pirates, I know my Cornish folklore – but it was sold in 1958. The money ran out. After that the Coppingers disperse, and dissolve, as families do.

Yet I must keep trying.

I am distracted. By a thumping noise, upstairs. Like someone dropping a modestly heavy object. Another bird in the house? There are no birds: Malcolm and Solomon imagined them.

I dismiss the noise and go back to my hunt for Coppingers. One in Somerset. A lawyer in Edinburgh. Ireland. Canada. More in Ireland, some old family there, the *same* family? I do not know. There are many, the Coppinger name is really not *that* unusual, so this might be fruitless. And now I hear it again. A dull, repetitive thudding, over and over. Like someone moving furniture, or someone hitting the floor?

This does not compute. I am alone in the house, it must be creaking wood, or a banging window.

I dismiss it again. How about searching for Coppingers in Cornwall? There are some. Bodmin, twenty years ago. A surf dude in Newquay. A rich older man in London. A publican in Saltash. Nothing that stands out . . . and now I hear it for the fifth or sixth time – this inexplicable thumping. For a moment my training says, hypnopompic hallucination? The mind *can* create noises and images out of nothing as it wakes, the same way it can hallucinate as it falls to sleep, and usually these mirages are auditory – but I am surely far beyond that. I've dressed, showered, had coffee.

This must be real. There is someone else in the house, there has to be.

Setting the mug on the table, I walk out of the kitchen.

Braced for an encounter with Solomon playing truant, or maybe Tricia doing some unexpected cleaning.

Thump.

Quickly I pass through the rooms downstairs, but all is quiet – and uninhabited. Another shaft of that winter sun illuminates the drawing room. The smashed-up Lego dinosaur has gone, replaced with an infantile drawing of soldiers with grotesquely long arms.

I hear it once more. The thumping: directly above. My skin begins to coldly tingle, because the noise seems to be following me. It was above me in the kitchen, yet now it is directly above me in the drawing room. It makes no sense – unless someone is simply trying to scare me. And I am feeling the prickles of fear.

Angry now, I stride into the hall and take the stairs – up and fast. The Gothic windows watch me, in their arched and studied sequence. Three, two, one. Up She Goes.

I try Solly's room first – empty. Malcolm's room? The same. The next room, also empty. Every room is empty, except maybe Grace's room – which has a stuffed toy in the bed, an old chewed-up teddy bear lying back on the pillow, its beady black eyes staring unblinking at the ceiling. It has been placed there, like it needs to sleep, but it can't sleep, its eyes gazing up and they are troubled, as if it too can hear these ridiculous thumps.

Now I hear footsteps, running fast down the stairs! So there *was* someone here. Racing from my room, I turn, but it is too late to see who is fleeing. I chase down the stairs so fast I almost fall, but I am still too slow. As I run across the darkened hallway, I hear the squeal of the back door in the kitchen.

When I get there it is wide open to the winter sun and the frosty garden.

I am mystified: it must have been Tricia, or Molly. Or maybe Miles, drunk, playing a joke. Or trying to freak me out.

Would an adult do that?

The puzzle will not be solved. Closing the door, as the clouds roll across, I decide to get going, get out, get a grip. Clean the kitchen and go and do more research at home. Picking up my mug, I carry it towards the dishwasher.

'Mummy, help me.'

The voice is so near it sounds as if it is in the kitchen. As if it is right behind me. If I turn, I will see it.

'Mummy. Help me. I'm scared of the water. *Mummy*.'

I turn around. Of course, the kitchen is empty. The voice comes from nowhere.

Now I feel as if I am observing myself. In slow motion. I can *observe* my own *fine motor movements* as I drop the mug from my trembling and horrified hands.

The mug shatters, loudly, on the tiled kitchen floor.

40

'Karenza? What happened?'

Miles has just walked in through the door of the kitchen and found the renowned forensic psychologist, who is meant to solve the psychological problems of his niece and nephew, crouched, trembling, sweeping the shattered shards of the mug into a dustpan, having been scared out of her wits – by what?

He says, 'I've never seen someone so pale.'

I stammer into silence, I don't know what to say.

Miles crosses the kitchen and holds out a hand, helping me to my feet. He gazes at me and makes a very good guess. 'You finally saw the ghosts of Baldhu?'

I mumble something; I do not quite deny it. Maybe I should simply admit it. That was a distinct hallucination; indeed, it was a sequence of them. I heard things that do not exist: I too am being *haunted*. And as I look back I realize this is probably not the first time. That bat in the cellar, it was not a bat, or a pigeon: it was a ghost, or something that reveals itself to the suggestible brain as a ghost. And the birds, I kept seeing birds, outside this same window! And then in the mirror in the bedroom!

Over these last weeks I have been haunted, I have only now realized, because it is now undeniable. And maybe it started the first time I arrived, on that drizzly day, when I saw the hunched, lonely figure in a hood. Was that really Tricia the cleaner? Or was it Eliza Tyack, hurrying away, a tiny babe hidden in her cradling arms? Darkshape.

And now this terrible voice.

Mummy. Help me. I'm scared of the water.

Miles is making tea. I stand up, brush myself down, literally and emotionally. I wonder if it is really that obvious to him that I am seeing things and am now scared. If it is, might he say something? Apart from the mortal embarrassment, this would ruin my already faltering career. The forensic psychologist who sees ghosts? *Yeah, she charges thirty pence an hour because she is mad, so no one uses her, and she never solved that case anyway.*

He looks my way. 'Calmer?'

He puts a mug down on the island in front of me and I take a chair, pick it up and sip from it. Noticing my hands, trembling still, but a bit less. 'Yes. Thank you.'

He laughs, reassuringly. 'It's OK. It can be terrifying, the first time.' A heartbeat of a pause. 'In fact, it can be terrifying the hundredth time.'

I look at him, helpless, defiant. 'But I don't believe in ghosts! Please don't tell anyone.'

He nods. 'Nor do I, nor do I.' A heartfelt sigh. 'But then, here we are. I won't tell anyone.'

I decide to be direct. 'Miles, if you believe Baldhu is haunted, is that why you don't sleep in the house?'

He blows cool air on his tea, and nods. 'Of course, I avoid it, if I can. Can't always do that, though. I must visit, they're my family. I love them. And funerals, birthdays, Christmas. Jesus – *Christmas* . . .'

'Is it worse at night?'

He shrugs profoundly, like there isn't any possible answer.

I ask, 'Why are you here anyway? Today?'

He gestures at the garden. 'The mine. It's been troubling us – we can't leave it uncapped till the council gets their act together, the wire isn't good enough, and the council want measurements first. Thought I'd help.'

He reaches into the pocket of his waxed jacket, produces a professional-looking tape measure.

I summon myself. Miles seems to respond better to direct questions than Malcolm or Molly. And in psychology you nearly always need to be proactive. At the same time, I am also thinking: I am alone with Miles, who grows as a suspect. I am *unsafe*.

But I am unsafe anyway.

'What about wells, Miles? Like, how wide is that well in the cellar? Enough for three people, if they're small enough? A woman and two babies?'

He stops fiddling with the tape measure and his eyes widen. For the first time since I've known him, weak, boozy, cynical-yet-amiable Miles Tyack looks completely astonished.

'You worked out the history?'

'I did. I worked it all out. Eliza Tyack, and her babies. Read the family bible, found a note in an old newspaper, the unnamed suicide, I put it all together. You told me the water from the well leads to the zawn. Eventually.'

He sets down the mug, stalls for another moment, then says, 'Nicely done. *Forensic.*' A loud, reluctant exhalation. 'Isn't it the most hideous story? Daddy didn't tell Mummy until they were married, by which time she had already moved in. That didn't do much for marital bliss. It's one reason we can't sell the house for what it's really worth, makes it so hard. Who would ever buy it, if they unearthed the truth?'

'Why didn't it ever make news stories? Why wasn't the woman identified as Eliza Tyack?'

He shrugs. 'This is all I know, the family story. She was an unmarried Tyack mother with twins, the shame was intense, so, apparently, we told everyone she'd gone to America, emigrated with a new husband. We didn't tell anyone about the suicide. We were a rich family, powerful, no one would come questioning.'

'And there was no evidence, no bodies.'

He nods. 'Exactly. They were down the bottom of the well. But eventually Eliza's body was dislodged, and months later carried off by heavy rains, but by then it was rotted and unidentifiable, and lots of streams lead to the zawn, and I'm not sure anyone important knew that one of them runs under Baldhu. The corpse found on the beach became a local mystery, then local folklore, then largely forgotten. No one worked out what the shoe meant.'

'Who else knows the whole story?'

He gazes into his mug as if its contents can foretell the future. 'Very few people. *Vanishingly* few. It's barely discussed. I reckon I heard Mummy and Daddy talk about it *twice*.'

The rain is spitting on the window; I persist. 'But Solomon knows, he is obsessed with that shoe, he throws shoes in the sea.'

Miles sighs guiltily. 'Yeah, well, ah, that might have been me. I was drunk, talking about Eliza Tyack with Molly. Solly was at the door. Damn those gimlets, eh?'

I file this away, too: Miles's guilt. Then I go on, 'Is that what haunts the house? The woman and the babies?' I catch at myself as I speak – but what choice do I have? 'I mean, I don't believe in ghosts, but if you did, I mean, if one did . . .'

He helps me out, half smiling, half sad. 'Is it Eliza Tyack wandering around? Is she the lady in the cellar, is she darkshape? Who knows, Dr Bray, who knows anything? Because I don't believe in ghosts either.' He pouts, licks his moist, red lips. 'But I sense them, I absolutely sense them; I sense the lady and her babies, so I don't like sleeping here. In the beautiful house in the lovely little valley. Beautiful, and terrible.' He tilts his head and continues, reflectively, 'One thing I have noticed is that the hauntings tend to affect Tyacks, and *only* Tyacks. Generally. Like it is a dynastic curse, handed to us by Eliza.'

'Tricia's not affected?'

He shakes his head. 'She just knows that Solomon sees things, and that gets to her. Apart from that I don't think she has witnessed anything directly.'

'No one else then. *Always* Tyacks?'

Miles nods, soberly. 'Well, that's what I thought. But now *you've* seen something, haven't you? Be honest. So that's a bit of a problem for my theory.' He scans my face, assessing. 'Are you able to talk about it now?'

'Sorry?'

'What was it exactly that you witnessed?'

I sip my cooling tea, listening to the endless drizzle. I might as well admit things. I don't think he will announce them to the world. 'I heard a thumping noise. Upstairs.'

'Yes.' He nods. 'Noises are common. Random bangs. Thuds. Often from the cellar. Sometimes you'll hear someone running down the stairs, and yet they never quite reach the bottom.' He winces. 'Perhaps that's just as well.' He glances my way: 'Anything else?'

I take a full breath and confess, 'Early on I saw a figure, in the garden, might have been . . . darkshape. Eliza Tyack. And just now I heard a girl's voice. A young child in here. She was saying, *Mummy. Help me. I'm scared of the water.*'

Miles gazes at me. 'Christ. That's quite bad.'

'I was scared.'

'Who wouldn't be?'

'You know I lost a daughter? To drowning?'

Miles nods, sadly. 'I heard. Ah. I didn't want to say anything.' Abruptly, he looks up at the window as if he can see my daughter Minnie tapping there. *Let me in, let me in, don't let me sleepwalk again . . .* 'You know, Karenza, maybe it's time to ask yourself if this is all worth it.'

'Meaning?'

'Meaning: you've done your best, and I know you'd love to help, but I wonder if you should let it go. Let *us* go. Let the mystery pass, go back home to your life. Maybe we *can't* be helped. The cursed Tyacks in our noisy old house, with the babies in the well.'

Another man telling me, yet again, to back off and go away? I say, noncommittally, 'Mmm.'

'Not least because this could be dangerous for you. Psychologically. Maybe even literally?'

I look at him. 'Why would it *literally* be dangerous?'

'It was clearly dangerous for poor, sweet Natalie, wasn't it? All the mad people here, in the haunted house. Her haunted kids sending her to distraction.'

'Are you implying she *was* murdered?'

'Perhaps. I honestly don't know. Or she was driven to craziness. I mean, *I* can barely sleep in Baldhu, and I was *born* here. God knows what it did to Natalie.'

Miles Tyack is telling me a certain truth. But it is just

one truth, and there are surely others. I say, 'No. I will not give up! *I do not believe in ghosts.* There must be a rational explanation. And these poor kids still need help. They need someone to stay sane and work it all out.'

'Well, yessss . . . they really do. *If* it can be done.' His frown is deep, disapproving. 'But maybe the rational explanation is this damn house is full of witches and ghosts, and a *sensible* person would get the fuck out, before it's too late.' His eyes meet mine. 'But good luck in your scientific quest, Karenza. If you can save us, bravo. It's like Rilke said—'

'Who?'

'German poet. Said, Life is maybe better if you don't understand. *Du musst das Leben nicht verstehen . . .* There's a lot of truth in Rilke. Walking that sad cliff by Trieste.' He casts an eye around the kitchen. 'You know, I'm sure Malcolm is hiding the absinthe.'

I allow myself a relieved smile; at least Miles knows when to crack a joke. 'If you find it, I'll have some.'

He stands up. 'I'm going to have a look at that mine first. Take the measurements. You'll be OK?'

I look up at him. 'Thanks, but yes. I'll be *fine.*'

He leaves the kitchen, heads out into the winter.

For a moment I sit here at the kitchen island of Baldhu. I have three choices. I can get in my car and drive to Falmouth and hug my cat, my big fat Gruffalo, or I can put in my airpods and block out the bitter, instant memory of that ghostly voice – *Mummy. Help me* – by listening to 'Useless Sacrifice' by Death Decline, or I can actually do my job. For which, among all this, I am still being paid. By Malcolm Tyack.

I shall do my job. I am a forensic psychologist. Picking up my phone, I continue my useless search, and this time I limit it to 'Coppingers' and 'Penzance'.

And I get nothing. I try 'Coppingers' and 'Skuse', 'Coppingers' and 'St Just', and 'Coppingers' and 'Chinese hand mirrors'. I am getting frustrated. I try 'Coppingers' and 'help', 'Coppingers' and 'pointless', and 'Coppingers' and 'wrecking', and 'Coppingers' and 'FFS'. Then I have a feeble brainwave, and I try 'Coppingers' and 'Natalie'.

And I get nothing.

One more go, quite desperate, I try 'Coppingers' and 'weddings' – maybe some woman changed her name?

And here it is. An ancient Facebook wedding photo. Diana Coppinger getting married in a Devon church to Aaron Curtis, becoming . . . my eyes widen . . . *Diana Curtis*.

Diana Curtis, a name I have heard several times. Because Diana Coppinger would become, of course, years later, Detective Chief Inspector Diana Curtis, out of Exeter.

She's the woman who led the investigation into Natalie's death, who was so *keen* to take charge of it; and she is by birth a Coppinger. All I know of her is what Kyle told me; she's a 'glory hunter' from Exeter, but of course she wasn't. She was somehow invested in this crime, and surely motivated to cover it up. Why, exactly? Protecting a close relative? Blackmail?

I stare hard at the photo, wondering if it shows any more clues. None that I can see, but I store it anyway. I also take a mental note, reaffirming what I thought: do not go to the police. I cannot trust them, I am not even sure I can trust Kyle.

But now I am on a roll. If the Coppingers are that important, what of the family in total? I remember what Ben said, from London.

The Coppinger crest. That was once legible on the mirror.

As soon as I browse for that, I get multiple images. The Coppinger crest is two eerie dolphins, either side of a flaming sword. And now it seems my lottery number really has come in, because I realize I have seen precisely this, before.

Mentally, I retrace my day trip to the kids' home. The sweet woman in Verran's corner shop, talking about the girls and the abortions and the men from London, preying on the easy meat. In that home, Petroc's, which is now being redeveloped. And I know it is being redeveloped because I saw the signs, and also the little crest on the peeling placard, at old St Petroc's Children's Home. And what did it show? Dolphins, exactly like the dolphins on the Coppinger crest.

That's why I had that mental image, peeling back the carpet, revealing the mosaic: the flukes of a dolphin.

I strongly suspect Coppingers owned that children's home. They were, after all, rich and landed until a few decades ago. And if they wanted to disconnect themselves from a scandalous place, where girls were abused? That would explain why the deeds for their sale have been taken from the lawyers: they decided to keep it all as discreet as possible. Erase the connection, until the psychogeography wears off, and everyone forgets.

Except me.

41

'The Kittiwake, Dad? Why here, all the way down in Falmouth?'

My father is sitting on the external wooden decking of the Kitty café. He looks cheery, and thirsty, as he gestures at the beautiful view of Gyllyngvase beach, and the rolling sea, and the green wooded headlands. 'Cos it's such a lovely day, after all that frigging rain. Make the most of it! Warm enough to sit outside.'

My father is not wrong. It's three days from Christmas and yet it could be May: one of those rare but not impossible sunny Cornish winter days. But I'm still confused; this is a long way to go for a drink: for him, on the little train from Truro. But he chose it.

'What would you like, Dad?'

'Pint of Tribute, darling. They do a lovely pint here.'

I step inside the Kittiwake, and I order Dad's pint, and a small glass of wine for my driving self. Taking them outside I see he has moved to the best table, with the best view.

'Love it here,' he says, accepting his pint with a smile. 'Reminds me of the view of the water at Devoran. Your mum loved that view.'

Dad seldom talks of Mum with me. The way I seldom talk of Minnie with him. They are the two places we *really* don't go. Dad took Minnie's death almost as hard as me. It defeated his conspiracy theories – it was so cruel and irrefutable – and yet it simultaneously made his quirks even worse: he escaped into his garden of madness. *You know they are changing our DNA so we can be surveilled?*

And yet Dad, today, seems less eccentric, less manic. More human. More worried about me. He was the one that asked to meet.

I sip my tiny glass of sauv blanc and he lustily downs his pint of Tribute.

He frowns my way. 'Got a call from Granny Spargo. 'Bout you.'

I roll my eyes.

'God, Betty is such a gossip. What did she say this time?'

Dad shrugs. He's wearing a neat zip-up woollen jumper, nice stripey shirt underneath, smarter than normal. I wonder if he has met a woman. He can still meet women, even in his seventies.

'She's worried about you, doll.'

'Worried why?'

Another big gulp of beer. 'Says this house and these kids, she's not keen. This case you're investigating in Penwith. Doesn't like it. Reckons you're a bit stressed.'

'OK . . .'

'And you do look pale, Kaz. Like you're not sleeping. These rich people up in that house. All a bit mad?'

It is hard to refrain from touching on the irony, the vividly piquant irony, of My Crazy Dad condemning something as 'a bit mad'. And yet, in this instance, I think Dad is right. Baldhu, and all that is happening therein, is *a bit mad*. Is more than a bit mad. I am sitting down and rationally discussing ghosts, as if they exist. Worse, I am hearing and seeing ghosts – because they exist?

Dad has been patiently guzzling beer as I think about this. He needs an answer. I give him a query. 'Dad, do you believe in ghosts?'

He sets down his empty pint glass. 'Well, that's a bit of a question from a scientist, isn't it? What's brought that on, Kaz?'

I take a deep breath, ready to tell. Because Dad is at least unshockable with mad ideas and bizarre stories. But he is also eyeing his empty pint glass. Meaningfully.

Dad doesn't have much money. He was never good at that little kayak-renting business in Devoran, it was Mum who made things tick, financially. So I *really* don't mind buying Dad a few pints. No one is here forever. Or is that true? Is Eliza Tyack here forever? Natalie Skuse?

The memory of that little girl's voice ices through me. *Mummy. Help me*. So unforgettable, and so horrible.

'If I tell you my story, you must promise not to tell anyone else ever. Swear on it, Dad?'

'Promise.'

'And if you do that I'll buy you ten pints.'

'Couple will be fine.'

I fetch the next pint of Tribute, hand it to my father, and in the mild December sunshine I tell him everything without giving names away. From the first arrival in the queerly scented hall to the sound of Solomon talking to his mum in the kitchen to my own near-death-by-drowning in the uncapped mine right up to the *thump thump thump*.

And as I offload all of this I see Dad's eyes widen in surprise, and perplexity, until he actually stops drinking his pint and says, loudly, 'Wait.'

'Sorry?'

I am halfway through the juiciest bit of the puzzle,

Eliza Tyack drowning herself and her kids. Yet Dad wants me to pause.

'Dad?'

He is strangely pale, in the winter sun. 'Karenza, describe this house to me, precisely?'

I do as I am told. The difficult roads there, the valley down to the zawn, Bathsheba and the woods, then the rattly windows and the modern kitchen.

'My, my,' he says. 'I maybe know this place.'

'What?'

'Yes. Baldhu? I'm never good at remembering names but I recognize the description.'

'What? How?'

'Because I reckon I might've been there, long ago.'

I gawp; he goes on.

'I can't say for sure, just rings a few bells.' He shrugs, unable to add more. 'Just a theory, that's all.'

'OK.'

I turn and look at the sea, blue and glittery in the December sun. Then I fill the brief silence.

'You know I'm spending Christmas at Baldhu this year? Malcolm wants help with the kids.'

Dad's expression is regretful, yet unsurprised.

'Granny Spargo said you might.'

'Of course she did.'

'I'm not gonna dissuade you, am I, sweetheart? You're welcome to join me and . . . whoever.'

'It's very kind, Dad, but not right this time.'

'All right, all right. Just . . . Good luck.'

He chuckles. With a hint of unease. We chat of old times, and it is nice and then the warmth abates. Dad says, 'OK, I reckon I'd better be going, sun's going in and I've not got a proper coat. Call me when you've had a chance to . . . settle in there.' He gazes at the ocean. 'I know you don't scare easy, Kaz, all those prisons. But maybe you should be scared, darling, just this once.'

He gives me an affectionate glance. Then he stands, we embrace, and I watch him as he heads down the decking, and as he walks with a definite pep in his stride, I realize he *must* have a new girlfriend, that's why he is dressed smartly, down here in Falmouth; he is incorrigible.

'Dad!' I say. 'You scoundrel, you've got some new woman, haven't you?'

He grins as he walks away. 'Gotta enjoy life! All too short! Phone me please: let me know you're safe!'

And then, even as I observe, Dad halts, and turns, and stares hard at the sea, which is greyer under the gathering clouds, and then he pivots to me. His face says: I have something else to say.

I rise and approach.

He says, 'It was a Christmas, ages ago. I've remembered when it was, when I went to this house. Baldhu.'

'Yes?'

'We got an invite, being family. And you came with me.'

My mouth falls open. 'I was there? And we're *family*?'

'Yes. Family. What are they called? These people at Baldhu?'

'Tyacks.'

He nods. 'Yes. That's 'em. Think they're cousins, on my dad's side. You know what West Cornwall is like. All that incest.'

'So I am also a Tyack, and so are you?'

'Guess so. In a way,' he muses. 'Not that it particularly matters, does it? Anyway.' His eyes are fixed on mine. 'For some reason one Christmas they invited us, the poor relatives, for a Christmas thing, stay overnight, but your mum wasn't keen and Loic was tiny, so in the end just me and you went, and . . .' He hesitates, as if debating how to phrase his next words. 'You hated it.'

'I did?'

'Yes. It was all rainy and cold and it never stopped raining, and you just hated that house, you must've been about six and you went properly mental. Like you were a toddler again.'

Dad is sniffing the breeze. It feels chillier now. 'Sorry to shock you like that, but it's better you know, I think. Right?'

'Absolutely. God. Uh, absolutely. I just – don't know what to say.' A pause. A long pause.

Dad makes an apologetic gesture. 'I really have to go. Silly to rely on winter sun. All gone. And my new friend is waiting, lives just up there!'

I am left on the decking, with the view of the emptying beach. That one singular glimpse of mildness is vanished, as if it was never real.

Picking up my phone, I send a message to Priya. I need more paranormal expertise. I need something. Anything. And I need it quick. But Christmas is coming, and everyone is busy, and we are hurtling towards the end. And we are all related.

Taking up our empty glasses, I retreat into the warmth of the airy café. And now I spy the owner, Ed Hartley, standing at the till chatting flirtatiously with a waitress. Maybe not gay then?

This is a chance.

I go up to Ed. He turns and smiles, but it is slightly forced: he'd rather be chatting up the waitress. Fair enough.

'Ed, sorry, do you have a moment?'

'For you? No.'

I stare at him.

He laughs, 'Jeez. It's a joke. What is it, Karenza?'

He leaves the till and his flirting and comes round the bar to be nearer me. I say, 'I want to know more about Miles Tyack. You said you know him. You said he was *volatile*.'

The smiley Ed is not smiling now. He shakes his head, with real sadness. 'Those poor children. That sad little girl. How is she, little Grace?'

'Not great.'

'Ach.'

'So, please. Help me, help the kids. *Why* do you think Miles is volatile?'

Ed exhales, and lifts his hands in a prayer, as if he can save us all, with his signet ring as a talisman. Or maybe to ward off my questions.

'I don't want to get involved, it's not my business.'

'Those kids!'

He meets my gaze, and at last nods.

'OK. OK. But *please* be discreet . . .'

'I will.'

'Have you ever noticed that Miles acts kinda guiltily?'

'Yes.'

'And also that he won't stay at the house? Don't you think that's rather weird?'

'He says it's because it's haunted.'

Ed offers a wry smile. 'Well. Maybe he's haunted by what he did. Think of it *that* way.'

A young female voice interrupts. 'Ed! Need help with the stock!'

He makes an apologetic gesture. I thank him and I zip my coat and go to the glass door.

As I exit to the road I hear a ping. It's a message.

From Dad, as if he's been listening in to this conversation with the Kittiwake owner, about the Tyacks.

Darling. You know who I didn't like in that family? The mother. Cruel and nasty. If something is wrong with them, maybe look there.

I almost yelp with frustration. This infernal mystery. My God! It is like the Cornish weather: one moment the clouds part and it all seems clear, and I can see the horizon, the ending, an actual solution. Then the clouds gather again, the drizzle falls, the mist rolls over, and I am as lost as ever.

And haunted like a Tyack. Because I am a Tyack.

42

My car is stacked with modest presents. I make the final turning into the muddy Baldhu Lane, where I see several other cars – rusted, rich, shiny, old – parked around the barns. Presumably the wider family or neighbours gathering. Molly, Miles, Malcolm. Others?

The recollection of that girl's voice stings, intrusively, as I turn the key to old Baldhu House.

Mummy. Help me.

Was I hearing myself, throwing a tantrum at Baldhu aged six? Can hauntings be explained as buried memories? I'd like to believe so, but how can that possibly explain all the other disturbances at Baldhu? It cannot.

Clearing my mind, I step into the sad, fragrant, gloomy old hall.

There is noise in the house.

And then I calm myself. It is just normal noises and normal voices. There are people drinking in the kitchen, a number of adults – Miles, Molly, multiple other family members I don't know, introduced as young cousins. They look like rich cousins. Then there are neighbours, Tricia, others.

The kitchen has pleasant Christmassy scents of mulled wine. Plates of blinis, smoked salmon, mince pies. Solomon and Grace come and go, playing some game, running between the grown-ups. It could almost be a normal happy scene of an affluent old Cornish family, on Christmas Eve, with no ghosts in the cellar and no suicides in a well. Or dead mothers on a beach. Mothers potentially murdered by someone in this kitchen.

Faces greet me, pleasantly enough, but Miles comes over and takes me by the arm. 'You're just in time. We're reviving a family tradition. Carols at St Levan.'

'The church?'

He steers me away from the drinking, chattering, canapé-eating people. 'Yes, the one down the coast. Rather lovely service. Natalie used to adore it, all the romantic candles – we . . . skipped it last year. She is buried there.'

I look at him, trying to hide my persistent suspicions of him.

'Miles!'

He turns. His sister is tapping her expensive watch. Miles nods my way, smiling, always smiling. 'We'd better go, service is in twenty minutes, we all need cars—'

I have already smelled the cinnamon-and-clovey mulled wine on Miles's breath. And probably some plentiful cognac. 'Let's take my car then.'

He gives me a slurred smile. 'Sensible woman. I'll do directions.'

Swiftly, the whole crowd decants from the house. Molly brings the kids, and we slide into various cars. The convoy parades down the lane, observed by damp brown cows. As we proceed, I get a sense of the family's importance, however faded now, and however parochial. Still quite something and, once, something quite profound.

The Tyacks of Baldhu are Going to Church.

As promised, Miles guides me down the narrow thorny roads, *go left, don't go left, go left, not that one, don't hit the standing stone, it's probably a warlock turned to granite,* then we all pull up in the narrow yard in front of a lyrically ancient Cornish church. It is tucked up tight in its moist green valley, with its weathered little tower, peering down the combe to the green-grey insurrection of the sea, forever battering the rocks.

Like a riot at the end of a boulevard that somehow never ends.

'Forgot how lovely it is, this church. Not sure I've ever been in. Don't really do churches, or religion, or . . . Weird beliefs.'

'Hah,' Miles chuckles. 'But, yeah, it is lovely, right? It's so old it was *rebuilt* in the twelfth century. And there's a seventh-century holy well down on the beach. And a Dark Age chapel. St Levan himself laid the stones.' Another chuckle. 'He's probably still in there, trowelling away. Maybe Natalie can hear him from her grave: it's over there.'

He notices my grimace, and grimaces in return.

'I'm sorry, there's so much *history*. And all these wells. All that water to drown in.' Now he glances at the Christmas Eve sky, which is bruised near to blackness with rain-bearing clouds. 'Especially this winter. Come on, let's get inside.'

Miles escorts me, making me feel faintly like a bride of a murderous husband. I hear in my head, once again, Ed Hartley's reluctant accusation of Miles. But not for long. As we step inside I gasp, quietly: the interior of the church is as exquisite as the location. I can see why Natalie loved it.

The church is dreamy, arcaded, medieval, shadowy, fragrantly infused with the prayers of centuries, and today it is decked with Jesus-is-born greenery, and lit with the flickery golden light of candles. It is also full of a hushed congregation, who all join in the carols as one, apart from Miles, who absolutely insists – uniquely – on singing 'Silent Night' in the original German. In between urgent sucks on his hip flask, like he is a hungry baby at the teat.

Stille Nacht, Heilige Nacht.

As the service comes to a darkened, Christmassy conclusion, the lights are dimmed so that only the candles illuminate the upturned faces of the worshippers, and only candlelight sends gently dancing shadows on the painted walls of the Celtic saints. I glance across the aisle at Solomon and Grace, who are standing between Malcolm and Molly, singing 'In the Bleak Midwinter', angelically, harmoniously, the image of blessed innocent kids of a lost Christian past, and so at odds with everything I have learned. Not a twitch from Solomon as he sings,

Snow had fallen, snow on snow,
Snow on snow,
In the bleak midwinter,
Long ago.

I cannot help it. This was one of Minnie's favourite carols as well. The shifting gold-jewel candlelight, the steepening winter dark outside, the beautiful twelfth-century stones, the sea that toils all alone and unloved, by the holy well on the cliff . . .

The tears for Minnie are falling down my face. I sleeve them away with my jumper. Miles looks across, as we all exit the church. He gives me a quick hug, as I gulp back the emotion. And as I command myself, I wonder: if this is what this lovely church service does to me, what is it doing to the family? Natalie's motherless kids?

And my opinion of Miles shifts every minute.

And yet Solly and Grace and everyone else seem perfectly calm as they climb in their cars, as the Tyack Clan makes its way across rainy Penwith, past the wild cairns of grey splintered granite, solemnly blackened by the wet.

I chide myself for my daydreams: I still have a job to do. And I have Miles to consider. As we steer between the stone hedges, he is texting on his phone, but I don't care; it gives me a moment to think, hard. Because time is draining. The police are corrupt. The Coppingers, wherever they are, are implicated, and linked to the police. And I am working out the puzzle, as fast as I can, even as danger surrounds.

'Miles, did Natalie have affairs? Was she unfaithful?'

For once, he is silent. I gaze across the car. He isn't just silent. He looks angry, he flashes me a glance I have not seen before. Aggressive. Wild.

'Do we have to go through this on Christmas fucking Eve? We've already got enough ghosts to deal with.'

I hesitate. I recall he is *really* quite drunk. I go on, 'I'm still trying to help.'

He glares again. 'Does this help though? Yes, she liked men. What the fuck does it matter? No marriage is perfect.'

'Where? With who?'

'I don't know!' He is actually shouting. 'Early on maybe – or maybe not. Some twat in Penzance, Truro, wherever. Goonhilly. Mevagissey. But *everyone* says this inane shit. And it absolutely might not be true.'

'Why not?'

'Because,' his voice is heavy, threatening, 'you don't know what she went through. And if you want to help the kids, this is not the road to go down. You'll drive straight into the fucking sea. Right over a cliff.'

He is now glaring ahead.

'You missed the turning.'

Abruptly, it dawns that he is not being metaphorical. I have actually missed the turning. Miles falls sullenly silent as I back up. And as I steer at last down the correct lane, which brings us closer to Baldhu, I understand *one* reason why he is in this lurid mood. I can see it in the way he stares ahead like a transfixed child: at the twilit heathland and the silhouetted cairns, the land of buried metal, buried water, buried memories. It is because he is genuinely terrified. It is not some fake game to cover for his guilty avoidance of the place.

He sincerely hates staying at Baldhu. Yet sometimes he *has* to visit, at 'funerals, birthdays, Christmas'. And now he is here. For Christmas. At Baldhu. What must be his annual nightmare. No wonder he is even drunker than ever: he is fortifying himself for what is to come.

And now we are all here. Baldhu. All parking up, stepping out and running under raised coats into shelter. Miles leaps from my car, sprinting to the house, and as he departs I notice he has left his phone on the car seat, forgotten it in his drunken hurry and fear.

It lies there, glinting metallically, like the hand mirror that shows you your death.

I cannot resist. It is breaking every social rule, but I lean and look and flick to quickly see what I can. Almost instantly, I see a list of recently called numbers and as I hastily scroll down, I spy one name. It is in capitals.

COPPINGER.

Miles knows a COPPINGER. And he is calling regularly. I want to press further and find the number, but the car door opens, and there's Miles, staring at me, holding his phone. He looks intensely alarmed.

I give him a big fat lying smile.

'You forgot your phone. I was going to bring it!'

He stares, and glares at me, then snatches the phone and runs back towards the house.

I gaze at Baldhu and Baldhu gazes back. The big old house has an air of ancient shock, its arched windows like raised eyebrows, surprised that we are all foolish enough to return to this fated place.

43

Christmas Eve at Baldhu House has, I discover, a serious kind of jollity in the encroaching dark. Sizeably crackling fires have been lit, even in rooms which are generally unused. Real live music is played by cousins with guitars, penny whistles, fiddles. Definitely not Death Metal. Elaborate games of hide and seek are ritually enacted for the children. Although the cellar, as Malcolm tells everyone, is entirely out of bounds.

But there are plenty of other rooms and attics and fat Victorian wardrobes to conceal a delightedly screaming seven-year-old. And they scream a lot, scampering up the stairs, toppling over medieval furniture, frightening away any ghosts.

Solomon has a quartet of friends over. They are as boisterous as him and they run around laughing almost as loudly as the many adults in the kitchen, who are once again attacking the creamy blinis and the devils on horseback and the endless silver platters of Helford native oysters.

Malcolm is getting drunk. Everyone is getting drunk. Getting drunk in Baldhu, I comprehend – not for the first time – means that you are generally stuck, unless you are prepared to jump in your car and beetle down an entirely lightless lane in the cloudy night and probably drive off the cliff at Percella Point. Alternatively, you could hike confidently across the heaths and moors and fall down a hoary old copper mine dug by the Phoenicians in 1500 BC.

'You all right?'

Malcolm is leaning close. Swaying by the kitchen door. But maybe it is me swaying. Too much booze already. My tongue is loosened. I have an urge to tell him my story, my dad's story: I am one of you, I am a Tyack, I am your cousin.

I actually start to tell him, 'My dad told me this story, it's so weird . . .' But then I have the good sense to pull up short. To veer away. Why should I reveal information? That's not the dynamic I want. And so I tell him one of Dad's mad conspiracy theories, instead of what I am really thinking: I am one of you, we are all family, I am even haunted like you.

I am also drunkenly and giddily thinking *I have a family again.* A big, rich, extended fascinating family, with drunks and bitchy sisters and musical cousins and ancient stories. This means I am no longer alone at Christmas, and I need not ever be alone again. I have nephews and nieces and everything, and even if the family comes with the dire curses of ten centuries, it is better than sitting alone in my flat with a cat and a lizard, until one day I die out and my pets die with me. And are mummified.

And Malcolm, as it happens, is sort of attractive without being handsome, and definitely masculine: that red beard, green eyes, big shoulders. And single. A bit like Jago . . .

No.

'Anyway, anyway, yes, I'm OK,' I say to Malcolm, who is almost leaning *over* me. 'Maybe a tiny bit too much wine, for now? Think I'll slow down. Have a walk, take the air.'

'Don't go too far!'

I step out of the noisy kitchen and ignore the noisy drawing room. And the thuds of the children upstairs. Hide and seeking. Making so many thuds. Like someone is up there and it isn't just the kids. Not just Solomon and Grace and the rest.

For the first time today, the unnerving creepiness of Baldhu returns, thud thump thud. *Mummy. Help me. I'm scared of the water.* Nope. I steady my dizzy self in the murk of the hall; the cellar door is firmly locked, no one can come up.

'I wonder if there is anyone still down there. In the cellar.'

'What?'

I'm startled: like I've touched electric wire.

But it is just Grace. In her dark dress, dark hair, pale skin, and standing all alone in the hall. Lost in its shadows.

'Grace! What are you doing out here?'

Grace gives me a shy, sad smile. 'Why shouldn't I be here?'

'I just – thought – you'd be playing hide and seek? Like everyone else.'

The whooping delight of the kids upstairs underlines the point. And also the slightly overloud thumps. That don't make sense.

Grace says, 'Oh, they're not my friends, they're Solomon's friends. They didn't ask me to play.'

The loneliness of the girl scrapes at my heart. I reach out a hand, almost cup the girl's cheek. 'Oh, darling, I'm sure they wouldn't mind.'

'It's OK,' she says, though something in her trembling lips says it is not OK, not today, not on Christmas Eve. 'I don't mind not having friends.'

'Grace—'

'Because I believe in parallel universes. Don't you?'

'Sorry?'

'Somewhere out there is a parallel universe, and that's where I will have a friend. Just one or two. But not here, there's no friends for me here.' She flashes a brave smile at me. 'I think I am too strange for friends, but I don't mind being alone. Not really. Not so much, I suppose.'

I consider myself. My own loneliness. 'Well, my God, Happy Christmas, Grace. I'm right here, and *I'm* your friend.'

Grace looks at me. 'You are?'

'Definitely. Girls together.'

Grace's mouth trembles momentarily again, showing her suppressed emotions. And then she leans forward once more, and this girl, this cerebral, lovely, lonely, scholarly girl who absolutely hates being touched, actually kisses me, just the slightest kiss on the cheek, and says, 'Happy Christmas, Karenza. I'm going to go and read now, where Mummy read, before things start happening.' She offers me a warning glance, but it is not unfriendly, it is maybe grateful for my company. 'They always happen at night and in the rain and in the winter. You'll see.'

I watch her go. The gloom soon engulfs her, and then me. That locked cellar door. The murky yellow light. Eliza Tyack and her twins.

Suddenly I'm desperate for freshness and a clearer head and no people, desperate to be back in my flat with Otto and El Gruffalo, to be in friendly Falmouth, with its shops and pubs and students. I can't do that, so I make for the front door and step outside, zipping my coat. The rain has disappeared. For now. The sky is momentarily clear and a billion stars and a shiny half-moon stare down on Baldhu, on Christmas Eve, and the noisy people inside, and the uncapped mine at the back of the garden.

For an hour, maybe two hours, I sit on a starlit bench in the chilly garden by the path that leads to the Zawn, listening to my own music. It is special soothing music. 'Peace Piece'. By Bill Evans. It is my sad, sobering music. I am frightened to go inside, but the cool night wind is good. The faint mineral scent of the nearby sea is like a balm, a veil of calm on my face. Peace piece.

My mind is clearer. I wonder if I should even go back inside, maybe I should simply quit. I remember Priya's warning that hauntings can end in death, telling me to stay away. Stay in *Falmouth*.

I think of Priya Hardwicke of Falmouth Uni, where everyone gossips about the Tyacks. I think about that lunch we had, in the Oyster Shack. And now, urgently, I think about all the people who have been to the Oyster Shack . . .

And, abruptly, it clicks together, with a satisfying snap.

I am a gladdened child solving a Christmas puzzle, out of a cracker, smiling to herself.

Falmouth University and the Oyster Shack.

Yes. Yes, yes!

Whipping out my phone, I examine the last evidence from Malcolm's suspicious and stalky file on his wife. Those bank statements. These are my latest trigger object: and my memory, my learned and necessary memory, my neurodivergent memory for symbols, faces, things, conversations, is so *good*.

Here. The Oyster Shack. The seafood restaurant right next to my flat.

Natalie was there *once*. And the payment comes at the same time as a payment to Exeter University. Which has made no sense to me, until now. Because at last I see the underlying logic.

On top of the Oyster Shack, there are also two payments to the Morgat, a little French café, very near Falmouth Uni's arty campus. One payment from five years ago, and one other payment at the Morgat – just before she died.

Falmouth: Exeter.

The sums spent are small, yet the Oyster Shack is quite pricey. It's as if Natalie was adding to a larger bill, being polite, buying a glass or two of wine. Coffees. Or a tip. As if someone else, someone richer, older, covered the bulk of the bills.

Falmouth: Exeter. How could Natalie Skuse have driven from Baldhu to Falmouth to Exeter and back? And then paid a small sum towards a nice seafood lunch? That is hours and hours of driving, at peculiar times. It makes no sense.

Unless of course the day when Natalie Skuse made that payment to Exeter University, it wasn't to Exeter University; it was surely to Falmouth University, but – as Dinah complained at the Kittiwake, 'It's so frustrating having to ask for everything from Exeter.' Technically Falmouth is financially and bureaucratically subsidiary to Exeter: as if Cornwall isn't yet trusted to have a university entirely of its own.

So Natalie Tyack was probably *really* paying Falmouth Uni. For what?

I can guess. I feel as if I already know. But I check the date, five years ago, when Natalie had that lunch at the Oyster Shack. Yes. Here it is. On the same day: a morning lecture in the Trevithick Room, Falmouth University. 'Ghosts and Ghosting: a Cornish Experience' – a lecture by Noel Oswell.

And the second time: another payment to Exeter Uni, the third of July, and yes, the very same day, another lecture. 'Paranormal Cornwall', by Professor Noel Oswell. That lecture was in the early evening, and then – after that evening lecture – they surely had *dinner* at the much more discreet Morgat.

A lunch can perhaps be excused, but a second dinner with the same man? That is likely an *affair*.

Was Malcolm's paranoia warranted?

I address my next questions in my head to Natalie.

Why would you go to these lectures at Falmouth Uni in the first place?

Because you are a young mother and you are frightened by your own house, which you believe is haunted, your kids are acting so strange, so you go to the only local expert: a professor at the local university, who is actually giving public lectures on paranormality and Cornish history.

The perfect man, and fifteen quid a go.

You are beautiful, lonely and scared. You like older men. He is wise and friendly; paternal, even. After the event you go up to him, he invites you for lunch and you discuss the haunting at Baldhu. You maybe flirt. And then you go to another lecture, and this time you do more than flirt. You have sex. And you maybe have sex again, several times?

'Jesus,' I swear, aloud. 'Noel bloody Oswell.'

I think I have a villain: I maybe have my murderer. He may even be Grace's father? Grace is ten years old, her mother's marriage to Malcolm is exactly the same age, so Grace was born around the wedding, and conceived nine months before. Did Natalie Skuse encounter Noel Oswell before Malcolm? Was her affair later a return to an old flame?

If Natalie was about to expose this affair, and maybe even Grace's true paternity, at that final lunch at the Morgat, shortly before she died – that would give him a motive for murder.

But how does he link to the Coppingers?

It doesn't matter immediately. I have him. Noel Oswell. He has a wife and family, he wouldn't want that shattered. He is a local figure of some renown.

It's him, I am certain of it. And now I have him in my sights, right in my target, I can hear his voice, boozily lecturing us at the Kittiwake. Spitting flakes of canapé, pompous and greedy, like a nasty form of Otto, consuming the powdery moths.

They have quite a history, the Tyacks, of Baldhu. Rumoured to be wreckers, in the seventeenth and eighteenth centuries. Even up to the nineteenth. Along with the Killigrews and the Coppingers – the cruel Coppingers . . .

He surely knew about Natalie's mirror, all along. She probably showed him.

44

Now I am more sober and lucid – and quite exultant about my sleuthing. I go back into the house, and I am surprised to find it is mostly quiet.

The party is definitely over. The fires have died down; cousins have departed. The core of the family is gathered in the kitchen. The core of *my* family: Miles, Malcolm, Molly, Solly and Grace. Sam lingers, too, but it looks as if he is about to go.

They are sitting on chairs at the kitchen island, Miles raises a glass of something alcoholic as I appear at the door.

'There she is, Dr Freud. We all thought you'd gone for some ill-fated walk.'

'I just needed a breather. Sorry. I'm not used to big family crowds, not any more anyway.'

Malcolm gives me a sympathetic smile. Molly says, with unusual warmth, 'Take a chair.'

'Thank you.'

'We're discussing tomorrow, how to ship Mum here from Penzance. Always quite a task.'

I sit down with my distant and extended family. I let them chat, content to be quiet yet part of everything. Sam is staying for a few more minutes, or so he says. Only Miles is still drinking. Everyone else is on tea and juice. Dishes have been cleared. An excellent plate of cheese and crackers decorates the table, but no one eats.

It all feels normal again. Until I notice Solomon.

He is twisting his face, detecting something.

It is the same unnerving face that sees birds, or his mother. Now I catch Miles's eye, and we both look at Solomon.

Solly is staring rigidly at the kitchen window now. Why? The rain has renewed, but it is just drizzle. A faint Christmas Eve soaking. The moon has come out from the clouds, there is some light out there.

'Darkshape,' says Solomon.

Whatever this word really implies – this family term – it freezes them all. I look around the kitchen. Everyone is staring, either at Solomon, or they are echoing Solomon's gaze, and staring at the kitchen window.

And now I can see it. And the blood in my veins is alchemically transformed to some freezing liquid.

Darkshape.

It is much worse than the figure I saw on my first visit here. It is like the silhouette of a woman, yet deformed, somehow hard to size, walking towards the window, very slowly. The darkness of the silhouette is a terrible blackness, sucking the light out of the night. And yet with sentience, and purpose.

Darkshape approaches. As she approaches the window I realize with horror that it really is just a *shape*. The shape of a sort of woman – but with a boneless, unnatural quality. There are no features, no face, there is less than nothing: like someone made a human-like void, in the moonlit world.

Eliza Tyack.

And now darkshape presses close to the window as if with her eyeless and featureless lack of a face she can see inside the bright modern kitchen, as if she wants to come in, as if she angrily has to come in, or maybe she does not believe the window exists and she cannot understand why she is stopped, like that *creature* in the cellar.

Darkshape is a faceless entity pressed hard against the window and pushing pushing pushing and trying to break the window to get in with her featureless shadows, and now darkshape bangs on the window – bang bang *bang bang* – and the window begins to ice, to frost, to turn quite white from some intense cold. It must surely crack any moment and then darkshape will be inside and the idea of this makes me want to scream; but Molly gets there first. She lets out a piercing shriek and Miles has a hand over his eyes, and now Malcolm shouts, 'Enough, Solomon, everyone, stop it!'

Darkshape is turning her sort of head, this way and that, arched and reptilian, as if she can see but she cannot see, and then she slides towards the back door, and Molly screams again, and Malcolm stands and turns *off* the kitchen lights and he grabs at his phone and switches on the torch, and turns it on the window and – there is nothing there, and then he opens the back door and there is nothing there, either.

Just the spitting of the rain in the silvery moon. No darkshape. No woman. No frosted window. No Eliza Tyack carrying her doomed little twins. No smeared non-face pressed to the window, or forcing the door open, trying to get at us. Nothing.

The silence is unreal. It is not silence.

I have never experienced shared terror before: not at this level. Maybe as a child watching a horror film too old for me. But this is far beyond that. The weird silence stifles the darkened kitchen. Almost everyone looks horrified. Maybe Sam looks more resolute than most, determined not to be scared. Did he even see anything?

Miles stands and turns on the kitchen light again. Everyone stares at everyone. Miles returns to the table, and he fills his glass from a wine bottle. Molly, with a trembling hand, shows her glass to Miles, and he refreshes it, liberally. Solomon is quietly crying. Malcolm stands and takes his son and picks him up and says, 'You've had a long day, it's time for bed, lad.' As if the boy is simply exhausted from too much football.

Miles offers me, likewise, a glass of wine. With equally shaking hands, I eagerly accept the offer. Deep red wine. It will be the only way to get through this.

As I sip, I realize the calmest person in the kitchen is little Grace, who seems entirely unfazed.

Now Grace leans close to me; she cups a hand so she can whisper in my ear. 'You see? It happens at night. That's when it *really* gets bad. This is just the beginning.'

45

At about 10 p.m. I creep upstairs into my bedroom and my bed, *my bed*, still half drunk, still recovering from that terror, and resolving not to drink so much tomorrow. I pop two sleeping pills because I have never so much wanted to be firmly unconscious for nine hours in my whole life.

Up to a point, it works.

I am so heavily sedated I only wake two or three times in the night, and it is not really waking, it is like half surfacing from the water with a snorkel mask still on. Everything is bleary; I vaguely sense things in the house, the noises, and thuds, the inexplicable thumps of things that maybe aren't people.

But the gravity of the sleeping pills does the job and drags me back down underwater, into sweaty sleep, down to the corals and the fish of my vague smearing dreams of tiny yachts and grinning foxes and a kiss with a man in a field with a beard and then it is Malcolm with a cat like El Gruffalo in his muscled arms. And Kyle crying in a mad animal café in Falmouth, and then it is my own mother in Devoran, before she died, dancing too fast with Minnie on the riverbank making me want to cry at the moment I wake up. Christmas Day.

Sad dreams.

I have had sad dreams, but they are probably better

than ghosts. After so much sleep I feel clearer, improved. I climb out of bed and draw the curtain to a grey but dry Christmas Day and I decide: today I will be professional, and *forensic*. Today I will not be a Tyack, I won't drink, I won't be scared by ghosts, I will merely observe, take notes, do my job, be as calm as Grace.

How does Noel link to the Coppingers, the crest, the Coppinger mirror? That is the bit I do not understand. Could Oswell be a Coppinger, after a name change? Or some kind of cousin?

And now I think about how to tackle Noel Oswell, when I cannot trust the police.

Brain buzzing, I shower, dress, descend.

Downstairs, Miles is already handing out the Christmas morning drinks in the drawing room by the roaring Yule fire – *the very best English fizz, darling, Gisborne Reserve* – to Molly and Malc and the neighbours and a couple more stray cousins, but I resist. I say Happy Christmas, and everyone says Happy Christmas, and a quick carol or two is laughingly sung, and it's as if everyone has forgotten or decided not to ever mention and therefore forget darkshape last night.

And that, I reckon, is one of the most sensible reactions I have encountered in my entire career of forensic psychology. I am beginning to understand that hauntings are psychological reality; I just can't explain them rationally – yet. But I will, I *will* solve the entire phenomenon of hauntings by Twelfth Night – I am good at this stuff.

At the same time I've begun to understand that the one way you probably get through hauntings is by accepting them. It is probably the only way. They happen, you shrug, you drink, you endure. You try not to kill yourself or throw anyone over a cliff. Then they go away, and you carry on.

And once I have solved the supernatural mystery, I can solve the natural mystery. The true deep dark mystery of what happened to Natalie Skuse. Maybe, probably, the two mysteries are intertwined, like my blood with the Tyacks. The people who are genetically haunted in Baldhu. That is what and who we are. Not Sam, not Tricia. And maybe not Grace?

Just us Tyacks. With our inheritance of memories, just as my cat is terrified of dogs it has never met.

Stirring from my reverie, I realize there is discussion of The Mother arriving from Penzance. Apparently Tricia's boyfriend Darren has been to collect her, and she will be here any minute. Even as this discussion concludes, Molly raises a hand and we all go quiet and there is loudness outside, a big engine, a van.

'Mummy is here,' says Molly. 'Happy fucking Christmas.'

Everyone troops outside and I see Darren pushing a gaunt and disapproving old woman in a wheelchair: Davina Tyack. Really quite old, scowling, with a scribble of absurd Christmas Day lipstick on her wizened face, and a chiffon scarf around her neck.

Davina glares shrewishly at me and says, 'Doesn't look anything like Natalie. She's much bigger.'

Miles gives me a shrugging glance, as if to say: *Yes, this is what she is like.*

Darren leans close to Davina, and says, loudly, 'All right, Mrs Tyack, we're going to take you inside, into Baldhu, for a lovely Christmas dinner.'

Davina scowls. 'If you must. This awful place. Look at it, such a dreadful heap.' She scowls directly at me, then at Darren. 'I'm not going to tip you, you're just servants, it's your job, Donald.'

Darren sighs. 'Happy Christmas, Davina.'

He looks as if he wants to thump Davina, but instead he pushes her towards the house and then Malcolm and Miles take over, pushing their mother in her wheelchair up over the threshold, into Baldhu, and everyone follows, like the courtiers of some evil disabled queen.

From this point I decide, even more than before, to abandon myself to whatever it is the Tyacks do on Christmas Day. I will float along: I will assist and observe. Inside the house I help Molly and Tricia serve Christmas nibbles, then the full Christmas dinner. Roast goose and Gran Reserva Rioja.

As we all eat, Davina asks the same mad questions at least seven times, going around the table one by one: *Where is Miles's wife? Is Natalie coming? Did I forget something about Natalie? Who are you? What is the point of you being here? What happened to that awful man from before? Did you find her birth certificate? Where is that rancid slut with the mirror?*

Sometimes I answer, blankly and flatly, as seems right, because this is what everyone else does. This is apparently how the family tolerates this cruel, demented mother and her rude, demented queries: with weary grace. Most of the time.

Every so often there is a thudding noise upstairs, or a running thump of someone coming down, even though everyone is in the dining room, and yet everyone ignores this, though nearly everyone flinches: except Davina, who scowls fiercely at me and says, 'Well, you're not even as *pretty* as that little trollop, from the Coppinger home, and you're obviously overweight – what's the point?'

I gaze at her. So she knows, in her delusions, that the Coppingers owned that place. It is the kind of oddly lucid fact that sometimes emerges in dementia. I flick a glance at Miles, to see how he reacts.

He is po-faced, and yet I also see a flush of something. A deeply concealed anxiety, and sadness.

The awful dinner continues. The only time I feel a desperate urge to intervene, to be the Tyack I apparently am, to get involved in this sad charade of happy family life and Christmas dinner, is when the goose is done, and the main course is cleared, and the fabulous plum pudding has arrived. It sits proudly in the middle of the table and Davina starts pointing at Grace and saying, 'Who is that *stupid* child?'

Then, 'Who is she? Who is this nasty girl, why is she so ugly?'

And, 'She's got nothing to say, Malcolm. You shouldn't let these common children into the house. She's nothing like Solomon. Solomon is my boy, you should be proud of him, not this pitiful mute.'

And again, 'Make that ghastly girl go away. She's obviously quite perfectly retarded. *Ugh*.'

Grace sits there, composed, calm and resilient, but I can see this is hurting her. That trembling mouth again. Grace is close to crying. Who wouldn't be close to crying, aged ten, hearing this disgusting abuse?

My anger is rising – my desire to defend Grace – and I am about to burst, but it turns out I do not have to intervene. Because first Solomon starts yelling at his granny, then he runs over and he hugs his sister, and then Davina Tyack says, again, pointing a trembling, wrinkled finger at Grace, 'Make her eat in the cellar. Daughter of that whore.'

And this time Malcolm stands up and says, 'Right, that's it. Happy Christmas, Mum, you tragic old bitch.'

Davina chokes, a little.

Malcolm goes on, loudly, 'We've all had a lovely time

and Darren's gonna take you home now. So you can be all by yourself for another year.'

Swallowing her food, Davina protests, 'But I haven't had pudding, Malcolm! Don't be ridiculous, you stupid boy. You were always so *stupid*. Molly, tell him! I want my *pudding*.'

Malcolm looks as if he is about to murder his own mother, but now Molly intervenes. She takes a spoon and scoops a big spoonful of the Christmas pudding and walks around the table and yanks open her mother's shocked mouth and rams the pudding into it, actually forcing the food between her mother's lips with her fingers. Davina is spluttering, gasping. Coughing up bits of pudding.

'There,' says Molly. 'Now you've had your lovely share of pudding, and you can go shit on your commode, you old crone.'

Malcolm says, 'Bye-bye, Mummy. Happy Christmas, see you next year.'

Desperately coughing up more raisins, Davina is brusquely wheeled out of the dining room by Darren and Sam, and then the entire table breaks into applause. As Darren's van speeds down the lane everyone apart from me – I am entirely bemused – everyone lifts their glasses and says, 'Thank God. Happy Christmas!'

Malcolm stares at me, realizing I am astonished. He says, 'Sorry if that shocked you.'

'No, it's just – ah – I mean—'

'What you need to understand,' he says, 'is that she was exactly like that *before* she became demented.'

Miles adds, 'If anything, she has *mellowed*. Must be the happy pills.'

Molly snorts with laughter, everyone snorts with laughter. And after that it is all somehow OK, and I sit here bewildered but also relieved. Maybe ghosts are easier than ghastly mothers?

I allow myself a tiny drink, still *observing*. Games are played, Grace and Solomon play with each other. Presents are affably exchanged. The afternoon turns into a torpid, overfed but contented evening and a few more adult games are enacted when the kids are in bed. And then I realize I have done it, I have actually done it, I have made it through one of the scariest Christmases ever, with my new extended family, and I stand and say, 'That was wonderful. Thank you, everyone. Especially . . .'

'After my mother went home?' says Miles, and again laughter cheers the room.

I murmur, 'She is certainly unique.'

And then I bid everyone goodnight and I leave the drawing room and cross the hall – where I ignore the repeated banging from inside the locked cellar door, where Eliza Tyack is obviously trapped – and instead go up the creaking stairs, carrying a big glass of Rioja as a sleeping draught, to my bed. There I tuck myself up and I decide: yes, I can do this. Bangs and black shapes? So what. *I will work out what this is*. I don't need sleeping pills, I am not scared. Human evil is scarier than dead humans. Davina Tyack is worse than darkshape.

I lie back, satisfied, a little tipsy. Sleepy. Confident. I am part of the Tyack family, in my family home. I have nearly solved every mystery; the last important pieces will soon be slotting into place. Noel Oswell, the Coppingers, the link through the kids' home. The pillow is soft and dreamy.

Sleep comes swift and profound . . .

Until I am woken in the depths of night – 3 a.m. – 4

a.m. – by a light. A strange, flickering but intense blue light. That then goes dark. At the bottom of my closed bedroom door.

What is that?

And then I hear the murmur of a childish voice, but it is not outside the door, it is somehow above me.

Mummy, I'm still here . . .

And then I hear a piercing scream: everywhere. And this truly terrifies me.

Because it is clearly my daughter.

46

I get up. I do not want to. I have to. Because the scream is not drunken, not laughter, it is the sound of someone in pain, or terror. Every five seconds, someone is screaming. Not words, more desperate wails. Icy and horrified.

And it is getting louder, and it sounds so much like Minnie.

Switching on the light, I prepare myself. To be empirical and scientific. I do not believe in ghosts; there is, simply, some as yet unexplained phenomenon occurring in Baldhu, and it has been occurring for many years, but it will be explained. Scientifically, psychologically, genetically.

If I can get over the horror of that scream.

I climb out of bed – and immediately gasp. My bare feet are in cold water. The room is scattered with frigid pools and lakelets of water. From where? I check the ceiling – there is no leak. There is no water running from the lovely bathroom. The water is simply here – like Eliza Tyack finally got out of the cellar, carrying her drowned and soaking twins, and came to see me, came right up close to the bed.

Mummy . . .

I slip a coat over my nightdress.

The screaming has begun again. It seems to be outside

the bedroom but not that far away. Presumably the whole house has heard it. Presumably the whole house will be running to the sound of the scream because it sounds as if someone is being tortured. And it could be one of the children.

Running to the door, I pull it open. The hallway is dark and empty: no one else is out here. I am alone, apparently unique in hearing this wretched girlish scream.

I slap on the light. The screaming spikes again, as if someone is being brutally stabbed. The landing is drenched in silvery trails of icy water. The screaming gets ever louder; I cannot tolerate this. The sound is now a continuous shriek, and with it comes a cool gust of air, like a wind is somehow blowing down the landing. It has the tang of the sea.

Where is everyone?

'Malcolm? Miles?'

No one answers. I shall not wait. The assailing shriek is so intense, I have to answer it: it really could be Grace. It sounds like a girl, and it is coming from a distant bedroom. The blue light I saw before is shining again, under another door at the far end of the landing.

The wind blows, and the scream sounds again. Every yard I walk it gets more insane, so loud now that it is painful.

Am I sleepwalking? Into the harbour?

I check myself. Literally: I look down at my arms and my legs. Check my surroundings. I am awake, and this is real.

The scream is peaking again, as if the torture, the anguish, is getting worse.

Walking fast towards the door the scream gets so profound that I cover my ears, because it hurts if I do not.

I am a few feet from the door. The blue flickering light dances around the doorframe. It is not a bedroom I know well. Not one that anyone sleeps in regularly. The screaming has now become more irregular, softer, yet more emotional. There are almost words in it. Perhaps words of pain, or apology.

'Mummy.'

I reach for the doorknob, preparing for my own lunacy. Yet resolved. Because I want to face the worst of this, because that might give me a scientific explanation. I might be terrified – yet in my terror I might find a solution.

But what if Minnie is really in here? Drowning? It might not be Eliza Tyack, it might be *Minnie*, my own daughter, drenched in the harbour water of St Mawes, walking the halls and bedrooms, then returning to this room, and ready to accuse her mother.

The screaming rises once more, and I open the door.

I stare at what I see, unable to comprehend.

It is Minnie.

My own dead and drowned daughter is floating in the room, about five feet above the rugless wooden floor. She is floating lengthwise to me: I can see all of her. Minnie is wearing yellow Primark pyjamas, the same pyjamas she was drowned in. She is suspended in the air in a horizontal position with her arms to either side in a crucifix shape, her head nearest the wall on the left and her bare feet pointing at the window on the right, and her bare feet are drooping as if off the edge of a bed.

My daughter's wide eyes are staring at the ceiling, and her long blonde hair falls vertically from her head. Her pyjamas and her hair are dripping cold water on to the floor. Her sweet face is tilted back so far it is as if her neck is broken and her mouth is wide open, terrified and shrieking, making that awful noise.

Screaming at the ceiling as if she can see something unbearable there. As if she has been levitated towards evil. And I wonder if I am witnessing the moment she died, she drowned, floating down on her back. It must have been terrifying and painful: there would have been no surge of peaceful neurotransmitters.

Minnie is moving slightly, as if alive, writhing, fighting something, but it is as if she is tied up, as if she has been physically suspended from the ceiling, or restricted in some other way.

I stare. The screaming is ebbing. Minnie's writhing subsides, and now the screams turn to moans, and here the lamenting noise turns to panting words.

'Daddy, Daddy, Daddy, Daddy . . . Oh Daddy . . .'

I stand rigid, and horrified, but determined to endure. This is a hallucination, yet this is also a real thing. It is both: it can be both, a dream can be real, reality can be a dream. The vision is not a ghost. It is not translucent, and it is not something in a silly bedsheet. This is a real girl, this really is Minnie, levitating in mid-air, five foot off the floor, with her face forced to stare at the ceiling, and I have seen enough, my willingness to endure is exhausted.

I cannot bear this. I am now the Merry Maiden, I am frozen in the stone of my terror. I want to cry but I am too sad, too horrified to cry.

I fall to the floor, sobbing at last, gulping, gasping, and I turn away, I crawl away – away away away. I lurch to the door and pull myself out of that room. I let the door swing shut behind me and I sprawl there for minutes, immobile, defeated, on the Turkish blanket on the scented polished floor of the old landing of Baldhu, in the Parish of St Buryan.

I am done, and yet I also feel Baldhu is done. The

flickering lights have gone. The tang of the sea is departed. I can smell old dust and beeswax: old Baldhu scents. Dragging myself to my feet, I stumble, like a wounded soldier without a comrade, down the landing to my bedroom. As I go, I see there is one door open. Miles's room. The light is on. I gaze in and see Miles sitting in the corner of his bedroom, trembling, his head sunk in his hands.

Everyone is being haunted in their own way. Baldhu is tormenting everyone. But – the realization of this punches me – it really is only people in the family who suffer. My scientific brain is coming to the rescue of my emotional brain, as she always does.

Miles *told me* the other day it is dynastic, a family curse; it only affects the Tyacks. Tricia, Sam, Davina, everyone else, they don't see it. They don't suffer. The *Tyacks* suffer. And now I am suffering. *Because I am part of the family*.

Calmer, calming, shaken, shaking, I retreat in bone-broken weariness into my room. I am thinking that a dream can be real, and reality can be a dream, and I remember that dream of Malcolm with a cat in his arms, a cat like El Gruffalo. I may not be a full-on *Freudian* psychologist, but I have read his immortal *The Interpretation of Dreams* and I know that dreams can be important. I clamber wearily into bed and take up my phone, and I begin to make notes.

Because I have the beginnings of a solution.

I have seen a ghost, and now I see the science. I don't want to go to sleep yet – I can't – so I will focus, through my red-rimmed eyes, on my notes.

I write it down, first slow, then fast. Very fast, my fingers trembling. Remembering that book I was reading on epigenetics.

I type it out as if I am explaining it to someone else, and that someone is the world.

It's called inherited trauma, and it is via a process called epigenetics. It means that terrible events can be handed down the generations, in our particular DNA or whatever, in a way we don't understand – terrible emotions, fear, dread, and so on. Even dangerous or extreme behaviour. Risk-taking, self-harming, suicidality.

There was a famous experiment done on mice. One generation of mice was electrocuted: tortured with shocks. As the mice were tortured they were simultaneously exposed to the scent of cherry blossom. So they strongly associated the smell of cherry blossom – a chemical called acetophenone – with pain and terror.

And so the mice then had baby mice and then those baby mice had more baby mice, three or four generations of mice, and when the scientists exposed the mice three generations down to the scent of cherry blossom, the mice exhibited fear, terror, horror, pain, like they were being electrocuted all over again. Yet they weren't. They had no personal memory of the scent, and they were never tortured. It was all waiting in their tiny mice brains. Inherited trauma.

It goes against everything we are taught, about Darwin, evolution, yet the experiments have been verified. The mice descendants had no reason to exhibit this terror, they had no personal experience, yet they were terrified, desperate to escape the aroma. Horror and pain can be inherited, especially if there is a trigger. The same way my cat El Gruffalo is terrified of tiny dogs, even though he has never been attacked by one. He has inherited the trauma of an attack from an ancestor.

The original trauma here is the drowning of Eliza Tyack and her twins. It is an inherited trauma that is epigenetic, so it only affects family members: Miles, Molly, Malcolm, their dad, not their awful mother – *she's not a Tyack. But Solomon, yes, and Grace – who knows? But obviously not Sam, or Tricia. But me? Yes, me: because I am, apparently, a Tyack.*

I stop typing.

I have my solution. But what is the *trigger*, what is invoking these fears at some times and not others?

I make my final note.

'What is the scent of cherry blossom in Baldhu?'

47

Boxing Day is apparently informal in Baldhu. Possibly because it is clear that nearly everyone in the house has been hideously haunted in some unique way overnight, and no one wants to talk about it.

The only person who talks is Malcolm, who tersely explains the Boxing Day deal when I edge into the kitchen.

'G'morning. There may be a family walk in the afternoon, we'll see. For now just come and go from the kitchen, eat leftovers from the fridge and grab a coffee . . .'

That suits me entirely. Fetching a plate of cold meats and a mug of coffee, I seek a quiet place. For an hour or two I work in the conservatory, with my laptop and phone, until I am satisfied I have the theory worked out. It is just missing one crucial piece.

'Hello?'

A sound.

Grace Tyack is standing at the door in jeans and a white hoodie. Bright-eyed and innocent – and friendly. She says, 'Happy after-Christmas, Karenza.'

'Happy after-Christmas, Grace.'

I am on the chaise longue where Grace usually reads. I feel a twinge of guilt, but Grace seems indifferent. She plonks herself down in an old armchair beside another pile of books, as the pale winter sun of the conservatory shines on her dark hair. Then she says, 'Apricity.'

I gaze at her. 'What?'

'It's a word that means the warmth of sunlight in winter. It's one of my favourites.'

I smile. 'Yes. That's a beautiful word.'

A silence surrounds us, a cocoon, even. Then she asks, 'Are we all going to die, Karenza?'

I look at her. It is hard to tell if she is mocking, or mock-serious, or entirely serious; I opt for neutrality. 'Not immediately, if I can help it.'

'That's good.' She muses. 'What are you doing now?'

She tilts her querying head at my laptop and notebook. This is quite a moment: what do I say? I decide that I may as well be honest. Grace and I seem to have developed an eccentric but precious alliance. And I have grown to like her, greatly. Time to bond even further.

'You know how this house is haunted, Grace?'

Grace yelps. 'Oh, my God, Baldhu is haunted?'

'Ah . . .'

'Yes, of course I know!' she smiles, sardonically. 'Karenza, I live here. I've seen my uncle Miles crying like a baby cos he's so scared.'

I nod encouragingly and go on, 'Well, I think I have worked out *why* and *how* it is haunted. And how it only affects some people.'

Grace, the scholastic girl of deep thoughts, the liker of the word *apricity*, the girl who wonders if we are all going to die very soon, nods in an inquisitive way and asks me to explain.

I take a breath and oblige. 'First you should know that I have a big fat cat. You must meet him one day.'

Grace grins. I go on, 'You'd like him. He's a character, eats too much, sometimes is a bit of a snob, but he means well. Anyway, the thing is . . . he has issues – like all of us.'

'I like him already!'

I smile at her. I can't tell her everything, but I can give her most of it. 'One of these issues is that he is scared of tiny dogs, and yet, weirdly, he has never had a fight or anything with a tiny dog. Isn't that strange?'

'Yes, it is.'

'But the other day I discovered why: it's because his *mother* was mauled by a tiny dog, even before Gruff was born, and he kind of inherited that.'

Grace frowns. 'So it was passed down? How?'

'It's called inherited trauma, and it's via a process called epigenetics. It means, basically, that terrible events can be handed down the generations.'

Grace nods, and I launch into it. For five minutes I give her the whole theory of inherited trauma, and the proof adduced, and the way I believe it applies to the Tyacks.

I am expecting Grace to be . . . what? Shocked? Confused? Disbelieving? But Grace seems untroubled. She sits there, chin cupped in two hands, and says, 'So, like, our great-great-grandma's scary stuff is in our blood? That's so weird. Cool, but weird.'

I can't help laughing. The sun seems brighter in the conservatory of quiet Baldhu. The *apricity*.

Grace asks, 'But this is only found in mice?'

I continue, 'No! Not just mice. Descendants of Holocaust survivors, survivors of war, starved prisoners, some families where there has been terrible abuse: there is evidence of inherited trauma there, too. It's all highly contentious. Some people think it's unproven, or nonsense – others think it's very real. We used to dismiss post-traumatic stress disorder in the same way, but now it's accepted.'

Grace sits back and meets my gaze. She says, 'You're talking about the well in the cellar, aren't you?'

Clever girl. I say, 'You know the story?'

'Yeah. I heard Miles and Molly talking about it. The suicide of Eliza Tyack, and her twins. Solly knows it too. So . . . in, like, *your* theory, Eliza Tyack is the original event, the horror, here in Baldhu?'

I am a little thrown. I had no idea Grace knew the whole story of Eliza Tyack. Yet she knew. She knows it all.

I say, 'Well, yes. Something like that.'

She frowns.

'But . . . why doesn't it happen *all* the time, Karenza? Why does it come and go? Why does it get so bad at certain times yet at other times everything is fine?'

I offer a shrug. 'That's the bit I can't work out. There must be a trigger here, specific to time and place maybe. But what is the trigger, the acetophenone, the scent of cherry blossom? What induces the visions?'

Grace looks beyond me, at the gardens beyond. 'I have an idea.'

I am partly excited, partly unbelieving, but this girl has insights way beyond her years. 'What? What's the trigger?'

Grace says, quietly, 'Could it be water? Heavy rains? Specially the heavy rains of autumn and winter? I mean, think about Uncle Miles. He always says it's worse in the rain and the dark. He really hates Christmas, and winter.'

The logic falls into place, in my mind, with another pang of physical pleasure. *Of course.* The original terror, the inciting trauma, happened during a time of heavy rain – the stream *engorged by winter rains* which swept away the body of Eliza Tyack, and maybe her babies.

Last autumn was also horribly wet, so bad that it caused a landslip to open up the mine at the back of the garden. Filling the mine almost to the brim. This year the rain is also heavy: the stream can be heard, rushing, at the bottom of the well. This is not common; I remember Miles mentioning this when they first opened up the well-shaft – 'all the heavy rain' they were having. .

Grace fills in my thoughts. 'And it's been really wet this year. It was really wet last year too.'

I interrupt: 'Do you remember the last time when it was this bad? Before last year, I mean?'

Grace frowns, thoughtful. 'Not really, but I kind of remember a time maybe . . . when Mummy got really depressed about four or five years ago. I remember her saying later it was maybe just the weather getting her down. I was tiny, though. Five or so. I can't be sure.'

I close my laptop triumphantly, saying, 'I can. That's it! That's our cherry blossom. The rains, the streams, the wells, the mines, the cascades of Bathsheba, the downpours of autumn and winter.'

'But it doesn't explain why my *mummy* is dead, though. She's not a Tyack. I mean, she wasn't, was she, Karenza? She wouldn't have had all these terrors or seen all the ghosts. She's not got the DNA thing so she couldn't have had the inherited epi-thingy.'

'Epigenetic inherited trauma. No.'

Grace nods and smiles, a little sadly. 'I'm going to miss the ghosts now you've explained them away.'

I pause, unsurely. And now Grace exclaims, 'Ah! I get it, they're *not* going away, are they, Karenza? Just because you've explained them doesn't mean they will stop.'

'No.'

'So we need it to stop raining forever, or the danger will get worse!'

I confess. 'Perhaps, yes. It could get worse. Alternatively, we could all leave Baldhu.'

She shakes her head, firmly.

'Daddy won't ever do that. This is our house for, like, eternity. And no one would buy it if they heard the real story, so we have to stay here with the ghosts.'

'I know.'

The two of us are quiet for a few moments. United. Silent. Thinking.

Then Grace says, 'Can I tell you something, because . . . I trust you now.'

I look at her. 'Of course.'

She takes a deep breath. 'On the night it – ah . . . the night . . .'

'The night Mummy died?'

'Yes.'

I offer as reassuring a smile as I can. 'Your dad says he found you in your room, all wet, like you'd been out, and you were saying you saw Mummy.'

Grace's face reveals a tiny twitch. But no more than that. She nods. 'He did.'

'So what *really* happened, Grace? You can tell me. We can work this out together. We worked out the ghosts, didn't we?'

Grace stares deep into my eyes. There are probably tears there, somewhere, but she will not let them fall.

'If I tell you,' Grace says, 'you promise you won't tell anyone else?'

'Promise.'

'All right.' She places her palms together, in her lap, as if she is getting ready to pray. 'That night, I – I woke up, and I heard Mummy downstairs, and she had been . . . sad for weeks, so upset, crazy even. She kept staring in that mirror all the time, like it was showing her something. And this night I was worried, and so I got dressed and I ran down and the door was open, and I saw her getting in her car. In the dark and the cold, and the rain. The rain!' Grace shakes her head, hesitates, eyes half downcast, then goes on. 'And I ran to the car, and I said, "What's wrong, Mummy, is it Daddy?" And, and . . .'

'And?'

Grace gulps. 'And Mummy hugged me, and she kept saying *It's not your fault, Grace, whatever happens, it's not your fault, I'm doing this for you. It's all for you. Whatever happens. It's not your fault.*'

Grace takes a deep, shuddering breath, suppressing the tears again.

'And then she said, *I have to go and meet someone, down by the falls, don't tell Daddy, don't ever tell anyone what you saw*, and she got in the car, and she drove away. And and and when she did there was someone else there watching.'

'Who?'

My heart slows and speeds. Is it Noel Oswell?

'Miles. Uncle Miles was watching. I don't think he saw me, but I saw him, and then he got in his car. And then I went upstairs. I never told anyone. I love Uncle Miles, he's funny. I love him.'

I gaze calmly across at her. So this explains the child's guilt. If your mother says *it's not your fault* and *I'm going to the falls* then very soon after she dies, and you somehow suspect your beloved uncle Miles, you would think: *it is somehow my fault*. And you would see, in your mind's eye, your mummy by the falls.

No wonder she has been so tormented.

Grace stares at me, seeking reassurance, and I smile back, as the warming winter sunlight, the apricity, disappears, and the sky clouds over. And then the first speckles of a new spate of rain gently rattle on the glass, becoming louder, as it hardens into a proper, drenching winter shower.

She says, 'You are really close to solving all this, aren't you? Just in time, maybe.'

'I hope so.'

'Congratulations, then. For being so forensic. But please hurry up before it gets *worse*.'

And then she laughs, mournfully, but soon she stops and stares at the rivulets of the rain now running madly down the glass. Like living things, scurrying to get to the ground, to soak into the earth, to engorge the streams that carried the bones of Eliza, and Daniel, and Lucinda, carrying them down Bathsheba Valley towards the waterfall of the primrose.

Grace gestures at the strengthening rain. 'Weather's turning again.'

48

The rain is so hard that the Official Tyack Boxing Day Walk is Officially Abandoned. I am in the garden, sheltering under a tree, with a sliver of signal, and I am phoning Dinah to get Noel's number. To give me options.

She answers, flustered, talks about her kids – it's Boxing Day! – but I insist.

'Dinah, please. This is crucial to the case, you can give me two minutes.'

'OK,' she laughs. 'You never stop working! Hold on a moment, it's not in this phone, new phone, but it's in my old one . . .'

I hear fumbling, as she searches. She returns.

'Here you go. Noel Oswell.' She reads the number out, then says, 'Oooh. Is he a suspect?'

I ignore her enquiry. I am thinking about her kids, I can hear them in the background. Something about the concept 'kids' makes me uneasy. It is probably because I don't see how Noel Oswell fits in with the Coppingers, and their ownership of the kids' home. I have so many pieces of the puzzle, probably all of them – all the carefully polished stones in the mosaic – but I have yet to fit them all together.

But I can feel my brain whirring: processing data at speed. I was so good at pattern matching and puzzle solving at school, even if I could not instinctively read emotions in faces and had to laboriously learn the craft. Perhaps that was nature's way of repaying me for neurodivergence.

So what is the pattern here?

Miles still lurks at the corner – or the centre – of the crime. He witnessed Natalie on her last night, yet he certainly never told the police, he kept that quiet; he was essentially inert. Why?

Miles is plainly involved in some way. I now have two people clearly implicated, Noel and Miles: yet I cannot tell the police, I cannot trust them. What else is there to do? Where do I go? Lost in this arthritic Penwith woodland, of ghosts and clues and murders?

I remember a poem my mum liked; she loved poetry, I never have. But she read a lot of it, and she loved a poet called Robert Frost, and she would always quote one line to me, when I was a troubled kid. *The best way out is always through*.

It always worked: that line always consoled me. So maybe my best way out is through. It is *straight ahead*. Attack the problem, call Noel Oswell, use that option. And surprise him with the truth. And record the call, seize all the evidence.

My fingers are not trembling, I am calm and determined as I key his number. And press Record, as I do.

He answers immediately, as if he knows this is urgent, almost as if he knows he is about to be interrogated and he cannot object.

'Noel.'

'Karenza Bray?'

'Yes.'

'This is a surprise, Happy Chris—'

I can hear Christmassy family noises in the background.

'Please. Shut up. I have questions.'

'Sorry?'

'Go somewhere quiet. This is about Natalie Tyack.'

That does it. The clever, egotistic and professorial Noel Oswell shuts up, and apparently goes somewhere quiet. The background noises have receded.

And then I let him have it, a broadside, everything at once, another technique: so much incontrovertible information he cannot resist. I speak loudly and fiercely.

As the cold, dropping rain trickles through the poplar trees, down my neck, and as I stand in the one corner of the Baldhu garden with signal, I overwhelm Noel with all the facts, and I even send a couple of photos. Natalie's bank statements, Falmouth Uni paid via Exeter Uni. His lectures on the paranormal showing the dates that tally *exactly* with her spending. The proof that they had some kind of relationship, and that they crucially met up *again*, shortly before she died. And he never told the police any of this, he's never told anyone this.

Which definitely means *guilt*. If you don't tell the police crucial facts during a potential murder case, you are in some way guilty or covering for another guilty person. I've done this job long enough to know *that*. And the same logic applies to Miles.

At last, I stop. I have been raving. I do not care. Noel is silent.

I say, 'Fuck this, Noel. This makes it look very much like you were involved with Natalie. You had an affair, you wanted it hushed, she threatened to expose you. Is that what happened?'

I don't entirely believe this, but I want to push him hard as I can.

He stammers, falls silent, then says, 'Why should I say anything?'

'Because you didn't tell the police, did you? Mm? And I am going to do just that, unless you tell me what really occurred.'

This is another bluff: I cannot trust the police, but he surely cannot know this. I am hoping the speed of my attack will throw him off balance.

I hear a steep intake of breath, like I have pierced something. Now he mutters, 'It *wasn't* an affair.'

'What was it then?'

'She did come to my lectures. She felt her children were acting strangely, the house, maybe haunted, though she hadn't seen anything herself . . .'

'And? Tell me everything.'

'We did nearly . . .'

'Have sex?'

'Yes.'

He sounds ashamed now as he explains, 'I wanted to, I mean, she was pretty and wanted my help. I was really . . . she was so much younger, we kissed, and we even got a room, but in the end, she said no. She got dressed. We didn't. She was faithful.'

I have the difficult feeling that I believe him.

He is begging me now. 'Please don't tell Angie this. It will destroy my marriage. Please – nothing actually happened. Natalie loved her family.' He sounds desperate, drowning.

I throw him a lifeline as the rain hisses on the Baldhu pines.

'Tell me everything else, then. Why did she come to see you that last time, just before she died?'

'She wanted advice.'

'Such as?'

'You know she had a mirror, a Chinese thing?'

I feel like lightning should be flashing, to match the drama.

'Yes. I know the mirror.'

'She was *obsessed* with that mirror; she said she'd worked out something. It was terrible and frightening for her, always had been, yet she would not let it go.'

I raise my voice again. 'Why? Why was that mirror so important to her? Because it came from her mum, right?'

Noel is silent.

'Noel! *Tell me.*'

At last, he says, 'Natalie told me, at one of those first meetings, a really big dark secret. The mirror didn't originally come from her mum, it initially belonged to Natalie's *dad*. Her mum stole it from Natalie's *father*.' I hear him sigh with sadness. 'You know she was an addict, Natalie's mother, right? I think Natalie's dad was only with her mum for a few weeks, God knows, maybe only a few hours! Anyway, Natalie's addict mother stole the mirror away, probably to sell it on and score drugs – but then she gave it to Natalie instead. One of the only nice things she did for her luckless daughter.'

The story is now unfurling in front of me: the last of it. I am scared of the ending, even as it emerges into view. Yet I have to know.

I say, 'Go on.'

'Also there was some . . . crest, some heraldic emblem. Connected with the mirror, maybe. Dolphins? Something, anyway. Natalie said at our final meeting she'd realized she'd seen it before. On a signet ring, on a man who used to visit her when she was a girl at the home. I don't know what that means, but it was truly tormenting her. I got the sense it was a secret so bad it was driving her close to suicide. I have no idea what that might be. Even now.' He sounds as if he is crying. 'She was such a beautiful girl, so clever, deserved so much better. I wanted to help, but she wouldn't tell me what this secret was.' Another pained sigh. 'I suspect, in the end, she killed herself. She discovered a truth so awful it made life unbearable for her. Something so bad she could never tell anyone. But – please believe me – I do not know what that was.'

I do believe him. I stare ahead, in horrible sadness, because I now have a sense of a secret so appalling it might drive you to suicide. Because the very final tesserae of the mosaic have been revealed, and it is indeed a dolphin, twin dolphins: as on the Coppinger crest.

Like the little emblem on the signet ring worn by Ed Hartley, owner of the Kittiwake Café, who so obviously keeps steering me away from himself.

I've seen that signet ring two or three times, but who notices these tiny details? Someone on the spectrum like me with unusual gifts, or maybe just someone lucky. No, someone like me.

I call Dinah.

'Again?'

'Dinah, I don't have time. Tell me, you remember when you spoke of Ed Hartley.'

'Er, what?'

'Ed. Ed Hartley? At the Kittiwake? Yes?'

'Oh . . . kay . . .'

I rush on: exhilarated, frightened, appalled.

'You said he was down here to be *near his kids*. What kids? Have you ever seen any sign of any "kids"?'

She hesitates, confused. 'Come to think of it, no. Isn't that weird? Why would he—'

'Doesn't matter. I think I know who this kid is. *A kid*. Thank you. Call you later.'

I close the call. Now I look again at the photo of Diana Coppinger's wedding. I cannot see a mother in the photo, I can see a father. The rich Coppinger in London? Probably. But no mother is pictured or mentioned at all. A divorce?

Could be. Next, with a tremor in my fingers, I google the names 'Coppinger' and 'Hartley', and I get just one result – but it is quite the result.

Edmund Coppinger-Hartley.

It mentions a small boy in a football team at posh Stowe School. This is Ed. This is him, as he was. In a football squad.

Little Edmund Coppinger-Hartley.

At some point after that, months or years down the line, Edmund must have dropped the 'mund' and become plain old Ed, and then he dropped the dodgy 'Coppinger' and become just 'Hartley', thereby becoming more matey, more cheery, more ordinary, but still actually a cruel Coppinger, and living in London. He was, surely, one of the men that came down from London to *prey* upon the pretty girls trapped at St Petroc's, the kids' home which his family conveniently owned. With the dolphins on the placard, their proud little crest, always giving them away, yet no one properly noticing.

Because no one notices these things, except people like me.

Ed Hartley – Edmund Coppinger Hartley – on his predatory visits to the home must have glimpsed that mirror at one point, and in the possession of beautiful, vulnerable, fourteen- or fifteen-year-old Natalie Skuse. He might have asked where she got it from, he would have gleaned the significance, he would have realized the scary or intoxicating truth: that he was looking at his own biological daughter.

Now I ponder it, he actually looks like Natalie, and therefore like Grace Tyack, the charming, handsome man, with the consequently pretty daughter. Yet Natalie would surely *not* have known Edmund Coppinger-Hartley – Ed Hartley by then – was her father, she can't have known, because she was actively looking for her father all this time, and yet ironically – beyond ironically – she was living in a kids' home that her biological father visited, a man who knowingly abused her.

The grim possibilities unfold. I have seen too much of this, in my work.

Genetic attraction. It happens.

As I stand here in the dripping Baldhu garden, I can hear the words in my voice, as if I am listening to a lecturer at the Bethlem.

Siblings who are separated at birth sometimes meet in adult life and, unaware of their genetic relationship, are deeply attracted to each other. Some scientists believe they are attracted *because* of the genetic closeness. In this theory – controversial and contested – the reason family members commonly do *not* break this taboo is called the 'Westermarck Effect'.

This refers to emotional bonding in a family unit which usually, biologically and psychologically, suppresses any overt sexual desire between siblings, or across generations, within a close family unit. Familiarity breeds disregard, or even disgust. However, if there is separation from a very early age, if the family members are dispersed, there is no 'Westermarck Effect', and as a result sad, dysgenic, incestuous things can quite easily happen if these people meet later in life. Family members can actually fall in love, fully and sexually.

Except, in this case, this is not remotely like love. This is an adult who knew the truth and a child that did not. So this was never 'consensual', let alone 'love'. It was always *rape*.

Right from the beginning.

I dwell on this because there is of course another, deeper logical outcome of this that makes me feel distinctly nauseous, almost dizzy with despair.

What if Natalie had one last sexual moment with Ed Hartley even as she first met Malcolm Tyack, thus explaining the timings of her first pregnancy and her hurried marriage?

That would make Grace potentially the daughter of the most terrible parentage. If the evil Ed Coppinger-Hartley is Grace Tyack's father, he is also her grandfather.

My clothes are soaking, my mind still races.

That is the kind of lurid, evil, family-destroying, soul-slaying secret that might prompt you to commit murder, in order to keep it quiet. Or to murder yourself: to commit suicide. Or it might make Ed Hartley, the genial owner of the Kittiwake Café, murder *you*, if he felt he was about to be exposed.

And that is the kind of secret that if you realized and witnessed it you might keep quiet even if you knew that murder was involved. You might then do that person's bidding, to keep the secret. If you were someone like Miles Tyack.

The rain patters. It is soothing – compared to my seething brain.

The solution to the puzzle is a moment of relief and of horror. The whole mosaic is displayed, and it is exquisitely made: simultaneously complex yet clear – and it terrifies.

Miles surely *knew* all this about Grace. That's the only thing that explains his peculiar behaviour, knowing but doing nothing, because what he knew paralysed him into inaction. He saw what happened that night, and did little, and ever since he's been protecting Grace from the possible life-destroying truth of her background, by protecting the identity of her incestuous biological father that must never be revealed.

Edmund *Coppinger*-Hartley.

That was perhaps who Miles was calling, frowning in the kitchen, the day he rescued me from the big black mine, maybe offering a warning.

I cannot risk this any longer. I have to take a punt, call my ex-husband. Desperately, in the cold and rain, I dial. The call goes to voicemail, and I shout into the phone. 'Kyle! Please pick up. Please please please. I know who it is! I know the killer. It's Ed Hartley. And he is being protected by Miles.'

49

Miles

My older brother strides with purpose towards the end of the gardens; as ever, I lag back. As I always do, I always did. Hiding sometimes. Disappearing at other times. Hiding behind furniture in the bedroom. Refusing to sleep at Baldhu, blaming it on my superstitious girlfriend, refusing to face the facts.

When we were boys I would escape his anger, fleeing somewhere in endless Baldhu, until he caught me, and hit me, and then Dad always had to separate us, the scent of whisky on his breath. Mummy was sunk in torpor, perpetually on the phone to her friends in London. Despairing of her wild boys, preferring her daughter, if she preferred anyone, or cared about anyone.

The endless drizzle persists; the garden is a silent hiss.

I am lighting a tiny cigarillo as I stroll. A new habit. He looks at me, questioning. I shrug, exhaling blueish smoke into the drizzly winter air.

'The whole world has given up smoking, so I thought I'd take it up.'

'Ever the rebel, Miles.'

'Well, yes. *Danke.*'

We stand by the gate at the end of the gardens, feeling as if we are at the end of everything. He and I used to run through this gate, run around the dunes and the carns, then down Bathsheba to Zawn Dorlam, wildly strip off, and dive into the sea.

There were good times at Baldhu. It wasn't always darkshape.

I puff on my little cigarillo, I can tell it annoys him. 'You know that Karenza has found out about the well?'

'What?'

'Afraid so, dear brother. The whole story.'

'I don't care, Natalie knows too.'

I look at him, squinting. 'Are you all right?'

'I am fine. I don't care who knows.'

I go on, 'She even knows about our poor dead Tyack twins, their tiny bones decorating the woodbines along Bathsheba. Perhaps that's why she is now seeing all the ghosts as well.'

He shrugs. 'What does it matter, now? She will pay.'

I laugh. 'Really? *What does it matter?* Who knows what else she might discover?'

'What do you mean?'

'For a start she might discover how much Natalie was...' I sigh. 'Broken. The ruby in the dust of Penzance. And then she could put two and three together and heaven knows. Make seven? Nine hundred? But still. You still don't get it, do you, how I am protecting you? How I have protected you all.' Anger rises. This time *I* could beat the utter crap out of *him*. I have spent a year with this obscene knowledge and this obscene guilt, all for him, and for them.

He ignores all this, like he can barely hear me. He says,

'Look, Baldhu is mine. And that means I need to fix that uncapped mine shaft, it's my responsibility. Let's do it.'

'On Boxing Day?'

'On Boxing Day!'

We have arrived at the lip of the terrible mine shaft. The tendrils of barbed wire look pitiful compared to the enormity of the wide black shaft which gapes, like a monstrous mouth rising to the green surface, eating the drizzle as if it is krill. Ready to eat everything.

'Jesus,' I say. 'I'm sure it's getting bigger. Like some kind of *tumour*.'

'All we have to do is get some planks, for now.'

'*Jawohl, Kapitän*.'

He cusses me. We stretch the tape, measure the width to get a sense of the depth, as best we can. I take notes. The rubble surrounds the shifting ground. He moves bizarrely.

I say, 'Christ. You're not trying to throw me in, are you?'

'Miles, *do* stop being a wanker.'

I laugh. 'I mean, that wouldn't be good, would it? Put yet another dent in Christmas. Far too much goose to go round.'

'Natalie doesn't like it, the mine being open.'

I eye him again. 'What are you on about? Are you that haunted?'

'You don't have any children, Miles, you wouldn't understand how it feels.'

'Thanks. You've gone completely mad. But that's sweet.'

Malcolm suddenly moves towards me, as if he really is going to throw me down the mine. He says, talking over my shoulder, in the direction of the house, 'I'm going to go do it. But you don't understand.'

Now he is silent again. Perhaps because my older brother is gazing at Baldhu with a new and endless horror. As if we are both kids again. *Make the darkshape go away. It is like a woman with a broken back. It is blacker than black.*

Then he walks away. I stand here for ages. For minutes. For an hour. Lost in my spineless determination to do nothing, say nothing, pretend I saw nothing, to save the family, let a murderer get away with it, avoid confronting a dangerous man. Just have a drink instead. Protect him to protect Grace. Otherwise, let it go. Why did Natalie tell me her fears?

She was so far gone at the end, that hateful mirror showing Natalie her own death.

Slowly, I walk back past the cairns towards the awful, beautiful house. As I approach the fateful iron gate I hear a voice by the trees.

It is Karenza Bray. She is almost shouting, every word quite clear.

'Kyle! Please pick up. Please please please. I know who it is! I know the killer. It's Ed Hartley. And he is being protected by Miles.'

And now I know my final duty.

I have no choice. She will destroy us all.

I move around the house to a different place where there is signal, and I dial *Coppinger*. Ed Hartley.

My heart is a dumb black stone in my chest.

50

I sit on a wet bench in a concealed corner of the garden and keep trying Kyle. No answer.

I've been sitting here for ages, trying to reach him, trying to think of some other salvation, maybe Dinah, maybe Priya – but no. And now it is getting dark, but I can't go in the house because of Miles.

But how can I leave the kids in there, in Baldhu, at risk? In all that madness? At last, I walk all the way around the darkening house to my car and I decide to get in. I am about to drive away, but even as I have my foot on the pedal, I pause, trembling. Where are the other cars? Something has happened. No. This is not right. I cannot flee, clutching the prize of my solution. What is that worth compared to my duty? The precious children?

I am a forensic psychologist employed by Malcolm Tyack, specifically to help the kids. And I think I love those kids now. They are part of me, and always will be, from now on.

Exiting the car, I crunch up the lane. The front door of Baldhu is swinging wide open, despite the rain. Stepping inside the hall, I shut the door. Securing our house.

The door to the cellar is also open. Tentative, I approach the small, dingy doorway. And those dank, slippery steps.

A fluttering noise makes me step back. I turn, to see a small black bird, flitting, panicked, around the hall. Like a trapped cranefly.

It is, I presume, another hallucination, thanks to our inherited trauma in this place in the rain. A ghost of a bird. Something to be ignored.

I go to the kitchen. It is empty. The back door too is wide open, gaping at the wet and darkened garden. I shut it, even as it ushers in rustling dead winter leaves to disturb the shiny modernity. There are mugs of half-drunk coffee on the island, and one plate lies in pieces on the floor.

Something has happened.

I run into the hall and then into the drawing room and there I find Grace, curled up on the sofa, staring at a book but with her eyes barely focused, as if she is half awake. As if everyone else has gone to another realm and Grace will soon follow them.

'Grace!'

The girl looks up. Her dark hair is tangled and frayed over her pretty face. Grace squints at me, as if she is trying to recognize me, and at last her face unclouds. 'Karenza, you came back.'

'Of course.'

Grace's smile is shy, but relieved. 'Thank you. I was lonely.'

'Where is everyone else, Grace? What's happened?'

'Oh it . . . it was major. It wasn't good.' She drops the book. 'Your thing. The epi . . . gen . . .'

'Epigenetics. Inherited trauma.'

'It got bad. *Really* bad, Karenza. Hundreds of birds. All these voices, they said. Solly was screaming in the cellar.' This resilient girl is frightened but trying not to show it. 'And Auntie Molly was down there, and she saw things too – and she grabbed Solomon and they, like, fled.'

'Where?'

'Dunno. Maybe to St Ives, to Molly's place.'

'And she left you here?'

'I wasn't frightened, I like it here. I didn't see the birds and I don't hear the voices.'

'And Uncle Miles?'

'He's here. Drunk. Probably upstairs.'

'And Malcolm? Your father?'

'He went after Molly, he was so angry.' Now Grace begins to tremble. 'I'm scared now. It's too strange.'

'Grace.'

'Yes.'

'I think you should come with me.'

'Yes?'

'We can get in the car, we can go, just for now, away from Baldhu. Away from the ghosts.'

Grace starts to cry, quietly. 'OK.'

She takes my hand, and we walk to the door, but as soon as we step outside, I see it. Dazzling headlights. A big, flashy car. So bright I can barely see. I hold a visoring hand to my eyes, and then I see who is getting out of it.

Ed Hartley. Or, rather, Edmund Coppinger Hartley. Someone has told him, someone – presumably Miles – has *warned* him. And now he has come straight here, to do what? Perhaps to do what he did before. Commit a murder, to slay another mother, the third in the line at Baldhu: Eliza Tyack, Natalie Skuse, Karenza Bray, the inheritance rolls on and on.

He walks purposefully up the long drive, I can barely make him out because of the dazzling car lights. Again I squint, and now I see it. A shotgun. Ed Hartley has not come here to offer explanations.

Abruptly, I kneel next to Grace. She is trembling, trying to be brave. Urgently I say, 'Go inside, go find your uncle Miles, even if he's drunk. Sit with him, please.'

'But—'

'*Please.*'

I know she will be safe with Miles. He might be in cahoots with Ed Hartley, but he has surely done all this to protect *her*.

She nods, then turns and runs.

But where do I go? Grace can entirely trust Miles, so she can go inside to safety; but I cannot. And Ed Hartley is thirty feet away and marching closer, intent on harming me or killing me. Certainly he wants to silence me. Where do I go? I can't go into the wilderness for fear of the open mine.

I have one choice, if it was ever any choice at all. I must run down to the zawn.

In the end, everyone goes to the zawn.

I know the route well. I run fast, the cold air burning my lungs. I stumble on rocks. I pray he won't follow.

Ed follows, equally fast. He shouts, *Stop!* The same way Miles once shouted *Stop!* to save my life, but Ed Hartley is not trying to save my life, he is maybe trying to take it, so I won't stop. Faster, I run, almost tumbling down the little valley, fast as Bathsheba, hurrying to the cliffs. I scrape my knees on rocks, they yowl with pain, my hair snags on brambles, I wheeze in the cold winter air, and I pull up short.

Ed Hartley, I realize, has a headtorch. He came prepared: the beam is strong, and it pierces the drizzle and the dark. I can hear him behind, almost smell him, and still he has that smoothing voice, not so charming now.

He calls out, 'Oh, do slow down, Dr Bray.'

I run on. I know where the path divides, I am just far enough ahead I might deceive him. I take the sudden dog-leg left to the zawn, praying he won't know the way.

My heart clutches as I realize: he knows the way. He is getting closer to me, his voice is ringing. Near near near.

'You silly woman—'

He is a brightness and a shadow. The drizzle is nearly gone, a moon is coming out. I can see his shadow behind me. The trees are thinning, my lungs are breaking open like split fruit, the pain of the cold winter air. I cannot go on much longer.

I climb the stile. I smell him again, his nice expensive after shave. Ridiculous. I run. I climb the second stile. He is barely two yards behind me. This is it: he will catch me. I am sprinting down through the open field that leads to the zawn.

And now the moon is full and bright and it sheds light, a lot of light, silver and antique, like a silver hand mirror in the sky, and the breath stings cold and harsh in my lungs, and now I can see the zawn and the dainty waterfall. I have one desperate idea of how I can avoid him, down by the sea, in a way he won't expect.

I hear his voice behind me as I approach the same treacherous cliff where Natalie fell – or was, of course, pushed. By him.

I look down.

'You really can't run any further. This is the end.'

I turn. His gun is raised. He is intent on my death. I cannot argue my way out of this.

I stop, and I turn. Defiant.

His gun is pointing right at my chest.

'Give me one last question. I can't go anywhere.'

He does not shift his aim. But he says, 'Why not? I rather admire your Sherlocking. You've earned it. Last question, please.'

'How did you lure Natalie here?'

His voice is cool, and businesslike. He's killed before, it is clear. A predator: maybe he was molested in his time, perhaps he had awful parents – but that is zero excuse. He knowingly raped his own underage daughter; he probably – possibly – impregnated her years later. I *know* men like him. He is one of the evil men I used to meet in psych units with anti-climb fencing, and furniture screwed to the floor, and mute prison guards and Alert buttons everywhere; but here I am on a Penwith cliff, in the moonlit dark, and he has a gun.

At last he answers.

'She asked to meet me here, threatened to expose me if I didn't come. I think she wanted to kill me. This is about the only place a small woman might have a chance. Against a man.' He sighs, abruptly. 'Or maybe she just wanted to be *here*. She used to come here as a child; once she actually came with me. Perhaps she hoped that would unnerve me, make me feel guilt.' He smiles. 'It didn't. Oh well.'

'You raped your own daughter, and you had a child by her. Grace Tyack.'

'Things happen, eh? But now I have a gun, and you have no choice. Jump and die, or I shoot. Jumping is so much better, because then we will say it's an accident, and the secret of Grace will never emerge. And she will be all right. I will see her occasionally, my own daughter, I won't ever tell her. Probably.'

I look at him. I smile blankly. He does really think Grace is his. He probably did move down here, to Cornwall, to be 'near the kids'. He knew Miles would protect him, despite witnessing the act, to spare Grace the truth.

'OK,' I say. 'I'll jump.'

I turn. I've made this estimate before. I look down, summoning all the rock-climbing knowledge of twenty-five years, and I step over the unstable rock-edge. I'm not going to jump, I believe there is a way down. I can drop to a little ledge, it looks drier, somewhat protected by the overhang next to it. I will hide under that. He won't expect this, he doesn't know I can rock-climb.

I take the deepest breath of my life – then I let myself drop.

'Karenza!'

I gasp as my chest knocks against the rocks, cracking a rib, maybe breaking something. But I am on the ledge, and now I am swinging under the overhang. This works. Made it, for a moment. But I am not far from Dorlam Brialli and the cascade spates in my face. The water is tumbling around me. If the wind shifts the flow, the ledge will become treacherous. I could easily fall. I don't know how long this can last. I could fall in a few minutes – that's if he doesn't find a way to shoot me.

He doesn't need to shoot me. He can just wait. And see me fall. It is obvious. I am about to die.

'Stop.'

Another voice. I crane to see, I can just about see. It is . . . Miles?

I stare, in amazement. *Miles?*

He also has a shotgun, a long shape in the bright glittery moonlight: it must be Malcolm's.

Miles speaks. He sounds as sober as I have ever heard him. 'I should have done this before, Ed. I was so stupidly weak. I was scared of you, of what you could do to Grace. I'm not scared now.'

'You know what I'll do, Miles. I'll tell the world, I warned you before.'

Miles replies, his voice full of scorn, 'Maybe. And maybe she'll cope, but whatever the case she doesn't need you around. It's your turn to jump.'

'Fuck off—'

'You—'

'Jump!'

A gunshot goes off. But I can still see two men. Up there. Fighting. So someone missed? Who? I can hear an urgent fight, a yell, one of the shotguns goes flying over the cliff, clattering onto the rocks. And now the two men are standing again – and then someone falls. Inevitably.

I hear the faint scream and glimpse a falling body.

A man lies crumpled on the rocks beneath, his eyes staring up at the sky, a large trickle of blood oozing from his skull; the moonlight is a curiously beautiful silver-crimson on the blood.

I am trying to see who it is. Through the endless falling water.

51

It is Ed Hartley who lies dead on the rocks at the bottom of Dorlam Brialli. The waterfall spatters his moonlit face, as it would have spattered Natalie Skuse, as it would have spattered on the sad, ruined face of Eliza Tyack, a hundred and fifty years before. It should have been me; it is not.

'Quick! Can you get back up? I can get a rope, somewhere.'

Miles. I reply.

'No, I think – I think I – can just make it, I used to climb.'

I move left, I find another precious dry handhold. I rise, then I find another dry foothold. And then for the second time in a few weeks I feel the strong arm of Miles Tyack as he rescues me from fatal danger. He exerts, and he lifts: he pulls me up. And now we are sitting here on the top of the cliff, on the safely solid ground. For a long time we say nothing.

Staring out to sea.

The moon is an avenue of pewter cobbles: it is a beautiful night. Cold, clear, lovely.

Finally, Miles says, 'No one can ever know why.'

'Of course not. Especially Grace.'

He leans and gives me a brotherly hug. And I think, Well, we actually are cousins. Both haunted by the waters of Baldhu, and now both haunted by the same knowledge – if indeed it is knowledge.

'I'll get the guns, drop them down the mine.'

'Good idea.'

He says, 'Another accident. Agreed?'

'He was going for a walk. It's a known danger spot.'

Miles laughs drily, sadly. 'I mean, it really is.'

'What about Grace?'

'She's fine. She's with Sam. A bit shocked, but she's fine. I saw him and you from the window and I dealt with Grace first.'

'Ah, good.'

There is a silence, then he says, 'I am sorry I was such a drunken fool – for a year! I knew it all. Natalie came to me in the last week, I knew about Ed and all that history . . . but I thought I was protecting Grace. I thought I was doing right. And I was kinda scared. I am a *dummkopf*.'

I give him a sisterly hug. Together we stare at the moon. And I say, 'But then you came good.'

52

Five Months Later

'That was fun,' I say.

Grace Tyack laughs. 'Yeah. Also ludicrous. I think I might be a bit old for superheroes now.'

'You're barely eleven.'

'Growing up! Not much choice in my family. But thanks for taking me.'

I chuckle. We are speeding through Newlyn, up the lovely sunlit road to Mousehole. It's our third visit to the cinema in five weeks. We really have become friends. Grace is a kind of replacement Minnie for me, I suppose, and Grace realizes I am a kind of replacement Natalie, a sort of mum, for now. It works for us both, but we don't talk about it. Not directly. It is best that some things go unsaid, forever.

Abruptly, in Mousehole, a hundred yards from the Ship, where the Maytime tourists are licking ice creams and admiring the sea view, Grace says, 'You can drop me here.'

'I can?'

'Yeah.' Grace Tyack is blushing, uncharacteristically. 'I'm . . . meeting a friend.'

'Ah, OK.'

'All right, Miss Forensic Psychologist, don't look so surprised. I made a friend! Amazing, huh? We play weird Korean video games.'

'OK . . .'

'And it's actually a boy. You better not tell Dad. You know how protective he is.'

'I promise.'

I lean over and push the car door so Grace Tyack can climb out. She really is growing up, her legs a little longer, her face a little narrower, the beauty of her mother emerging. But also the height of her father, of Malcolm Tyack, or of her father and grandfather Edmund Coppinger-Hartley? Who knows? No one knows for sure: and that is how it will remain.

Because Natalie Skuse and Ed Hartley are dead, and the secret dies with them. That is the only way.

Grace pauses, turns, and gives me a brief but meaningful hug, and then she is out of the car, running off, then gone, to go see her friend. A boy.

Growing up fast.

I start the car again. And drive the last miles to Baldhu. It has been dry for weeks, a long, sunny spring, so the lanes are crackly rather than muddy, and the cows hide in the shade of the sweet little trees, and Baldhu House looks cheerful and grand in the brightness, with its magnificent views down to Zawn Dorlam.

As I park, I see Darren and some other men, installing windows in the barns. Putting glass in the frames. Apparently the restaurants are doing well. Tourism is good in Cornwall this season, and the summer promises more. Malcolm Tyack is making money, and Baldhu benefits.

He greets me in the hall, and we go into the kitchen. We chat about nothing much, which is, clearly, absolutely fine by both of us. We talk about Solomon's football team, and Grace's amazing reading skills. The proud father, without a hint of doubt. If there is doubt he will never show it. Like a proper father. I wonder if there is any doubt in his mind? He might genuinely never have got that close to the truth. A truth, if it is even a truth, that is now buried forever, thrown down a mine, which is now capped off.

Only once do we touch on anything sensitive.

'What if you have another rainy winter?'

He laughs. 'We'll take a winter holiday in the Canaries. A long one. We can afford it.'

'You're not worried at all?'

'We'll cope, Karenza. Now we know more, now we understand, thanks to you, we'll cope better.' A gruff but affable smile. 'It's just a load of noises basically. Almost nothing. Even Miles is sleeping here occasionally. Brings his girlfriend. They even talk of marriage! He still drinks too much, but maybe less. Hah. But anyway you know all this, you and Miles, he says you have lunch sometimes.'

'We do.'

Malcolm talks about the house, the renovations, and as he does I marvel at the description of everything we went through, all those weeks of terror, as 'almost nothing' and 'a load of noises basically', but I don't say anything. I finish my coffee and go outside and get in my car. Malcolm merrily waves me off. My last sight of him is as he strides over to the workmen, giving orders.

This is our house. We are the Tyacks. We will not leave. Can't sell the damn house anyway, not with all those ghosts.

* * * * *

'These cronuts, they still get me. If I lived here I'd put on six stone in three months. Don't know how you resist.'

Dinah napkins crumbs away; I smile at my friend. I am waiting for the last few questions Dinah has not asked. They must be coming. So far it's mainly been small talk, or short explanations, in my local café, and Dinah has to head off in a few minutes to do stuff at the uni.

My friend smiles. 'So, how is everything, now the inquest is over?'

'Good.'

'It was quite brisk, wasn't it?' Dinah asks. 'I mean, done and dusted so quickly. Accidental death?'

'As far as I can tell, everyone was happy with that.'

'And no one else wants to investigate further?'

'Why should they? He slipped. For everyone, that's the best, and of course that's what happened. And the police stuff is out in the open, how DCI Diana Curtis née Coppinger tried to protect her brother. Edmund Hartley-Coppinger. Guess there will be a trial soon enough, and she will plead guilty for a shorter sentence. For all intents and purposes, it's done.'

Dinah nods, as if she knows not to ask more. Instead, she enquires, 'And what about you, now, after all this time?'

'What do you mean?'

'What's your opinion now, professionally? Still epigenetic, inherited trauma?'

'Mmm. Probably.'

'That's quite an ambitious theory, seriously out there.'

'I hear you,' I say. 'And maybe it's wrong. But I have a hunch it's the truth.'

'Perhaps it was simple psychological contagion? As in, group hallucination? That's the other possible answer.'

'Yeah,' I say, sipping the last of my flat white. 'Or maybe Baldhu is just bloody haunted, and full of ghosts.'

Dinah smiles, unsurely. 'You don't believe that? You're not leaning in to all this ghost stuff, are you?'

I hold her gaze, then shake my head. 'No, course not. And besides, it's truly not great for my CV, so I don't talk about what I saw. I know *something* happened. I'm sure there's a scientific explanation, and I believe I might have found it, but I'm not going to boast. However . . .'

'What?'

'Priya Hardwicke did say one very profound thing. In the middle of all that craziness.'

'Which was?'

I set down my empty coffee cup. 'She said, when there are hauntings, the thing is, people hate them, even if they are unreal. Haunted people spend the rest of their lives avoiding anything like that. And I feel the same.'

'Great. So you're not going to do any more ghost cases!'

'Nope. I'll stick with upper-class coke addicts. Enough bangs and thuds for one life.'

She laughs.

We rise and pay the bill and weave out into the sunny plaza by the Maritime Museum where the seagulls are eating chips. We hug and say goodbye and then I return to my flat.

El Gruffalo is lying on the kitchen counter. He graciously permits me to stroke him, before rolling over to think about Aristotelian logic. I walk into the living room and look out at the wonderful view of Carrick Roads and the Fal. The skiffs and the yachts, the Navy and the lifeboats. The vivid business of the sea – I still love it. I also look at the beautiful silver hand mirror on the shelf. Malcolm insisted I keep it. He said they'd had enough of it. I rather like it. A souvenir. It doesn't frighten me.

Now Otto stirs and gazes at me, suspiciously, with one swivelling eye. As if he knows I have been lying.

And he is right: I have just lied to Dinah.

If I can get another supernatural case, something inexplicable, I am sorely tempted to seize on it. I am now fascinated. When I walk the cliffs of Bedruthan or Kynance, or the riverside paths of the Helford, I listen to podcasts about paranormal experiences. Trying to understand. I keep hoping that Kyle will call me with a new case. Someone apparently reincarnated in Redruth, a curious poltergeist in Polperro. Anything.

But nothing. Instead I have my normal clients, and tomorrow I will go and see Granny Spargo, and flirt with Jago on the boat to St Mawes.

Otto looks hungry. He is using both eyes now. Examining me.

'All right, Otto, I'll get you some food. But I want an answer.'

Otto clutches his favourite twig.

'Should I get a man, do I need a husband? Dad says I do. Everyone says I do.'

Otto remains resolutely grey. Not a no, but not a yes. Neutral. Your call.

'Fair enough. One more question.'

The twig moves faintly. Otto licks an eyeball, lavishly. I say, 'I'm thinking of taking on more spooky cases if they come along. Whaddaya reckon, big mistake? The last job nearly frightened me to death.'

For a moment Otto does not react. Then he seems to

change colour, to the faintest of greens. It is a delicate, beautiful green. Like the clean green waters of Frenchman's Creek, where they flow over the sifted golden river sands, into the deeper, lovely, welcoming depths of the River Fal: the place where the waters mingle, and greet, and say Yes.